THE

DRAGEAL

WAR

BOOKS BY DOT CAFFREY

The World of Drejon Series
The Power Trilogy
Awakened
Cursed
Conquest

THE DRAGEAL WAR

A WORLD OF DREJON NOVEL

DOT CAFFREY

DragonCat
Books

For those who asked...

CHAPTER ONE

"I DO NOT UNDERSTAND, brother. Why do you have such a hatred for the others?" Pheunaf asked.

"The real question is, why you do not?" Darchok answered her question with his own.

The black and gold feathered dragon waited for him to continue.

"They are all vermin. Parasites. They take everything, our hunting ground and game, and they give back nothing of value. And, worse yet, none of them, especially your precious humans, are even tasty to eat." Darchok smirked fully expecting a rise from his sister.

The younger drageal fought the urge to take the bait. Surely he was joking. He had not truly eaten any of the other races, had he?

"You are not funny, Darchok." She stared at him wondering about the origins of such a deep-seated hatred, the likes of which she had not seen in anyone else in the clan.

"I make no jokes, dear sister. Merely speak the truth." He patted her on the head as he would a dragonlet.

\#

The next morning the sun shone and the air was crisp as Pheunaf took to the sky, trying to erase Darchok's words from her mind. She soared above the clouds, too busy savoring the contrast of the cold air and the warm sun playing on her feathers and the joy and exhilaration of flight to notice the land below changing from her craggy mountaintop to lush green foliage where the others lived.

She turned toward home when a screech, like nothing she had ever heard, shattered the silence. Though she did not know what it was, she knew she must help it.

#

Pheunaf had almost reached her room unnoticed. Almost.

"Where have you been?" Jocel asked approaching her from the side hall. "Your mother is livid that you have once again shirked your chores."

"I was flying. I will go to Mother in a moment."

Jocel put his hand on her shoulder. She turned and the thing she held started to wail.

"What have you got there?"

"Nothing," she said and entered her room.

"Nothing does not sound like that. Show me."

The young drageal opened her hand to reveal a now quiet but squirming pink body.

"What are you doing with a human infant? Do not tell me you have taken to stealing children."

"Of course not. I found it beside a dead one at the bottom of a ravine."

Jocel shook his head. "You found it and thought it a good idea to not only take it, but to bring it here?"

"I had no choice," Pheunaf said just above a whisper.

"That makes no sense."

"I know."

"You cannot keep it. You must return it to where you found it."

"If I do, it will die."

"Good," Darchok said from the hall. "Death should be the fate of all humans."

"Darchok!" Jocel snapped. "I will not tolerate such talk in my house."

Darchok growled under his breath and retreated.

"You must return it. Surely the other humans are looking for it."

"No!" Pheunaf cried. "You do not understand. I do not understand. I just know I must keep it."

"You cannot. You, we, know nothing of the needs of a human, especially one so small. It would be far more compassionate to kill it now, swiftly and painlessly, than to let it suffer because of your ignorance."

Pheunaf glared at him. "If you will not allow me to keep it, then I will leave. I will go elsewhere and raise it on my own."

"Child..."

"I cannot explain. I only know I must raise it. I must find a way, if not here then somewhere else."

The conviction in his daughter's voice, no, in her entire being, surprised Jocel. He had never seen her so resolute. He watched her cradle the infant in her arm and realized there was more to this than sheer determination. He just did not know what.

"Since it is obvious I cannot change your mind, daughter, I suggest you and the infant visit Dylys."

"Dylys?" Pheunaf gulped.

Jocel nodded. "She is the only one in the clan likely to have information on humans. And, I know someone outside who may also be able to help you. I will contact her."

"Thank you, Father."

\#

Pheunaf cautiously approached Dylys' cave. One never knew how the ancient one would react to visitors. Some days she was cordial and others you feared she would set you ablaze.

"Dylys. Are you there?" Pheunaf called out.

There was no reply. Pheunaf called again and was ready to leave when the silver feathered drageal appeared.

"What do you want?" Dylys growled.

Pheunaf took a deep breath. Facing Dylys in a foul mood was always a challenge. Many a young drageal had fled in fear from her presence at one time or another, Pheunaf included. But that was not an option today.

"Father sent me," Pheunaf said, trying to keep her voice calm.

"Why?"

The young drageal opened her hand and held it out for Dylys to see.

Dylys looked at it and snorted. "What am I supposed to do with that? I do not eat humans."

Pheunaf quickly closed her hand and drew the babe back to her. "It is not for eating!"

"Let me have a closer look." The young drageal hesitated. "I will not harm it."

Pheunaf again showed the baby, now awake and squirming to the old drageal.

"Hmm. It is a male and, from the looks of him, very young, perhaps only a few days old. Where did you get him? You did not steal him, did you?"

"Of course not. Why would I do such a thing?"

Dylys shook her head. "Well, there was a time..." her voice trailed off. "You still have not told me why you have him."

Pheunaf told the old drageal how she found him—of his ear-splitting shrieks, how as soon as she plucked him from the ledge he quieted, and that once on the ground, how he crawled to her and looked deeply into her eyes. "I could not look away or leave him."

"That does not seem possible. One so young should barely be able to squirm, never mind crawl. Are you sure he crawled to you?"

"Of course, I am not stupid, nor did I imagine it."

"I did not mean to say you did. But..." Her voice drifted off and she stared into the distance.

Pheunaf then put the child on the ground and took a step away. The child immediately followed her.

"Extraordinary," Dylys said. "What could this mean?" she asked under her breath and then turned to Pheunaf. "What do you intend to do with him?"

"Raise him."

The old drageal shook her head. "Killing him now, while he is too young to know what is happening, would be more merciful than having him suffer because you, we, have no idea how to tend to his kind."

"NO!" Pheunaf cried. "There must be another way. Do you not know someone who could help us, help me, learn what to do for him?"

Dylys did not reply. "Then I will find out on my own," Pheunaf snarled.

"How?" Dylys asked.

Pheunaf faced the old drageal, and it shocked Dylys to see the tears in this one's eyes.

"I do not know, but I will. I must."

Pheunaf turned to leave, but Dylys stopped her.

"Why not leave him near a human village? Someone there would take him in and care for him."

Pheunaf shook her head. "No. That will not do."

"Why?"

"I am not sure," Pheunaf whispered and looked away. "It makes no sense, but I feel the nearby humans would cause him great harm."

Dylys smiled. "If you feel that strongly, then it must be the truth. Who is to say how? Still, keeping him will be a huge commitment and one that might, despite your best intentions and actions, not be successful in the end."

Pheunaf nodded. "I know."

"Are you aware how different human babies are from dragonlets?

Pheunaf did not respond.

"They are helpless for quite some time and need constant attention for several years before they are as self-sufficient as a dragonlet is at a few months. Are you willing to take on such a task?"

Pheunaf looked down at the tiny pink bundle still in Dylys' hand. "I have no other choice."

At that moment, the baby began to cry.

"Why is he doing that?" Pheunaf asked.

"He is probably hungry." The old drageal began rocking him, and he stopped crying, but only for a moment. "Yes, I am sure that is it."

"Should I get some meat chunks for him?" Pheunaf asked.

Dylys smiled and shook her head. "Only if you wish him to choke."

Pheunaf looked confused.

"Have you already forgotten how different human and drageal

babes are?"

"What am I to feed him?"

The old drageal thought for a moment. "In my cave there is a large crock of broth. Put some in a small bowl. Bring it and a clean cloth here."

Pheunaf did as she was told, returning with the requested items.

"How cool is the broth?" Dylys asked.

"It is warm to the touch."

"If you think it warm, it is likely to be too hot for him. Fan it until it feels almost cold."

Pheunaf complied. When it felt cool enough, she held the bowl out to Dylys. "Now, what?"

"Wrap the cloth around your talon, dip just the tip into the broth and gently place the cloth near his mouth."

Pheunaf did so and was surprised to see the baby immediately suck the liquid from the cloth. Dylys nodded her approval.

"After every few sucks, dip the cloth back into the broth and repeat," Dylys said.

"How many times do I do this?"

"That will depend on him."

"That is not a very good answer."

"But it is. Every babe is different, be they human or drageal. Some will gorge until they make themselves sick. Others will stop at just the right amount and there are those who are so fussy they will barely eat a thing."

"I hope he knows to stop," Pheunaf sighed.

Dylys agreed.

After what seemed like a long time, the baby would take no more.

"Ah, so it seems you got your wish."

Pheunaf nodded. "How often will I need to do this?"

"As often as he requires it. And, before you ask, he will let you know." She paused and looked off into the distance. "I wonder, do I know anyone who can help you with the other challenges you will face?"

"Father said he knew someone. I think he went to find her."

"Good. Now, take the babe home. One more thing, he has neither fur nor feathers, so will require something to keep him warm. A soft cloth will do."

Pheunaf nodded and departed.

"Good luck to you both," Dylys said when they were gone.

#

"Were you able to find someone to help us?" Pheunaf asked upon Jocel's return.

"Yes, we will meet her tomorrow in a place about an hour's flight from here."

"So soon?"

"We thought it best for the child to do so."

"Of course," Pheunaf said. "Father, I did not know you knew any humans."

"I do not. My friend is a chetoga." Pheunaf looked puzzled. "A race of intelligent ferret-like beings. She and I met many years ago and have been friends ever since. It is she who knows many across the different races."

The young drageal nodded. "Will she bring a human with her?"

"Yes, I would think so. You should bring the child as well."

"NO!" she snapped.

"Why not?" Jocel asked.

"What if they try to take him from me."

"I would not allow them to do so."

Pheunaf still looked concerned.

"The human might be able to show you things to help care for him. It is your decision, child. I will not force you," Jocel said. "So, you say Dylys decided he was a male, eh? Where is he?" Jocel asked.

"Asleep, in my room. Mother and I set up a temporary bed for him."

"Good. Have you decided on a name? One cannot expect to go through life without one."

The young drageal looked away.

"What is it?"

"I would like to call him Zabaneja, after grandfather," she said and quickly added. "If that is all right with you, Father." She hoped it would not offend him that she dared to name a human after such a beloved drageal.

"It is a good name and it will help him be strong, just as my father was."

#

Pheunaf walked to her room and found Darchok blocking the doorway.

"Get out of my way, I need to go to Zabaneja."

"What did you call it?" he roared. "First, you darken our home with that thing's presence, and now you dishonor us by naming it after grandfather. How dare you?"

"Father did not seem to think I was dishonoring the family, nor his father. He said it was a good idea so grandfather can watch over him and help him through the trials of his life."

Darchok growled and stormed away.

CHAPTER TWO

"I AM GLAD you changed your mind and are bringing him," Jocel said as they took to the sky.

Pheunaf nodded, hoping it was not a mistake.

"Ah, there they are," Jocel said, pointing to two figures in the empty clearing.

Zabaneja fussed when they landed. "I see he, like you," Jocel said, "prefers to soar the skies rather than be earthbound."

The drageals approached the chetoga and her companion, a human.

"Ah, so this is the pair I have heard so much about," Kalini, the snow white chetoga, said in perfect dragealian.

Pheunaf looked at her father and then at the small figure in front of her. "How do you know our language?" she blurted out and then looked away, embarrassed by her rudeness.

The others chuckled.

Kalini walked closer to the young drageal. "Ah, yes, that. Did your father not tell you about me?" She gave a stern look to Jocel.

"He said you were a remarkable being, but did not elaborate."

Kalini shook her head. "I do not speak dragealian or any other language that is not my own. I possess a gift, one might call it magic, which allows me to understand others as if they spoke my tongue and for them to do the same when in my presence."

Pheunaf nodded, though she did not understand.

"I am honored to meet one so young and noble enough to save the life of another not of her own kind," the human said.

Pheunaf managed only a whispered thank you, embarrassed by the praise.

"Allow me to introduce my friend, Filemena, and I am Kalini."

Pheunaf nodded.

The old woman, bent and crooked, slowly approached the black and gold feathered drageal and reached out her arms. "May I hold him?"

Pheunaf did not know why, but she immediately handed the baby to her. She watched Filemena tickle his chin and coo at him.

"His name is Zabaneja," Pheunaf said.

Kalini smiled. "Zabaneja, eh? After your grandfather. That is quite the honor you bestow on the child."

"I think it appropriate."

"As do I," Kalini said.

Filemena walked away, and Pheunaf was surprised she was not in the least bit concerned that this human might try to steal her child.

"Come, Pheunaf, you and I have much to discuss," Filemena called over her shoulder.

Pheunaf did as she was told and followed the old woman.

#

Filemena, still cuddling Zabaneja, sat on a nearby rock. The drageal sat beside her.

"Tell me, Pheunaf, why do you feel yourself capable of raising a human child? Especially one so young."

The young drageal was taken aback by the question. She was told humans were not so direct. Without hesitation, Pheunaf told Filemena everything, even things she had not told her father or Dylys. The old woman listened without response or reaction. Only when the young drageal finished did she speak.

"I must say, had anyone else told me such a tale of what the babe did, I would call them a liar. A human child so young should not even be able to turn over on his own."

"That is what Dylys said," Pheunaf interrupted.

"Yes, I am sure she did." Filemena looked into the babe's face for several moments, then returned her gaze to Pheunaf. "It is truly remarkable you were able to save one so young. I am quite impressed with you, so I will not tell you what a difficult task you are embarking on. The others have already told you that more times than you wanted to hear." Filemena grinned. "Even in the short time since we met, I can tell you will not change your mind about the decision you have made."

Pheunaf nodded. "Can you help me?"

Filemena threw her head back and roared with laughter, a reaction no one was expecting. "Of course, I can. And I will."

Pheunaf's sigh of relief made the old woman smile.

"There is much to tell you, far too much for you to understand right now or to remember, but I have a bit of magic of my own that will help."

Pheunaf did not know what to say, so remained silent. The old woman put her hand on the drageal's head and closed her eyes. In the next moment, Pheunaf's mind was flooded with images and ideas that flashed across her mind and then were gone.

Filemena removed her hand, sat on the rock and released a

heavy sigh. She saw the look of concern on the drageal's face. "Do not fear. When the situation arises and the time is right, my words will rise to the surface of your thoughts and you will know what to do."

"I hope so."

"I know you do not want to hear this, but I must say it. Even after all we have discussed and knowing your determination, I believe it would be better if you gave the child to someone of his own kind." Before Pheunaf could respond, Zabaneja began fussing and crying in the old woman's arms. Filemena shook her head and laughed. "Perhaps, I was wrong. It seems this child, like you, may know better than I what is best."

"I do not understand."

"From what you have told me, it may be that you two are fated to be together." She handed the baby back to Pheunaf and stood. "Yes, I do believe you two are extraordinary beings. And, this world has quite a future planned for you both."

Pheunaf wondered what the old woman meant, but before she could question her further, Filemena returned to the others.

#

"You seem both relieved and concerned," Jocel said after the others had gone. "Was Filemena not able to answer your questions?"

Pheunaf shook her head. "She said she gave me all the information I will need to know, but even now I cannot recall anything she said."

"Well, that does not sound like a good thing."

"I think, because of the way she imparted it to me, she said it was her little bit of magic, it will be fine."

"Her magic?"

Pheunaf nodded and told him what Filemena had done and

what she had said about their future.

"Why do you find that amusing, Father?" she asked when she saw him smiling.

"I am not surprised to find Kalini's associates also possess powerful, albeit different, skills. The real question is, are you all right with how she did it? Do you think it will work as she said it would?"

"I can only hope."

"Well spoken, child. Now, it is time for us to leave. We should not be in the air with Zabaneja after dark."

"I do not understand. He is not afraid of the dark. And I will not drop him."

Jocel shook his head. "Those are not my concerns. I fear it will get too cold for him, and the light cloth he is wearing will not be sufficient to keep him warm. It is too bad we did not think to bring additional coverings for the trip home."

"Oh, my, I forgot about that."

"It is as much my fault as yours, child." He patted her on the shoulder. "I did not think we would be out long enough to warrant such an item."

Pheunaf was relieved Jocel did not think her totally irresponsible, even though at the moment she did.

CHAPTER THREE

AFTER ABOUT SIX MONTHS, Zabaneja cried almost constantly. Nothing Pheunaf tried, not even flying, made him stop for more than a few minutes.

On an afternoon flight, she hoped might give the others a rest from the never-ending noise, she suddenly realized what was happening. She turned back toward the mountain, praying this would be the answer.

#

"Is everything all right?" Amarysa asked as she rushed into the room.

"Of course, Mother," Pheunaf replied. She watched her mother scan the room and smiled. "If you are worried about Zabaneja, there is no need. I remembered Filemena's words about this."

Amarysa breathed a sigh of relief as she saw Zabaneja sleeping quietly in his bed. "I do not understand."

"Human babies are born without teeth. When they get them, it is painful and the only way they can respond is to cry."

"How did you dull his pain?"

"I put a tiny amount of aykopyra on a cloth and allowed him to suck on it."

"Ah, so even the humans know that use of fermented brews."

"Apparently, but she did caution me to use just the tiniest amount and also that it may not work the entire time."

"And then what will you do?"

Pheunaf shook her head. "I am not sure."

#

As feared, the small amounts of the fermented liquid soon lost their effectiveness. Pheunaf saw the incessant crying was an irritant to everyone, especially Darchok. She sensed her brother was just barely holding himself back from hurting Zabaneja, regardless of the consequences from Jocel. She needed to find another solution to the problem. Sadly, there was no further insight from Filemena.

"Zabaneja and I are leaving," Pheunaf announced to her mother.

"Leaving? What do you mean, leaving?" Amarysa asked. "Where will you go?"

"I found a small unoccupied cave, isolated from the others, a short distance from here. If we live there, even if he cries all night, I will be the only one he disturbs."

"Why not just toss him off the mountain?" Darchok said as he entered the room. "That would solve this and every future problem he will cause."

"Darchok!" Amarysa snapped.

He withdrew, cursing under his breath.

"I am sorry, Mother," Pheunaf said. "I did not realize he was here."

"Nor did I. You know, moving away does not actually address the true nature of the problem."

"Yes, but it will be just a matter of time until this is over."

"Did you not tell me the old woman said it could take up to three years for all his teeth to appear? Are you really planning on staying away, on your own, for that long?"

Pheunaf took her mother's hand. "If I must. But I think this will be over sooner than that. He seems to progress so much faster in everything he does. I have a feeling it will only be a short time before the worst is over and he is once again the sweet child he was before."

"Well, it seems you have considered all the possibilities."

Pheunaf nodded. "I do not see any other way. I know his crying bothers you and father almost as much as it does Darchok, though neither of you would ever come out and say it."

"Have you told your father of this decision yet?"

The young drageal lowered her eyes. "Um, I was hoping you would do that for me."

"Of course," Amarysa laughed.

#

"What is that?" Darchok sneered at the rock wall encircling Pheunaf's new cave.

"It is to keep Zabaneja from wandering too close to the edge of the mountain," Pheunaf said.

"Just let him fall. If he is too stupid to know better, perhaps it is best to be rid of him now, before he takes up any more of our time. That damned human has already cost more than he is worth."

"Why are you here?"

"I wanted to make sure you were doing all right, little sister, now that you are all alone," he hissed.

The civil words did nothing to hide the menace behind them. As usual, she chose to ignore his veiled threat. "We are fine."

"Wonderful. I would hate for something to happen to you. Although, that thing is another matter entirely."

Pheunaf scooped Zabaneja up in her arms and entered the cave without addressing Darchok further.

"Are you not going to invite me in?" Darchok called, his voice dripping sarcasm.

"Go away."

"As you wish, sister," he said as he laughed.

#

"Is Zabaneja still crying all the time?" Amarysa asked during a visit.

"Not as much as before, although he does have his moments. I swear he is getting louder than he had ever been when we were in your home." Pheunaf immediately regretted her words.

"What do you mean, my home? It is your home as well, child." Amarysa looked at Pheunaf, then shook her head. "You are not planning on coming back, are you?"

Pheunaf looked away.

"Do not turn from me. Tell me the truth. Are you planning on staying here alone?"

"I am not alone, I have Zabaneja."

"I see."

"Mother, I know you are not happy with my decision…"

"That is an understatement, dear."

Pheunaf nodded. "And, Father will not be happy either."

Amarysa smiled. "An even greater understatement."

"This is something I must do. Zabaneja is my responsibility, and I cannot continue to rely on you and father shouldering so much of the burden of tending to him."

"Burden?" Amarysa snapped. "Do you think we consider Zabaneja a burden? How dare you?"

"That is not what I meant. Oh, I am making a mess of this." Pheunaf walked to her mother and took her hands. "I do not want you to think of what should be done for him ahead of what you should do for yourself. You have already done that for all your children and now it is time for me to do so for mine."

"I see you have given this quite a bit of thought. You are no longer a child, so I cannot force my will upon you. But know this, whether you live in my cave or your own, I will always think of what is best for you, for Zabaneja and for all my children."

"Thank you, Mother. Will you tell Father my decision?"

Amarysa chuckled and shook her head. "Oh, no. Not this time. I told him you were moving out when it was meant to be temporary, because you were too much of a coward to do so. But this decision, this action, must come directly from you."

"I was afraid you would say that." Pheunaf turned away with a half-hearted smile.

#

"He has gotten so big these past months," Amarysa said as she and Pheunaf watched the toddler running around.

Pheunaf nodded. "I think it is time to find a playmate for him."

"Why now?" Amarysa asked.

"He lives amongst drageals so, he must learn to interact with them," Pheunaf said.

Amarysa chuckled. "I see, I wondered if perhaps he, as all

children do at this age, was getting a bit too rambunctious for you to deal with."

"Well, he is quite energetic."

"Are you not afraid he will get hurt?" Amarysa asked.

"That is a possibility, but…"

"Might it not be better to wait until he is a bit older, a bit bigger? Until he can better understand?"

Pheunaf shook her head slowly. "He will not be full grown for many years, and even then he will never be as large as even the smallest drageal. I do not want him to be alone or with just us for all that time. He may as well find out now what he can and cannot do around the others. He is finally steady on his feet—seriously, the only time he stops moving is when he sleeps—so a playmate will be good for him. And, there is plenty of room here for him and a dragonlet to romp around so he will be somewhat safe."

"Do you have anyone particular in mind?"

"Nanetscka. She is small for her age and does not seem overly aggressive."

"Yes, that is an excellent choice. Have you approached her mother?"

"Not yet. I wanted to see what you thought of the idea first. Do you think her mother will object?"

Amarysa thought a moment. "I have never heard her voice any animosity towards humans, but that might be different if it comes to having her own child associating so closely with one."

"I never thought of that."

"It is just something you must keep in mind and, if she prefers not to have Nanetscka play with Zabaneja, you must not take it as a personal affront to either you or him."

Pheunaf shook her head. "That may be difficult to do."

"I know, but you must remember, as much as we love Zabaneja, others in the clan may just be tolerating him from a distance. Not with the same hatred as your brother, just not willing to become too closely associated with him. Just be prepared to have your request turned down."

#

"His dragealian has improved," Amarysa said.

Pheunaf chuckled. "It is all Nanetscka."

"I see. They do seem to get along quite well together. She was a good choice, my dear."

"Yes. She is careful around him, but not too much so. She seems to instinctively know just how much roughhousing he can handle," Pheunaf said. "You know, it would not surprise me if the two of them do not figure out a way to fly together very soon."

"Really? Are you concerned about that?"

"A little, but they both seem very sensible about the whole thing. I hear them talking it over and I must say, I am quite impressed with the way their minds work. I do not think I would have been so logical when I was their age."

"Will they come to you for advice?"

"I am not sure. To be honest, I think they have struck upon a near-perfect plan already. They just need a bit more time to realize it."

"I will ask again, are you not worried? What if they attempt this near-perfect plan of theirs and it goes awry?"

Pheunaf shrugged and chuckled. "That, dear mother, is why I keep such a close eye on them. If they attempt it, I want to be near, just in case..."

CHAPTER FOUR

NO MATTER HOW OFTEN they flew together over the next few years, it was never enough for Zabaneja. Too soon, Nanetscka holding him to her chest with her arms wrapped around him became cumbersome and uncomfortable for both. He feared it would not be long until he could no longer fly. That thought created within him a sullenness he could not mask.

"What is the matter with you?" Nanetscka asked.

"Nothing. Why would you think such a thing?"

Nanetscka slapped him on the back. "You really are a terrible liar. Tell me, what is making you so mopey?"

The young boy shrugged and looked skyward.

Nanetscka stared at him for a long moment. "Wait, I know."

Zabaneja was surprised, yet not shocked, by her reply. She knew him better than anyone. Even better than his mother.

"I have no idea what you are talking about. I told you there is nothing bothering me."

"So you say, yet that is not how you are acting. I understand." She waited a moment, but he did not respond. "I would be in a much worse state if I feared I could never fly again."

"I still do not know what you mean." Zabaneja turned from her.

She reached to stop him. He tried to pull away, but she tightened her grip. "If I am wrong, why are you trying to run?"

"I am not running. I have more important things to do than listen to your nonsense."

She released him and he walked away.

"All right then, go. I guess you do not want to hear the plan I came up with to let you fly."

He stopped and turned to face her. "What plan?" he asked, trying to act nonchalant, but not succeeding. "What do you mean?"

She laughed. "I knew it. The idea of not being able to fly is the cause of your mood."

"Whatever you say." He dismissed her with a wave of his hand. "Tell me, what is this plan of yours?"

"You have gotten too big for any of us to hold you in flight as we once did..."

"Yes, I already know that."

"I was thinking, instead of holding you, what if you sat on my back?"

"It sounds simple enough and logical."

"Do not act so surprised," she said with a laugh.

"Well, logic is not your strong point."

"True," she smirked. "But it makes sense, right?"

"I have never seen or even heard of a drageal carrying anything on its back."

"Neither have I. But is it because we cannot, or we have never had a reason to?"

Zabaneja shrugged.

"If you think about it, the second reason sounds far more likely. It is doubtful our backs are not strong enough, but the need never arose since even dragonlets are able to fly almost as soon as they are born."

"True."

"I think we should try. What is the worst that can happen?"

"You mean besides me falling off your back and plummeting to my death?" Zabaneja asked only half-jokingly.

"Exactly!"

"Well, that would make Darchok extremely happy."

"That, my friend, is the last thing I want to do."

"Glad to hear that. Now, how are we going to do this?"

"I have not yet thought out all of the details."

"Why does that not surprise me?"

"Hey, I at least thought of a plan which is more than you did. You were content pouting like a spoiled dragonlet."

Zabaneja was going to protest, but the smirk on Nanetscka's face just made him smile.

"Yes, I know. You are the great thinker and I am the sullen one. But you have yet to tell me the part of your plan you already know."

"I doubt there will be a problem with you sitting on my back, right before where my wings start," she said, craning her neck and pointing her chin in the general direction of which she spoke. "Try getting on," she said as she lowered herself to the ground.

He nodded. He tried to remain calm, but the possibility of being able to fly with less discomfort than before, excited him.

"What is the problem?" Nanetscka asked after a few moments.

"Unless I grab your feathers, which I am not of a mind to do, I cannot get a handhold to climb up."

"Hmm. You could tug on them a little."

"No, I would need to pull a lot harder, probably to the point of damaging or pulling them out. Which neither of us want to happen."

Nanetscka nodded.

The pair stood looking, first at each other and then at their surroundings. At the same moment, the two friends shouted 'the rock!' and laughed.

Zabaneja ran to the large nearby rock and climbed on it. Nanetscka stood beside it, again lowering herself so he could climb onto her back.

"Next problem," Zabaneja said as he tried to settle himself.

"What?"

"Well, unless I move far up your neck, I cannot straddle you. You, my dear drageal, are too wide," he said with a chuckle.

"No, you, human, are too small."

Both laughed again.

"Seriously, though, how much farther forward would you need to be?"

"Let me see," he said and shimmied toward her neck. Finally, he got to a point where, while he could get his legs around the sides of her neck, it did not feel comfortable for him. And, from the way Nanetscka twitched, it was not good for her either.

"If that is the spot, well..." Nanetscka began.

"I agree, this will not work."

He shimmied back closer to where he had originally been sitting. "And, there is another problem."

Nanetscka sighed, afraid her plan to help him contained even more flaws than she had anticipated.

"I need something to hold on to or else I will fall off," he said as he slid off her back onto the rock.

They looked at each other, their faces showing dejection at their failure. Over the next few hours, they tried to find a solution; each would start a thought and then shake their head as they realized its flaw, until both had exhausted all of their ideas.

"It was a good try, my friend," Zabaneja said. "And, I thank you."

"No, we cannot quit. It is a good plan, we just need to find a way to make it work."

"Is that not what we have been trying to do?"

"There must be something we missed. Something we have not thought of."

"Or, it is just impossible."

"Zabaneja!" Nanetscka cried. "I am shocked. I thought you loved flying."

"I do. But there comes a time when one must face reality, and this may be that moment." He turned away.

"No. I will not accept that."

"I think we must, Nanetscka. There is no other choice."

He turned, waved farewell and walked away, leaving his friend shocked to witness his seemingly calm acceptance of failure.

"Well, you may have given up," she said when he was out of earshot, "but I am not about to. I know there is a way to make this work and I will find it. And then, you and I will again soar through the skies with the wind in our faces."

#

Over the next few weeks, Zabaneja became more and more reclusive. He avoided everyone. Even when friends came looking for him, he would not see them. He barely left his room.

Only in the middle of the night, when everyone else slept, would he venture out, climbing to the highest point he could reach. He stood motionless, staring at the stars and enjoying the wind as it whipped around him. On more than one occasion, he felt tears of remorse and loss running down his cheek, knowing this was as close as he would ever again come to the sky.

"What are you doing out here at this hour?" Pheunaf asked,

jolting him from his trancelike state.

"Mother. I am sorry, I did not realize you were there." He wiped the tears from his face. "I could not sleep."

"Hmm." She moved closer. "If that is the case, then you have not been sleeping very much lately, since you are here every night, regardless of the weather."

"I do not know what you mean."

Pheunaf laughed. "My dear Zabaneja, you should know better than to try to lie to me."

He looked at her, but said nothing.

"Now, tell me the real reason you come here night after night."

"It is nothing." He turned away from her, then whispered under his breath, "Nothing anyone can help with."

"But, dear child, how is anyone to help if you do not tell us what is wrong?"

Damn, he thought. *After all this time, you would think I would remember how good a drageal's hearing is.*

"There is nothing you or anyone else can do to help."

He turned to walk away, but Pheunaf stopped him.

"Tell me."

"I do not wish to talk about it."

"Tell me," she repeated, her voice a whisper.

"No."

"Tell me," she said once more, this time her voice almost not there.

Legend said drageal eyes could mesmerize anyone who stared too long and too deeply into them. He was not sure if that was true for all drageals, but he knew looking into hers always forced him to tell the truth, regardless of his wishes. And this night was no different.

In the next breath, he broke down and told her of his sadness and frustration over never again being able to feel the exhilaration and joy of flying. He cursed the first time he flew and how, even though he was a mere babe, he still remembered. As those words escaped his lips, he regretted them.

"I am sorry, Mother. I do not blame you. Flying is as natural to a drageal as breathing. And, perhaps, in time, I can look back on the memories with happiness. But not tonight."

Pheunaf's heart broke to see her son, still a child, hurting so. "Surely there must be a way."

"Nanetscka thought she had a plan to have me fly on her back, but..."

"But what?"

"It just will not work. There is no way I can hang on without injuring her and, as much as I may love flying, I have no desire to fall from the sky to my death or to hurt my friends."

"Well, I am very glad to hear that. But surely we can find a way. Perhaps some sort of seat or rope contraption."

"I do not understand."

Pheunaf smiled. "I have heard humans create apparatuses to be used to help them control or ride on things like horses, and such. Maybe we could fashion something like that for you. Though, I will admit I have never actually seen one." She tilted her head to one side in thought, "We should check with the others, perhaps one of them will know how such things are fashioned. Give me a bit of time to talk to them and let us see what we can find out."

"And if no one knows?" Zabaneja tried desperately to suppress the excitement building within.

She patted his head. "Then you and I will need to find the answer."

Zabaneja nodded, now grinning from ear to ear.

"Until then, son, do not give up hope. Even if this is not the solution, we will find one. I promise."

#

"How dare you even think to do such a thing?" Darchok shouted. "The very thought of it is demeaning. It is not bad enough we have had to endure that thing's presence all these years? And now... Now, you propose this? I cannot imagine having anything, especially a lowly human, riding on my back."

"I do not recall anyone asking you to do so nor for your opinion, brother," Pheunaf said, upset with herself that she had not checked to ensure he was not nearby before bringing the subject up. "We all know what you think, whether we want to or not. If you have nothing constructive to offer, go away and let us continue our discussion."

Darchok saw the disapproval on his parents' faces and stormed out, grumbling under his breath.

"You realize, child," Jocel said once sure Darchok had departed, "others may share that opinion."

"But, Nanetscka is the one who thought of the idea. No one is forcing her to do this against her will."

"Still, there is a chance not everyone will care about that, even if it is the case."

"Fine, then I will be the one whose back he rides on. And just let any of them comment to me about it," she snapped.

"Now, now, calm down. That is not what I am saying," Jocel went on. "I have every intention of helping you find a way to let Zabaneja fly. Denying him flight would be nearly as bad as taking it from us."

#

Everyone in the clan, short of Darchok and his friends, helped in both the design and creation of Zabaneja's flying apparatus. They scouted nearby settlements for ideas, which they then created by weaving long ropes of vines and such into straps and a seat, which could be attached to a drageal's back. In only a few attempts, an apparatus that worked well for both Nanetscka, as well as any other drageal, and Zabaneja was complete.

"Are you sure you want to do this for a real flight?" Zabaneja asked.

"I am sure," Nanetscka replied. "We know it works near the ground so why would it not do the same aloft?"

"I still worry it might impede your flight."

"And, I think you are afraid." Nanetscka laughed and winked. "Come, help me put it on."

Once the seat was in place, Zabaneja shook his head. "I am still worried this will hurt you once we are more than a short distance from the ground."

"The only way we will find out is to try. So, either get in it or admit you are afraid."

"I am not afraid," he said. "After all, what is the worst that can happen, besides death?"

"Precisely!"

The two friends laughed and Zabaneja climbed into the seat-like contraption attached with straps around Nanetscka's neck and torso. He tied himself in and realized he could either lean all the way forward and hug Nanetscka's neck or sit more upright.

"All right, then, I am ready... I think," he said.

"Good, then off we go."

Zabaneja felt a slight wobble in her ascent from the additional weight, but it took no time for her to adjust and soon, the pair soared high into the clouds.

Zabaneja enjoyed the flight even more than usual from his new vantage point.

"That was magnificent. I have never experienced a flight like that before. You did not have any problems with me on your back, did you?"

Nanetscka shook her head. "A little when we first took off."

"It was the extra weight, right?"

"Yes, that and the fact that my balance was shifted a bit, but as soon as I adjusted for it, all was fine. You did a great job as well. I realized after we took off I had not told you how to lean when I banked, but you already knew, because you did it perfectly."

Zabaneja shrugged. "Just seemed the natural thing to do."

#

Soon enough, Zabaneja's other friends, and even some of the adults, wanted to try out the flying seat.

The added attention increased Darchok's anger at what he considered an affront to the entire drageal race. He vented his fury by increasing the ferocity and malice of his verbal assaults toward Zabaneja. And he was quick to remind the boy if he sought help from his mother or grandfather, there were other ways, more vicious ways, he could employ. The drageal took great joy in terrorizing the boy, knowing he would endure the threats in hopes they would go no further.

CHAPTER FIVE

"WHAT ARE YOU DOING INSIDE?" Pheunaf asked. "It is a beautiful day, the sky is clear, the air just brisk enough to tickle your feathers. Why are you and your friends not aloft?"

Zabaneja shrugged but did not reply.

Pheunaf walked to his side and put her hand on his shoulder. "What is wrong, child? You are not ill, are you?"

He shook his head. "No, I am fine," he replied in a voice so soft even her drageal ears had to strain to hear him.

"Hmm," she said. "Well, you certainly do not seem to be acting that way. It is not like you to sulk."

He pulled away. "I said I was fine. Just leave me alone!" he shouted and stormed out of the house.

Pheunaf stood there, stunned by his reaction, wondering what was bothering him.

#

"So, the others, your so-called friends, have at last seen you for what you really are, and they have decided you are not worth their time," Darchok hissed at the boy.

Zabaneja glared at his uncle but did not reply. Even at his best, he could barely hold his own in a discussion with Darchok, and now, well, he did not even want to try.

"Your silence tells me you have come to the same conclusion."

Zabaneja shook his head. "No. You are wrong. They are still my friends."

Darchok laughed. "You say that, yet I see none of them here. As a matter of fact," he paused, put his hand to his chin and tilted his head, "I cannot remember the last time they were, can you?"

Rather than answer, Zabaneja tried to leave, but his path was blocked.

"Afraid to face the truth?"

The sound of Darchok's voice, so dripping with contempt, angered Zabaneja.

"As if you have any idea of the truth, UNCLE," Zabaneja said, emphasizing the term he knew would anger the drageal.

Darchok threw back his head and roared. "Do not ever call me that, whelp. I am not your kin. The fact my sister has burdened both our family and our clan with the shame that is the likes of you is immeasurable."

As the drageal continued his tirade, the same one heard for as long as he could remember, Zabaneja seized the opportunity to escape. He returned to his room and realized a small part of him feared maybe, just this once, Darchok was right. "No," he said to the empty room. "There is another explanation. There must be."

#

How can I have been so blind? Why have I not noticed his friends have not been around lately? Pheunaf chided herself after overhearing the conversation between Darchok and Zabaneja.

She wondered why he had not come to her? Why he had endured the abuse? She gasped as she feared Zabaneja actually believed her brother's hateful words. She would deal with that problem later. Right now, she needed to find out what was really going on.

#

"Nanetscka," Pheunaf called as she approached the young drageal's home. "Are you there?"

In the next moment, a flurry of blue feathers appeared.

"Pheunaf, so nice to see you."

"I was wondering if you would give me the riding seat."

Nanetscka looked puzzled. "Why would you want that?"

"I am going to fly with Zabaneja," the older drageal replied.

Pheunaf wanted to lash out at the young drageal, Zabaneja's first friend, for abandoning him without so much as a word of explanation. Yet, she knew that would serve no good purpose.

"It seems it has been some time since last you flew together. And you know how he is. Keep him out of the sky for more than a few days and he gets fidgety. If I did not know better, I would swear that boy was at least part drageal."

Nanetscka smiled until Pheunaf's words sank in.

"Oh, my," Nanetscka sputtered. "I guess it has been a little while since I have seen or flown with him. I have been, well," the young drageal looked away, embarrassed, "a bit busy, and just lost track of the days."

It was the young drageal's reaction that made Pheunaf realize what age Zabaneja's friends were and what stage of their lives they were entering.

Nanetscka closed her eyes and tried counting the number of

days it had been. After a few moments, she shook her head. "Oh my goodness, has it really been that long since I have seen him?"

Pheunaf nodded. "It has."

"I am so sorry."

"It is not me you need to apologize to."

"Of course. I will go to him now," Nanetscka said and turned. "Wait, did you want to fly with Zabaneja, or will you allow me to?"

"No, child, you fly with him. Having rarely used that thing, I would more than likely make quite the mess of it."

#

Returning home from meeting with Nanetscka, Pheunaf realized she knew nothing of human sexual desire. When did it awaken? And, more importantly, what were the consequences should it go unfulfilled? Could Zabaneja's isolation from his own kind bring him harm, or worse? She prayed humans did not react with madness like drageals did. An image of Zabaneja going mad and throwing himself off the mountain to his death flashed in her mind and she was filled with horror.

As her fear heightened, she was overcome with calmness and Filemena's words filled her mind and she realized it was time to see the old woman again.

She went to find her father to arrange a meeting.

#

"I am so glad we are flying again," Zabaneja said as he and Nanetscka soared toward the nearby mountaintops. "I was beginning to think I had done something to offend you and the others."

"What do you mean?" Nanetscka asked.

"Well, it seemed that everyone was suddenly avoiding me. Darchok said it was because you finally realized how worthless I am."

"You did not believe him, did you?"

"I did not want to, but it has been quite some time since I have seen anyone," he confessed.

By now the pair had landed on a nearby mountain top. Zabaneja climbed down from his perch on her back. As he walked around the drageal and stood by her side, he looked up. "So, what was everyone doing? Why were you avoiding me?"

"I was not avoiding you," she said, "it was just I got, um, well, busy."

"Doing what?"

"Well, things. You know."

Zabaneja shook his head. He was becoming annoyed at her. "If I knew, I would not be asking, would I?"

Nanetscka gulped. Though the older drageals were comfortable discussing mating and such, she was not, especially not with Zabaneja.

"Do not get angry with me," she snapped, masking her discomfort with annoyance. "It is time to go home."

Zabaneja wondered what had he done to warrant Nanetscka's displeasure, as he climbed into his seat. The two flew home in silence.

"Ask your mother what is going on. I am sure she will tell you," Nanetscka said as she headed for her home.

#

"I wondered when you would think of this," Jocel said.

"And, had I not? Would you have just let me blindly carry on, not realizing I could be harming him?"

Jocel ignored his daughter's sharp tongue. "I have already

contacted Kalini, and she has set up a meeting."

"I am not giving him up!"

Jocel put his arm around her and hugged tightly. *You may have no other choice, child,* he thought, but would not say until they knew more of what Zabaneja's future might hold.

"We will meet with Kalini in four days."

Pheunaf drew in a breath and looked away.

"I know you are worried, but we have no answers to the questions that are plaguing your mind."

"I know. "

"Will you bring Zabaneja with us?" Jocel asked, already sensing his daughter's response.

"No!" she snapped. And then, softening her tone, added, "There is no need to right now."

"Are you afraid?"

Without wanting to, she nodded.

"Of what?"

"I am not sure. I just know I do not want him there. Perhaps next time."

"If that is your wish, child."

He did not need to look at her to know the source of her fears. Since she first found him, Zabaneja had been her entire life. The boy had never voiced a desire to be with his own kind, but Jocel sensed Pheunaf feared that meeting another human, might make him want to go with them. Still, he knew Pheunaf would always do what was best for the boy though losing him would be devastating.

#

"Is something the matter, Mother?" Zabaneja asked.

Pheunaf was startled. She had not heard him enter. She was lost in thought about the upcoming meeting later that day, as well as what her father did, and more importantly, did not say.

"Of course, not. Why would you even think such a thing?" she replied, trying to calm herself.

"You seem very preoccupied. I cannot remember the last time you did not hear me approach, and I was not even attempting to be quiet."

Pheunaf smiled, but did not answer.

"I am going out. Nanetscka and I are going for a flight to the eastern mountains."

"Ah, it is certainly a lovely day for it." She looked at him and shook her head. "You really need to think more about yourself when you fly. Go put on something to keep yourself warm, it will be extremely cold and I do not need you getting sick again."

Zabaneja smiled, leaned in and kissed her face. "Yes, Mother."

Something is definitely going on with her, he thought. *Or am I just overreacting?* Nevertheless, he could not help but feel something was amiss not only with her, but with so much around him.

CHAPTER SIX

Jocel kept a wary eye on Pheunaf as they travelled to meet the chetoga. "You need to calm down, child. All will turn out for the best."

I wish I shared your sentiment, she thought as they circled above a clearing some distance from the place they had last met the others. "Where are we?" Pheunaf asked.

"Where Kalini told me to meet her."

\#

A few moments later, Kalini emerged from amongst the trees followed by a human male.

"No matter how many times I see you land, I am still in awe of how silent and graceful the act is," she called out.

The chetoga turned to the man and said something the drageals could not understand. The man, his eyes wide open in awe, nodded.

Jocel took a step forward, bowed his head slightly and introduced both himself and Pheunaf, knowing Kalini's magic would translate his words.

"I am Aneesyma," the man replied. "Long have I heard tales of the majestic drageals, but I never expected to see, never mind actually speak to one. I must say, the tales do no justice to your actual presence."

Jocel nodded.

"Where is Filemena?" Pheunaf asked.

"Sadly, she is no longer of this world," Kalini said and saw the look of surprise in Pheunaf's eyes. "You know, she was extremely old for a human. Even at our last meeting, though she did not tell you, she knew she would never see you or Zabaneja again. But she felt honored to have met you both."

"If she is not here, who can I trust to help me with Zabaneja?"

"Aneesyma," Kalini said and pointed to the man beside her. "He is wise and a good friend."

The human bowed to Pheunaf but said nothing.

"Where is the boy?" Kalini asked. "I hoped you would bring him. I hear from Jocel that you have devised a method for him to comfortably fly with you."

Pheunaf did not respond.

"This is quite the isolated place," Jocel said, changing the subject. "We saw no towns or villages anywhere nearby. Where do you live, Aneesyma?"

"My home is a three-day ride from here."

"And why are we meeting so far from it?" Pheunaf asked, sounding a bit more suspicious than she meant to.

Rather than being insulted, Aneesyma smiled. "My homeland, Hammarsh Keep, is densely populated, both within and outside its walls. Your arrival any nearer could very well have led to a riot—one sparked by fear or astonishment or both. Either way, I do not think we could have gotten much accomplished."

Jocel and Kalini nodded, but Pheunaf did not respond.

"So, Pheunaf, tell me about this boy. Zaban..." Aneesyma struggled with the name.

"Zabaneja," Pheunaf said, correcting him.

"I am sorry. That name does not roll off a human's tongue as easily as it does a drageal," Aneesyma replied. "From what Kalini tells me, he is about twelve years old."

Pheunaf nodded.

"Ah, a good age. Young enough to fear his parents and toe the line, but old enough not to have to be watched every moment of the day."

"I give him no reason to fear me." Pheunaf snorted. "I am no monster."

"Forgive me, Lady, I did not mean to imply such a thing. I am sure you have raised him well. Perhaps, the word fear is not exactly the correct one for what I meant. At least not actual fear. I meant to say, the way I remember it when I was that age, the child still feels the parent must be obeyed at all costs."

Aneesyma was glad to see Pheunaf relax a bit.

"Alas, when he reaches puberty, that may change in an instant."

"Puber..." Pheunaf struggled to pronounce the word.

Aneesyma thought a moment, looking for the words—the right words—to explain. "Puberty is the time in a child's life, be they boy or girl, when their bodies change, mature. And boys bodies mature faster than their minds."

Pheunaf still looked confused.

"To put it bluntly, it is when they begin to mature sexually."

"Ah, yes," Jocel replied. "That is what we are here to discuss."

"Well, I will answer any of your questions as honestly as I can."

"Go on, daughter, ask him."

"I had hoped to speak to another female. Like Filemena."

"A woman, no matter how wise, could not tell you what the boy will really be experiencing. Only what she has heard," Aneesyma said. "Now, please ask me what you wish to know and let us ignore each other's embarrassment."

Pheunaf nodded. She was beginning to like this human. He had a sensibility about him. Over the next few hours, Pheunaf and Aneesyma discussed her concerns. Both were so fixated on their conversation, they failed to notice Jocel and Kalini wander off to the other side of the clearing.

After many questions, Pheunaf looked away and was silent for several moments.

"You still seem unsettled. What weighs so heavily on your mind that you fear to ask?"

For the first time since they met, she smiled. "You are indeed perceptive, Aneesyma. Very much like my Zabaneja. There are still a few things that worry me."

"And what might they be?"

"When drageals reach the age of sexual awareness, they need to find a partner to satisfy their physical desires. If unable to do so, many have been known to go mad, sometimes to the point of diving to their death."

Aneesyma shook his head in awe at her words.

"Do humans experience the same thing? Should I worry about Zabaneja in that way?"

Aneesyma reached for her hand. "Ah, now I understand. No, humans do not react that extremely to not being able to relieve their sexual desires."

Pheunaf released the breath she had been holding.

"However, though not directly related to his burgeoning sexual awareness and desires," Aneesyma continued, "do not be surprised if your once pleasant-natured boy suddenly becomes sullen and outright combative." He chuckled. "I hope that even in the depths of frustration he would start a fight with a drageal, even a little one."

Pheunaf smiled. "No, that would not be a pretty sight at all."

"I sense there is still something else on your mind."

"Filemena suggested I should send him back to live amongst his own kind as he approached manhood. Do you think that is necessary?"

Aneesyma rose and walked a few steps away. "That is not an easy question to answer," he began. "If you are asking if he will die from never having associated with his own kind, I must emphatically say no, human contact is not a requirement for his survival."

Again, Pheunaf let out a sigh of relief.

"On the other hand," Aneesyma continued, "if you are asking whether I think he should have the opportunity to live amongst his own kind, that is something of an entirely different matter; one I respectfully decline to answer. It must be up to you and him to decide what is best for him and for his happiness. Will he be happy never finding a mate? Never doing things with beings with similar abilities? That is something I am unable to answer. I think you have some time before you need to consider that. Let him grow a bit more. Watch him and see how he reacts to his maturation. If there comes a time when you, or the two of you together, feel his quality of life in the long run would benefit from his being with humans, have him go to the humans."

Pheunaf did not respond for several moments, and both she and Aneesyma sat in silence.

"And, if I come to that decision? How will he be able to join a human group? He only speaks dragealian. Only knows our ways," Pheunaf said after a time.

Aneesyma again touched her hand. "If, my dearest Pheunaf, that becomes your decision, have Kalini contact me. I shall bring him into my household and help him transition into life amongst humans."

"That is very kind of you, Aneesyma. But what if you dislike him?"

Aneesyma laughed, deep and hearty. "My Lady, if he was raised by you I know for certain I will be immediately endeared to him."

Pheunaf lowered her eyes.

#

"What still troubles you?" Jocel asked when he and Pheunaf were alone.

She thought for a moment. "I am relieved to know he will not attempt to end his own life if he does not find a female."

"But..."

"I am still worried about him. About how he will react to the changes Aneesyma spoke of and with no one for him to talk to about them and what he should do or feel or... well, any of it. If I am to understand Aneesyma, humans are not nearly as instinctive in these matters as we are. I am torn. Not sure what to do. How to handle this. Should I just wait to see how he reacts to the changes in himself and his body? Or, should I send him off to live with the humans? And, if that is the decision, when? Should he go now, before any of the changes begin, or should it be later?"

She breathed a heavy sigh and shrugged.

"I understand your dilemma, child."

"Simply understand, or are you going to give me a solution?"

Jocel looked at her with just the slightest glint of amusement. "It is not up to me to decide Zabaneja's future. He is, and always has been, your child and, therefore your responsibility."

She was not really surprised by her father's response. Still, a small part of her hoped he would tell her what to do.

He put his arm around her and hugged her tightly. "You know I will be here to offer advice, but, in the end, the decision must come from you."

She nodded.

"Well, Aneesyma said you had some time. Perhaps as long as a few years, so why not put the decision aside for the moment? Enjoy the time you have left with him…"

"Left with him?" she snapped and pulled away. "So you actually believe I should send him away?"

Her reaction surprised Jocel. "That is not what I said. If you had let me finish… What I was going to say, before you jumped to your erroneous conclusion, was, you should enjoy the time you have left with him while he is still a child. And remember, if the time comes when you feel the need, we can bring Zabaneja to meet with Aneesyma to just talk things out."

"Of course, why had I not thought of that?"

Jocel smiled. "Let us head home."

They made the return journey in silence.

CHAPTER SEVEN

"WHY ARE YOU ALWAYS watching me, Mother?" Zabaneja asked.

"I do not know what you mean, son. Why would I be doing such a thing?"

He shook his head. "I am not sure, but it seems lately, you are always staring at me with a strange look on your face, one I have not seen before."

Pheunaf laughed. "I think you are developing quite the imagination, young man."

\#

It was more than a year before the first signs of the thing Aneesyma called puberty appeared. It started with his voice. From one word to the next, his voice would deepen then rise then crack, much to the amusement of all but him.

Though he did not show any major behavioral changes, he became a bit more sullen and withdrawn. Pheunaf was concerned and arranged another meeting with Aneesyma. This time, she decided to bring Zabaneja along. She prayed it was the right action.

#

"What do you mean you want me to go on a flight with you?" Zabaneja asked, his voice full of annoyance. "Where? Why?"

"There is someone I wish you to meet."

"Who?"

"You will find out when we get there," she replied as they finished attaching the seat to her back.

She nodded to him to get on and, in between gripes and grumbles, he did as he was told. She chuckled inwardly at how, regardless of how much he argued, he would do just about anything if it meant he could fly.

It did not take long for the pair to reach their destination.

"So, where is this mysterious drageal I am to meet? There is no one here," he said, his tone insolent.

"Patience, boy. They will be here soon enough."

Zabaneja rolled his eyes.

Within a few moments, there was a rustling noise from the direction of the wooded area. Zabaneja thought it odd, any drageal bigger than a newborn would not be able to walk through the dense foliage.

He turned and saw two figures. The first looked remarkably like a ferret, but there was something unique about it. Something he could not define, but he somehow knew it was not a ferret. The other was a human, a male, similar to himself, but at the same time different. The human was taller and broader than Zabaneja and had yellow hair that hung loosely across his shoulders. The boy wondered who he was and, more importantly, why had his mother brought him to meet of all things a human.

"Do not stare, son. It is rude. You do not wish to be thought impolite by our friends, do you?" Pheunaf asked.

Zabaneja did not respond.

"Ah, Pheunaf, it is good to see you again. It has been far too long," the ferret-like being said. "You have indeed done a good job raising him, just as Filemena knew you would." She then turned to the boy. "And, you, young man, must be Zabaneja. It has been quite some time since last I laid eyes on you. You were just a babe, all pink and squishy, and look at you know. I have heard so much about you over the years."

"Well, I have never heard anything about you," Zabaneja replied rudely.

"I suppose not," the man said, ignoring the boy's tone of voice, "so allow me, this is Kalini and it is her magic that allows us to understand each other, since I assure you, I cannot speak, nor understand, dragealian or, for that matter, chetogan."

"Chetogan?" Zabaneja asked.

Kalini grinned. "Yes. I am a chetoga, and that is my language."

Zabaneja flushed with embarrassment.

"Please forgive him. I did not tell him the reason for our flight here," Pheunaf said.

"And you still have not," Zabaneja snarled.

"Do not speak to me in that tone of voice," Pheunaf said, annoyed by his attitude. "I am your mother and these are my friends, and you will be polite to both them and me. Do you understand?"

The sharpness of her voice made Zabaneja redden. "Yes, Mother. I am sorry."

"It is not me you need to apologize to."

Zabaneja turned to the others, his face even redder than before, but before he had a chance to respond, Aneesyma spoke up.

"There is no reason for him to apologize. We understand his

confusion and mistrust."

"Well, I do not. He has no reason to mistrust anyone I would introduce him to," Pheunaf said and turned to Zabaneja. "Have I ever, even once in your entire life, done anything to hurt you? Or put you in a situation that had the slightest possibility of doing so?"

Zabaneja shook his head and lowered his eyes. "No, Mother, you never have," he replied just above a whisper.

"Then you should know I would not do so now."

Zabaneja neither looked up nor answered.

Pheunaf turned back to the others. "I am so glad you could come, and on such short notice."

"We were glad to hear you wanted to see us again," Kalini said.

"And, I for one, was even more excited when I heard I was finally going to meet this young man," Aneesyma added.

Zabaneja looked up into the man's eyes. They were icy blue, like the color of frozen mountain pools. And while they did not hold the same depth and power as those of a drageal, the boy sensed a sincerity within them that made him relax.

"I apologize for my rudeness. It is just I have never encountered anyone like either of you before. And..."

Zabaneja's words drifted off because, in truth, he did not understand why he had acted as he had. And that happened more and more lately. He would suddenly go from being in a good mood to being argumentative for no apparent reason.

After a moment, he turned to his mother. "So, why did you bring me to meet these two?" he asked, his voice now calm.

"Because, son," Pheunaf began, "you are at an age where..." Now it was the drageal's turn to struggle with finding the right words to express a concept she did not fully understand.

Aneesyma did not allow her to struggle long. "If I may, Pheunaf, perhaps I can explain."

Zabaneja snapped his head around, the anger returning to his eyes, and glared at the man. "My mother is perfectly capable of speaking her own mind without the aid of a human."

The others, especially Pheunaf, were taken aback by the contempt Zabaneja showed for the word 'human', as if its very utterance left a foul taste in his mouth.

"I am sorry, Zabane... I am sorry, your name is difficult for me to say," Aneesyma said and put his hand on the boy's shoulder.

The young boy glared at him and pulled away.

"Stop it, Zabaneja. Aneesyma is here to help us."

"Help us? We need no help."

"Child, you are growing up. You are changing, both in body and in mind. And, I, as much as any drageal, hate to admit I cannot do everything myself. Right now, I am not certain I know how best to help you through these changes. I am not human. I have no idea what you are going through. Therefore, I have sought the help of a human, one who can explain what is happening to you."

"Nothing is happening to me. I am fine. Just as I have always been," Zabaneja snapped.

He turned to leave, but she lightly grasped his shoulder. He tried to pull away. She pulled him close and hugged him tightly.

"We both know that is not the truth," she whispered and lifted his face toward her. "Take this, for example," she said and ran a finger lightly over the side of his face. "You never had hair on your face before."

He tried to wriggle out of her grasp, but she would not let go.

"I am only here to help you," Aneesyma said. "To let you know what to expect over the next few months and years. And how to cope with some of them in the unique living arrangement you have."

Zabaneja once again took offense at the man's words. Words the boy took as an insult to his family and the drageals. He broke free from his mother's grasp and leapt at the man, knocking him to the ground. But, in the next moment, without even seeing the man move, Aneesyma was standing over him with his boot on Zabaneja's throat.

The boy tried to move, tried to push the man's foot away, but Aneesyma countered his resistance, pressing harder on Zabaneja's throat, making it difficult for him to breathe.

"You may sling words of abuse at me all day, young man, without the fear of retaliation, for I will make allowances for your youth and the stupidity that comes with it. However, I will not afford you such license if you choose to attack me physically."

Aneesyma turned to Pheunaf, half afraid the drageal might strike at him for his actions against her son. He was relieved to see the opposite reaction from her. He turned his attention back to the boy, still squirming, but far less so, under his boot.

"You have now been told more than once this day that we are here to help you, yet you fail to accept that. While I am not going to hurt you, do you think you will see the same end if you attempt such a silly action against one of the drageals? If you launched yourself at Darchok, would he let you off with a warning or even just a cuffing?"

Zabaneja's mind was immediately filled with images of the many things Darchok had threatened to do to him.

Aneesyma watched as the boy's expression changed from anger to abject terror, assuring him the threats the boy had endured were far worse than anything the man could have imagined. He removed his foot from the boy's throat, bent over and offered a hand to help Zabaneja up. This time, the boy accepted, clearly shaken by what he had conjured in his mind.

"I am sorry, I do not know what came over me?" Zabaneja said as he rose and brushed the dust from his clothes.

"But you see, I do. I know what came over you and I can help you."

"You can make these strange feelings go away?"

Aneesyma shook his head. "Not completely. They are a part of growing up, of maturing from a boy into a man. But I can give you ways to help deal with them and tell you of other changes that will occur."

This time, Zabaneja did not deny nor argue. He just nodded. "I think I would like that."

"Good," Aneesyma replied with a smile. "Let us take a walk, and we can talk. I will tell you all I know of what you are going through."

Zabaneja nodded, and the two walked off toward the trees.

#

A part of Pheunaf was afraid as she watched Zabaneja and Aneesyma walk away. Afraid Aneesyma might steal her son from her. That he had men waiting amongst the trees, waiting to grab him and ride off with him before she even knew what was happening. The rational part of her knew Aneesyma would do no such thing. She breathed a sigh of relief when the two stopped and sat upon two large rocks near the edge of the forest.

Kalini, who had been silent to this point, reached over and touched the drageal's hand. "You know you have nothing to fear from Aneesyma, do you not?"

Pheunaf looked down at the chetoga. "Sometimes, Kalini, I think your magic is more than just allowing us to speak to each other. Sometimes, I think you can see into another's mind, into their thoughts, as well."

"I do not know what you mean."

The drageal chuckled. "Yes, I am sure you do not."

"It does not take magic to know what you are thinking, at least not in this situation."

"Really? And, pray tell, what would that be?" Pheunaf asked, her voice strained.

"You fear Aneesyma will tell you Zabaneja should come with him. And, in the dark recesses of your mind, you worry Aneesyma might steal the boy from you."

Pheunaf was shocked. "So, you can indeed read my thoughts."

Kalini shook her head. "No. I am also a mother, and every mother fears the loss of her child, even when it is something as normal as them going off with a mate to start a life and family of their own. And, my dear drageal, you have the added complication that your child is not of your kind, so I can only imagine what fears that conjures up in your mind."

CHAPTER EIGHT

"THE TIME HAS COME, BOY," Pheunaf said a year or so after his first meeting with Aneesyma.

"For what?" Zabaneja asked.

"For you to leave."

"What? What do you mean?"

"It is clear, to me and to everyone else, you have no desire to remain among us."

"That is not true. You know that. This is my home. You and the clan are my family. The only family I know, have ever known."

Pheunaf fought to hold back her tears. "Be that as it may, your behavior as of late—your sullen moods, belligerence, and outright rudeness—does not support that. On more than one occasion, you have even gone so far as to curse your existence here."

"But Mother, you know I did not really mean those things. They were only spoken in anger."

"Perhaps, but your outbursts of anger have become more and more frequent. And your actions during those outbursts are becoming intolerable. It is only a matter of time before there is a physical confrontation."

Zabaneja looked stunned. "I will change, I swear. I will go back to the way I was."

Pheunaf smiled and stroked the side of his face. "I do not think that possible. You are no longer that child."

"What will you do to me? Surely you would not send me off on my own, would you? I do not know if I could survive by myself."

Pheunaf shook her head. "I would never do such a thing. You are my son and I love you, no matter what you do. But we do not live alone."

"And?"

"I have decided to send you off to live with the humans."

"NO! You cannot do that to me."

"Yes, I can and I will. It is the only way. You need to be with your own kind. They will be able to help you deal with these changes."

"But I do not want to go. I do not want to leave you or the clan, this place," Zabaneja said, his voice barely above a whisper.

"I know, son, but there is no other way. It is my fault. I should not have been so selfish to think I could provide you with all you needed to grow and thrive. I should have listened to the old woman so many years ago and let you be raised by your own kind. It is my fault you must now endure this turmoil."

"Do not send me away, Mother. Please let me stay."

Pheunaf shook her head. "I cannot do that."

"Where will I go?"

"I have made arrangements with Aneesyma. He will take you into his household and help you."

"But I cannot even talk to him, not without Kalini's magic."

She smiled. "You will learn. Just as you learned to speak dragealian, you will learn Aneesyma's language."

"Is there no way I can talk you out of this?"

"No."

"When will I leave?"

"Tomorrow."

Zabaneja was shocked. "That soon? That will not even allow me time to say farewell to my friends."

"I suggest you do so this night."

#

As Zabaneja walked outside, he heard a low, guttural chuckle. He did not have to look to know who it was.

"So, at last, we are to be rid of you," Darchok said as he stepped out of the shadows.

Zabaneja did not reply.

"I always told you this day would come, eventually, all, even my dimwitted sister, would see you for what you truly are."

The boy was in no mood to listen to his uncle, but at the moment, had no choice. The drageal positioned himself so Zabaneja could neither advance nor retreat from where he stood.

"Yes, uncle," Zabaneja sighed. "You were right all along."

Darchok snorted. "Well, I am glad you have finally faced the truth. So where is she sending you? To some new master who will treat you like the filth you are? Or perhaps she has found some beast looking for an appetizer to its meal."

Zabaneja shrugged.

"Come now, boy. Surely, you know something."

Zabaneja shook his head. "No. Mother has told me nothing, merely that I am to leave very soon."

A flash of anger crossed Darchok's eyes. "She is not your mother. You have been nothing more than a pet to her. To her and all the others you foolishly thought to be friends. But now, now, you have outlasted your usefulness as even that. So, we will at last be rid of you. You and your filthy habits and foul odor. Had I been in charge of this clan..."

"Yes, yes, uncle, I know," Zabaneja interrupted. He shook his head in exasperation. "You have been saying the same thing to me for as long as I can remember. So, at last you can enjoy your life without the stench of something not drageal constantly offending your delicate nose."

With that, the boy squeezed past the drageal and returned to his room, Darchok's sadistic laughter echoing in his wake.

Zabaneja sat mulling over the words of both his mother and uncle. And, in a short while, they took on the same meaning. He was no longer wanted here. And, as that realization became his reality, he became angry and decided to leave on his own. Tonight. With no farewells. Without his mother taking him to Aneesyma to become whatever it was the human had in mind for him.

He packed his few meager belongings—a stone from the first place he remembered flying, a feather shed by a beautiful bird he had seen perched in a tree, and a few other trinkets. He waited until he was sure Pheunaf was asleep, until he could hear her soft breaths in the quiet of the night, then slipped out.

He was not sure where he would go, or even how far he could get from his mountain home on foot. Was there even a land route off the mountain? And, if so, would it be so dangerous it might lead to his death? Did he even care?

As he made his way to where he hoped a path would be, Zabaneja was glad there was a bit of moonlight. That would help him see where his footfalls should be so he would not fall from the mountainside. For the briefest moment, he thought of throwing himself off the mountain. But only for a moment. No, he would not now nor ever do such a thing, because it was not in his nature. He also refused to ever give Darchok the satisfaction of knowing he had affected him.

#

The trek down the mountain was slow and arduous. Even with the moonlight, the path, when there was one, proved treacherous. As the sun rose, he realized he had not gotten very far.

He wondered if anyone would look for him and hoped they would just let him go. His thoughts were disturbed by a sound imperceptible to the untrained ear, the slight whoosh of a drageal in flight. He was not sure if it was someone looking for him or just one out on a morning flight. He flattened his back against the rock, hoping not to be seen.

"Well, well, well. What have we got here?" Darchok chuckled. "Is that a speck of dirt clinging to the side of my mountain? Perhaps, I should pluck it off and drop it into the abyss so my mountain can once again be clean and pure," he continued, his voice more menacing with each word.

Zabaneja did not reply. He had no defense should Darchok decide to do just that. And, unless someone saw him, someone not afraid to speak against him, it would be thought Zabaneja had merely slipped and plummeted to his death. If anyone even cared.

"Or should I carry it away and drop it in someone else's territory and let it be their bane, not mine?" Darchok continued.

Zabaneja did not need to look at Darchok to know he was gloating.

"So, uncle…"

"How many times must I tell you not to call me that? You are no kin of mine, vermin," the drageal snarled.

"Be that as it may," Zabaneja continued, not sure why he was trying to goad the drageal. After all, Darchok, not he, was in the position of power. A few heavy wing flaps and Zabaneja would be pushed off the mountain without the drageal ever touching him, and with no one ever knowing the drageal had a hand in the boy's demise.

"It does seem you are finally getting your desire. You are to be rid of me."

Darchok snickered. "True. But I face a dilemma. How rid of you do I wish to be?"

Zabaneja sighed knowing Darchok was preparing one of his long speeches. Again, unsure why he did so, the boy taunted the drageal.

"Please, uncle, spare me the rhetoric. We are both aware of the precariousness of my situation and the advantage you hold. So, either let me pass or pluck me from my perch and drop me into the abyss. I have listened to your rantings my entire life and do not wish to hear any more of them."

"Why, you little whelp!" Darchok sneered. "I had thought of allowing you to pass unharmed, but now... Now that you have shown me such contempt, merely dropping you to your death does not seem punishment enough."

Zabaneja swallowed trying to dislodge the lump in his throat realizing he had gone too far.

"Your memory is apparently short or, more likely, you are stupid. Have you forgotten all those things I told you? All the ways I can hurt you? How much I can make you suffer before I finally grant you the relief of death?"

"No, Darchok, you are wrong. I am neither stupid nor is my memory short. I remember every threat. Every insult. But I no longer fear you. If you do choose to kill me in whatever way you find appealing, then so be it. The guilt for that action will be on your head."

"Ha! As if anything as inconsequential as you would cause me pause, let alone guilt."

"Yes," Zabaneja said and looked away from the drageal. "I understand that. But what of your sister, my mother, when she hears of your part in my demise."

The drageal laughed. "And just how will that happen? We are alone. There is not another set of eyes for miles. Who is going to tell her?"

Now it was Zabaneja's turn to laugh. "You. Not to her face, of course. At some point, you will feel the need to brag about this, about how you finally rid yourself of the noxious being that infested your household. And, when you do, it will get back to Mother's ears. And, even if you deny it, she will believe what she heard, for she knows you. Everyone in the clan knows you. And no one feels you are above such an act. We all understand what you are capable of."

Darchok's nostrils flared and for a brief moment, Zabaneja felt certain he would soon be incinerated where he stood. But the fire breath did not appear.

"That may well be true. But I will deal with Pheunaf when, and if, the time comes because, it will be worth it to be rid of you once and for all. Your mere departure leaves the door open for your return. I must ensure that is not an option. I will not only close the door, but forever seal it."

The drageal slowly flew closer to the boy. Zabaneja closed his eyes, took a deep breath, and prepared himself for death.

"Darchok! What are you doing?"

Zabaneja opened his eyes and saw Darchok's defeated look at the sound of Pheunaf's voice. He growled under his breath and turned toward her.

"Sister. So glad you arrived. I was on my morning flight and saw something on the mountainside. When I approached, I saw it was Zabaneja. I was just trying to discover why he was here and get him to come back home with me."

Pheunaf did not believe her brother's story. He may have just stumbled across him during flight, but it was doubtful he was trying to help Zabaneja.

"Thank you, brother. I will see he gets home safely."

The large red drageal nodded, he turned to Zabaneja and whispered, "This is not over, boy. Do not think you have won."

Won? I have not won. Not unless Mother has changed her mind about sending me off to Aneesyma, Zabaneja thought. *Do you think death, even a painful one, is the ultimate punishment? Ha! Exile from all you hold dear, your home and loved ones, is a far worse sentence.*

As soon as Darchok was gone, Pheunaf flew in closer and gently plucked the boy from the path. She clutched him to her chest and took off. To Zabaneja's surprise, she flew in the opposite direction from both home and the usual place they met the others.

CHAPTER NINE

"WHAT WERE YOU THINKING, BOY?" she asked when they landed.

"Does it matter? Why did you not just let Darchok do away with me? At least that would have been a quick demise rather than being subjected to who knows what at the hands of Aneesyma."

"What in the world are you talking about?"

"You know very well, Mother. You are sending me off to Aneesyma to be his pet or worse."

Pheunaf could not help but let out a bit of a laugh. "My dear boy, you and that imagination of yours, urged on, I am sure, by a few words from my brother have truly outdone themselves this time."

Her laughter, even stifled, irked the young boy. "Do you deny you are exiling me to a life where I know no one, know nothing. Dammit, Mother, I do not even speak their language."

"It is not an exile, son."

"Really? Then what do you call it?"

"I call it an opportunity for you to grow. To become the man you were meant to be."

Zabaneja snorted and turned away.

"Child, think about it, not with your emotions and the pain you are feeling, but with your mind. Do you seriously think I would ever, under any circumstance, send you to a place where you would be hurt? Do you think that little of me and the love I have for you?"

He knew from the waver in her voice she was in as much anguish and turmoil over this situation as he was—perhaps even more. But his anger would not let him openly acknowledge that.

"You say that, but still you insist on sending me away, do you not?"

"It is in your best interest."

"Bah!"

"You know Aneesyma is a good man, and he has been a good friend these past few years. Do you really think he would do something to harm you? That he would offer to take you into his own household only to abuse you?" Her voice cracked as she spoke, and Zabaneja's anger dissipated.

"But, I do not want to go, Mother. I do not want to leave you and the others."

He ran to her and threw his arms around her. She closed her massive wings in front of her, wrapping him within them.

"I am sorry, Mother, I did not mean to accuse you of..." he said, struggling with the words.

"Shh, child. There is no need to apologize, I understand. This is painful for us both. As much as you do not want to go, I do not want to send you away."

He pulled back and looked up into her face. "Then do not make me go. Let me stay."

She smiled. "Ah, if only I could. But this is something that must be done. Something I have always known would happen no matter how much I tried to deny it."

"But, why? Why must it happen?"

She opened her wings and gently took him by the shoulders to face her. "Because, you are growing into a man. A human man. One with needs. Needs you have already seen your friends satisfy. Needs that in time will make you hate me for not letting you fulfill yourself."

Zabaneja looked confused.

"Trust me, son. This is for the best."

He again shook his head. "I do not, I cannot, believe that."

"I know."

The pair stood in silence for several moments until Pheunaf finally spoke. "It is almost time. Aneesyma will be waiting for us."

Zabaneja wanted to cry out, to protest, to try one last time to convince his mother she should change her mind and allow him to stay. But he knew it would be nothing more than futility, a waste of time, so he merely nodded.

"Do you wish to get your flying seat?"

He shook his head.

"Will it not be uncomfortable flying in my arms for that distance?"

"I will be fine if you will," he replied. A part of him hoped she would drop him into a deep ravine during the flight, but he knew that would never happen.

She nodded, and the pair took off.

Halfway to the meeting point, Zabaneja regretted his decision. The memory of this, his last flight, would be anything but wonderful. This memory would be of a tedious, uncomfortable journey, so unlike all the others he had taken before.

#

"I see we are early," Pheunaf said.

"Mother, how will I communicate with Aneesyma and the other humans. I do not speak their language, and it would be highly unlikely any of them speak dragealian."

"Yes, it would be quite odd to find another human speaker. I am sure Kalini has a plan. She is almost as meticulous as a drageal," Pheunaf said with a chuckle.

Zabaneja did not share his mother's expectations.

A few moments later, Aneesyma and Kalini emerged from the brush.

"So good to see you both again," Aneesyma said as he bowed to Pheunaf and then patted Zabaneja on the back. "Well, son..."

"It is Zabaneja. I am not your son," the boy snapped.

"My apologies, Za... bah... new... jear," Aneesyma said, mangling the pronunciation of the boy's name. "I did not mean to offend you. I was going to say you have grown quite a bit since the last time I saw you."

"Yes, and so has his appetite. He eats near on as much as most drageals his age," Pheunaf added to help ease the tension.

Aneesyma laughed. "Oh, I am sure he does. Most boys his age seem hellbent to eat every morsel of food they can find."

"I have a question about all of this," Zabaneja said, his sullen tone in contrast to the others.

"Only one?" Aneesyma replied.

Zabaneja darted toward Aneesyma and grabbed him by the collar. "Do not make light of what I say. I am no child, do not treat me like one."

Aneesyma grabbed the boy by the wrist and with only the slightest movement brought Zabaneja to his knees.

"That is the second time you have laid your hands on me. And it will be the last. If you ever again touch me in anger," Aneesyma leaned in and whispered in the boy's ear, "I will have your head."

Zabaneja was surprised. Though there was no anger, and certainly no volume in Aneesyma's threat, he felt more afraid of the menace hidden inside Aneesyma than he ever had of Darchok and his rantings.

Aneesyma released Zabaneja and took a step back. "Do you understand me, boy?"

Zabaneja nodded. "It will not happen again, I promise," he said and stood up.

"So, what was your question?"

"Does Kalini live with you?"

Now it was Kalini's turn to chuckle. "I dare say not. Chetoga are not suited for that sort of household."

Zabaneja was not sure what she meant, but was now more concerned with other matters at hand. "Then how will we communicate? I have no desire to be mute or to be looked upon as the dumb animal who merely grunts and points at what he wants."

Aneesyma put his hand on Zabaneja's shoulder and, though he tensed, the boy did not pull away. "Have no fear of that, my boy. I shall teach you to speak and understand the language of my people."

"But it takes years to do such a thing. What am I to do in the meantime? If that is the best plan you can come up with, I would rather be left alone to die."

"Stop overreacting and let Aneesyma explain," Pheunaf said.

"Thank you, Pheunaf. You are indeed correct in your assessment, young man. Under normal circumstances, it would indeed take more time than we have. So, Kalini has devised a way to speed up the process."

"How?"

Aneesyma cocked an eyebrow as he looked at the boy.

"Yes, I understand it will use her magic. I am not stupid," he snapped. "I was asking how she will use her magic on me, on us?"

"Let me explain." Kalini described the plan. When she finished, she looked at Zabaneja. "You do not look convinced."

"It sounds simple enough, but I am not sure it will indeed work."

"Well, we will just have to wait and see."

Zabaneja turned to ask Pheunaf what she thought, only to find her gone.

"Where is she? Where is my Mother? What have you done with her?" he cried.

"Calm down, boy. We did nothing to her. She departed," Kalini said.

"But, she... I... We did not say goodbye," Zabaneja whispered.

Kalini walked to him and took his hand. "She felt it was best this way."

Zabaneja did not know what to do. He wanted to run and scream and call her back. Instead he clenched his fists, dropped to his knees, and roared at the empty sky.

His companions stepped away to allow him time with his grief and anger.

#

Once his voice was spent, Zabaneja approached Kalini and Aneesyma. He did not apologize for his behavior; he was not sorry for his actions.

"Zabaneja," Kalini said, "I have something for you. Something Pheunaf asked me to give you."

The boy looked at the chetoga and saw a small pouch.

"What is it?" he asked.

"She did not tell me, she merely said to give it to you."

He held out his hand and Kalini dropped the pouch into it.

Zabaneja looked down at the soft, heavily gilded cloth and closed his fingers around it.

"Thank you," he whispered.

Kalini wanted to ask why he did not immediately open it, but refrained. Perhaps the boy had an inkling what was in the bag and how it might affect him and wanted to be alone when he saw it.

CHAPTER TEN

"IT IS TIME WE MOVE ON," Aneesyma said. "I do not wish to be here when night falls. We need to get to shelter."

Zabaneja was confused. He had never been afraid to be anywhere, night or day. The only time he and the drageals sought shelter was during storms.

"I see no storm approaching," the boy said. "Why do we need shelter?"

"You are no longer amongst drageals."

"I am well aware of that," Zabaneja snapped back.

This may be far more arduous than I imagined. He takes even the most innocent statement as insult to kin and self. Aneesyma wondered if he had the patience for it.

"That was not meant as an insult. If a drageal, even a small one, was near, no wild animal would dare approach. That will not be the case with the three of us. We do best to get somewhere where we will find both comfort and security."

Zabaneja did not respond, he just continued glaring at Aneesyma.

"Now that is settled," Kalini said, hoping the lilt in her voice might lighten the tension between her companions. "I suggest we get started."

She turned to Zabaneja. "It will take several hours to get to the cabin we will stay at for the next bit of time."

"Cabin?"

"Oh, forgive me, I forgot you are not familiar with the customs or lifestyle of humans," she replied. "A cabin, or a house or various other names, depending on its size or lack thereof, is the structure where humans reside."

"Like our aeries and caves?"

"Similar. The one we will be staying in is made of wood and is, you will find, very small compared to what you are used to. After all, it is meant to house creatures the size of humans, not drageals. But you will find it to be warm and comfortable, and it will keep us safe from the weather and all but the largest predators."

The trio left the clearing and entered the woods. Zabaneja kept looking around and upward, reaching out to the trees and occasionally stopping to touch the moss or grass. As the forest thickened and the path narrowed, the trees crowded in upon them. Zabaneja's awe at the beauty turned to a deep sense of confinement.

"How much further?" he asked, praying the cabin would afford more openness. "The air is so thick in here, I can hardly breathe."

"Ah, yes. Sorry. We had not thought that the closeness of our route might cause you discomfort. But it should not be too much longer before we arrive," Kalini replied.

"If everything is going to be like this..." Zabaneja did not finish his thought.

"No, it is not all like this," Aneesyma replied. "Though I sincerely doubt you will find many places with as much open space as you are accustomed to."

Zabaneja scowled. Yet another thing he had to give up and for no good reason. With each step, the trees seemed to close in on him and his breathing became labored yet the others were having no such reaction. He took a deep breath, or at least as deep as this stifling atmosphere would allow, and squeezed the pouch in his pocket. At that moment, he wanted to both curse his mother and run back to her, begging to be allowed to stay with her and the drageals. But he did neither, he just trod on following the others.

With each step, he feared he could take the closeness no longer and then they were at the edge of a clearing. Small, but at least there was open space and Zabaneja could again breathe and see the sky.

"I told you it was not a long trek through the trees," Aneesyma said.

Ha! Zabaneja thought. *It felt like an eternity.* "It was long enough," Zabaneja snarled, not trying to conceal his anger.

"Be that as it may, we are here now. We already laid some supplies in for our stay, so it should be pleasant enough."

They continued into the clearing and Zabaneja stopped. "Do not tell me that tiny box is where you expect me to stay."

"As a matter of fact, it is," Kalini said.

"It is not even large enough to house a dragonlet." Even from the outside he could see this was a far cry from his home with stone halls and ceilings so wide and high even the largest drageal never felt cramped.

"That may very well be. But there are no dragonlets here, so it will be quite large enough for a chetoga and two humans." Aneesyma cursed himself for allowing his annoyance to show.

Zabaneja did not respond. He merely followed the others inside. He surveyed his surroundings, an action that did not take long since the room was quite small.

"I cannot stay here."

"You can and you will. It may not be as large as my castle, and certainly far smaller than your home, but it is sturdy and clean and more than large enough to accommodate the three of us," Aneesyma replied.

"There is no air to breathe."

"Do not be absurd."

"But…"

Aneesyma turned on his heel and stood in front of the boy. "There is no but. Whether you like the situation you are in or not, is none of my concern. What I do care about is keeping my promise to your mother, to help you find your way in the human world."

"I do not want to."

"And I do not care what you want."

Zabaneja was taken aback by the man's response and he stood silently staring at him.

Aneesyma pointed to a corner on the far side of the room. "The bed roll over there is for you. Go put your things away and then come outside and help us prepare the evening meal."

Before Zabaneja could respond, Aneesyma was gone.

#

"You need to have patience, Aneesyma," Kalini said as the two stood a distance away from the cabin. "He is just a boy. And a confused one at that."

Aneesyma nodded. "I know. I know. But he is already frustrating me so, and we have just barely begun our journey together."

Kalini smiled. "And we both know this is only the beginning."

"Yes, I expect things to get far worse before they get better. If they ever do."

"Again, patience."

"Not my strong suit, eh, old friend?"

She laughed. "Not in the least. And yet, you accepted the task of taking the boy in, having at least some inkling of how hard a job it would be to assimilate him into human society. I have wondered why you made such an offer. Surely it was not just on a whim. That is not like you."

Aneesyma shrugged and looked off into the distance. "I am not sure. Perhaps it was the desperation I saw in Pheunaf's eyes; her fear that, after all these years, after all her efforts, she had failed the boy."

"And do you think she did?"

He turned and saw Zabaneja standing there.

"Not in the least," he said. "In fact, just the opposite. From what she told me, the human you were found beside was the first she had ever seen up close. So, to take on the responsibility to raise you, knowing absolutely nothing of what you would need then or in the future... well, that shows either great compassion or enormous stupidity. Or maybe an outrageous ego thinking one could do anything they set their mind to."

Zabaneja felt the hairs on the back of his neck stand on end at the man's words.

"I, for one," Aneesyma continued before giving Zabaneja a chance to lash out, "think it was out of compassion—blind compassion mixed with a bit of naivete. Regardless, her heart was in the right place." Aneesyma walked over to the boy and put his hand on Zabaneja's shoulder. "Do you have any idea what she went through, the ridicule, the shunning and the rest, just to keep you?"

Zabaneja looked confused.

"I did not think so. Pheunaf is not one to share her woes with others, especially one she holds so dear. Apparently you were never told that when Pheunaf first brought you to the drageal camp, it was not only Darchok who wanted no part of you."

"What are you talking about?"

"It was a hard fought battle for her to keep you, a human, and a helpless infant at that, amongst drageals."

"Are you saying everyone hated me? That they felt like Darchok?"

"No. Most were actually concerned for you, for your safety. You were so tiny and everyone else, even the smallest of dragonlets, was so much larger. What if you were trampled to death? Others, well, they just did not think it right for a human to be there amongst them and perhaps, on some levels, they were correct."

"What do you mean they were correct? Are you of the same mind as my uncle? That races should stay separate?"

Aneesyma took a deep breath. He had to remind himself that it was the boy's emotions, his heart and his youth reacting.

"Really? Do you sincerely think I feel that way? Do you see who I travel with?" Aneesyma asked, trying to sound as calm as he could.

Zabaneja looked over at the chetoga sitting silently on a rock, seemingly ignoring them.

"I do not believe as your uncle does. I do not abide by the idea that the human race is the only one that matters, that all non-humans are useless or worse. What I believe, dear boy, is that it is difficult for one to be raised by a group that is not their own. Unless, of course, they are looked upon as a pet."

"I was no pet!" Zabaneja sneered.

"I am fully aware of that."

Zabaneja glared at Aneesyma.

"You must admit, by growing up surrounded only by drageals, you have missed out on many things that make a human human."

"That makes no sense. I was content and nothing you or anyone else has said has convinced me it is a good idea for me to go with you."

"Are you saying you do not feel even the smallest amount of jealousy when you see your friends going off together? Knowing that is something you cannot and will not be able to experience?" Aneesyma asked.

"I have no idea what you are talking about."

Aneesyma smiled but did not respond.

"My friends are drageals. If they do not mate when they reach a certain age, they will go mad or worse. I do not have any such requirements upon me."

"Perhaps. But, perhaps, you are just too uninformed to know what is happening to you or why. Surely you have seen the changes in your body."

"My body is growing, that is all. That is natural. All creatures become larger and stronger as they get older. I am no different."

"And, what of your behavior? Do you know what is causing those changes?"

"My behavior is the same as it has always been. This conversation is pointless." Zabaneja said and turned back toward the cabin.

"Yes, of course it is," Aneesyma laughed. "It has always been in your nature to get angry and lash out at those around you for no good reason, as you are doing now."

Zabaneja glared then turned on his heel. "I have every reason in the world to be angry right now. You, for whatever reason, have somehow convinced my mother she should abandon me and hand me over to you. You say it is for my own good, but I fail to see that. So, am I angry? More than you know."

He turned and stormed off.

#

"The boy has a point, you know. Nothing you or Pheunaf has said or done has given him any reason to believe this punishment of exile…"

"It is neither punishment nor exile," Aneesyma snapped.

"Now who is getting angry for no reason?" Kalini smiled. "And, while it may not be to you, it most certainly feels as such to him. And, I daresay, at some level to Pheunaf as well."

Aneesyma shook his head and smiled. "You are right, my friend. As always."

"Ha! Do not sound so surprised."

"What am I, we, to do to convince him this is in his best interest?"

Kalini shook her head. "Ah, that is the dilemma. But, for the moment, I am hungry and the grumbling from your belly tells me you are as well. And, it seems the beast you put on the spit to roast is ready, though I daresay I will never understand why you insist on burning up perfectly good meat before you eat it. Disgusting!"

"So, you have told me on countless occasions. Well, I suppose we should call the boy. I am sure his belly is as empty as ours."

CHAPTER ELEVEN

PHEUNAF HATED LEAVING Zabaneja without giving him a final embrace. But she knew if she had touched him or looked into his eyes, she would never have been able to leave, and he needed to be in the human world... at least for now.

She hoped he would eventually come back to her, but that needed to be his choice, not hers. Once alone in the sky, she could no longer contain her emotions and she wept. Wept until she could barely see. Until she could no longer weep. Only then did she travel the final leg of her journey home.

She was glad no one was nearby when she landed. She was in the wrong state of mind for company. All she wanted to do was go to her son's room, to feel his presence, savor his scent one last time before it dissipated even from her keen senses.

She reached the doorway and was horrified by what lay before her. Every inch of the room—floor, walls, and ceiling—was smeared with a thick, sickeningly sweet smelling sap. And, in the middle of the floor was a pile of ashes, the remnants of the few items Zabaneja had left behind. Things she had planned to cherish.

Pheunaf did not need to wonder who had done this. It was

obvious.

She raced to her parent's cave to find the culprit. "Darchok!" she roared as she reached the entrance.

"What is it, dear sister?" he said nonchalantly, approaching her.

"Why did you do it? Why did you destroy Zabaneja's things?" Pheunaf asked.

"It was the only way to finally rid ourselves of the last remnants of that vile creature you forced us to endure. My only regret is he was not amongst the things I burned. That would have been delightful." Darchok snickered.

His words enraged her. She leapt at him with a ferocity neither of them had ever seen in her. The speed of her attack and the surge of strength she unleashed caught Darchok off-guard, and, to his surprise, she knocked the much larger drageal to the ground. Before he could react, she grabbed him around the neck and prepared to slash his throat with her talons.

"What is going on?" Jocel called as he rounded the corner to see his two children literally at each other's throats.

"This time he has gone too far. I will no longer tolerate him," Pheunaf growled and moved her talon closer to Darchok's throat.

"Daughter!" Jocel shouted.

Pheunaf's hesitation was enough to allow Darchok to regain control and throw her off. He prepared to attack her, but Jocel stepped between them.

"Enough! Both of you!"

The two drageals took a step back but continued to glare at each other.

"Pheunaf, I know it has been a trying day, but what could he have possibly done to make you act so? To put yourself in danger?" Jocel asked.

She told him what she had found upon her return and what

Darchok said, bristling at the smug look on her brother's face.

Jocel shook his head and turned to his son. "We have endured your malicious rants and viciousness far too long. This time you have gone too far. As of this moment, this is no longer your home. Leave! Now! You are no longer welcome here."

"What? How dare you? You force me out of my home, my birthright because of that... that thing she has forced upon us these past years?" Darchok lunged toward his father.

With just a flick of his hand, Jocel sent his son sprawling across the room. The elder drageal shook his head. "Not only are you no longer welcome here, but as of this moment you are no longer my son. Begone! Now!"

Darchok slowly rose. "I will not forget this injustice, old man!" he shouted and stormed out. "You will pay for this! Both of you!"

Jocel approached Pheunaf and put his arm around her shoulder. "I know how upset you are, child, but you cannot go after him like that. You are lucky your action shocked him enough that he did not hurt you."

"Had you not stopped me, Father, he would no longer be an issue."

"And you would have regretted that for the rest of your life."

Pheunaf glared at him, not sure she would have.

"I think it best you move home. At least for a little while." When he saw her ready to protest, he added, "Your mother and I do not think it wise that you be alone with just your thoughts at this time and now with Darchok in the state he is in..."

"I would rather be alone."

"Please, dear," Amarysa said from the doorway. "At least for tonight."

The tone of her mother's voice broke through the rage and sorrow, and Pheunaf relented. "Perhaps just this night."

#

Darchok was livid as he left the cave, his home. How could he have allowed her to get the best of him? This would not be the end. He would get his revenge. Too bad the little whelp she so dearly loved was gone. Doing away with him in front of her would be sweet beyond belief.

Darchok did not return home that night or the next. When he did, Jocel met him, blocking the entrance.

"What are you doing, Father? Let me pass."

"This is no longer your home and you are not welcome here."

"What do you mean?" the stunned drageal asked.

"Too long have I tolerated your cruelty, but no more."

"Are you saying I am banished from the clan?" Darchok asked.

Jocel shook his head. "I do not have that authority. I can only ban you from my home."

"I should not be the one suffering this indignity. She is the one who should have been banished when she brought that, that thing into our midst."

Jocel did not reply, he merely stood staring at his son.

"Will you at least let me pass to gather my things?" Darchok asked, still seething.

The older drageal remained silent and pointed to a pile at the side of the cave entrance.

Darchok snorted and glared at his father. After a few moments of failed intimidation, the younger drageal gathered his belongings and departed, grumbling.

He took to the air to clear his head and cool his temper and squelch the desire to rain the fire of his current wrath down upon his father and sister. And even he knew that would not be good. So, he flew, high and fast, to decide what to do.

#

"Why did you do that, Father?" Pheunaf asked as Jocel re-entered the cave.

"It is something I should have done years ago. Perhaps when you first brought the babe here."

Pheunaf thought a moment. "No, I think it would have been far worse for Zabaneja if Darchok was not under your roof. Only recently have I realized the horrors he exposed the boy to."

"As have I, and I am ashamed for being blind to them all those years."

"We both were," Pheunaf replied. "I wish Zabaneja were here so I could tell him how sorry I am for my lack of vision. Why did I not see? Why did he not speak up?"

Jocel took her hand and smiled. "Because, my dear, he is your child and like you have always done, and likely will always do, he tried to solve the problem on his own."

"Even if his only solution was enduring it?"

"Just as you always did."

"Me?" Pheunaf asked.

"Yes," Jocel replied and pointed to a featherless scar just under the top edge of her wing. "You did not come to me for help when Darchok did that, did you?"

"No."

Jocel chuckled. "And neither did Zabaneja. He may not be your natural child, but he certainly inherited your independence and stubbornness."

She turned away. "Nevertheless, I sent him away. Banished him from the only home he ever knew."

"You did not banish him," Jocel replied. "You are giving him the opportunity to become the man he should be, whether it is amongst humans or drageals."

"I do not think he sees it like that."

"He will, child. He will. And when he does, he will thank you for giving him the chance to choose his own life's path. Not many of us get that luxury, you know."

Pheunaf turned toward her father. "You say that. I say the same. Still, they are mere words. Words that do little to comfort the pain of separation I am feeling. Pain I can only imagine is far worse for him, alone in an unknown land, with beings who the only thing they have in common is they are human."

"I will not deny it will be difficult for him at first," Jocel said. "But he will adapt. No, he will thrive just as he did here. You raised him well, daughter."

As much as she wanted to believe her father's words, Pheunaf could not help but feel she had abandoned her son.

CHAPTER TWELVE

ANEESYMA HANDED ZABANEJA a plate, and the boy stared at it. "What is this?"

"Dinner."

Zabaneja poked and sniffed at the steaming mass. "It certainly looks like nothing I have ever eaten. And, it smells disgusting. Have you no meat?"

"That is meat."

He poked at it again, turning it over on the plate and shaking his head. He saw Kalini gnawing on the carcass of a rabbit.

"No, THAT is meat!" he said, pointing at the chetoga. "This is, well, I have no idea what this is."

Kalini nearly choked, trying to stifle her laughter.

"At last, a human who understands the correct way to eat. Here, come sit by me, Zabaneja, I have an extra one."

Zabaneja nodded, walked over and sat beside the chetoga. She handed him a rabbit, and he reached into a pouch on his belt and pulled out a small sharpened stone.

"Unlike the drageals, and, I see, you as well, I cannot abide by the fur," he said as he skillfully skinned the rabbit. "But the meat, ah, now that is a different story." He sank his teeth into the skinned carcass, tearing a chunk of bloody meat from it.

Aneesyma watched in awe.

Kalini laughed. "Do not act so surprised, my friend. The boy grew up with drageals. Have you ever heard of a drageal eating anything but meat off the bone? Or, for that matter, starting a fire other than to burn something?"

Aneesyma shook his head. "I guess I had not given that part of it any thought."

"Then it is a good thing I did, else you would have burned all the meat and he would have had to starve. Slow down, child," Kalini said, turning back to Zabaneja. "We are in no hurry to finish and there is more if you want it. I do not want to be the one to tell Pheunaf you choked during your first night in our care."

Zabaneja nodded and slowed down, but only a little.

"Are you hungry enough for another?" Kalini asked as she saw the boy throw the rabbit's last, now clean, bone to the ground.

He wiped the remaining blood from his mouth and face with his arm and shook his head. "No, thank you. My belly is quite full."

Hmm, Aneesyma thought. *This may present a problem. I cannot have the boy entering society eating raw meat off the bone. That will not bode well. Ah, well, yet another task to add to the list of things to teach him. The art of eating cooked food.*

#

Later that night, the trio sat around the fire. Another thing Zabaneja was not accustomed to. He listened as the others playfully argued over the differences between cooked, apparently that was what the humans called the burned mess they ate, and raw meat. Their banter reminded him of home, and he remembered he would never again share in the company of his family, and a gloom once again came over him.

"What is the matter?" Aneesyma asked.

"It is nothing, I was just thinking of home."

"Well, thoughts of home should not make you look so sad," Kalini added.

Zabaneja turned toward her and glared. "They do when you know you can never return there."

"Is that what you think? That you can never go back?" Aneesyma asked.

"That is what exile is, is it not?"

Aneesyma drew in a breath and shook his head. "Ah, that explains a great deal about your attitude."

"So, Pheunaf did not tell you?" Kalini asked.

"Tell me what?"

The chetoga turned to Aneesyma. "I thought she had explained to him."

"As did I," Aneesyma replied. "Perhaps, she did not want to influence him."

Kalini nodded.

"Tell me what?" Zabaneja demanded. "Stop talking as if I was not sitting here. Tell me what you mean."

"Zabaneja, this is not an exile. You can return to Pheunaf and the others in your clan," Kalini said.

Zabaneja's face lit up. "Really? Good, then I want to go now. I do not understand, if I can go back, why I was even brought here in the first place."

The boy jumped up and was ready to run back to the cabin to retrieve his belongings.

"Hold on. You can go back, but not just yet," Aneesyma said.

"You are speaking in riddles."

"Come. Sit. Let me explain."

Zabaneja did as he was told.

"First, you must know, must realize, your mother loves you very much. And, this separation pains her as much, if not more, than it does you."

The boy looked as if he was going to interrupt, and Aneesyma raised his hand to stop him. "Yes, I know. Right now you cannot believe that to be the truth. But, believe me when I say it is."

Zabaneja shook his head. "No. If she loved me, she would not have abandoned me."

Aneesyma wanted to laugh but did not. "You are not abandoned. You are here with us."

"You are neither my clan nor drageal. You do not matter."

"Now you sound like your uncle," Kalini said. "If that is truly how you feel, then you do not matter either since you are not drageal."

The boy glared at his two companions but did not respond.

"Your mother sent you to us to give you the opportunity to decide," Aneesyma said.

"Decide what?"

"To decide, once exposed to both cultures, which you wanted to remain with."

Zabaneja sat in silence. Aneesyma was not sure if the boy believed him.

"So, you are saying after you teach me your culture, the culture of humans, and I find it lacking, I can return to the drageals."

"Yes, if that is your wish. Or you can stay with the humans."

"I sincerely doubt that will happen," the boy snorted.

"Perhaps not, but whatever you decide at that time, it will one made out of choice, not coincidence."

"How long will it be before I can tell you I want to go back and you take me there?"

Aneesyma did not feel threatened or hurt by the boy's tone of voice and attitude. To some extent, he understood. He remembered that, at about Zabaneja's age, he was sent far away to a strange land, with strange people—different language, odd customs. The difference was, Aneesyma knew the reason he was sent away. Even so, he remembered the feelings of pain and abandonment. Only now, after so many years did he finally understand the purpose.

He had to find a way to get Zabaneja to understand, now, not twenty years from now, that this would indeed help him. Aneesyma's mind argued with itself over just how that would or even could be done.

"Your mother and I decided a period of five years..."

"Five years!" Zabaneja shouted. "Are you out of your mind? Why not just say forever?"

Again, Aneesyma ignored the boy's outburst and continued. "We decided five years would give you sufficient time to not only learn the differences between the cultures, but to mature enough into manhood to be able to make an intelligent decision regarding your future."

"I am old enough now and if what I have seen of your behavior is any indication of what the rest of your kind..."

"It is your kind as well," Aneesyma corrected.

"Not by choice."

Kalini laughed. "Silly child, no one be they human, drageal, chetoga or anything else has a choice in what they are. The only thing you can choose is who you become, what you do with your life as whatever race or kind you are."

Zabaneja bristled at being called a child. "Regardless. As I was saying, before you rudely interrupted me. I am old enough now and have seen enough of human ways to know I want to go back to the drageals."

"No," Aneesyma said flatly.

"What do you mean, no?"

Kalini could see Aneesyma's patience wearing thin, and his temper nearing the surface. The chetoga touched his hand. He looked at her. She gently shook her head, but said nothing.

He nodded, fully understanding her action and was, as always, awed how she sensed his emotions so well. He took a deep breath.

"Your reaction to everything we say, emphasizes the fact you are acting emotionally not rationally. The look in your eyes when Kalini called you child, your insistence that you and I are of different ilk, and so many other little things you have done or said in the short time we have been together, merely act to reinforce my opinion that you are still too young, too immature, to make any such decision."

Zabaneja glared, hatred in his eyes, but said nothing.

"I know the time seems like an eternity, it did to me as well when I was sent away from my home and family, but you will see. Soon enough, it will be time to make the decision, and though you do not believe it now, it will be the hardest thing you will ever do."

The boy silently glowered at his companions.

"And who is not to say that you may decide to divide your time between the two worlds," Kalini said.

Aneesyma looked at her. He had not thought of that possibility.

CHAPTER THIRTEEN

I DO NOT CARE what they say, I will never want to stay with the humans. I will always return to the drageals, Zabaneja thought as he tried to make himself comfortable in the tiny box they called a cabin.

He heard the shallow breathing of sleep coming from his companions, but sleep eluded him. Even with his eyes closed, he felt confined. After a while, he rose, grabbed his blanket and went outside to sleep in the open under the stars. His eyes barely closed before he was asleep.

#

"I told you he did not run away," Kalini said as she and Aneesyma approached the sleeping Zabaneja.

The boy sat up and rubbed his eyes. "And, where would I go? I do not know where I am. Even if I did, I have no way of getting home."

"He does make a good point," Kalini chuckled. "Are you ready to eat, boy? I have some squirrels."

Zabaneja nodded.

"I hope we can be on a bit friendlier terms today. I really am not the enemy. I am only here to help you," Aneesyma said between bites of food.

"I know," the boy said.

"That is good to hear. So, where shall we begin? Language? History? Customs? What do you wish to learn first?" Aneesyma asked.

"To be honest, I have not given it much thought. Until just a short while ago, I had no interest in anything you had to say to me. But now, now I want to hear, to learn everything."

Aneesyma and Kalini looked at each other and then at Zabaneja and saw him holding a rock. No, it was more than that. Even with most of it hidden, they realized it was a gemstone of a kind and color neither had ever seen before.

"May I inquire what you have in your hand?" Kalini asked.

Zabaneja opened his hand to reveal a large purple gem.

"This? This is what my mother asked you to give me. It is one of her most valued possessions. And if you know anything about drageals, we, unlike other dragons, do not collect hoards of shiny gems. This may be the only one my mother owned, and she gave it to me. So, I know she expects me to return it to her." He swallowed hard, trying not to break down, but his voice, still that of a boy on the verge of manhood, cracked with every word. Then he smiled. "That means she expects me to return to the drageals."

"Is that not what we have been telling you?" Aneesyma asked.

#

"How is this going to work?" Zabaneja asked as they began the first lesson in language. "If we speak our own tongues without Kalini's magic, it will be incomprehensible."

"True," Kalini said. "I have made it so you will hear Aneesyma's words in his language and, at the same time, your mind will translate them to dragealian. Hopefully, that will allow you to more quickly associate the two languages."

"If you say so," Zabaneja said with more than a hint of skepticism.

"It will be a bit different from the way we are speaking now, but I think it will work."

"Will Aneesyma be learning dragealian as well?"

"Sadly, no," Kalini said.

"We talked about that," Aneesyma chimed in, "but decided that, for right now, it was more important for you to learn my language. Perhaps, in the future, we can reverse roles and you can be my teacher."

Zabaneja was taken aback. When Aneesyma spoke, he heard gibberish but in his head the words were dragealian.

This is going to take some getting used to, he thought.

#

"Be good crash words into another head not hard work learn," Zabaneja said in the human language at dinner on the fourth evening after his lessons had begun.

Aneesyma nodded. "Very good try, but I think you meant to say, 'Would it not be wonderful, if one could merely put an entire language into another's head without the hard work of learning it?' Is that right?"

"Yes," Zabaneja said in human and then slipped back into dragealian. "Why do they add so many extraneous words? Just say what you need to and get on with it. Such a strange way of speaking,"

Kalini laughed, "I agree. Humans do, indeed, have a penchant for using more words than needed to get a point across."

"However," Aneesyma said, guessing what the boy said after

hearing Kalini's response in his own tongue, "if you are going to function and live among us, you must learn how to speak in a manner that will both be understandable and make you sound like a man of intelligence who belongs there."

"Understand. Think silly. But will learn to do," Zabaneja replied, trying to add the additional words he thought were superfluous.

"We have complete faith in you. And," Aneesyma said, "now that you have gotten a decent grasp on many of the words for both things and concepts you will need, we can move on and concentrate on how to actually speak the language."

"I am excited to learn more," Zabaneja said, carefully choosing every word to make it sound correct.

"Perfect. Both in sentiment and composition."

#

"It is almost time for me to go," Kalini told Aneesyma after Zabaneja had retired.

The man nodded. "Yes, we have kept you far longer than I had anticipated."

Kalini smiled. "Actually, you are farther along than I expected."

"Really?"

"Yes. That boy has both a penchant for learning and superior intelligence. He picked up the language very quickly, even with all the grumblings I heard from you both." She chuckled at the memory of the sight of them during the first few days.

"I thought so, too. And, he is learning the customs even faster. He is an amazing young man."

"And, on the subject of customs..."

"No. I have yet to bring up mating," Aneesyma said, already

knowing where she was heading. "I have not found the right time, the right opportunity. Or for that matter, the right words."

"Silly humans, always so reticent to speak of the natural cycles of life. And, in his case, it should actually be easier than if he was, say, your own son. He knows what mating is and has probably seen it occurring, likely on more than one occasion. Drageals, like most races, save you humans, are not shy about what they are doing."

"Yes, but that was between drageals. I daresay, our ways are far different."

"Of course, you are not in flight," she said and laughed.

Aneesyma grinned. "At least not outwardly."

"But seriously, sex was one of the main reasons he was brought to you to live among his own kind."

"I am well aware of that."

"So, when are you going to discuss it with him? I really think you need to do so while I am here and you have the benefit of my magic to translate."

"No, I am planning on a different way of introducing him to sex."

"Oh, really?"

Aneesyma nodded. "One that will not require translation, so it will need to wait until you have gone. Your presence may be difficult to explain."

"I believe I can guess what you have planned," Kalini laughed. "You know, there just may be hope for you yet, human."

#

"What do you mean you are leaving?"

"Zabaneja, I need to go home. I have responsibilities and you do not need me anymore. You and Aneesyma can easily speak to each other now. As a matter of fact, I lifted the spell a few days ago."

"I know, but still…" He turned away from the chetoga. "I do not wish you to go. First, Mother. Now you. It seems as of late, everyone I care about leaves me."

Kalini walked to him and took his hand. "Child, you knew the time would come when I would have to leave. Like a drageal, a chetoga does not easily fit into the human world. At least, not with most humans."

"That is very true," Aneesyma said as he approached. "In the few short years you have been alive, you have already experienced things most beings never will, no matter how long they live."

Zabaneja stood in silence.

"I am not abandoning you, child," Kalini said. "We will remain friends, and, if the need arises, there are ways for us to communicate. But for now, I must bid you both farewell."

"I do not like this, not even a little," Zabaneja told Aneesyma as the last glimpse of the white chetoga disappeared into the woods. "Will you leave me next?"

Aneesyma put his hand on the boy's shoulder. "No, you will not be rid of me that soon, nor that easily."

"What are we to do next?"

"Tomorrow I am going to take you to meet someone."

Zabaneja was a bit shocked. "I am not ready to meet anyone. What will I say?"

"Do not worry, boy, she will not care whether you talk or not."

"She? A female?"

"Yes, a woman. A dear friend of mine. One with some very special talents. Someone who will introduce you to an aspect of your life you have yet to discover. One I am sure you will enjoy like nothing you have experienced so far."

"I do not understand."

Aneesyma smiled. "You will. You will."

CHAPTER FOURTEEN

"WELCOME, LORD ANEESYMA. It has been quite some time since you have graced my home with your presence," the woman standing in the doorway said.

Zabaneja was surprised to hear her call Aneesyma 'Lord'. Did that mean Aneesyma was a noble? They had discussed class structure, but he never mentioned anything about his status. Or did this person just call everyone by that title?

"And that has been my loss, Pajeau," Aneesyma said as the two embraced and he kissed her on the cheek.

She smiled and turned toward Zabaneja, who took a step back.

"Ah, you must be Zaban... Forgive my inability to pronounce your name, I am not good with languages that are not my own."

Zabaneja's first thought was to rudely tell her she had him at a disadvantage, but then recalled what Aneesyma had told him about talking to people, so, he said, "It is fine."

She smiled and took Zabaneja's arm and walked him through the door. Aneesyma grinned and silently followed.

Pajeau released his arm and walked to the side table. She returned with a tray of drinks.

"Sit, sit," she said as she put the tray on the table and handed each of them a glass. "Here is something to quench the thirst I am sure you got on your trip here."

After they had finished their drinks, Pajeau came over and took Zabaneja's hand. "Follow me, young man."

He looked at Aneesyma and saw him smiling. "Go on."

#

Zabaneja did as he was told and followed Pajeau up the stairs, and down another narrow, stifling hall to a door. She opened it and Zabaneja was relieved to see the room was almost as large as the cabin he recently stayed in. He looked around and saw it filled, more like cluttered, with all manners of things. Sticks of fire, candles he thought they were called, sat upon almost every flat surface, while dark, heavy fabrics, thankfully pulled aside to allow light in, hung from the windows. Against one wall was a large bed with sheer fabric hanging from the ceiling around it. All of it, save perhaps the window drawings, seemed to serve no purpose which added to his confusion about this place.

"Do you know why you are here, young sir?"

"No."

"Well," she said and began unbuttoning his shirt.

"What are you doing?" He recoiled from her and the strange feelings she was causing within him.

Pajeau was stunned by his reaction. No one, especially not one of his age, had ever reacted so.

"Were you not told why you were brought here?" she asked and reached out toward him again.

"No. I was told nothing." He took several steps until his back was against the wall.

"I am going to educate you in the art of lovemaking," she said with a smile. "Do not worry, I will not hurt you, in fact, it will be just the opposite."

She reached for him again and this time he had no escape from her touch. She unbuttoned his shirt and gently ran her fingers over his chest and belly. He held his breath, trying to control the strange sensations she was causing. She ran her fingers over his crotch and grasped his manhood. He wanted to protest, but the sensations racing through his body did not allow him to speak.

Pajeau loosened his trousers and pushed them down from his hips, lowering herself until she was kneeling in front of him. She removed first his odd foot coverings and then his trousers. Even without looking, she knew he was holding his breath. She smiled and took his fully erect manhood in her hand and then her mouth.

Almost immediately, Zabaneja's entire body quaked with a sensation he had never before experienced. He let out a moan as he felt something he could only describe as an explosion within himself. His entire body felt as if it was shaking, his knees went weak and he had to lean on her to keep from falling. He felt her tongue lick the end of his now limp shaft and then as a sense of steadiness returned to his body, he straightened up.

"What did you just do to me?" he gasped.

Pajeau stood up and smiled. "Did you enjoy it?"

"I am not sure."

"Ah yes, Aneesyma told me you had never been with a woman before. I had assumed, like most boys your age, you had found a way to relieve, how should I put it, the tension."

Zabaneja looked confused as he stood naked beside her.

"It seems you are even more of an innocent than I imagined." She took his hand and led him over to the bed. She motioned him to sit, and he obliged. "I, we, will remedy that situation and, when I am through with you, not only will you know the joys of being pleasured by a woman, but I will teach you something else. Something that will endear you to all women, especially those you will be the taking for their first time."

He did not understand what she meant, but as she leaned toward him and stroked his face, his body once again responded.

She smiled. "And, my dear, with this face and that," she pointed to his manhood, "women will clamor to be with you."

"I do not understand."

"Later, dear boy, we will talk about that later. Right now..." She dropped her robe to the floor, revealing her naked body. She was confused that he had no reaction to the sight of her, but gently pushed him back upon the pillows and climbed on top of him.

#

She proceeded to introduce him to the joys of sex, first for his pleasure and then for hers. And, not surprisingly, she enjoyed his education almost as much as he did. She was amused that she had almost forgotten the extent of both the stamina and enthusiasm of the young. She smiled as he drifted off to sleep when he was finally spent.

She lay beside him and found herself intrigued by the young man and his relationship to Aneesyma. The only thing she was told prior to their arrival was that Aneesyma wanted her to introduce a young man to his first sexual experience. She thought it odd. He had never asked such a thing of her, though he knew she had performed such a service for many young men, himself included.

From the moment the boy had entered her home, she felt there was something different about him. Something more than just his unpronounceable name and odd speech patterns. The way he looked around her house and room, as if this was the first time he had ever seen such things. And now, after this initial encounter, she found him more naïve than anyone she had ever met.

Who was he? Could he be Aneesyma's son? His bastard? She shook her head, knowing it was not her place to question the Lord of the Keep. Still, theirs was a unique relationship. By some terrible stroke of fate, they had fallen in love at their first meeting, even though both knew their stations made a life together impossible. But even that knowledge did not stop their love from happening and continuing, even after all these years. The questions continued to fill her mind and as her curiosity won out over her sense of decorum, she decided, proper or not, she needed to know the truth.

She rose from her bed and quietly left the room.

CHAPTER FIFTEEN

"AS USUAL, you tire men out long before they do you," Aneesyma said with a chuckle as she entered the sitting room.

She smiled as he pulled her onto his lap and kissed her on the cheek. "Do you have any energy left for me?"

Even after a full day of sexual satiation, his touch aroused her. "I will always have energy to be with you, my love. Shall we retire to the other room, or shall we be bawdy and feed our lust right here?"

Aneesyma laughed and rose from the chair with her in his arms. "I, for one, am long past the days of rolling around on a hard floor when a soft, comfortable bed is nearby."

"As am I," she said and kissed his cheek as he carried her to the other room.

#

It surprised neither of them that their passion, even after all these years, was the same as it had been when they first met.

"So, tell me of this boy you have brought to me to educate," she said as she cuddled next to him.

"There is not much to tell."

"I sincerely doubt that."

He smiled and hugged her tightly. "I never could get away with telling you anything but the truth, now could I?"

"Tell me, is he your son? Your bastard?" The words blurted from her mouth before she could stop them.

Aneesyma pushed himself up on one elbow and stared at her. "Why would you ask such a thing?"

She shook her head and tried to turn away, but he took her chin in his hand and held her face so she had to look at him. "I am sorry, I know it is not my place nor are you under any obligation to answer, but..."

And, at that moment, she realized why she cared if the boy was his son, bastard or not. She was jealous that someone else would bear his child. She chided herself for the foolishness of such a notion. Still, it was not her head feeling that way, it was her heart.

"But what?" Aneesyma asked, surprising both of them with the sharpness of his tone.

Pajeau tried to get up. She wanted to escape his touch, his glance, but he would not let her go. Would not even let her sit.

"It is just the oddity of the situation. Out of the blue you tell me you are bringing a young man to me, a special young man, for his initial foray into sex. And when you arrive, well, let me just say he was not quite what I expected."

"What did you expect?" he asked, his tone of voice once again softer.

"I do not know. The son of some noble or high ranking merchant whom you offered to do a favor for."

"And what is to say he is not?"

Pajeau smirked. "This is me you are talking to, My Lord." He winced, knowing he had irritated her into addressing him formally, but said nothing as she continued. "If he is either of those, I am the Empress of the World."

Aneesyma did not respond.

"The boy has no social skills and can barely speak, yet I sense it is not due to a lack of intelligence. No, it seems to be more likely a lack of experience. Which of course leads to the question of why you, a noble of this kingdom, would be so interested in a lad of foreign origins. Unless..." She did not complete her thought, she felt she did not need to.

"I am disappointed that you think the only reason I would offer him assistance would be if he were of my loins."

"That is not what I meant. It is just that... oh damn, I do not know what to think, other than both the situation and the boy are odd."

"I am not odd," came an angry voice from the doorway. "How dare you say that?"

Both Aneesyma and Pajeau jumped, startled by Zabaneja's appearance.

"Do not speak to Pajeau that way, boy," Aneesyma said as he rose from the bed and retrieved his trousers.

Pajeau did not move except to turn her head toward the wall. "The boy is right. It is not my place to say such things."

"Now, now," Aneesyma said, "I think this is all a misunderstanding. Neither of you has all the details of the situation. Let us discuss this together over a cup of tea... or something stronger."

Zabaneja glared at Pajeau then turned and walked away.

Aneesyma finished dressing and took Pajeau's hand. "Please join us."

She nodded.

#

"Why were you so rude?" Aneesyma asked as he and Zabaneja sat down.

Zabaneja glared at him but said nothing.

"I asked you a question, I expect an answer. Why would you speak to her in such an abusive manner?" Aneesyma asked as Pajeau joined them.

Zabaneja glared at them, his anger boiling over. "Did you not hear what she called me? She called me odd. I am not stupid, I know what she meant, she thinks me a lesser being than herself."

It was only when he saw the stunned looks on his companion's faces that Zabaneja realized he had been speaking dragealian.

"I knew he was not of this land, but what is that language he speaks? It is nothing I have ever encountered from any of the foreign travelers who have crossed my threshold. It does not even sound human. Have you brought a changeling to my house? Or is he a demon?" Pajeau cried and tried to head for the door.

Aneesyma gently took hold of her arm and stopped her.

"So, now she thinks I am not only odd but a devil as well," Zabaneja shouted, this time in the human tongue.

"Sit down, boy!" Aneesyma said, his tone commanding obedience.

Zabaneja hesitated a moment and then sat.

"It seems I must explain what is going on here." Aneesyma said and turned to Pajeau. "I had hoped you would not delve any further into who he was beyond that it was me bringing him to you." He shook his head and smiled. "I should have known better."

Pajeau bowed her head. "I am sorry. I overstepped my bounds as both Guild member and friend." She raised her head and looked first at Aneesyma and then turned to Zabaneja. She reached across the table to touch his hand, but the angry young man pulled away. "And, to you, dear boy, whoever you are. I also apologize. There is no excuse for my outburst."

"There is no need to apologize to either of us, Pajeau," Aneesyma said.

Zabaneja snorted but said nothing.

"Nor is there a need for you to do so either," Aneesyma said, looking at Zabaneja. "If anyone is to blame, it is me. I should have been more open as to what was going on."

Pajeau and Zabaneja were surprised by his statement.

"My dearest Pajeau, you and I have known and loved each other for many years now, and I count you as one of my closest confidantes, yet, I was not wholly honest with you." He touched her hand, and she smiled. "And that has led to misunderstandings, anger, and hurt feelings and pride. A situation I will now attempt to rectify."

Pajeau and Zabaneja nodded.

"Pajeau, I must ask you not to reveal anything about him or his past without his permission."

Pajeau's curiosity was piqued even further. What was the boy's secret that Aneesyma was initially reticent to disclose it and now as he did, he requested her silence about it? "Of course."

"First, he is not my child, bastard or otherwise, though I would be proud to call him son if he were. Nor is he a changeling or demon or anything else of that ilk. He is a young man with a rather interesting past."

Aneesyma walked around the table and stood behind Zabaneja and put his hands on the boy's shoulders. "All we know of his past is the one we think to be his mother was killed when he was but a day or so old and, by some miracle, he survived."

Zabaneja squirmed in his chair.

"And who raised him?" Pajeau asked.

"I was raised by a clan of drageals," Zabaneja replied.

Pajeau gasped, both in awe and a bit of disbelief. "Really?

Drageals? So you are saying they are indeed real? I thought they were just myth, legend."

Zabaneja snorted.

"They are not myth. They are as real as you and I. And the tales we have heard do not do them justice," Aneesyma replied. "I have yet to find the words to adequately describe their beauty and majesty."

Pajeau drew in a breath, trying to imagine what they were like. "But how? How did a drageal raise one so young? I mean, I am not saying I know anything about how drageals raise their young, but I would think just the mere size difference would lead to all sorts of issues."

Aneesyma waited for Zabaneja to reply, and when the boy did not, he continued. "Yes, I am sure there were, but early on Pheunaf, the drageal that took him in..."

"My mother," Zabaneja interrupted.

"Yes, your mother, I meant no disrespect. Early on, his mother, Pheunaf, found a wise woman who lived a few days' ride from here."

"Filemena?" Pajeau asked.

"Yes."

"I knew her," Pajeau said and smiled. "She was far more than a mere wise woman."

"So I have been told," Aneesyma replied. "Well, Filemena was able to give Pheunaf advice on what to do to ensure the boy's welfare."

"Why did Filemena just not take the babe and raise him herself?" she asked, looking at Zabaneja. "Would that not have made more sense?"

"My mother would not just discard me like the carcass of a dead animal," Zabaneja snapped, his voice dripping with contempt.

"Watch your tone. Pajeau asked a valid question."

The boy looked at Aneesyma and turned away.

"Something Pheunaf could not explain compelled her to keep him and, apparently, Filemena agreed."

Pajeau nodded and thought for a moment. "Why then is he with you?"

"It was not my choice," Zabaneja grumbled under his breath.

"No, it was not your choice," Aneesyma replied to the words he was not supposed to hear and then turned back to Pajeau. "As you can see, he is of that age when even the kindest, gentlest boy becomes a rebellious, obnoxious soon-to-be man. Not to mention, the impending birth of his sexual awareness and the tension that would have added to his and everyone else's lives, especially with no release available to him, could have led him into some harrowing situations with the drageals. So, it was decided he needed to be introduced to his own kind."

"More like banished," Zabaneja said, this time not attempting to hide his words.

Aneesyma shook his head. "I thought we had discussed that, and you were not only aware, but felt a bit more comfortable about the situation."

Zabaneja did not reply.

"You will have to forgive his attitude, as you can tell, he did not come willingly to me, and we are the first humans he has ever had any contact with."

"I understand."

"Really? You understand?" Zabaneja shouted. "Were you torn from your family and everything you loved and thrown into a world where you knew nothing and could not even speak the language?"

Zabaneja was taken aback by his own reaction. He, too, had thought he had come to terms with his situation. But, now, this place... this woman... every thing that had gone on today, well... he just could not explain, nor did he understand.

"That is where you are mistaken," Pajeau said, barely above a whisper. "I, too, was wrenched from everything I knew, everything and everyone I loved. And, even though I could speak to those in my new surroundings, everything they did, not to mention my new duties, were as foreign to me as we are to you."

The sorrow in Pajeau's voice tugged at Aneesyma's heart. He knew some of her history in the brothel, but not until this moment did he realize how it still affected and tormented her. He wanted to run to her side and cradle her in his arms. But this was neither the time nor the place for such an action.

Pajeau looked into Zabaneja's eyes. "So, to some extent, I understand what you are going through."

Zabaneja wanted to ignore her words, her emotions. Wanted to rail at her once again. Tell her she could not possibly understand anything about his situation. But he could not, because, in that moment, he realized she did.

"I am sorry. I was not aware of your past," Zabaneja said.

"Nor I of yours," she replied and reached across the table to take his hand. This time, he did not pull away.

She turned to Aneesyma and wagged her finger at him "You! Well, there is no other way to say it but outright. You are an idiot!"

"Idiot? Do you not think that is rather harsh?"

She shook her head. "I think not! Even with all you knew of his upbringing, you brought him here with no knowledge of what was going to happen? And chose to leave me in the dark as well. Surely you must have known I would sense something was different about him."

"Umm," Aneesyma stammered in response to his well-deserved chastisement. "I guess I was not thinking."

Pajeau threw her hands up in the air. "That is an understatement. I certainly hope you think more when it comes to ruling your lands." She turned back to Zabaneja. "I apologize for all the misunderstandings, on both of our parts, here today. I do hope you will forgive me."

Zabaneja nodded. "As I hope you will forgive me."

Pajeau again took his hand in hers and smiled.

"As for you," she said, turning her attention back to Aneesyma.

"Yes, yes. I will admit it. I was an idiot. It will not happen again."

"Well, I hope not. How many other boys raised by drageals are you planning on bringing to me?" Pajeau laughed.

"None, I hope. This one is more than enough to handle."

"Well, now that all the misunderstandings and drama are over," Pajeau said and then added, "They are over, correct?"

"I certainly hope so," Aneesyma replied.

"Then I believe it is time to get supper ready," she said.

"That sounds like a grand idea," Aneesyma replied.

#

"Why have you not touched your roasted rabbit? Do you not like rabbit? I think I have some other meat, it was cooked yesterday, but is still good."

"Um, no, it is not that," Zabaneja said.

Aneesyma slapped his hand to his forehead. "Damn! Another thing I forgot."

Pajeau looked at him.

"He prefers his meat raw."

"Raw?"

"Drageals do not cook food save broth for the ill," Zabaneja said.

"But you are not a drageal, dear boy, and humans eat their meat cooked." She reached under the table and put her hand on his lap and was not surprised at his body's immediate reaction to her touch.

Zabaneja blushed and Aneesyma chuckled.

"Please leave the boy alone so he can enjoy his dinner."

"It is fine, I do not mind," Zabaneja said, his voice slightly strained.

"I bet not."

"Seriously, dear boy, unless you only plan to eat alone, you had best develop a taste for cooked meat. Most young ladies, at least those you want to have dealings with, will not take kindly to a man tearing raw flesh from a bone. And, the ones that do, well... take my word, you want to get as far away from them as possible."

"That is what I have been trying to tell him," Aneesyma said. "Well, maybe not the ladies part, but..."

"All right. I will try it again, for you Pajeau, because the last time I did, it tasted vile."

"Believe me, it will be worth it to you," she said and touched his manhood again, "and your loins in the long run."

CHAPTER SIXTEEN

"WHY ARE YOU NOT WITH HER?" Zabaneja asked as the pair rode off the following morning.

"What do you mean?"

"It is obvious, even to me, that you both clearly have feelings for each other."

Zabaneja watched as a deep sadness came over Aneesyma's face. "There are many things that keep us from being together."

"Such as?"

"Remember when we spoke of classes in the human society, in my land?"

"Yes."

"That is what is at play here, I am a noble and cannot be with one of her class."

"I do not understand."

"It is a long story, dear boy. One that began with our first meeting, a meeting very similar to yours, and I believe I was the same age you are. Unlike you, I knew why I was brought to her. She was, at that time, just one of the many guild whores and by chance, or perhaps by the cruel hand of fate, she was the whore hired to introduce me to sex."

Though Aneesyma had been reticent to discuss the topic before once he began it was like the floodgates to his heart opened up. As if he had been waiting to tell his story, their story, to someone.

"So, because of who I am, who I am supposed to be, I have had to live without the one I love."

Zabaneja shook his head. "I do not understand the benefit of your class system. Amongst drageals, all are the same."

"They have a clan leader, correct?"

"Yes, but that role does not seem to carry the same restrictions as yours."

"Ah, that might be a nice way to live," Aneesyma replied as much to himself as to Zabaneja.

"So, where will I fit in?"

"I had not given that any thought. There are seven main classes in our society—noble, diplomat, merchant, peasant, farmer, servant and soldier," he said and gave a brief description of each.

"Well, I am obviously not noble."

"Or peasant or farmer," Aneesyma added. "That leaves servant, merchant, diplomat or soldier.

Zabaneja laughed. "Somehow, I do not see myself doing well as either merchant or diplomat."

"No, those roles would not suit you at all. Nor would servant."

"So, I will become a soldier."

"Yes, I think you might fit very well into the palace guard."

Zabaneja thought for a moment. "When we get to your home, our relationship will have to change, will it not?"

"Yes, I am afraid so. At least in public you will need to show a modicum of formality that will be new to you," Aneesyma said. "Damn, what was I thinking? Or not thinking. If nothing else, I should have thought to introduce you to the formalities of life within the Keep from the beginning. Or have gotten someone else to be the one that met you."

Zabaneja did not respond. He already knew Aneesyma well enough to realize the man was not really talking to him, but rather trying to work out the problem that plagued him. Zabaneja waited silently while Aneesyma grumbled, mumbled and argued with himself.

"I have a solution," Aneesyma said after a few moments. "I have always planned to introduce you as someone I had met on my journeys beyond our borders."

"Well, that is true."

"Right. We will maintain the formality of our relationship as much as we can and, on those rare occasions when one or both of us make a mistake and perhaps acts too friendly, we can blame it on the fact that your land has different customs."

"Again, true."

"Yes, and as long as we do not go into too much detail as to where you come from, we should be fine. And, to be honest, and I am again sorry to only think of this detail now, we will not really have much contact with each other."

"I do not understand. Are you also abandoning me?"

"Not abandoning. You see, if you were coming in as a trained soldier, one with experience, I could instill you in my household guard with little trouble. But..."

"Ah yes, I see. I have no training and therefore if you did put me in such a position and the need arose for me to defend you, I would be of little use."

"Yes. What I can do is bring you in as a trainee for the palace guard. I have a man, a good friend and the captain of the guard, Guentza, who I implicitly trust. He will look after you in my stead."

"What of my background? Will people not question it? You

told Pajeau she was not to tell it to anyone else; is there a problem with others knowing?"

"Perhaps not an actual problem, but people are often fascinated or frightened by that which they do not know or understand..."

"Like Pajeau was?" Zabaneja interrupted.

"Yes, much the same situation, but on a larger scale. The problem is, the two groups might pester you to the point you feel persecuted or at least annoyed. And, please do not take this the wrong way, but, until you become better versed in the social amenities and dealing with people, I think this will be best."

"I suppose that makes sense."

"To be honest, your appearance alone will raise enough questions and gossip."

"And, will you tell Guentza of my past?"

"I do not plan to, but Guentza is also a very perceptive person and he, like Pajeau, may need to be told more than everyone else. But I assure you, he, too, will keep whatever he is told in the strictest confidence."

"I think you actually have thought this out more than you give yourself credit for, Lord Aneesyma."

Aneesyma looked at the boy.

"That is the correct way of addressing you, is it not?"

"Yes, it is. It seems strange hearing it from you."

"Well, I am not sure how long it is until we arrive at your home..."

"Our home," Aneesyma interrupted.

Zabaneja ignored the correction and continued. "I think it is best that I get used to calling you by your proper title."

"You are probably right." Aneesyma sighed.

CHAPTER SEVENTEEN

THREE DAYS LATER, the pair were in sight of the Keep wall. Zabaneja stared in awe.

"Is it not what you expected?" Aneesyma asked.

The boy shook his head. "I am not sure what I expected. This is so much bigger than both the cabin and Pajeau's houses put together. It is almost as large as my mountain."

Aneesyma laughed. "Zabaneja, those are not the walls of my house, my castle. They surround the Keep grounds. There are many buildings, homes and places of trade within the Keep."

"Ah, yes, I remember," Zabaneja said, but still did not fully understand.

Aneesyma described the various structures within the grounds and those that surrounded the walls. The farms, the shops. But soon he stopped when he saw Zabaneja was not really paying attention. Rather, the boy was staring at the wall.

Aneesyma tried not to laugh at the sight of his companion, mouth agape, eyes wide, as they rode through the gates of the Keep.

"It is so loud and crowded. And the smells," Zabaneja said and crinkled his nose in disgust.

"This is nothing. Wait until you see it on market day, that is when it will be truly loud and crowded."

The boy looked at Aneesyma. "I do not think I wish to see that."

Aneesyma laughed. "Come, I will take you to meet Guentza using the back streets. They will be less of an assault on your senses."

Though Aneesyma called the back streets empty, they were so narrow, with buildings and people everywhere, Zabaneja felt even more stifled.

"I am not sure I can live in such a place. There is no sky; no air to breathe," Zabaneja said, and then after a moment's thought added, "Your Lordship. "

"It will take some getting used to, I grant you that, but in no time at all you will adjust."

Zabaneja shook his head and hoped Aneesyma was right. But, as they turned down one narrow street after another, Zabaneja became more and more anxious for light and open space. And, the ability to breathe.

At last, they turned another corner into an open courtyard. Zabaneja let out a sigh of relief and followed Aneesyma towards a large building. Before their horses came to a complete stop, two young boys came running. Both bowed and took the reins as Aneesyma and Zabaneja dismounted.

"Is Guentza inside?" Aneesyma asked.

"Yes, My Lord," one of the boys replied.

"Good," he said, then turned to Zabaneja. "Follow me."

They entered the building and Zabaneja was surprised to see it was a large open room with beds stacked two or three high along the outer windowed walls. In the middle of the room, there were several tables with benches on either side.

As soon as the men sitting at the table saw Aneesyma, they jumped to their feet and put their hands to their foreheads.

"Lord Aneesyma, it is good to have you home again," one man said.

Zabaneja noticed it was not until Aneesyma acknowledged the men with a nod did they bring their hands to their side.

"It is good to be home. Please, go back to what you were doing."

"Thank you, sir," one said as the group sat back down.

"Is Guentza in his office?"

"Yes, sir, he is."

"Thank you," Aneesyma said, and directed Zabaneja to a hall on the right.

"What was that movement, with their hands, those men did when they saw you?"

Aneesyma looked confused. "Oh, you mean this?" he asked and mimicked what the others did.

Zabaneja nodded.

"That is called a salute. It, like bowing, is a show of respect. You will see I receive both or either, depending on who I am greeting. Others, like Guentza, will receive a salute but only from the soldiers and guard."

"Why?"

"Why do they respect us or why do we receive the show of respect from different people?" Aneesyma asked, forcing Zabaneja to explain.

"I understand a show of respect and why. But, yes, why is it from different people?"

"Remember what we spoke of about class and status?"

Zabaneja nodded again.

"That is why. My role as Lord of the Keep dictates that all who come in my presence must show certain signs of respect—a bow or curtsy, a salute, or sometimes a mere bowing of the head. And, of course, they always address me by my title, not just my name and that is something you will need to remember."

The boy blushed a little. "I am sorry, Lord Aneesyma, I forgot."

"I understand, but others will not, so please be careful," Aneesyma said and put his hand on the boy's shoulder. "Ah, here we are."

Aneesyma rapped sharply on the door.

"Enter," a gruff voice from the other side called.

Aneesyma opened the door, and the man seated at the desk jumped to his feet and saluted Aneesyma as the others had.

"I am sorry, Lordship. I did not realize it was you knocking, else I would not have been so rude."

Aneesyma laughed. "If you responded any other way to a knock on your door, I would fear you were ill or worse."

Guentza walked across the room and the two men embraced. "It is good to have you home again. You were away far too long this time."

"As always, it is good to be back."

Guentza took a step back and looked at Zabaneja, then at Aneesyma. "And who might this strapping young lad be?"

"Before you get any ideas, he is not kin," Aneesyma said, seeing the look on Guentza's face. "Why does everyone jump to that conclusion?"

Guentza chuckled. "Everyone? You brought the boy to Pajeau?"

Aneesyma nodded.

"Well, I bet that was one hell of a meeting, especially for you, boy." Guentza looked at the sullen lad and laughed. "Well, if you were able to convince her the boy is not kin, then who am I to argue. So, if he is not kin, who is he, and why do you bring him to me?"

"As you can tell, he is not from around these parts. As for his history and any other details of his former life, well, I will leave that up to him to decide to whom and how much he wishes to reveal. Know that while he is under my care and protection, he should not be afforded any special rights or privileges. Save the fact he has only recently learned our language and our customs. Other than that, he should be treated as any other new recruit to the guard would be. As for his name, I will let him tell you that."

"I see, Lord Aneesyma," Guentza said and turned to the boy. "And your name?"

"My name is Zabaneja."

"Zabana... what? Too long. Too difficult to say or even remember. I will call you Zab."

"No, you will not!" Zabaneja snarled. "My name is Zabaneja. I was named after my great grandfather, a fine and noble dr..." Zabaneja caught himself, "man and I will not allow you nor anyone else to besmirch his name by bastardizing it. Therefore, if you wish to address me, you will call me by my given name."

Guentza looked at Aneesyma, who nodded. The guard captain, a very large man both in height and girth, stood in front of Zabaneja, towering over the young man. "When you are in my charge, I will call you anything I want, be it your name or an obscenity, and you will answer to it. Do you understand?"

Zabaneja glared at Guentza. "Then I will not be in your charge," he said and turned to walk away.

"Come back here!" Aneesyma shouted.

The boy stopped and turned toward him. "I will not take such abuse," Zabaneja growled.

Guentza grabbed the boy by the collar and shook him. "And you will not speak to his Lordship in that tone of voice or with that lack of respect."

Zabaneja turned and glared at Guentza, then looked back at Aneesyma.

"We spoke of this before. You know what I expect of you. What you need to do."

It surprised Guentza that Aneesyma would tolerate such an attitude from the boy and wondered who exactly he was if not the Lord's bastard.

"But..." Zabaneja sputtered.

"But nothing." Aneesyma turned to Guentza and nodded, and the man released his grip on Zabaneja's collar. "Guentza, did you, when you first suggested it or will you in the future, mean any disrespect to his ancestor by calling him Zab?"

"No, Lordship," Guentza responded. "The reason I gave was the honest one, his full name is too long and difficult to say."

"So you see, Zab," Aneesyma said, reinforcing the fact he agreed with Guentza, "there is no disrespect meant. Your great grand-father's honor remains intact."

Zabaneja bristled, but did not reply. He knew he had lost this battle.

"And," Aneesyma continued, "as for you being in Guentza's charge. You are! And you will obey his every command whether he tells you to lick the floor with your tongue or anything else. Do you understand?"

Zabaneja glared, first at Aneesyma and then at the now smirking Guentza, but from the tone of Aneesyma's voice, he knew better than to argue. "Yes, My Lord, I understand."

Guentza strode to the doorway and called to one of the men in the outer room, who was almost immediately standing by his side. "This is Zab. He is a new recruit. Get him outfitted and find him a bunk then introduce him to the others."

The young man nodded and walked over to Zabaneja and offered his hand. Zabaneja reluctantly took it.

"Welcome, Zab. Come this way. Do you like cards?"

"I am not sure what that is."

A huge grin came over the young man's face. "Oh, we will show you how to play."

"I said to show him around, not take the shirt off his back the first day he is here. If I find you lot are..." Guentza said.

"No sir, I promise we will do no such thing."

#

"So, Aneesyma," Guentza said, dropping the formality of title once they were alone. "What is the truth behind this boy?"

"I told you."

Guentza laughed. "You told me the surface tale, one with little detail and less substance. That you allow him to speak to you in the manner he did, tells me there is much more to your relationship than you are letting on. And while you insist upon denying him as your bastard, well..." Guentza looked at Aneesyma for any response and saw none. "What other logical conclusion can one come to that would abide by such behavior being tolerated?"

Now it was Aneesyma's turn to laugh. He looked at the captain and shook his head. "I warned the boy I would have to tell you the truth, all of it, or else you would not stop digging until you found it."

"So, I am right. There is more to this than what you originally said."

Aneesyma nodded and told Guentza all there was to tell about Zabaneja.

Guentza shook his head as if doing so would make the words more real, more believable. "Had anyone but you told me this tale, I would have called them liar."

Aneesyma laughed. "That, my friend, is what Pajeau said."

"Yes, I assumed she was told the truth as well."

"You know Pajeau," Aneesyma said with a chuckle.

"Not as well as you do." Guentza smirked and patted Aneesyma on the shoulder.

"Yes, well, even so, you know once she sets her mind to something, she will not give up until she completes her mission."

"And when you brought Zab to her, she naturally assumed he was your son."

"Apparently that is what both of you did."

"So you say she educated Zab, eh? Was that before you told her who he actually was?"

"Yes."

"I will bet you anything, she thought he was your son, and that is why she took him on."

"Yes, you are probably right. But now she knows the truth about him. As do you."

"And you need not fear either of us will ever reveal any of it to anyone without your permission."

"It is not my permission that is needed, it is his."

CHAPTER EIGHTEEN

ZABANEJA FOUND his sleeping arrangement to be one of the worst things about being at the Keep. As the newest recruit, he was relegated to a lower bunk in a tower of three in the corner furthest from the windows. Every night he would sneak outside to sleep under the stars.

"Why do you insist on sleeping on the cold, hard ground?" Guentza asked.

"It is what I am accustomed to. I cannot breathe in there. I feel I am being consumed by the walls, the ceiling, the mass of bodies."

"Well, you cannot sleep out there anymore."

"I do not understand. Why not? I am not bothering anyone. I am not in anyone's way."

"It is not proper. And soon enough the seasons will change and it will be too cold for such a thing. I have found you better accommodations."

"None of the other bunks will be any better," Zabaneja sighed, anticipating Guentza's idea.

"No, it is not any of the other bunks. Follow me."

Zabaneja walked behind Guentza toward one of the nearby

buildings.

"No, this cannot be better, look how tiny it is," Zabaneja said as they approached.

Guentza did not respond, but beckoned the lad to follow him around back to a staircase. They climbed to the roof where Zabaneja saw his bedroll and a few things lying in a pile on the far side of the flat roof.

"You can sleep here."

"Really?" Zabaneja asked, not able to hide his excitement. "This is near perfect, so much closer to the sky and the stars. Are you saying I can stay up here and not have to sleep in that closed box?"

"Yes and no," Guentza replied.

Zabaneja turned to face Guentza. "Even in my short time among your kind, I have found that is never a good answer."

"You must assimilate into life here. And, unfortunately for you, that means sleeping indoors, and, for now, in the general barracks."

"You said I can stay up here, did you not?"

"Yes, I did, but I want you to learn how to sleep in the barracks."

"I do not understand."

"Here is my plan. Sleep up here every night for the next few months. Then sleep in the barracks for one or two nights at a time. Slowly increase the number of nights you are sleeping indoors until they outnumber the number of nights outdoors."

"It sounds reasonable."

"Good, you can begin tonight."

#

"Now, you, too, are handing me off to another," Zabaneja said as feelings of abandonment rose again to the surface.

"It is not my place to be with the new recruits every moment,"

Guentza said. "You have already gotten more of my attention than most. It is the norm for new recruits to be taken under the wing of another soldier, one with a similar background."

Zabaneja snorted. "So, he was raised by drageals too?"

"Of course not. I meant when Rikar first arrived, he spoke a dialect most here could not understand, and he knew very little of the formal language. He will help you without ridicule, for he remembers what it was like," Guentza said.

"What does he know of me?" Zabaneja asked.

"Only that you are of foreign birth, new to this land's ways and language," Guentza replied. "That will allow you to explain any mistakes you may make either in action or word. As for the rest, as Lord Aneesyma said, it is up to you to decide how much of your former life you wish to divulge to Rikar or anyone else for that matter."

Zabaneja nodded.

"I can already see it is not in your nature to ask for help, but if you are going to succeed here and make some semblance of a decent life for yourself, you need to learn your way around. Rikar is a good lad, a bright lad. Much like yourself. Give him a chance to help you. From what I understand, you will be with us for five years, it will be up to you how that time goes," Guentza said.

Before Zabaneja could respond, there was a knock on the captain's door.

"Enter," Guentza barked.

The door opened and a large lad, likely about Zabaneja's age, slowly entered.

"You sent for me, sir."

Guentza motioned him closer. "Yes. Rikar, this, as I am sure you know by now, is Zab. I want you to take him under your wing. Like you once were, he is new to this land and will need help with both language and customs."

Rikar nodded and the two boys left the room.

#

"So, Zab, from what I have heard, you dislike the confines of the barracks. Prefer to be on the roof, eh?" Rikar asked as they walked out into the courtyard.

He still cringed at the shortening of his name, but had already decided getting anyone to call him Zabaneja was a battle he would not win, so, like it or not, he was stuck with the name Zab.

"Yes, I grew up on a mountain. I like to feel the wind and see the sky," Zabaneja said.

"I understand. Before I came here, I spent most nights tending my sheep on the side of the hills. But you will get used to being indoors," Rikar added.

"I doubt that. I cannot see myself ever liking being cooped up," Zabaneja snapped.

Rikar laughed and gave Zabaneja a friendly slap on the back. "Oh, I did not say you would like it. But you will get used to it."

Zabaneja smiled. Maybe Rikar did understand, at least a little.

"So, Alexandrashi is new to you, right?" Rikar asked.

"Alexandrashi? What is that?" Zabaneja answered Rikar's question with questions of his own.

"The language of this land. Did you not know that was what you were speaking?"

Zabaneja shook his head. "No. I was not told its name. But I thought this place was Hammarsh Keep."

Rikar smiled. "It is and the Keep is one of the many provinces within the kingdom."

"I see."

"Well, I will say, whether you knew what it was called or not, you speak it well. Better than I did when I first got here," Rikar said.

"Really? But I thought you were of this land," Zab said, obviously confused.

Rikar laughed again. "Yes, I guess I am, in a manner of speaking. My home was quite remote. It was not even a village, more like a few scattered thatched huts. We had few dealings with anyone outside our own group, so we did not speak proper."

"Do you miss your home? Your family?" Zabaneja asked.

"I miss the land and the openness. But my home and my family are gone. Not sure what happened. I was out in the fields for several weeks and when I returned everyone was dead. Guess it was a fever or something. I was so afraid, I just ran. Ran as far and as fast as I could. Left everything behind, even my beloved sheep," Rikar said, his voice cracking and his eyes welling up with tears. "That was a year or so ago."

"How did you end up here?" Zabaneja asked.

Rikar shrugged. "Not sure. I kept running until I could run no more. No idea how long I ran, but I sure must have covered a lot of distance because this is nowhere near where I started. Last I remember, I was hungry and tired and laid down. Actually, I think I fell down by a tree. Next thing I knew, I woke up in a soft bed with a man in uniform looking down at me. That was Guentza. Apparently, he had come upon me while out with a scouting or hunting party. Told me he was not sure I was going to make it, I was so skinny." Rikar laughed and patted his belly. "Hard to believe I was ever skinny, eh?"

Zabaneja smiled.

"As soon as I was able, Guentza got me started as a recruit. Much like you are now."

"And did you have someone to help you figure out what was happening?"

"Oh yes, and tell you what, my speaking was a mess. Thinking back on it, I have no idea how anyone figured out what I was trying to say. You speak a great deal better than I did, so you have that going for you."

"Thank you," Zabaneja said, trying to imagine how poorly Rikar must have spoken.

"But enough about me. Tell me about you. Everyone wants to know. You were brought here by his Lordship, were you not? How did you manage that? I have barely ever seen a glimpse of him and you rode with him. Are you a noble? Should I be calling you Sir Zab?" Rikar asked.

Zabaneja tried to gather his thoughts. He was not expecting to be so bluntly questioned. From what he had heard from Aneesyma, people often skirted such questions. "Lord Aneesyma is acquainted with my family. That is all I am at liberty to say."

"Acquainted with, eh? Hmm, well that opens up an entirely different set of questions now, does it not?" Rikar asked with a twinkle in his eye.

"Can we talk about something else?" Zabaneja pleaded.

Rikar was surprised at the tone of Zabaneja's response.

"All right. I was just teasing. You understand that, right?" Rikar asked, afraid he had offended the one he hoped would be his friend.

Zabaneja nodded. "I am not an idiot."

"Did not mean to imply you were, but when I first arrived I did not know such a way of interacting even existed. Where I came from, my kin said what they meant and meant what they said. Took a bit of time for me to learn about teasing. Still have trouble with lies. Not very good at spotting them all the time. How about you?" Rikar asked.

"Pretty good with teasing, so-so with liars. Depends on the lie and the person telling it, I guess."

"Well then, we will have to stick together to see if we can figure out who the liars are."

"Guess we will." Zabaneja replied, realizing he liked this fellow.

"Did Guentza tell you anything of your duties? Nah, he probably expects me to do that. You and I will be working together. The work is not hard, mainly just standing watch. But there will be weaponry practice. How are you with a sword?" Rikar asked.

Zabaneja shook his head.

"Knife? Bow? Spear?"

Zabaneja shook his head no to each of them.

"Any weapon at all?" Rikar asked in total surprise.

"None," Zabaneja replied.

"Where did you grow up that you have no knowledge of any of those?" Rikar asked. Before Zabaneja could reply, Rikar went on, "Never mind. I know you cannot tell me."

Zabaneja nodded.

"Does Guentza know about your lack of weapons skill?"

"Not sure. I do not think the subject ever came up." Zabaneja said.

"Well, we are going back there right now to bring it up. Even though standing watch is not dangerous, I am not about to do so with someone whose only knowledge of a knife is buttering his bread."

Guentza was surprised when the two boys returned to his office and shocked at what he was told. He immediately changed Rikar's schedule from night watch to only weapons practice with Zabaneja, a change that did not please Rikar.

CHAPTER NINETEEN

THAT NIGHT RIKAR and some of the others took Zab to the local tavern expecting to get him drunk so he would tell them the truth of his background. Little did they know, the alcohol served in the keep's tavern was like drinking well water compared to the aykopyra the drageals brewed. Throughout the night, they challenged him to drinking contests, and he met each one, matched them drink for drink and never faltered. In the end, when no one else could lift a glass, he helped drag them back to the barracks.

At morning muster, only Zab seemed unaffected by the previous night's escapades. And his drinking prowess gained him a level of respect among his fellow soldiers, but also had them looking for other challenges to lay before him.

\#

After morning muster, a sickly-looking Rikar led Zabaneja to the weapons training building, a large wooden structure on the opposite side of the Keep from the barracks.

"Well, you may have out-drunk me last night," Rikar said as

they entered the building, "but even in the state I am in I should be able to beat you at sword practice."

"I certainly hope so," Zabaneja said with a laugh, "since I have never even held one. As a matter of fact, I had never even seen one until you showed it to me yesterday."

"That, my friend, is beside the point." Rikar laughed.

The class began and the weapons master, Sabouren, detailed what the class was to do. She approached Zabaneja, still not fully believing the boy had never held a weapon of any kind. It took only a glance at the way he held the practice sword for her to believe what she had heard.

"You can drink these men under the table, yet you do not know how to hold a weapon. The mystery surrounding you grows deeper, young man." She chuckled and walked away.

By the end of the class, Zabaneja was bruised on every inch of his body from hits he had received.

"You would have been dead a hundred times over before you blocked your first shot, boy," Sabouren said, "but at the end you were showing some promise. I am sure you will do better tomorrow."

"Thank you, ma'am," Zabaneja said, surprised to receive even the smallest of compliments.

"Rikar, make sure he gets a good soak tonight. What is he scheduled to do next?" the master asked.

"I was to start him on reading."

"Perfect. Go back to the barracks and get him in the tub now. He took quite a beating and I want him able to move tomorrow." She smiled at the grimace that crossed Zabaneja's face. "He can start his reading exercises while he soaks."

"Yes, ma'am," Rikar said.

"I am not sure a mere soak is going to help," Zabaneja said, rubbing his arm.

Rikar laughed. "Be thankful she is letting you do this now, the longer you wait the less effective it is. And this place has some very good salts that when added make the soak far more effective than mere water alone."

Zabaneja nodded, still not sure any amount of soaking would relieve the pain he was already feeling.

#

"Settled?" Rikar asked, and before Zabaneja could answer, he continued. "Good. So, you do not know how to read, eh?"

"Not a word." Zabaneja said.

"Well then I am your perfect teacher, because I could not either, and now I can read and write as well as most of those with proper schooling. And, pretty soon, you will be able to as well."

"If you say so."

CHAPTER TWENTY

THE FOLLOWING DAY, another female joined the weapons class. Oddly, her appearance was met with snickering and snide remarks the other females in the class did not elicit. Zabaneja was confused. When asked, the only thing Rikar could think of that she was a noble.

"But some of the males are nobles," Zabaneja said. Rikar shrugged.

"Well, I for one will make sure she gets no special treatment from me," one of the males proclaimed. "I do not care if she is a weak little girl, or a pampered noble."

"She seems neither weak nor pampered," Zabaneja said as he watched her take a practice sword and slice the air with it.

"And you are aware," Rikar added, "there have been many females throughout history that were both master swordsmen, or should that be swordswomen, as well as ferocious warriors."

"Like Sabouren?" Zabaneja asked. Rikar nodded. "In my homeland there are many female warriors, and not a one of them could ever be called weak or pampered. At least not if you wanted to live should they hear you."

"And where is your homeland, again?" one of the other boys asked with a grin.

"Far from here," Zabaneja replied.

"Some day, Zab, we will get you to tell us your mysterious history," someone else said.

"Perhaps." Zabaneja said with a smile.

#

A few moments later, Sabouren entered, and the room quieted.

"Ah, Rusalei, you have arrived. I heard you would be joining us. If you are half as skilled as your late mother, you shall be a star pupil in no time at all," Sabouren said.

The young woman nodded as if trying to hide the fact she was blushing. "I will do my best, ma'am."

"That is all we can ask," the master replied. "I have heard you have some skills already. Is that true?"

"I have been known to play with my brothers from time to time."

"And have you ever bested them?" Sabouren asked.

"On occasion."

A collective gasp and murmurings of 'she bested her brothers?' could be heard.

Zabaneja turned to Rikar. "Who are her brothers? And why is everyone so surprised she bested them?"

Rikar smiled. "Her brothers are probably the best swordsmen in the entire kingdom, not just the Keep."

"Yeah, I am sure they let her win so she would not cry," one of the young men, Lurian, said a bit louder than he had meant to.

Rusalei did not respond.

"Well, young man, let us put that theory to the test. You will be her partner and at the end of the lesson we can decide if Rusalei's brothers were humoring her," Sabouren said.

The boy flushed crimson and nodded. "Yes, ma'am."

"Good. Now, all of you, to work." The master retreated to her perch to watch and comment on the goings on in the class.

#

During class, the master shouted words of both encouragement and criticism. "Good block." "Strengthen your stance before you strike." And so on, words that were never cruel or demeaning even if the student, usually Zabaneja, was not doing well.

But today she seemed to take special delight in riding Rusalei's partner, Lurian. Every time the young woman blocked his shot or hit him with her blade, which was quite often, the sword master made sure to acknowledge it.

With each comment, Lurian's anger grew. It did not take long for him to stray from the forms of combat allowed in the class, those not meant to seriously hurt anyone. With each strike it was clear, his aim was to injure her. No, it was more than that, he wanted to break her. The cracking noise of wood against wood increased with each strike Lurian made against her weapon, impelling the others to stop to watch.

"He looks as if he wants to kill her," Zabaneja said. "Why is the master not stopping this?"

Rikar shook his head. "I do not know, but I am sure she has her reasons."

Even Lurian's friends were shocked at the savage look on his face as he continued to lash out at Rusalei. The master watched in silence.

"You will not beat me," Rusalei said calmly as she blocked yet another of Lurian's attacks.

"And why is that, girl?" he asked, his words like venom.

"You attack blindly, out of anger, with no thought of what you are doing and no pretense of disguise. I know exactly what you are going to do. Where your next strike will be."

The boy growled and lashed at her and, once again, Rusalei anticipated his blow, but this time when she blocked, she twisted her blade and wrenched the sword from her opponent's hands, sending it flying across the room and into the wall.

"And I am better than you will ever be," she said.

Lurian, his face almost purple with rage, lunged at her, but his path was blocked and the others restrained him.

"You were beaten fairly, Lurian. Even when you chose to attack on a level both uncalled for and prohibited in this class, she maintained her composure," the weapons master said and descended from her vantage point. "I do not expect nor will I tolerate such behavior from anyone. Go, cool off and, when you are in a more reasonable mood, return for my decision about your future here."

Lurian pulled away from those holding him and stormed out.

"You are truly your mother's daughter, Rusalei. You fight with the same technique and calmness she did," Sabouren said.

"Thank you, Master."

"I think a ten minute break is in order, people." The master headed for her office to the right of the large arena.

As soon as the weapons master turned to leave, the others gathered around Rusalei, bombarding her with compliments and questions. All but Zabaneja, he went outside to the water pump to get a drink. Soon enough, the others followed and everyone stood milling around chattering.

At the end of the break, everyone returned to the training room. As usual, Sabouren sat on her perch, readying herself to give instructions for the next exercise, Lurian made his way to the front of the group. He looked up at Sabouren and then at Rusalei. "May I have permission to speak, Weapons Master?"

Sabouren nodded.

Lurian turned to face the others. "I wish to apologize to everyone for my despicable behavior this morning." He turned to face Rusalei. "And to you, Lady, I am especially sorry. I do not know what came over me to make me act so."

"It is alright, Lurian. I understand. To be honest, the first time I bested my eldest brother, he had a very similar reaction."

She held out her hand, and he took it. "I hope we can be friends."

"As do I," he said, and then turned to Sabouren. "Weapons Master, I ask your forgiveness for dishonoring both you and this class by my actions. I humbly request to be readmitted. I vow there will never be a recurrence of the incident."

The weapons master nodded.

"Back to training everyone. Rusalei, I would like to see you in my office," she said and pointed the way.

Rusalei followed, wondering why Sabouren wished to speak to her. She had not seemed upset at her besting Lurian. Had she done something else to displease her?

Sabouren sat behind her desk and waited for Rusalei. By design, there were no seats for the trainees. She liked them to feel a bit ill at ease, at a disadvantage, when they came before her.

"I am befuddled, young lady. Why are you here? Can you enlighten me?" Sabouren asked.

"Excuse me, ma'am? I am not sure I understand. I am here to learn the art of swordsmanship and weaponry."

The weapons master pounded her fist on the large wooden desk, making Rusalei jump. "Bah!" she exclaimed. "Just now you easily bested one of my top students without working up a sweat, so you do not require any training."

"In his defense, I do not think Lurian was at his best," she said.

"Perhaps," the weapons master replied, eyeing her with a bit of suspicion. "Still, I wonder about your motives. You could easily be one of my assistants instead of a student. So, why? I can only think of two reasons. Either you wish to get closer to one of the boys or you are trying to get away from your family."

She watched as Rusalei reddened.

"I have no idea what you are talking about, ma'am. I am here for the sole purpose of learning. There is no reason I would want to escape from my family."

"And what about the boy? Which one might it be?"

"What!" she shouted. "You are wrong. If I wished to meet a young man, I most certainly would not need to stoop to subterfuge to do so. I am not one to chase. I am appalled you should even suggest such a thing!"

"If you say so, Rusalei." The weapons master smiled. "All right then, go back to class. Partner with Rikar and Zab. And do go easy on Zab, he is very much a novice."

Rusalei nodded and tried to hide the smile that crossed her face.

"So, it is one of those two, eh? But which one?" Sabouren said to the empty room. "Neither of them are in your social class by any stretch of the imagination." She chuckled and then added, "Well, this may make for an interesting term."

#

"Wait a minute," Rikar said after Rusalei told him she was to practice with them. "We are nowhere near your caliber of expertise nor station."

"I thought there was no station in this class other than the master. As for your skill level, maybe I can help you improve," she replied. "Unless you have a problem partnering with me."

"You realize we will not be a challenge for you, other than amusing you with our lack of skill," Zabaneja said.

Rusalei laughed. "Do not let Rikar fool you. He is already quite accomplished for the short time he has been here and from what I have seen, you are coming along very well, too."

As soon as the words left her lips, Rusalei regretted them. How could she explain she had been watching him? Ever since she first saw him ride in with Aneesyma, the scruffy looking awkward boy had caught her attention and her curiosity.

"And how do you know our skill levels, My Lady? Have you been spying on us?" Rikar asked with a grin.

She looked at him. "Not spying. Let us just say I like to know my enemies as well as my allies."

Zabaneja remained silent. He was not quite sure what was going on.

"So, let us begin," Rusalei said, taking command. "Let me see up close what you two have been up to and what you can do."

It did not take long for the three to become a well-organized team.

"You know, Zab, I am impressed with the way you anticipate your opponent's moves, but you still handle the weapon too clumsily to be able to follow through," Rusalei said as the trio was putting their weapons away at the end of class.

"Am I to take that as a compliment?"

"Of course. I think once you feel more comfortable with the sword in your hand, you may surpass both Rikar and me."

"Now you are just making fun of me." Zabaneja stormed away.

Rikar shook his head. "I am sorry. He has a difficult time seeing his own talents."

Rusalei smiled. "Well then, Rikar, that will be our job, to make him realize how good he is."

"I like that," Rikar said.

CHAPTER TWENTY-ONE

"I DO NOT UNDERSTAND why I am being given this responsibility," Zabaneja said when told he was to be put in charge of dealing with new recruits. "I have not been here as long as most of the others. Surely one of them would be more capable..."

"You are not being given anything, young man. You have earned it," Guentza said. "If I, or Lord Aneesyma, thought anyone else more capable, they would have been given the task."

"As if An...," Zabaneja started and caught himself, "Lord Aneesyma has any idea what I am doing."

Guentza shook his head. "His lordship gets regular reports on your progress and is well aware of everything you do, both on and off duty."

"I find that hard to believe. I have not seen nor spoken with him since he abandoned me to you."

"Have you forgotten he told you he would be watching? Just because you are not aware of it, does not mean it is not true."

Zabaneja did not respond.

"Here is a list of your duties, study it. We have new recruits arriving tomorrow who will need your attention. "

"Yes, Captain."

#

"Have you given any thought to what you want to do when we finish training?" Rikar asked as the pair returned to the barracks after conducting a weapons training session with the new recruits.

"What do you mean?"

"You cannot be serious, man. We only have a few months left as recruits."

"But I have not been here as long as you have. Surely I need more time..." Zabaneja said.

"Normally, that would be the case, but you, my friend, have shown an extraordinary ability to quickly learn everything that has been thrown at you. So, now it is time for us to move on."

"Move on? Where?" Zabaneja asked.

"The army or the guard are the two most likely courses."

"I did not realize that. I assumed we would be Sabouren's assistants, and I would continue to work with the new recruits," Zab said. *Unlike you, my friend, I do not have a choice. I am bound to stay in this place for a few more years.* "What are you thinking about doing?"

"The army. I think I have spent enough time in one place."

"Really? I thought you liked it here."

"I do, but you should understand, I want to be somewhere with more open space. I have to say, I am surprised you want to stay here," Rikar said.

Zabaneja smiled. "I guess I have become comfortable here. Since Guentza no longer forces me to sleep inside the barracks, I get a little taste of the open sky."

"I am glad. I have to say when you first got here I did not think you would stay. You acted like a caged animal, I fully expected to wake one morning to find you gone. But it is good you adjusted. And, with you staying here, I will not be surprised to hear you are the next captain of the guard."

"Now you are making fun of me."

"All right, perhaps not captain of the guard just yet. But I sincerely doubt Guentza will let you remain in your current duties for very long."

"I think this is a very important position," Zabaneja said.

"Your abilities would be wasted in that position for any length of time." Before Zabaneja could protest, Rikar added, "You really do not realize just how talented you are, do you?"

"I am not sure what you mean, but thank you for the kind words."

#

It did not take long for Rikar's words to come to pass. A few months after joining the guard, Zabaneja was promoted to Guentza's aide.

"Where are we going?" Zabaneja asked.

"We report the routine goings on of the Keep to his lordship on a daily basis. And to the council whenever they meet."

"I see."

"For now, you will accompany me to listen and learn. Eventually this will be your job, and I will come along only on rare occasions. The most important thing to remember is to speak only when given permission to do so. Do you understand?"

Zabaneja nodded as the two men arrived at the council chamber. Guentza knocked and waited for permission to enter.

He delivered his regular report, bowed and motioned Zabaneja to leave.

"Gentlemen, stay a bit," Aneesyma said.

"My Lord," Guentza said after the others had departed, "if it is all right with you, I will get back to my duties and allow you and Zab to visit."

"As you wish, Guentza. I will send him back to you soon," Aneesyma said. "I am sure you have a great deal of work for him to do."

Guentza nodded.

"It has been a long time since you and I have spoken, Zab. But I have been keeping an eye on your progress here."

"So I have been told, My Lord."

"I am sure you have. But it does not sound like you are happy."

"It is not my place to be happy or not with what you do, My Lord," Zabaneja said with more than a hint of disdain.

"Can we, for a few moments while we are alone, drop the formalities?"

"If that is your wish," Zabaneja said.

"How have you been, Zab? Truly been?" Aneesyma asked.

"I have adjusted, I guess."

"Adjusted, but not happy? Do you still miss your home?"

Zabaneja glared at him. "How dare you ask me such a question? Do you think there is something so magnificent in this place that it would make me forget my homeland? My family?"

"That is not what I meant. I know you will never forget your homeland."

Zabaneja continued to glare at Aneesyma.

"Oh, come now, Zab. You cannot still think I am the monster you once did."

"No, not a monster. But you did bring me here and then abandoned me with little knowledge of what was going on."

"You do not release a grudge easily, do you?" Aneesyma asked.

Zabaneja smiled. "A drageal trait, I guess. Some habits are harder to get rid of."

Aneesyma laughed. "Perhaps, but I get the sense that regardless of who raised you, you would still be the same."

"Perhaps."

"Now, what about your new position? Are you enjoying it?"

Suddenly a thought struck Zabaneja, and he was appalled. "Was it your doing that I was put in this position and the one before? Because, if you are affording me special privileges..."

"No, I had absolutely nothing to do with the positions you have achieved. You have done all of that on your own. Guentza has nothing but praise for you, and we both know he does not do so easily or falsely. Ever!"

Zabaneja nodded. "That is true."

"You know, he is so struck with you and how you conduct yourself, I think if I let him, he would make you Captain of the Guard and he would be your aide."

Zabaneja shook his head. "That is ridiculous."

"Perhaps."

CHAPTER TWENTY-TWO

AS WAS OFTEN THE CASE in the months after Zabaneja began delivering the daily reports, Aneesyma requested he remain after the others had left.

"Was there something that concerned you in today's briefing, Aneesyma?"

"No, nothing like that, but there are other things we need to discuss."

Zabaneja was confused.

Aneesyma smiled at the boy's reaction. "How long have you been here, Zab?"

"Three years."

Aneesyma laughed. "Not quite, but almost."

"Why is that important? Do I not need to stay here five years before I can leave?"

Aneesyma was disappointed that Zabaneja's first response was to talk about leaving. He had hoped the boy had come to enjoy life at the Keep enough that he might want to stay on.

"True. But your mother and I made plans for you to visit her halfway through that time."

"What? I was never told that."

"No, we thought it better not to tell you until I saw how you fared in this environment."

"And what if I do not wish to return here once I see my mother again?" Zabaneja asked.

"Is that a possibility? Would you renege on our agreement?"

Zabaneja glared at Aneesyma. "It was not my agreement. That was between you and my mother."

"Ah, I had hoped by now you would have lost your anger over that."

He too had thought he had done just that. He had even grown fond of Aneesyma and looked forward to the times they spoke. But now, with the mention of seeing his mother again, all the old emotions came flooding back into him.

"I guess not," Zabaneja replied, shaking his head.

The sadness in Zabaneja's voice surprised Aneesyma.

"About the visit to see Mother," Zabaneja continued with a smile, "when will we meet her? And where? She certainly cannot come here."

Aneesyma laughed. "No, her coming here would not work on a myriad of levels. We will meet in the same place we met before."

"When?"

"We leave tomorrow, before sunrise."

Zabaneja drew in a breath. "So soon? Why did you wait until now to tell me of this when you obviously have been planning this all along."

"I thought it best to keep your excitement to a minimum amount of time. You are excited, are you not?"

"Of course, I am. What of my duties?" Zabaneja asked.

Aneesyma smiled at his young charge's concern about his responsibilities. "Guentza is aware of your background and our relationship, and though I have not told him all the details of our trip, he will ensure all is taken care of here."

Zabaneja chuckled. "I had forgotten he knew. Now, I need to be on my way if we are to leave in the morning, I need to prepare. How long do you think we will be away?"

"Ten to twelve days. That will allow time to travel leisurely both there and back and to give you a few days to visit with your mother."

"That will be nice," Zabaneja said.

"All right, then. I will meet you at the north gate an hour before sunrise."

Zabaneja nodded and left. It was not until he reached his own room that he realized he had not asked Aneesyma how Pheunaf would know when and where to meet them. Had the two of them been in contact all this time? Why had Aneesyma not told him? No, that could not be. Surely, if there was a way for Pheunaf to keep in touch with Aneesyma, she would have done so with him. He would have to remember to ask.

#

"So, it is time, eh? Do you think they will be there?" Jocel asked.

"Of course," Pheunaf said emphatically, trying to convince herself as much as her father. "Why would they not?"

"It has been a long time, and I am sure Zabaneja has gone through a great many changes in his life."

"Are you saying he has forgotten me? Forgotten us?"

"Of course not, child. It is just..."

"Just what? That Darchok was right? That as soon as my son was among his own kind, he would discard his time with us?" Pheunaf railed.

"I did not say that. I know Zabaneja will never forget you. Just as you will never forget him. But it has been a long time, and you have had no contact with either Zabaneja nor Aneesyma. Might it be possible that Aneesyma has forgotten? The boy was not told he would get to see you now, right?"

"We decided it would be better for him not to know," Pheunaf said.

Jocel put his hand on Pheunaf's shoulder. "That was a time of great emotional upheaval for you and Zabaneja. The decisions you made came from your desire to do what was best for him."

Pheunaf looked at him and smiled.

"When will you leave?"

"In a few days. I know it will only take a few hours to get to the meeting place, the same place we first met Aneesyma, where I abandoned Zabaneja..."

"You did not abandon him. You gave him an opportunity."

"Bah, you did not see his face."

"No, but I saw yours."

"Perhaps. I hope he realizes that."

"Do you wish me to go with you?" Jocel asked.

Pheunaf looked at her father, trying to figure out if he wanted to go with her merely to see Zabaneja or to be there to comfort her if they did not show up.

"No, I will go alone."

"If you change your mind, let me know. I would really love to see my grandson again."

#

It was difficult for Pheunaf to be patient until it was time to leave to meet Zabaneja. Finally, she could wait no longer and departed a day earlier than she had planned. She knew they would not yet be there, but she wanted to be waiting when—there was no if—Zabaneja arrived. She wondered if he feared she had forgotten him. That she would not be there. If that thought crossed his mind, even for a moment, she wanted to make sure she would be the first thing he saw as soon as he entered the clearing.

She arrived and was alone. She hoped Zabaneja was as excited about their meeting as she was, so perhaps they would arrive early as well. But it did not matter, she would wait.

#

Zabaneja did not sleep at all that night. He sat on his rooftop perch and stared at the stars. No matter how he tried to deny it, though he missed home and family, he missed flying even more. He dared not hope, but did anyway, that his mother would bring the flying seat to allow him to again soar above the trees.

He arrived at the gate hours before Aneesyma. Had he known the route, he would have gone ahead and let Aneesyma catch up. Instead, he paced, unable to stand still, until at last he heard Aneesyma's approach.

"I am early and, not surprisingly, you are already here," Aneesyma said with a chuckle. "How long have you been here waiting?"

Zabaneja shrugged as he mounted his horse and the pair set off.

CHAPTER TWENTY-THREE

"CAN YOU NOT GO any faster?" Zabaneja asked.

"It is a three-day ride to our destination, Zab, and if we push the horses beyond their capability, we will be forced to travel on foot and who knows how long that will take," Aneesyma replied.

"I am not asking to push them to their death, but at the rate we are going we will be lucky to be out of sight of the Keep by nightfall."

Aneesyma laughed, but did not pick up his pace.

At midday, the pair stopped, much to Zabaneja's chagrin. Aneesyma reminded him they needed to eat and, more importantly, the horses needed a short rest.

"You might as well sit and enjoy your meal, Zab. I know I will," Aneesyma said.

Zabaneja grumbled, gobbled down his meal then paced or fidgeted with the horses until they could once again be on the road.

"Not surprisingly, my young friend, we are ahead of schedule. If we start out again tomorrow at sunrise, we might be able to reach our destination just after sunset. A full day early," Aneesyma said as he tended the horses when they stopped for the night.

"That will be fine with me," Zabaneja responded.

"You know if we arrive early, Pheunaf will not be there."

Zabaneja chuckled. "Oh, she will be there. It would not surprise me to find she is already there waiting."

"Really? Why would she be there so early?"

"You do not know my mother very well, do you? She knows I am coming, and she will want me to see her as soon as we enter the clearing. She is my mother."

"Of course. You realize that Kalini will not be there," Aneesyma said, "so you will need to act as interpreter."

The boy nodded.

#

The next day the pair set out before sunrise and rode at a faster pace than the previous day, taking an even shorter break for lunch, hoping to arrive at their destination before the sun went down.

"How much longer?" Zabaneja asked as they were once again on the road.

"At this rate, probably an hour or so."

"Wonderful."

About an hour before sunset, as Aneesyma had predicted, the pair approached the clearing.

"She is there, I know she is. I can sense her," Zabaneja said and picked up his pace.

#

Pheunaf felt Zabaneja's presence long before she scented him. She smiled and waited.

Zabaneja rode into the clearing, saw his mother and, as tears of joy filled his eyes, jumped from his horse before it came to a halt. He hit the ground and ran to her open arms.

"Mother," he cried and buried his face in her feathers. "I have missed you so much."

"And I you, son," she said and wrapped her wings around him.

Aneesyma followed a few moments later, dismounted and gathered both horses. He did not approach the pair. This was their time to be reacquainted.

#

"Mother," Zabaneja said as Pheunaf opened her wings. "I am so sorry for the way I spoke to you the last time we were together."

"I know, son, I know," she replied as she wiped the tears from his cheek. Tears he did not try to hide. "Now, let me take a look at you, my boy."

Zabaneja took a step back.

"You have grown, my son."

The pair walked toward Aneesyma. "You did a good job with him, Aneesyma, as you said you would," Pheunaf said. Zabaneja translated.

"Thank you, Pheunaf. I did very little. The man he has become is all due to the way you brought him up."

"Thank you. Your words are very kind."

"And now, I will take my leave," Aneesyma said.

"Your leave?" Zabaneja asked. "Does that mean I am going home?"

"No, not yet, Zab. I am going to the cabin we stayed in previously to allow you and your mother some time together without my intrusive presence."

"You are never an intrusive presence, Aneesyma, you are a valued friend," Pheunaf said.

"Thank you, My Lady, but be that as it may, I will leave you two alone for a bit. I shall return in the morning."

Without waiting for a response, Aneesyma took the horses and departed.

#

"He is a good man," Pheunaf said.

"Yes, Mother, he is."

"I am glad you have at last come to that conclusion. That was not your opinion of him the last time I saw you."

Zabaneja shook his head.

"Now tell me what you have been doing. How is your life among the humans? Have you made friends? Met a mate? I see your dragealian has not suffered, though I am sure you find little use for it there."

Zabaneja laughed. "Mother, you are acting like I usually do. Asking a barrage of new questions before I have a chance to answer the previous ones."

Pheunaf smiled and asked Zabaneja to tell her all that had gone on in his life since last they met. When he finished, he asked about the clan and his friends and family.

"What? Grandfather made Darchok leave his house? I can only imagine that Darchok did not take kindly to that."

"No, he did not."

Suddenly Zabaneja got quiet.

"What is it, son?" Pheunaf asked.

"Nothing, Mother," he replied.

She laughed. "We have not been apart that long that I cannot tell when there is something troubling you."

"I am ashamed at the way I acted the last time we were together.

I was so angry. I truly thought you abandoned me and then at the Keep I had little contact with Aneesyma. So, in the matter of a few weeks, it seemed everyone I either loved or trusted had abandoned me. It took a very long time for me to understand that was not the case."

"I see you now understand, but I feel you have not fully forgiven me. Am I correct?"

Zabaneja looked away. "Well..."

"I understand, son. Believe me, I do. I cannot tell you how many times I have cursed myself for sending you away. And, I know I would feel the same way if I were in your place."

"Really? It is good to hear that you understand how I feel."

"But you have not told me if you have found a mate."

"No, no, I have not. To be honest, I have been so busy I have not really had time for such things."

"That is too bad, but you still have time there. Perhaps you will find someone."

The pair talked until Zabaneja fell asleep against the soft pillow made by Pheunaf's feathers.

CHAPTER TWENTY-FOUR

A SHORT TIME AFTER the sun rose, Zabaneja stirred and Pheunaf cooed to try to lull him back to sleep.

He looked up at her and smiled. "Still trying to comfort me, eh, Mother?"

"Always, my son. Always."

Zabaneja rose and stretched. He looked around as if searching for something or someone.

"Did you misplace something?"

"Not really. I was just... oh, never mind, it is nothing."

"No, you are looking for something. I can tell," Pheunaf said.

Zabaneja smiled. "I never could fool you."

"Tell me what you seek?"

"I hoped you might have brought my seat so we could take to the sky for one more ride. But I do not see it." Zabaneja looked at the ground. "It is probably for the best."

Pheunaf pointed to an outcropping of rocks by the group of trees to her left.

"Really? Are you saying you brought it?"

"Well, go see for yourself," she said with a smile.

Zabaneja could not contain his excitement. He ran to the rocks and let out a cry of joy. He came running back to his mother, carrying the seat with the straps dragging along the ground behind him.

"Can we go now? Please?" he asked.

"Of course. But have you forgotten you need to mount the seat from the rocks? That is why I left it there."

Zabaneja shook his head. "You are right, how silly of me. I was so excited at the thought of flying again, I forgot the logistics."

"Well, drag it back over there and we will be off," Pheunaf said and headed for the rock.

#

Zabaneja quickly affixed the seat to her back, climbed into it and strapped himself in. As soon as that was accomplished, Pheunaf turned towards him, winked, and in a flash they were aloft.

Once in the air, even without looking, she knew he was grinning from ear to ear. She was glad she had brought it, there had been a brief moment when she had considered leaving it at home. She worried whether it would be worse for him not to fly now or to fly and not be able to do it again until the time he made his decision whether or not to come home?

But as she felt his excitement, the joy he experienced from even the small amount of flight time, she knew her decision had been correct.

#

It was not until the sun was high in the sky that drageal and rider silently landed in the clearing. Once on the ground, Zabaneja untethered himself, dismounted and unstrapped the seat. Only when he and Pheunaf began to walk back to the middle of the clearing did they notice Aneesyma, who sat where they had last met the evening before.

The two approached him, and he stood.

"That was amazing! I have never seen such a sight. I cannot fathom how fantastic it must feel to be so free. No wonder you always have that look of longing in your eyes when you look at the sky."

Zabaneja looked at his mother, and she nodded.

"Would you like to experience that feeling yourself? How would you like to take flight with Mother?"

"What? No. I could not. I mean, am I not too large for the seat you ride in?" Aneesyma stammered.

Zabaneja chuckled. "I do believe Aneesyma is frightened. What do you think, Mother?"

"You should not tease him so, son. Just because you think flying is as natural as breathing does not mean any other human does." Pheunaf turned to Aneesyma. "I understand if you are reticent about such an endeavor."

"Thank you, Pheunaf. That is kind of you to say."

"But the seat will accommodate you, so, if you change your mind, I would be more than willing to take flight with you."

She saw his dilemma. On the one hand, the boy within, wanted to taste the adventure, but on the other, the man, the leader, hesitated.

"I will consider it, My Lady. Thank you again."

"Bah, he is afraid," Zabaneja said and laughed. "That is all there is to it."

"I will admit, I am apprehensive," Aneesyma began.

"No, you are afraid," Zabaneja said, taking great delight at teasing his master.

"All right, I am a little afraid," Aneesyma admitted, then

grinned broadly. "But, how can I pass up such an offer? If you are indeed willing to grant me the privilege of flying with you, I would love to."

"Wonderful. Let us go now." Pheunaf turned back to the rocks where the seat still rested.

"Now?" Aneesyma said, his voice cracking a little.

"It is a perfect afternoon," Pheunaf replied without looking at him. "The sky is clear, the temperature mild and almost no wind. As I said, perfect."

Aneesyma stood frozen for a moment until he felt the nudge from Zabaneja.

"Go. It will be fine. Mother would never let anything happen to you."

#

"I think I see, at least a little, how hard it has been for you to be landbound. I am sorry for not understanding that from the beginning. Only now, after experiencing the exhilaration of flight, even for that brief moment," Aneesyma said, "can I see how difficult it has been to be denied something so magnificent, something you did your entire life. I am sorry I was not more aware of your sacrifice. Why did you not tell me?"

"How could I? I never saw you," Zabaneja said.

"I am sorry about that, as well. I guess I failed to make it clear Guentza was my representative. If you needed something from me, you could have gone to him."

Zabaneja did not respond.

Aneesyma put his hand on the boy's shoulder.

"I assumed you would know."

#

"I have to thank you, Aneesyma," Pheunaf said as the three sat together.

"For what, My Lady?" he asked after Zabaneja translated.

"For taking such good care of my son."

Aneesyma shook his head. "I have had very little to do with it. I am ashamed to say my duties have kept me away from him for a good part of the time he has been in my land. Any success he has had in his maturation into a fine young man has been from the integrity and ethics you instilled in him."

Pheunaf gave him a strange look. "Am I to understand you left him to fend for himself? If that is true, why did I allow him to go with you?"

"Forgive me, Pheunaf, I have not made myself clear. Though I was not the one who watched over him, I left him in good hands."

Aneesyma looked to Zabaneja for help. When the boy was not forthcoming, Aneesyma said, "Please, Zab. Tell your mother I did not abandon you."

Zabaneja smiled. "Hmm, it might be interesting to see her reaction if I do not."

"You would not do such a thing, would you?"

"What are you two saying, Zabaneja?" Pheunaf asked when the boy did not translate what he and Aneesyma were discussing.

"Please, Zab, you know I did not abandon you. Guentza not only watched out for you, but he kept me informed of how you were doing on almost a daily basis. Please tell her that."

Zabaneja smiled, turned back toward Pheunaf and began to speak.

Now it was Aneesyma's turn to wonder what was being said. Drageals show little facial expression, at least nothing noticeable to those not intimately acquainted with them, so he could not tell how she was reacting other than the fact she had made no move toward him.

At last, after what seemed an eternity, Zabaneja turned back to him with a grim expression, but then he broke into a smile. "My mother still thanks you for all you have done for me."

Aneesyma let out a loud sigh of relief, and Zabaneja laughed.

CHAPTER TWENTY-FIVE

ALL TOO SOON, it was time to leave. Zabaneja did not want to return to the Keep. He wanted to soar again with his mother and the other drageals. He wanted to go home. But, after some discussion and debate, he conceded to Pheunaf and Aneesyma's wishes that he continue his stay amongst the humans.

Naturally, before the visit ended, Zabaneja and Pheunaf took one last flight together. And while it seemed to him to be over in the blink of an eye, he could tell by the position of the sun they had been aloft for several hours.

The next morning, after Pheunaf bid Aneesyma farewell, he excused himself to the edge of the wood to allow mother and son time to say their goodbyes.

This time, Pheunaf did not sneak away and Zabaneja stood staring up at the sky long after she had disappeared from sight. Finally, he took a deep breath and turned to Aneesyma.

\#

"I have to tell you, Zab, there was a small part of me that

wondered if you were going to be truthful in your translations," Aneesyma said as they left the clearing.

"What do you mean?" the boy asked. "You are not still upset about the threat I made, are you? You know I was only teasing."

"Well, there was a moment there where I was not quite sure. But that is not what I am talking about. I meant when we were discussing your return to the Keep. I know you would have much rather flown off with her than be riding with me. Though, I do hope there is a part of you, even just a small part, that wants to remain with us."

Zabaneja did not reply.

"I do not think it would have been that difficult to twist either of our words to the other to make them say what you wanted. So, I am honored that you are coming back with me now to fulfill the bargain we made."

"You are very right in saying I would have much preferred to go home with Mother. But you are wrong in thinking I could have lied to her. She has a way of looking at you, no, it is more like she is looking into you, to find the truth. So, had I tried to lie or even distort the truth, she would have known. It is said most drageals have that ability, and Mother is the best I have ever seen. Why do you think she was willing to allow me to go with you?"

"I see," Aneesyma said. "I will have to keep that in mind for any further dealings with drageals."

#

The return journey to the Keep was at a far more leisurely pace than the trip to the clearing. But Aneesyma did not mind. He knew Zabaneja needed time to sort out his feelings.

"Have you told anyone about your background? Your family?"

Aneesyma asked as they rode.

"You mean besides you telling Guentza?"

Aneesyma nodded. "You know I had no choice, correct? He had to have a reason that made some of your unusual behaviors and habits understandable."

"Yes, now I do, but then I did not."

"So, you still have not answered my question. Have you told anyone else of your history?"

Zabaneja shook his head.

"Really? Not even Rikar? I would have thought as inseparable as the two of you have been, well... Is there a reason?"

The boy shrugged. "I guess the situation where it would have made sense to tell him never arose."

"I see."

"Why do you ask?"

"I was just curious," Aneesyma replied.

"What will you tell the others about our absence?" Zabaneja asked to change the subject.

"Ah, dear boy, that is the best part about being the Lord of the Keep," Aneesyma began with a laugh, "no one questions your actions."

#

"How was your visit with Zabaneja?" Jocel asked.

She managed a weak smile. "Too brief, Father. Too brief."

Jocel chuckled. "Anything short of him coming home for good would be too brief a visit for you, my dear."

Pheunaf smiled. "I suppose you are right."

"Tell me everything. How is he doing? Is he well? Is he happy?"

"He seemed fine, but I am not sure."

"Did he say something?" Jocel asked.

She smirked. "It was not what he said, it was what he did not."

"What do you mean?"

She shook her head. "I do not know. There was just something."

Jocel took her hand. "You are his mother. No matter what he says or does, you will always want more for him. Especially when it comes to happiness."

"Perhaps. But still, there was a sadness in his eyes. Or perhaps an anger. I fear he has yet to forgive me for sending him away."

"Did you ask him?"

"Yes. He said it was my imagination."

"But, you did not believe him?"

"I want to, but there was a sorrowfulness in his demeanor. In his words and..." She turned and looked off into the distance.

Jocel chuckled. "He is so like you, my dear."

"What do you mean?"

He shook his head and smiled. "Do I really need to tell you? Do you truly not know?"

She looked at him and nodded. "Yes, I suppose I do. Still, I fear he is not happy."

"Not happy or that he will not return to you, to us?"

She smiled. "Both."

CHAPTER TWENTY-SIX

"WELCOME BACK, my Lord. Zab," Guentza said as he met the pair outside the stable. "I hope your journey was successful."

"I believe it was," Aneesyma said as he and Zabaneja came to a stop beside the captain of the guard. "Do you not agree, Zab?"

"Yes, Lord Aneesyma." he replied as the pair dismounted.

Aneesyma threw his arm around Guentza in a bear hug. "It is great to be home, my friend. I assume all went well here."

"Of course, My Lord."

"Oh, so I am not needed then, eh?" Aneesyma said.

"That is not what I said," Guentza replied and both men laughed.

"I will tend to the horses, My Lord. Did you wish me to bring your things to you or will you take them with you now?"

"Bring them to me when you are done here."

"Of course, sir."

Once Zabaneja was out of sight, Guentza turned to Aneesyma. "So, are you planning on telling me where you two actually went and what you were up to?"

Aneesyma smiled. "Are you saying you do not believe what I

said before?"

"You did not expect me to, did you?"

"No, not really," Aneesyma said and laughed. "You could ask Zab about it."

Guentza shook his head. "Then I will never hear anything. It would be easier to steal the eggs of an eagle than have Zab speak of himself."

"Well, you know more about him than anyone else here. And, who knows, maybe someday he will feel comfortable with you and everyone else to let you into his private life and thoughts."

"I understand his reticence and have no intention of prying," Guentza replied.

"I did not think you would," Aneesyma said, patting his friend on the back. "But I also know you are a bit disappointed, and maybe even a little hurt, that he does not feel comfortable enough with you to share."

Guentza did not respond.

#

"The horses have been tended to, My Lord, and I have brought your things," Zabaneja said as he entered Aneesyma's chambers.

"Thank you, Zab. You can put them in the corner," Aneesyma said.

Zabaneja did so and accepted a glass from Guentza.

"Guentza was just asking about our trip," Aneesyma said.

"I thought you had said all went well," Zabaneja said.

"Ah, so I did," Aneesyma replied with a smirk. "I was wondering if you had anything else to add."

Zabaneja shook his head and glared. "I have nothing to add to what you have already told him, My Lord."

Aneesyma chuckled and turned to Guentza.

"Now, tell me what has happened in my absence."

Guentza briefed Aneesyma on the goings on around the Keep. "As I said, nothing unusual, just the normal day-to-day business."

"Well, that is good to hear, but even if something out of the ordinary had happened, I am sure you would have dealt with it."

"Thank you, My Lord, your confidence in me is appreciated. Now I must be going." Guentza placed his glass on the table.

"I will send Zab along in a bit," Aneesyma said.

"As I surmised," the captain said with a smirk and departed.

#

"What more do we need to discuss that we have not over the last few days?" Zabaneja asked.

"I really think you should consider confiding in Guentza," Aneesyma replied.

"Confide what? He already knows my past. What more is there to tell him?"

"You could talk to him about recent events, about how you are feeling about everything? About things going on in your life. Things that are troubling you."

"There is nothing troubling me. And, even if there were, I would not need to confide in anyone. I can handle my problems by myself."

Aneesyma laughed. "That is exactly what I expected you to say. But you need to change that attitude. Surely by now you know you are amongst friends. Amongst people you can trust. People who care about you."

"I know that," Zabaneja began. "I mean, I understand that the people I have met here would never do me harm, but it is not..."

Zabaneja hesitated, and Aneesyma put his hand on the boy's shoulder.

"Not the drageal way," Aneesyma said, finishing his sentence. "That was what you were going to say, was it not?"

Zabaneja nodded.

"Even drageals share their feelings and their thoughts with others, with their own family and friends, do they not?"

Again, Zabaneja nodded and looked away.

"Oh, I see," Aneesyma said. "You still do not really consider us, humans, your friends, do you?"

"I do not know. I mean, I understand you and Guentza and even Rikar care about me. But…"

The boy shook his head.

"I understand, Zab, I truly do. I had hoped by this time, you would have changed your opinion, but I see now that you are not there yet."

Zabaneja looked at Aneesyma, but said nothing.

"Perhaps, in time, you will. Just know we are here for you when you do."

"Thank you."

"Now, off with you. I am sure Guentza has a lot for you to catch up on."

Zabaneja smiled. "I am certain of that."

"And there are probably a few wenches in town who have been missing your company."

The boy's face reddened. "I doubt that. There are many others who can satisfy them as well as I can."

Aneesyma laughed. "That is not what I have heard. Now, off with you, see what Guentza needs you to do and then, well, a night of drinking and wenching will probably do you a world of good."

CHAPTER TWENTY-SEVEN

RUSALEI WAS EXITING the barracks office as Zabaneja approached.

"It is good to have you back, Zab. I have missed you..." Rusalei sputtered. "I mean, I have missed hearing your reports, Guentza's presentation is so dry."

"Thank you, My Lady. It is good to be back," he lied.

"So, I suppose there is no point in asking you where, or what, you and Lord Aneesyma were up to while you were gone, is there?" she asked with a sly grin.

Zabaneja shook his head. "You will need to ask His Lordship for details, My Lady. I am not at liberty to say."

"Of course," she said. "That is exactly what I expected to hear."

Zabaneja nodded. "If there is nothing else, My Lady, I must be on my way. I am sure Guentza has a lot for me to do."

#

"Did Lady Rusalei speak to you?" Guentza asked.

"Yes, how did you know?"

"She was just here, telling me how much more enjoyable your delivery of the daily reports are," Guentza said with a chuckle.

"Um, yes, she did mention that to me."

"I do believe the lady fancies you, lad."

"That is ridiculous, Guentza. I mean seriously, look at her and look at me. She is nobility and I am, well, I am not."

"That may be, my boy, but I still think she fancies you. Perhaps she has heard of your way with the ladies and wants to sample your prowess," Guentza said with a twinkle in his eye.

"How dare you speak of her in that way? She is a lady of the highest caliber, she would never do such a thing."

Guentza laughed. "Hmm, you seem to come to the lady's defense rather quickly, boy. Could it be that you feel the same for her?"

"Do not be ridiculous."

"I have known many a noblewoman, who is more than happy to spread her legs to receive a man beneath her class."

Zabaneja jumped to his feet and grabbed Guentza by the throat. "Do not ever speak like that about Lady Rusalei again. If I hear of such a thing, I will slice your throat."

Zabaneja glared at Guentza, released him and stormed out of the room, leaving the shocked captain rubbing his neck and grinning from ear to ear.

"I think I struck a nerve with the boy," Guentza said to himself once he was sure Zabaneja was out of earshot. He rubbed his neck. "I will need to remember to mind my words on that subject from now on."

As he returned to his quarters, Zabaneja wondered why he reacted so aggressively to Guentza's comments. He shook his head. It did not make sense, but he did not know why.

CHAPTER TWENTY-EIGHT

MANY IN THE CLAN hoped that, with Zabaneja's departure, Darchok's anger would lessen despite his expulsion from his father's house. Too soon, their hopes were dashed. Even with the human child no longer among them, Darchok's tirades against all beings that were not drageals became more frequent and vicious. To the dismay of many, he also attracted others to his cause. Before long, the clan elders would tolerate it no more; Darchok and his followers were exiled.

Darchok spewed fire into the sky above as he and his followers departed the mountaintop they had called home.

"Where shall we go now?" Ysernon, Darchok's childhood friend and ardent follower asked.

"To the other clans. Surely the others are not of the same mind-set as that one was," Darchok replied.

Though they acquired additional followers from each clan they visited, none were willing to give Darchok and his followers refuge. As they departed from the last clan's mountain, Darchok decided that, since no one else would have them, they needed to form their own clan.

Yet even being the head of his own clan did little to make Darchok happy. His clan was small and held no prestige amongst the others. But that would change. Soon, drageals and all others would learn the depth of his hatred as they tasted his power and revenge.

#

"It is time to show the others our ideals are more than just words," Darchok said.

Ysernon nodded. "Where shall we begin?"

"There is a large human city some distance from here. We will raze it and annihilate its occupants."

Ysernon looked concerned.

"You object?" Darchok snarled.

"Only the chosen target."

"Why would that be?"

Ysernon took a deep breath. He knew to tread carefully when disagreeing, even slightly, with Darchok. "Surely you realize most of our clan are young, some have never killed before, not even for their own food. Perhaps our first target should be a place that would offer no resistance."

"Resistance? What resistance can humans mount against us?"

"Nothing of any consequence, to be sure. But a large city will have some defenses in place and even if they are ineffectual, none of us has ever been shot at or attacked in any way. So, though it would indeed have no real effect on us, it could unhinge the resolve of some of the young ones. Instead, let their first taste of killing be targets that will flee in fear at the mere sight of us. Such a reaction from their prey will surely bolster their confidence and whet their appetites for more."

Darchok pondered his friend's words. "I do not understand

such an attitude, but I see your point. I will leave it to you to find a suitable objective."

Ysernon nodded.

"Do not make it too small, else you will suffer my displeasure."

"Of course, I will find one that will be to your liking," Ysernon said, knowing Darchok's threat was not an idle one.

#

"This is a good day for our initial attack upon the humans," Darchok said to his assembled clan. "The clear skies will let them see our approach, and we will be able to observe their terror as we burn not only their homes but their bodies as well."

Darchok and Ysernon were the first to swoop down upon the humans who, at the mere sight of them in the sky, screamed and scattered in terror. The pair descended, unleashing a stream of inescapable flames upon the land and its inhabitants below. Slowly, as the others saw the delight the two took in the devastation, they joined the assault.

When it was clear nothing—plant, beast or human—remained alive below, the drageals triumphantly rose through the smoke and shouted Darchok's name.

#

"This day has been the first step, albeit a small one, in our quest to cleanse this world of those beings that do not deserve to breathe our air," Darchok jubilantly shouted to his clan gathered on their mountaintop.

All cheered.

"And, now, let us celebrate," Darchok continued.

Another cheer went up, and the assembled drageals broke off into groups to enjoy the aftermath of the destruction of the human settlement.

Ysernon walked with Darchok.

"So, what is our next move, Darchok?" Ysernon asked.

"You mean our next target?"

Ysernon nodded. "Do you think there will be retribution?"

Darchok turned and grabbed Ysernon by the throat. "Retribution from whom? Humans? Bah, why would I fear humans? You saw how they fled at the mere sight of us. We had not singed a hair on their heads, and they screamed in terror. What could they do to us?"

He released Ysernon and began to walk away.

"I did not mean the humans, Darchok," Ysernon replied, rubbing his neck. "I meant the other drageals."

Darchok turned and glared at him.

"Do you not worry that they will retaliate against us for what we have started?"

"Hah!" Darchok snorted. "I fear them no more than I do anyone else. Most will not care. And those who do are too old and weak to do anything about it. We have nothing to fear from them or anyone else."

Ysernon nodded.

CHAPTER TWENTY-NINE

"ARE YOU CERTAIN?" Jocel asked.

The drageal nodded. "I saw the aftermath with my own eyes."

"And you are sure it was Darchok?"

"Who else could it be?" The young drageal looked at him sideways. "If not him personally, most definitely his followers."

Jocel shook his head. "I knew he hated the humans, but I never thought he would actually do such damage to them."

"I am sorry. I know he is your son, but..."

Jocel scowled. "Son or not, he must be dealt with. Such actions are unacceptable from anyone, be they my son or anyone else's. Those who were slaughtered must be avenged."

The young drageal was taken aback at Jocel's response, not so much the words, but the controlled, but still apparent, rage behind them.

"We need to notify the others," Jocel said.

"Others?"

"We are not alone in this. His followers, his new clan, came from all others. They, too, must come to terms with this tragedy. Then we must decide what needs to be done."

"Of course."

"Go, seek out the elders and tell them what you have told me. Have them meet me at sunset."

The young drageal nodded and departed.

#

"What is it, Father?" Pheunaf asked as Jocel entered the cave.

He told her what he had learned.

"I cannot believe he actually followed through with his threats."

"Nor can I," Jocel replied.

Suddenly, Pheunaf cried out. "Oh, no! What about Zabaneja? I must warn him."

"Stop. Darchok does not know where the boy is. If he did, that would have been the first attack. Instead, this took place on the opposite side of the world from Aneesyma's land. Zabaneja is safe." *For the moment.*

#

As Jocel arrived at the meeting, a few of the others instantly became silent.

"You have been informed of the recent happenings," Jocel said, disregarding the sidelong glances from some, "and are, I am sure, as appalled as I. Such actions cannot be tolerated and therefore must be dealt with."

"Even if the culprit is your son, Darchok?" asked one who had quieted at Jocel's approach.

"Even if?" Jocel chided. "Do you think anyone but Darchok is responsible for this atrocity?"

"And if the only way to stop him..." someone started.

"... is to kill him?" Jocel finished the thought.

"Um, yes."

"If it should come to that, I would not hesitate to be the one to do it," Jocel said.

Those gathered nodded their agreement.

"But, that is easier said than done, and we cannot do it alone," Pheunaf said from behind them.

"Daughter, I did not expect you here."

She laughed. "I am sure you did not, since you failed to invite me."

"Be that as it may," one elder said, "she is here now, invited or not, and I am sure has an opinion. And I agree, we cannot stop them alone. We must seek the help of the other clans, all whose kin joined Darchok."

"And how will we know which clan to approach?" another asked.

"We need to contact all of them," Pheunaf said. "I cannot believe there will be any clan who will not wish to stop Darchok and his plan of annihilation."

Let us hope that is true, Jocel thought.

#

Pheunaf arrived at the clan of her mother's family and was met by her uncle, now its leader.

"To what do I owe the pleasure of your visit, niece?" he asked.

Pheunaf looked at him, unsure if he was baiting her or he had not yet heard the news.

"Unfortunately, Uncle, there is no pleasure in this visit."

"Oh? So it involves your brother then, eh?"

She nodded.

"I am sure you have heard he has left our clan," Pheunaf said.

"Left? I heard he was exiled," her uncle said.

"If you know that, I am sure you know the reason."

"I know his side," he said. "He came here seeking asylum."

"And an ally?" she asked.

"Yes. He did ask for that."

"But he is not here, so may I assume you did not agree."

The elder drageal shook his head. "No, I did not. I am pained you thought I would consider such a thing."

"And I am hurt that you tried to play games with me. I am no longer a child, you know."

He smiled. "That is true. But you have yet to tell me, why are you here?"

"Have you not heard what Darchok and his followers have done? Or are you once again playing games with me?" Pheunaf asked.

"No," he laughed. "I am not playing games. I truly have heard nothing more of your brother's actions since he left here, angry at my refusal of aid or alliance."

"Did any of your clan go with him?"

The old drageal nodded. "A few. Young ones. Hot heads. Why?"

She told him of the attack, the destruction of the human settlement, and watched his reaction. She was glad to see he was shocked at the tale she told.

"Long has he railed about destroying every race that was not drageal," she said. "But I doubt anyone believed it was anything more than rantings. Until now."

He drew in a breath. "I cannot believe he actually did that."

"I am not lying, Uncle."

"That is not what I meant. But like you, and everyone else, I, too, thought his threats merely the rants of a misguided youth. That he actually followed through, well..."

"Yes. And now we have to decide what to do about him and his followers."

"What do you mean?" he asked.

"We have to stop him," Pheunaf said.

"And how do you plan on doing that?"

"That is why we are contacting all clans. His followers were recruited from each of them, so everyone should be involved in this."

"I see," he said. "And could this concern for humans have anything to do with that son of yours? With Zabaneja?"

She wanted to emphatically deny his statement. It was, after all, not really an accusation, but she could not. "I would be a liar if I said Zabaneja did not play at least a small part in my desire to stop my brother. Even if I had never met nor seen a human or any other race, I could not stand by and allow Darchok, nor anyone else, to cause such destruction."

He took her hand. "Nor can I, niece. I pledge my clan's assistance with this task."

"Thank you, Uncle."

"Well, now that the formalities are over, tell me about that boy of yours. How is he doing? I bet he was happy when Darchok left."

"Zabaneja is not with the clan at this time," she said.

CHAPTER THIRTY

NO FURTHER VIOLENCE against non-drageals was reported over the next month or so, leading some to believe the attack they heard of was a lie, or at least an exaggeration.

"Would you like to view the devastation that was wrought upon the land and its people?" Pheunaf asked.

No one accepted the offer.

"So what are we to do now?" one of the elders asked. "I fear there is no way for us to know where another attack will happen, if indeed it ever will."

"We need to find Darchok and his people," Jocel said. "Let them know we want to meet, to come to an understanding, a truce of sorts, to cease his reprehensible actions."

The others agreed and word was sent out to all corners. Soon enough a reply was received, and a meeting arranged.

"Do you think we can actually reason with him?" Pheunaf asked as her father prepared to meet with her brother.

Jocel shook his head. "I do not know, but we must try."

Pheunaf looked at him. "I wish you would let me go in your stead, Father."

"No, I am the one who must face him." He kissed her on the head and departed.

#

At the appointed time and place of the meeting, Jocel and representatives from the other clans waited.

"He is over an hour late," one of the drageals said. "Do you really think he is coming?"

"This is his typical action," another said.

"How much longer are we to put up with his disrespectful behavior?"

Jocel pointed upward. "I believe he is here."

Darchok and Ysernon landed and slowly approached the others. They stood in silence, glaring at the representatives from the various clans.

"You know why we have asked you here, Darchok," Jocel said, breaking the silence.

Darchok did not respond.

"We wish to discuss your behavior against the humans and what can be done to reach an agreement to ensure no further incidents will occur."

"No, old man, that is not why I am here." Darchok reached out with his talon and nonchalantly sliced across his father's neck, nearly decapitating the old drageal. Before anyone could react, Darchok and Ysernon were gone.

The remaining drageals stood frozen in disbelief for what seemed an eternity. As the shock wore off, one approached the lifeless body. She looked back at the others and shook her head, but said nothing. There was nothing to say, at least not yet.

#

Pheunaf cursed herself for allowing Jocel to go to the meeting. She should have been the one to approach Darchok, not her father. What was Darchok thinking? Was his hatred of their father so intense he did not anticipate the consequences? Did he think he and his small band of miscreants could take on and defeat the forces of all the other clans? Or worse, did he just not care?

The last option sent a chill down Pheunaf's spine. It was by far the most terrifying. Could it be Darchok and his followers had, indeed, forsaken sanity for violence?

She shook her head to clear it. This was not the time to determine motivation. This was the time to plan, to decide whether they should go on the offensive and actively seek out and destroy Darchok or should they take a defensive stand and wait for his next move. Neither option was without fault.

She joined the others and accepted their condolences. As the last of the attendees arrived, Pheunaf waited for someone to break the seemingly endless silence, but no one did.

"I did not expect to be the first to speak. As a matter of fact, I did not expect to speak at all," she said. "It has been many ages since drageals had to fight an enemy. And, we have never had to go against our own kind."

Heads nodded and murmurings of agreement sounded among them.

"It now seems obvious, Darchok had no desire to negotiate. He wanted to instigate a conflict," she continued.

"Jocel's death is a tragedy, but are we sure this was not merely the act of son against father? Are we sure Darchok will actually bring his violence against the rest of us?" Uhlahf, the leader of another clan asked. "Is this really our fight or just yours, Pheunaf?"

Murmurs of both agreement and dissent swept through the crowd.

"I do not share your opinion, Uhlahf," another of the clan leaders said. "Pheunaf, my clan stands behind you in whatever course of action you decide."

"As do we," several of the other clan leaders said.

Uhlahf shook his head, still not convinced.

"You were not there, brother. You did not see the look in Darchok's eyes," Brendirum said. "This was no mere family matter. Darchok is deranged, mad. If we stand by and do nothing, he will burn this world and eventually, whether you like it or not, we will be involved. By then, it may be too late to turn him back." He glared at his brother. "We can face him now or face him later, after he has tasted blood, too much blood, of human and drageal alike."

Uhlahf was surprised at Brendirum's reaction. "Is that your true belief, brother?"

"It is. If we allow Darchok to go on, we will all suffer," Brendirum said.

"Then, Pheunaf, you have the support of my clan as well," Uhlahf said.

"Thank you. But I do not think I am the one to lead."

"Your father always spoke of your abilities, your leadership qualities. He knew you would one day lead your clan. Ask anyone here if those were not his feelings, for he never missed an opportunity to tell that to anyone who would listen," Brendirum said with a smile.

"I was not aware of that," Pheunaf whispered.

Brendirum looked at the others. "I am willing to accept Pheunaf as leader. What say the rest of you?"

Pheunaf looked around, surprised to see all were in agreement.

"If that is your wish," she said, "I accept."

#

"Do you think word has gotten back to Darchok of the alliance of the clans?" Brendirum, now Pheunaf's second-in-command, asked. "If so, would he dare strike any of the clan strongholds?"

"Who is to say what he knows or does not," Pheunaf said. "I do not think he would target any of the clans outright. That would be too insane a move, even for him. For now, if he is to attack us, it will be where he can find small groups alone and away from both defenses and shelter."

"You are probably right."

"Yes, but while we may remain safe, I fear the same will not hold true for humans and others. Whatever Darchok is, he is not a fool. He knows they cannot defend themselves. And he will go after the weakest first."

"Do you truly believe he will carry out his threats to annihilate all things not drageal?" Brendirum asked.

"Sadly, I do. I have no clue why, but he has always harbored a deep hatred for the others. We must find a way to warn them."

"How? Unlike you, I have had no dealings with humans nor any other beings."

She smiled. "My dealings with other races is quite limited. It was my father who knew many others."

The two looked at each other in shock.

"No. You do not think? Could it be?" Brendirum asked, not really having to define what he was asking for they both knew.

Pheunaf shook her head. "I would hope that was not his purpose in murdering our father. But it cannot be discounted."

Brendirum nodded.

"Still, his motive is not what matters. My father, the one who would have been our emissary, our link to the other races, is gone, so we must find another way. We need to reach out to the other clans, to see if anyone has any relationship, no matter how slight, with any of the others."

"I will send the messages."

"Please do and let us pray that my previous contact is not all we have," she said.

Several days later, Brendirum returned.

"Have you heard from the others?" Pheunaf asked.

Brendirum nodded.

"Your expression tells me it is not good news."

"No. No one has ties to the others. Too long have we isolated ourselves, mired in our own lives."

Pheunaf turned away in frustration. "How can we hope to protect the others if we have no way to contact them? If only I knew how my father reached Kalini..." She shook her head and took a deep breath. "Still, I will not leave the others to Darchok. We must find a way to protect them."

Brendirum drew in a breath. "That sounds like a near im-possible task."

"You mean truly impossible, do you not?" She smiled. "The feasibility of accurately predicting where he will strike next is dismal at best, but we cannot sit idly by and do nothing."

"I agree. Perhaps if we get everyone together, we can find the more isolated and lightly populated regions that would likely be most appealing to Darchok's plans and patrol those skies."

"That is a good idea."

#

Pheunaf returned home and sat with her head in her hands. Then she felt a sensation within her mind, and she immediately knew what to do.

"I am off," she said when she found Brendirum.

"Where?"

"To find a way," Pheunaf said, and left without further explanation.

#

Pheunaf flew to the place she had last met Kalini, certain, for some reason, the chetoga would be there. To ensure she was neither being watched nor followed by any of Darchok's devotees, she did not go directly there. Only after she was sure she was alone in the sky, did she head toward the meeting place.

She landed and was alone. For just a moment she feared she had imagined the voice in her head, but then heard a rustling in the bush and Kalini emerged.

"My friend," Kalini said.

"It has been quite a while," Pheunaf said.

"You wonder how I knew you needed me, do you not?"

The drageal nodded.

"Since the day your father brought you to see me all those years ago, I have kept my eye on you and Zabaneja."

"Then you are aware of what has been going on. Of what my brother has done. Of my father's murder," Pheunaf said.

"I am. And I fear there are worse horrors yet to come."

Pheunaf was only half surprised at the chetoga's statement. "Then you know why I am here."

Kalini nodded.

"Do you have a plan?" Pheunaf asked.

"It is already in play."

"I do not understand."

"I have already begun to get the message of Darchok and his attacks out to those likely to be in his path," Kalini said.

"Will they be able to stop him?"

"Stop him? No. Those bound to the land will not be the ones to do that. And, unfortunately, not all of the air will rise to the task. The best the landbound can do is prepare ourselves for Darchok's wrath."

Pheunaf nodded.

"I know you fear for Zabaneja, for what will happen should Darchok find him. Know, when the time is right, I will contact both Aneesyma and Zabaneja about what is going on."

Pheunaf smiled. "Thank you. But what of you? Even now, I fear for your safety. Though I took precautions coming here, one can never be too sure."

"Do not fear, dear Pheunaf, you were not followed. I am in no danger. Unfortunately, I cannot say the same of you and the other drageals that will stand against your brother and his hatred. I know you do not see it now, but you are indeed the correct drageal for the task ahead."

"I am honored with your confidence, though I am still unsure if it is founded."

#

When the clans next met, Pheunaf was less than happy with the outcome. Several failed to attend and sent no excuse.

"I am sad to think so many of our kind have chosen the path of inaction. Still, I am heartened to see so many willing to stand against this madness," Pheunaf said.

All gathered nodded in agreement.

"Good. As you know, the first thing we must do is find where

Darchok and his followers are. Our scouts have been unable to find him. Has anyone else found anything?" Pheunaf asked.

Heads shook.

"There are regions which we have not scouted," one of the drageals said. "The clans who chose to stay away were supposed to look in those places."

"We must assume there will be no information from them, so we must complete the tasks previously assigned to them. Let us hope Darchok does not mount any more attacks before we can confront him,"

"Agreed," everyone said in unison.

CHAPTER THIRTY-ONE

ZABANEJA FELT an odd sensation in his mind, as if someone was summoning him to make his way outside the Keep's wall, and he felt compelled to comply.

As the sun began to set, he stood at the gate for a moment then slowly walked through it and down the path. He entered a stand of trees to his left and within a few paces saw Kalini sitting on a rock.

"I am glad you came, dear boy," Kalini said.

Zabaneja laughed. "Did I have a choice?"

The chetoga did not respond.

"Why did you lure me here?"

Kalini shook her head. "Do you still not trust me? Have you not yet forgiven me?"

"That is not it. I no longer hold any animosity toward you or anyone else. But you have yet to tell me why you are here. Why you sought me out after all this time."

"I have news of your clan. Unsettling news."

"Mother? Has something happened to mother? I saw her recently, and she was fine."

"She is well for the moment. Are you aware of your uncle's exile from the clan?"

"No, only that grandfather banished him from his home."

The chetoga explained the situation, then added, "But it has gotten worse."

"Worse?"

She nodded and told him of the attack on the human settlement and his grandfather's murder, both at the hands of his uncle.

The young man dropped to his knees in despair. "I always knew he hated me, but Grandfather? How could he do such a thing?"

"Ah, if we knew the answer to that, perhaps we could have stopped him. But there is more?"

"More? You said mother was safe."

"Yes, she is safe, for the moment."

"What does that mean?"

"War is imminent. And, your mother is leading those who oppose Darchok."

Zabaneja shook his head slowly, trying to digest the chetoga's words. "I must go home. Right now."

"No. You cannot."

"What do you mean? If I am not to go home, then why did you tell me what you just did?"

"To warn you," Kalini said.

"Are you saying I am in danger? Wait, if I am in danger then so is everyone here at the Keep. I cannot allow that to happen. I must leave immediately."

"You are not in direct danger. I came to warn you about what is coming. And leaving will not protect these people if Darchok is not stopped."

"If I am not to join my mother and my clan, how can I help defeat him?"

"Your part in this conflict will come, but not just yet."

Zabaneja shook his head again, but did not argue further.

A rustling of leaves behind him made Zabaneja turn and put his hand on the hilt of his sword. Kalini did not move. In the next moment, Aneesyma appeared.

"Kalini, I knew that was you in my mind. But why are you here, so close to the Keep?" Aneesyma asked, then saw Zabaneja. "Hmm, if you have already summoned Zab, I can only surmise whatever you are here for concerns his clan."

Kalini nodded. "Your instincts are as sharp as ever. Yes, my business concerns the drageals. Drageals and humans and all the rest of us."

"That sounds ominous," Aneesyma said, "as if you are talking about war."

"I am."

"I do not understand," Aneesyma said.

Kalini explained all she knew of what had occurred, including details she had not previously told Zabaneja.

Aneesyma shook his head when she finished. "How could this happen?"

Kalini looked at him. Both knew the question did not have an answer, so she did not try.

"But what are we, those of the land, to do against the power and might of the drageals?"

"For the moment, all we can do is prepare to defend ourselves."

"And how will you, we, defend ourselves from dragon fire?" Zabaneja asked. "Have either of you ever been near it? Ever even seen it?"

Kalini and Aneesyma both shook their heads.

"Well, I have," Zabaneja said. "And let me tell you, even when not invoked in anger, it is terrifying."

"We can only imagine..." Kalini said.

"No, you cannot!" Zabaneja shouted. "That is the problem. You have no idea what you are in for if the drageals attack or even if you are caught in the crossfire."

"Well, then, what are we to do? Sit around and wait to be incinerated?" Aneesyma asked.

"Of course, not," Zabaneja replied.

"I think Zabaneja was only trying to make sure we had an idea of what we will be up against if this war comes to our doors," Kalini said, trying to dissipate the escalating emotions of the two men. "Is that not right, young man?"

Zabaneja nodded.

"He does have a point. Even the most heavily armed human settlement will have little effect on drageals. And those of us without such things will be in even greater danger."

"What are we to do?" Aneesyma asked.

"For the moment, Pheunaf and her contingent of drageals will do their best to keep Darchok at bay."

"But you said they had not yet confronted each other," Zabaneja said.

"It will be soon."

"And what happens if Pheunaf is unable to do that, to keep Darchok contained?" Aneesyma asked.

Kalini shook her head. "I do not know. I cannot see much beyond the fact a conflict between drageals is coming."

"We must warn the rest of the kingdom and the lands beyond," Aneesyma said.

"No, not yet."

"What do you mean?"

"Warning them now would do no one any good. Most will not believe you, and those who do would raise a panic that could be worse."

"So, you would leave them unaware of the impending danger."

"Of course, not," Kalini said, shaking her head. "Those in Darchok's path will be warned and assisted. When it comes time, if it does actually come to that, it will be decided what should be done."

"You have always been right before," Aneesyma said, "so I will trust your counsel now."

"Be that as it may," Zabaneja said. "I want to return to my people. To my mother."

"No," Kalini said. "As I told you before, this is not the time."

Zabaneja looked as if he was going to protest until Aneesyma put a hand on his shoulder.

"Do not fear, dear Zabaneja," Kalini said, "I will keep you informed of your mother." *And she of you.*

Zabaneja found himself reluctantly agreeing to Kalini's plan.

From that night forward, Zabaneja found Kalini to be true to her word. He did not know, nor was he sure he wanted to, how she was able to creep into his mind and tell him things. Nevertheless, she did. And he was happy to hear his mother remained safe.

CHAPTER THIRTY-TWO

THE SKY ABOVE the four young, frolicking drageals suddenly darkened. They looked up and saw a large number of drageals hovering above them. At first they took no notice; if they knew of this place, why would others not?

In the next moment, an ear-splitting screech was heard as the larger drageals descended at full speed upon the youngsters. Two of the newcomers attacked the smallest of the youngsters and forced him into a death spiral toward the ground. The others tried to flee, already aware of their friend's fate, but the newcomers were larger and faster than the young ones and two were overtaken. The last of the group was able to flee when the attacker pursuing her suddenly turned away.

As she fled, she was torn between returning to aid her friends or going for help. She realized there was little she could do against the attackers so she flew at top speed home to tell the others.

As soon as she arrived on her mountain, she raced to the elders, shouting to them of the trouble her friends were in. At first they did not believe her, but when she mentioned the presence of a large red drageal among the attackers, the clan elders knew she spoke the truth. Once calmed, the young drageal led the others to the site of the attack.

Little hope was held for the survival of the three drageals left behind. As they neared the site, their worst fears were confirmed when their senses were assailed with the stench of burning feather, flesh and grass.

The elders instructed the young survivor to stay with the healers while the rest of the party descended to search. They followed the scorch lines on the ground and quickly came upon the charred remains of two of the youngsters. Knowing nothing could be done for the dead, the other drageals continued what they feared would be a fruitless search for the last youngster. As they were about to give up, they heard a faint cry from deep within the ravine below. They swooped down and found the last youngster, badly injured but still alive. The healers were immediately summoned to its side.

"I cannot believe even Darchok would do such a thing. These are his kind," one of the drageals said as they awaited the healer's determination of the youngster's fate. "I thought he only hated things not drageal."

The clan leader shook his head. "I fear this is only the beginning of how his madness against all who are not of like mind with him will manifest. We must get word of this incident to the other clans, especially Pheunaf. All must be warned."

"Do you really think he will repeat this incident?"

The clan leader glared at him. "How can you not? Quickly, go to Pheunaf and tell her what we have seen today. I will send more details as we find them out. Right now, the youngsters need tending."

#

"Why did you allow that one to escape?" Darchok growled as

they landed on their mountain.

"What good would it have done," Ysernon said, scrambling for an explanation that would not anger his leader, "to have killed them all? Had we done that, who would know the attack was your doing? You did plan on taking credit for it, did you not?"

Darchok slapped him on the back. "Good thinking, my friend. Now they will all fear me as they realize they must join me or die."

Ysernon managed to nod.

"Come, let us celebrate another victory and the start of our new world."

"I will be along shortly, start the festivities without me."

Darchok laughed and went to join the rest of his clan, jubilant over what they had done.

Ysernon walked to the other side of the camp then took to the sky. He needed to clear his head, to digest what had happened because, except for killing other drageals, especially children, Ysernon actually agreed with Darchok's philosophy.

"I was beginning to think you deserted me, old friend," Darchok said as Ysernon landed.

"Why would I do such a thing?" *Where could I go?* he thought. *No clan would have me after today's incident.*

"You did not seem overly happy over today's attack. Not to mention, you did not celebrate with us and now you return well into the night looking sullen. What else am I to think but that you are having doubts about our cause?"

Ysernon shook his head. "That is not true." Still, he knew he could not say what he truly felt. That he did not agree with the killing of drageals, the others, most definitely. But were they not fighting to keep the world for drageals only?

Darchok squeezed his friend's shoulder until his talon began to dig into it. "I sincerely hope not," he hissed and then let go. "Well, I am off to bed. Until tomorrow then."

Ysernon nodded as he rubbed his shoulder.

#

"This has been my greatest fear," Pheunaf said after receiving the news of Darchok's attack on the young drageals. "I had hoped it would never come to pass, I should have known better."

"There is no way you could have foreseen this happening," Brendirum said.

"Perhaps not the time nor place, but I should have been more forceful in warning the others of my concerns. We need to spread the word of this to all the other clans," she said, "to heighten their alertness. We must find safe havens for the young and the non-fighters."

"And for the rest of us?"

"A council must convene to determine our plans for the war against him."

That is the first time she has called this a war, Brendirum thought as he departed.

CHAPTER THIRTY-THREE

"IT WILL NOT BE LONG before the conflict between the drageals spreads beyond the sparsely populated lands," Aneesyma said. "I fear the time for you and I to be the only ones aware of this is coming to an end."

"I have been thinking the same thing," Zabaneja said.

"We must inform our people of the situation before war arrives over our heads."

"That is good. But what will you tell them? Will they not wonder why you have knowledge of happenings so far from your borders?"

"That is the part of the plan that involves you," Aneesyma said.

"And what might that be?" Zabaneja asked.

"You must now reveal your identity, your family, your ties with the drageals."

"I do not understand the purpose of such a revelation."

"It is as you said, how would I know of such things going on so far from my own land when even those closer to the actual fighting do not. I must have a way of explaining it."

"And you can think of no other plan?"

"Well, you or I could claim to be a seer, a wizard. Would that be better?"

Zabaneja chuckled. "That is amusing but far from believable. Even less believable than the truth."

"I thought that too," Aneesyma said. "Since Rikar is here with the troops from his unit, he should be the first you tell. And you may want to tell Rusalei as well."

"Why Lady Rusalei?"

Aneesyma laughed. "Oh, I assumed you and she were friends. Close friends."

"What are you saying?" Zabaneja snapped as his face flushed. "Of course we are not. Such a thought is preposterous."

"Hmm. I guess I am mistaken. I thought the friendship you two had when you were trainees had blossomed or at least continued. Is that not the case?"

"Those were different circumstances. We have both settled into roles that do not afford us the luxury of childhood friendships."

"Even so, I think she and Rikar should be the first to be told."

"If that is your wish but, regardless of who is told first, the real question is how do I tell them. I mean I cannot just come out and say, 'Oh, by the way I was raised by drageals', now can I?"

"No, that would not work. That is why you should tell those two first. Then they can help you decide how to tell the others," Aneesyma said with a slight smirk. "Shall I summon them?"

Zabaneja shrugged. "If you think that best. Have you considered they may not believe me?"

"Guentza and Pajeau did."

Zabaneja lowered his head.

"What is it? Surely you are not ashamed of your life with the drageals."

"Of course, not!" Zabaneja snapped. "I would never feel that way."

"Then what is it?" When Zabaneja did not reply, Aneesyma continued, "You cannot be worried about the circumstances around how Pheunaf found you, are you?"

"Well, why not? Was not the human who bore me murdered by her own kind? There must have been a reason."

Aneesyma was surprised that even after all this time, Darchok's malicious words still held such sway over Zabaneja.

"Oh, for goodness sake, those two are your dearest friends. Do you really think so little of them that an incident over which you had no control will change that?"

"I am not sure."

"Well, I am!" Aneesyma declared as he rang the bell for his page.

#

"You summoned me, Lord Aneesyma," Rusalei said as she entered the chamber and saw Zabaneja and Rikar.

"Yes, Zab has something he needs to discuss with you. Something he has previously not revealed to anyone."

Rikar laughed. "Are you saying we are finally going to hear about your past?"

Zabaneja squirmed in his seat.

"We are! Well, it is about time."

Aneesyma glared at the young man. Rikar immediately apologized and fell silent.

"We are hoping you two can help him determine how best he can tell everyone else his history."

"Why now?" Rusalei asked.

"And, why does he have to tell everyone?" Rikar asked.

"There are things happening in the world outside the Keep that could affect us all, and Zab's upbringing may have an impact on how certain things will be handled." Aneesyma looked at the others and saw both puzzlement and alarm. "But we will discuss that later. Right now, you two need to hear what he has to say."

"Of course," Rusalei said.

"Good. We will discuss the other details when I return."

#

Rusalei and Rikar sat in silence, waiting.

Zabaneja fidgeted in his seat, first looking down at the table and then to the side. On more than one occasion he looked up seemingly ready to speak, only to shake his head and look down again. After a few minutes, Rikar stood, walked over to the sideboard and poured three glasses of mead.

"Here, maybe this will help," he said as he put the glasses on the table.

Zabaneja picked up the glass and took a long sip of the sweet liquid.

"I know you have always wondered about my background."

"We are not the only ones," Rikar said with a chuckle.

Zabaneja half-smiled.

"Are we to be the first ones in the Keep to hear your tale?" Rusalei asked. "Besides Lord Aneesyma, of course."

Zabaneja shook his head. "Guentza knows. Aneesyma told him the first day I arrived."

She laughed. "I remember that day. You were quite scruffy and looked like a frightened kitten, hissing and growling to make yourself scary to those around you."

Zabaneja's face reddened. "I am sure that is true. But it was not a kitten I was trying to emulate, it was a drageal."

"You aim high," Rikar said.

"It was all I knew."

It took a moment for his words to be understood. "Wait. What? All you knew? What do you mean by that?" Rikar asked.

Zabaneja did not respond.

"No. You cannot possibly be saying you have seen a drageal," Rusalei said.

He nodded.

"I grew up knowing nothing of humans," he began.

"You say that as if you consider yourself to be something else," Rikar interrupted.

"My earliest recollection is looking into the large eye of a black and gold drageal, my mother, Pheunaf."

"Your mother? A drageal?" Rikar blurted out.

"Yes, my mother, the only mother I have ever known is a drageal," Zabaneja said.

"But how?" Rusalei asked.

Zabaneja recounted the tale of how he came to be raised by drageals. When he spoke of how he was found beside the dead human, thought to be his mother, his voice dripped with animosity as he recounted how he had sometimes overheard the others saying the humans had killed her and left him to die.

"So that is why you have so little regard for us," Rikar said.

"You knew?" Zabaneja asked.

Rikar nodded. "You did try to hide it most of the time, but every so often... well... I could tell."

"I am sorry, it was not directed at you," Zabaneja said. "At either of you..."

"Why did you come here?" Rikar asked.

"It was not my idea or choice. My mother thought I needed to be exposed to those of my own kind, humans, at least for several years. I, of course, disagreed then as I do now, but as you can see, one rarely wins an argument with a drageal."

"Well," Rikar let out a breath in a whistle, "that explains a lot—your intense anger at everything, your lack of knowledge about any kind of weaponry and so many other things."

"I suppose so," Zabaneja said.

"Do you plan to return to the drageals?" Rusalei asked.

"Yes, as soon as I am allowed."

Rusalei looked away. "Are you saying you regret your time here? That you dismiss those of us who consider you a friend?"

"That is not what I meant," Zabaneja said.

"But you do not consider this your home," Rikar said.

"No. My home is with my clan. With the drageals."

"I am sorry to hear that," Rusalei said, not trying to hide the sadness his words caused her.

"Would it be any different if you were sent to live with the drageals for a time? Would you not want to come back to your home as soon as you could?" Zabaneja asked.

"That is different," Rikar said.

Zabaneja shook his head. "No, it is the same. Exactly the same."

The three friends sat in silence for a few moments.

"I am happy you are not angry at the lies you were told," Zabaneja said.

"Well, in all honesty, we were never actually told any lies," Rikar said. "I was only told you were from a distant land, which is, in fact, the truth," Rikar said.

Rusalei nodded.

"But I do not understand. Since you are so proud of your life with the drageals, why would you hide it?" Rikar asked. "That is far more interesting than the background of anyone else in the Keep, even His Lordship."

"We thought it best. Too many questions, I guess. And if you remember, I was not very friendly back then," Zabaneja laughed and shook his head. "As time passed, it just became easier not to speak of it to anyone but now I must."

"Why?" Rusalei asked.

At that moment, the door opened and Aneesyma entered. "Because a war is going on that may soon come to our doorstep."

"War? War between whom? I have heard of no war," Rikar said.

Rusalei nodded her agreement.

"A war between drageal factions. One who hates everything not drageal and the other who values all life. Right now, their war is far from here, but we cannot be sure how long that can continue. So, we must warn those in other lands," Zabaneja said.

"And you need to explain how we know of this when no one else does," Rusalei said.

"Yes. And, I must decide what I should tell the others. Do I need to tell them all, all that has been told to you or just part of it. And if only a part, which part?" Zabaneja asked.

"Well, I think all you need to say is you were found and raised by drageals," Rikar said. "And leave it at that."

"And what if they ask how I came to be here?" Zabaneja asked.

"I will handle that question," Aneesyma said.

CHAPTER THIRTY-FOUR

THE NEXT DAY, Zabaneja told the tale of his upbringing to the council. Once that was done, he wondered how Aneesyma would have him reveal it to everyone else. Too soon, and, to his utter dismay, he found himself standing beside Aneesyma at the top of the castle steps before a gathering of almost everyone in the Keep.

"I have called you all together, here, in our home, to discuss a matter of great importance," Aneesyma said, addressing the crowd below. "War is looming. Maybe not today, and if we are very lucky, perhaps it will never reach us. But we must be prepared in the event it does."

"War?" the cry went up from the crowd.

"With whom? We have seen nor heard of no conflict, never mind war," one elderly gentleman shouted.

"The war is between the drageals," Aneesyma began.

"Bah! Drageals have not been seen in ages, if they ever were. They are myth. Fantasy," another shouted.

A nervous Zabaneja stepped forward to the surprise of the gathered crowd. None had ever seen him speak to more than a few people at a time.

He cleared his throat and began. "Drageals are no myth, no fantasy. They are as real as you and I."

"And how would you know such a thing, boy?" a voice shouted.

"Because I have lived amongst them. Before I came here, my home was with a drageal clan," Zabaneja said.

"Nonsense! Do you really expect us to believe such foolishness? Where is your proof?" someone shouted.

"I am his proof," Aneesyma said, stepping forward to stand beside the young man. "I have met the drageal who raised him, and I am here to tell you, in no uncertain terms, drageals are as real as we are."

A shocked murmur flooded the crowd. Some of them still did not want to believe, but if Lord Aneesyma said they were real…

"If they are indeed real, My Lord. Why has it been ages since anyone, save yourself, has seen them?"

"Drageals feel no need to reveal themselves to others. They live high in the mountains, away from other groups. In reality, even if one was in the sky above you at this very moment, you would not know it unless it chose to let you do so. They soar high above the clouds, well out of sight of even the keenest eyes. But now, they are in conflict. A conflict I fear will, before it comes to an end, involve most races of this world."

The crowd was confused and on the verge of panic.

"Do not fear," Aneesyma began, reining in the crowd. "The danger is not imminent."

"Then why tell us of this to begin with?" someone shouted.

"Because others face that danger and we need to warn them and everyone else. We need to prepare," Aneesyma said. "You must remember, drageals are not constrained by things which hinder land-bound beings. They know not of boundaries nor need roads to travel upon. Their path is almost always clear and if it is not, they soar above or around it."

"But how do we defend or even prepare?" another voice cried out.

"That is where Zab comes in. Why, after all this time, he has finally revealed his background. He has the means to keep in contact with the drageals and will be able to warn us, and others, if their battles are near."

More questions were asked and answered, and when the crowd seemed satisfied, and their fear level under control, Aneesyma dismissed them.

#

"I am still not sure this was the right thing to do," Zabaneja said after the crowd dispersed.

"Why not?" Aneesyma asked.

"What did we accomplish other than frightening them?"

"Do you think it would be better for them to awaken to the flames of a drageal attack?"

"Of course, not."

"Well then, how would you handle the situation?"

Zabaneja shook his head. "No. You are right. They needed to be told."

Aneesyma put his hand on the young man's shoulder. "I am not looking to be told I am right, Zab. I want you to understand why I did what I did. And why I did it at this point in time."

Zabaneja looked at him but did not reply.

"Do you understand?"

He thought for a moment. "Not really."

"Think about it. What will the guard be doing from this day forward?"

"Guentza and I discussed increasing the numbers on watch in the towers, and on the wall, guards with spyglasses."

"Exactly. And that is the correct action to take. But how would the people react if suddenly they saw that with no prior explanation?"

Zabaneja nodded. "Of course. By telling them what we did, they will feel more secure when they see that we are on the lookout for potential threats."

"And, as an added benefit we can enlist them, especially those who live outside the walls, to aid us. It also served another purpose."

"What is that?"

"Revealing your relationship with the drageals, the people will assume there is some means of communication between you."

"But we did not explain how."

Aneesyma smiled. "No, and we never will. Generally, people do not want to know how things work, especially if it is out of the scope of their everyday life. Most are content to view it as either 'just the way it is' or 'magic'. And, for those who do want more details on how it is done, well, good luck. I do not know about you, but I have no clue how most of this happens. Do you?"

Zabaneja shook his head and laughed.

CHAPTER THIRTY-FIVE

:IT HAS BEGUN.:

Zabaneja bolted out of bed as Kalini's words invaded his mind. She did not need to elaborate. His first thought was to go to his mother.

:Do not fear. Your mother is fine, but there have been casualties on both sides. And I fear it will not come to a quick end.:

Zabaneja quickly dressed and raced to talk to Aneesyma. He tried not to appear overly excited as he approached the castle. It was not unusual for him to be running off to meet Aneesyma at all hours of the night, so his appearance elicited no more than a nod from the guard on duty.

He found the door open and Aneesyma waiting within.

"I knew you would be coming."

"So, you too have heard the news from Kalini."

"Yes."

Before Zabaneja could continue, there was a quiet knock on the door and a young servant boy entered with a tray of tea and biscuits.

"Well, it is not like we were not expecting it. No one expected Darchok to surrender. But I am very happy to hear Pheunaf is safe,"

Aneesyma said after the servant had left.

"Yes, but for how long?"

Aneesyma put his hand on the boy's shoulder. "I wish I could give you a guarantee..."

"I need to go back. To be with her. To help her," Zabaneja said. "I know I am supposed to stay here for a while longer, but..."

"No. What help could you be to her?"

Zabaneja wanted to protest, but as Aneesyma looked at him, he knew the older man was correct.

"As you have been told already, your time in this conflict has yet to come. For the moment, your place is here and your mission is to assist us so that, if it comes to it, we can defend ourselves against Darchok."

"I understand."

"Did Kalini give you any details? Where it took place?" Aneesyma asked.

"No, not really. She did say no other races were in danger at this time," Zabaneja replied.

#

Several months after the start of the war, Zabaneja once again awoke to Kalini's voice.

:*There is a battle is near the Keep,*: was all she said. All she needed to say. Zabaneja flew from his bed and ran to his rooftop vantage point. As he peered into the sky he saw a flash of light far in the distance. Untrained eyes might think it lightning, but he knew better.

He ran to tell both Guentza and Aneesyma the news and was glad to find them together.

"Do you think Darchok has found you?" Guentza asked.

"If he had, he would have already attacked us," Aneesyma said.

"Of course. I must put the guard and others on alert for what may come," Guentza said and left.

"I cannot sit idly twiddling my thumbs. I will go outside and help the others prepare," Zabaneja said and departed.

#

Zabaneja entered the courtyard just as the blackness of the night was shattered by spewing fire in the sky directly overhead. In the next moment, he was overtaken by the stench of burning flesh and feathers and saw a drageal falling from the sky. The burning mass crashed into the clock tower of the castle before landing in the courtyard. Zabaneja ran to it but saw it was already dead. He looked to the sky, praying its opponent did not follow it and was relieved to see it had not.

Zabaneja would have liked to grieve for the drageal, but it was dead and there were other things that required his attention—fires needed to be extinguished, wounded needed to be tended to. He saw Guentza and several guardsmen racing out to take control of the situation, allowing Zabaneja to search for Aneesyma.

Zabaneja ran past the devastation in the building the drageal had crashed into and to the castle. As expected, the household staff were already mobilizing to handle whatever issues might arise.

He called to a page, asking Aneesyma's location. He held his breath, waiting for the boy's reply, hoping Aneesyma had not left his rooms in the other wing. The boy turned to Zabaneja, his face smudged with dirt and soot, and shook his head. Zabaneja nodded and ran towards the residence wing.

"What is going on, Zab?" Aneesyma asked when Zabaneja found him.

"A drageal has crashed into the south wing's clock tower and the courtyard."

"Are we under attack?"

"No, we were just in the path of their fight."

"I see. Is anyone hurt? Dead?"

"I do not know. Guentza has already taken charge in the courtyard, so as soon as he has things under control, I am sure he will report to you."

"Of course. And what of the damage to the castle?"

"Your staff are already taking control of that."

"We must gather the ministers to decide what to do."

"I will have someone find them and send them to your study. The study will be safer than the throne room."

"Of course." Aneesyma turned and headed toward the study.

Zabaneja directed several servants to fetch the ministers and send them to the study to meet with Aneesyma before he headed back outside to see what needed to be done. When Zabaneja returned, he found Aneesyma alone.

"Guentza's preliminary report says there are many wounded, but as of yet, no deaths. There is also extensive damage to the tower in the south wing."

"I see. Let us hope the death toll does not get too high," Aneesyma replied.

It only took a few moments until the ministers arrived.

"Ah, I am glad you are all safe." Aneesyma motioned for everyone to sit.

"I do not understand what is going on," the elder minister, Haoule, said as he entered. "Are the drageals attacking us?"

Zabaneja shook his head. "No. From what I can surmise, two or more drageals were battling overhead, one was mortally wounded and crashed into the courtyard."

"Are we in any additional danger?" Rusalei, the youngest and only female minister, asked.

"No. I believe we were just in their path and are not in any further danger at the moment," Zabaneja replied.

The door opened and Guentza entered. He bowed deeply to those gathered and then approached Aneesyma.

"What is the situation, Guentza?" Aneesyma asked.

"The fires have been extinguished, and we have begun to clear away the smaller debris. Once the sun rises, we will be more able to ascertain the full extent of the damages."

"And our people?" Aneesyma asked.

"It is not as bad as it could have been, but it is not good." Guentza looked down and shook his head before continuing. "The wounded number in the fifties, most of those were in the tower. Their injuries range from minor cuts and bruises to massive trauma. And, though no one has died yet, there are at least ten or more victims the healers feel will not make it through the night."

The group shook their heads but said nothing.

"That is not good to hear," Zabaneja said after a few minutes. "Had this happened during the day, this tragedy would have been far worse."

Guentza cleared his throat and turned toward Zabaneja. "There is also the matter of the dead drageal. What are we to do with it?"

"Can we not just chop it up and bury the pieces outside the city walls?" the third minister, Tuzzern, grumbled.

Everyone in the room looked at the old man with disgust. Zabaneja, about to rudely reply to the insensitive minister, was stopped by Aneesyma lightly touching his arm.

"Tuzzern, once again your insensitivity and stupidity astound me," Aneesyma began. "Drageals are not mindless beasts, they are as intelligent as humans and deserve the same dignified treatment in death as we would afford one of our own."

"What would you do if you heard a drageal treated one of our fallen in the manner you described?" Rusalei snapped. The others nodded at her retort.

Tuzzern's face reddened at the chastisement he received both from his lord and more so from that woman-child he thought had no business on the council.

"Then what are we to do with it?" Tuzzern's lack of contrition was not lost on anyone. "Are we to just let it lay there until it rots and drives us from our homes with the stench?"

Aneesyma nodded to Zabaneja, who took a deep breath to calm his anger before he answered. "Pheunaf will determine what to do with the body," Zabaneja said.

"And if it is not one of hers?" Tuzzern interrupted. "Do you intend to bring the other one here?"

"Do not be silly, Tuzzern," Zabaneja replied, barely able to contain his disdain. "Pheunaf will decide what to do with him regardless of which side he fought on."

Tuzzern snorted, but after catching the glare from Lord Aneesyma, decided not to reply.

"How will we contact Pheunaf?" Rusalei asked.

"We will not need to. She is probably already making arrangements to come here. I would be surprised if we do not hear from her by morning," Zabaneja finished.

"That is all well and good for that," the elder Haoule, who had been to this point silent, said "but what of the bigger problem? If the drageals are battling in the air, how will we defend ourselves from more incidents like this?"

Zabaneja shook his head. "I have no answer for that."

Everyone in the room, especially Aneesyma and Guentza, were

surprised Zabaneja had no plan.

Aneesyma put his hand on Zabaneja's arm. "I am sure Pheunaf does. But until she arrives, we must keep our people calm." The others nodded. "So, until then…"

Tuzzern left the room first, not even acknowledging the others. Rusalei and Haoule were in conversation as they left. Zabaneja and Guentza began to follow but, as they reached the door, Aneesyma stopped them.

"Gentlemen, please remain."

The two men did as told.

"So, is what you told the others the truth?"

"For the most part," Guentza replied.

"And you, Zab? Did you reveal all you know?"

Zabaneja coughed. "As always, My Lord, you read me too well. I always wondered, since the first time we heard of the conflict, if we would be able to avoid becoming involved. And now the battle has been brought to our doorstep. However, this was not a direct attack on us, we were collateral damage and the battle has already moved away from here."

Both Guentza and Aneesyma nodded.

"But, remember that is not to say this cannot occur again or that we will not be the target of Darchok's wrath in the future. Especially if he learns I am here."

"So how will we defend ourselves against this threat?" Guentza asked.

"Perhaps if we align ourselves with Pheunaf's group…" Zabaneja said.

"If we join with Pheunaf, what is to stop Darchok from attacking us even if he is not aware of your presence?" Aneesyma asked.

"That is the dilemma. Right now, Pheunaf and her forces are able to keep Darchok's group concentrating their wrath on them, but..."

"It will probably not be long until he decides to come after all the landbound as well," Guentza finished Zabaneja's thought.

Zabaneja nodded.

"So, you are saying that regardless of what we do or do not do, sooner or later we will likely become the target of Darchok's wrath," Aneesyma added.

"Exactly," Zabaneja said. "That is why we need to talk to Pheunaf."

"But how can you be sure she or one of hers will come?" Guentza asked.

Zabaneja smiled. "I know my mother."

Guentza nodded.

"Drageals are fiercely loyal to their own. I am certain they are aware a drageal fell and will come for it, even if it is not one of theirs," Zabaneja added.

"I see," Guentza said.

"With your permission, My Lord, I would like to go stand beside the drageal until they arrive."

Aneesyma nodded and the two men rose and left the room.

CHAPTER THIRTY-SIX

"DO YOU THINK it is a good idea for you to stay with the drageal? You have yet to sleep," Guentza said as they walked down the hall. "I could get one of my men..."

Zabaneja stopped. "No. I will do it. It is my duty."

"I am sorry, I meant no offense."

Zabaneja put his hand on Guentza's shoulder. "I know. It is that... well, be he one of Darchok's or Pheunaf's forces, he is still one of my kind."

"No need to explain, I understand. At least allow me to bring you something to eat while you wait."

Zabaneja nodded. "I would appreciate that. Also, could we cover the body?"

Guentza smiled. "That has already been done."

"I should have known. Thank you."

#

Zabaneja stood beside the fallen drageal and waited for its companions, or possibly its adversaries. Just before sunrise he heard someone approaching. He turned, expecting to see Guentza or one of the guardsmen, but instead saw Rusalei approaching with a jug.

"My Lady, what are you doing here? The sun has yet to rise. You will catch your death in this cold night air."

Rusalei smiled. "You, of all people, should know I am not that fragile, Zab."

Zabaneja flushed and bowed his head. "I did not mean that, Lady Rusalei. It is just that last evening's meetings lasted so late, I assumed you would be sleeping."

"I do not understand why you insist upon such formalities between us. Are we not friends?" she asked. "You were never like this during our training."

"That was then, My Lady. We were students. Now, well... things are different."

"Bah," she said and shook her head.

"You still have not told me why you are here."

"I thought you might want company in your vigil, if you would allow me."

"Thank you, My Lady..."

"Zab, regardless of your perception of our stations, I still consider you a friend, so I would greatly appreciate it if you would call me by my name, rather than my title."

"That would not be proper, My..." He stopped himself.

She looked at him and shook her head. "Dearest Zab, always one to stand on protocol. Let us do this, when we are alone, you call me Rusalei and during official functions or when others are around, you can call me 'My Lady' or 'Madam Minister' or whatever silly term you come up with."

"I will try, My... Rusalei."

"How long do you think it will be before Pheunaf's people arrive?"

Zabaneja pointed to the sky. "Right about now."

Rusalei looked where Zabaneja indicated and saw three dark spots in the early morning light.

"You were right, if you had not shown me where they were, I would have not even noticed them."

"And, they are not even trying to hide."

As the drageals came closer into view, Rusalei gasped.

"They are beautiful, are they not?"

Rusalei nodded. "Where will they land?"

"In the clearing outside the wall. If you would be so kind, please inform Lord Aneesyma of their arrival while I greet them."

"Of course."

#

Zabaneja waved to the drageals slowly circling overhead, took a deep breath, strode out the gates and stood at the edge of the open field waiting. He immediately recognized two of the them—the blue feathered Nanetscka and her mate, the purple feathered Vainen. He was glad these two had been chosen since they were friends.

Zabaneja approached the group. "Nanetscka. Vainen. It is good to see you both again," he said in dragealian.

"Sadly, it is not under better circumstances," Nanetscka replied and then smiled. "Allow me to introduce you to the third member of our party. This is my brother's dragonlet, Phrynia."

The smaller golden feathered drageal glared at her aunt for calling her that, but said nothing.

"Tell us what happened," Vainen said.

Zabaneja related the incident from the previous night.

"Were there any fatalities amongst the humans?" Vainen asked.

"Not yet, but the healers hold little hope for a handful of them."

"We are sorry," Vainen said.

"And the drageal?" Nanetscka asked.

"He died before landing. I am sorry to say it was not an easy death for the poor thing."

"Death in battle rarely is," Vainen said.

"Do you think it is one of yours or one of Darchok's?"

"We are not yet sure. Several of our comrades are still un-accounted for," Nanetscka said and shook her head. "I am sorry our conflict has spilled over to your world. But I suppose we are fortunate it happened here, where you are. I am not sure how we would have dealt with this elsewhere."

Zabaneja did not respond.

"You stood vigil by the fallen one all night, did you not?" Vainen asked.

Zabaneja nodded. "Regardless of whose side he belonged to, he deserved respect."

Phrynia snorted.

"Do you have something to say, Phrynia?" Nanetscka asked.

"If it is one of Darchok's, it deserves nothing."

Nanetscka turned to face the young drageal in a movement so fast, Zabaneja did not even see it.

"So, should Zabaneja have just left the carcass exposed and unwatched?"

"If he is one of Darchok's, yes."

"And if he is one of ours?"

Phrynia muttered something incomprehensible.

"Exactly as I thought," Nanetscka continued. "You speak without thinking."

She turned to face Zabaneja again. "Please forgive the insolence of my niece. She is young and well..."

Zabaneja nodded. "As we all were at one time. I do not believe all of you will fit into the courtyard..."

"I understand," Nanetscka said. "I will go."

"But I wanted to go," Phrynia said in the closest thing to a whine a drageal can muster.

"And your father wanted an obedient daughter," Nanetscka said. "I guess none of us will be happy today. And do not even think about snorting at me, child. I will have none of that."

"Yes, Nanetscka."

Zabaneja ignored the young drageal's chastisement and continued. "I should warn you, there will likely be humans gathered to get a glimpse of you. They mean no disrespect, they are merely curious, none have ever seen a drageal."

"No offense taken. I remember the first time I saw a group of humans, I had the same response," Nanetscka said with a grin.

"I will meet you inside the wall," Zabaneja said and walked back to the gate as Nanetscka took to the sky.

Nanetscka landed and saw Zabaneja had been correct in his assessment. Even if the fallen drageal had not been lying there, her entire party would not have fit in the space.

"You were a little rough on your niece, old friend."

Nanetscka sighed. "That child will be the death of me. She has no control of her emotions or her tongue."

"You said it yourself, she is young."

They approached the fallen drageal and saw Rusalei and Aneesyma standing silently beside it. Zabaneja pointed to Aneesyma and said, "This is Aneesyma, the man in charge of my care while I am with the humans."

Nanetscka and Aneesyma nodded to each other.

"And this is Rusalei," he said, turning toward her. "She is one of the council ministers. She has kept vigil with me this past night."

Rusalei looked shocked at hearing Zabaneja speak in the foreign tongue she surmised to be dragealian.

"Is she your mate?" Nanetscka asked.

Zabaneja was noticeably caught off guard by his friend's question. "Of course not," he stammered.

Nanetscka chuckled as he squirmed. "I am not so sure of that, old friend. No matter, please tell them I am honored to meet them."

Zabaneja translated Nanetscka's words of greeting. Aneesyma and Rusalei bowed deeply to her as Zabaneja walked to the fallen drageal and uncovered its head. He saw the shock come over Nanetscka's face and watched as she struggled to maintain her composure. The humans stood in silence until the visibly shaken drageal was ready to speak.

"Yes, he is one of ours," Nanetscka whispered, her voice cracking. "He is Vainen's younger brother. Thank you for caring for him."

"It was my privilege."

"We must determine a way to remove him from here and take him back to our people."

"I understand. Please know if you require any assistance from us, we would be honored to help in any way we can."

Nanetscka put her hand on Zabaneja's shoulder. "Thank you."

The drageal turned and departed the courtyard. A few moments later, after the others were given the news, there was a loud shriek that was immediately squelched.

Rusalei looked to Zabaneja for an explanation.

"This is Nanetscka's mate's brother," Zabaneja began. "And the cries came from the younger drageal, Phrynia, Nanetscka's niece."

Rusalei's eyes welled with tears. "That is horrible. Is there anything we can do to help them?"

"I am not sure. I have already told her we will do whatever we can to assist her to get him back to my people."

"You are indeed an honorable man, Zab. A good and honorable man."

#

Later that day, after the drageals had some time to grieve, Zabaneja escorted several of the Keep's master builders outside the gates to help discuss how the body might be moved.

"If he were in an open field," Nanetscka said, "we would lay the cloth next to him then two of us would roll the body onto it while the third ensured the cloth stayed in place. Once that is done the corners of the cloth are tied together and we attach additional ropes so that we can lift the body and raise it aloft. However, we cannot do so with him where he is."

As Zabaneja translated, the builders nodded and immediately began talking amongst themselves, almost oblivious to the presence of the others.

"As I understand, only one drageal can fit into the courtyard, is that correct, Zab?" the senior builder asked.

Zabaneja nodded.

"Would that one be able to lift the body or part of it enough to allow us to put a few rollers under it?"

Zabaneja relayed the question.

"She thinks they could do that. But how would putting something under the body help?"

The builder chuckled and explained they would use a series of rollers and after the first rollers were under the body, the cloth could be put on the next ones and eventually after all of the rollers were under the drageal the cloth would be too. At that point they could tie the ends together and attach the ropes as they normally would and the drageal in the courtyard could bring them to the other drageals waiting overhead.

"That is a genius plan," Nanetscka said. "Please tell your people we are very impressed with both their knowledge and ingenuity."

The builders beamed at the compliment, and it was agreed they would perform the operation the next morning.

#

Before the removal of the body got underway, Zabaneja said farewell to Nanetscka and the others.

"I hope we will be seeing you again," Nanetscka said as she and Zabaneja hugged. "And next time under happier circumstances."

Zabaneja nodded, afraid to speak lest he break down.

#

It took several hours and a few failed attempts before the drageal's body was positioned so that Nanetscka and the others could remove it. In the end, the operation went rather smoothly.

As Nanetscka picked up the last rope, the one she would carry, she and Zabaneja called out a final goodbye to each other.

Zabaneja, along with most of the Keep's occupants, watched as the drageals flew off. Once out of sight, the crowd dispersed, but Zabaneja stood for some time staring upward into the now empty sky.

"Do you wish you had gone with them?" Rusalei asked.

"It was not possible."

"That was not my question."

"Of course I do," he said more harshly than he intended. "Had there been a way, I would have, but..." His voice softened and looked down at the ground. "That is not to be for a long time."

Rusalei tried to reach out to comfort him, but he pulled away.

"I am sorry, My Lady, you must excuse me. I have duties to attend to," he said and dashed off.

CHAPTER THIRTY-SEVEN

"OUR SOURCES TELL US the battles have moved away from the Keep and the kingdom of Alexandrash, but this may not last forever," Aneesyma addressed his council a few days after the drageal incident. "We can no longer be the only ones aware of the war above us. We must decide how to tell the others and devise a plan to deal with what may come."

The council members reacted with both agreement and confusion and all, including Aneesyma, looked to Zabaneja. Not surprisingly, the young man had some ideas. As he had suggested to Aneesyma earlier, he advised they join forces with Pheunaf and enlist additional support from their King and the other kingdoms, since the war had the potential to spread across the entire world. Haoule and Rusalei saw the merit in the suggestion but had questions. Tuzzern, on the other hand, disagreed not because of any lack of merit in the proposal, but out of sheer malice.

"Tuzzern, while I welcome discussion, and even disagreement, I do not appreciate your hostility. If you cannot add anything constructive, well..." Aneesyma rose and walked across the room.

Tuzzern was stunned. "Are you removing me from the council?"

Aneesyma did not respond.

"I see. You now wish to have only your bootlickers as advisors." Tuzzern growled and jumped up.

"You know that is not true," Haoule shouted.

Aneesyma raised his hand to silence the elderly minister, and Haoule quieted.

"I am sorry you feel that way, Tuzzern. In your heart, you know the truth, but, no matter what I say, you refuse to listen."

Tuzzern remained standing, his face red with rage.

"It will give me no pleasure to see you leave the council," Aneesyma continued. "Over the years, you have given, first my father and then me, valuable advice. However, as of late, your offensive comments directed at individuals or, in this case, an entire race have no constructive value other than to feed your personal anger."

Tuzzern pushed his chair back and stormed out of the chamber, slamming the door behind him. All in the room sat in stunned silence.

Aneesyma returned to his seat. "Now, in addition to dealing with the issue of the impending conflict, I also need to find someone to fill a vacant council position."

"Do you not think he will come back once he calms down?" Rusalei asked.

"I doubt it," Aneesyma replied.

"Ever since his son died in that hunting accident, he has been unable to find pleasure in any aspect of life. Still, that is no reason for him to try to drain the joy from everyone else," Haoule said.

Aneesyma nodded and cleared his throat. "Back to the business at hand—the war. Zab, do continue."

Zabaneja reiterated what he had been saying before Tuzzern's tirade. He stressed that even if they did nothing, they could again become collateral damage or worse, the target of an attack.

"Will Darchok not be more inclined to attack us if he finds we have aligned ourselves with Pheunaf?" Rusalei asked.

"Possibly, but if Darchok defeats Pheunaf…"

"Yes, we are all well aware of what would happen then," Haoule said. "So Zab, how do you think we can assist the drageals? After all, the battles are in the sky and we are landbound."

"I do not know."

Aneesyma, who had been silent to this point, looked at Zabaneja. "But I surmise you have an idea."

"The seeds of one. I think the first thing we need to do is contact the drageals."

"So," Aneesyma said, looking at his ministers, "what counsel will you give me on this matter? Or, do you wish to discuss this outside of my presence and return to me with your suggestions?"

"I have no issue discussing this matter with Haoule in your presence, My Lord," Rusalei said.

"Nor do I," Haoule replied.

Aneesyma nodded.

"Let me begin, Zab, by saying I respect your position in this situation," Haoule said. "But, that being said, I am still not wholly convinced what you propose, siding with Pheunaf's faction, does not, to some degree, come from your relationship with her and the drageals. How can we be sure your plan is the best or the only possible solution for us?"

Rusalei threw her hands in the air and shook her head. She seemed ready to voice her disagreement when Aneesyma raised his hand and she stilled herself.

"I will not deny my relationship with Pheunaf. However, it is my knowledge of the evil lurking within Darchok that tells me we must do something."

"And what will that something be? How will we be able to assist

Pheunaf's drageals?" Haoule asked.

"I am not sure. Perhaps we cannot help at all."

The others in the room were shocked at Zabaneja's response.

He continued, "We must first find out if the drageals would accept our help at whatever level it could be offered."

"Can you guarantee we will not merely be used as fodder for Darchok's attacks?" Haoule asked.

Zabaneja shook his head. "My knowledge of Pheunaf and most drageals tells me they would never do anything so ignoble as that to anyone. I am also certain that, if Pheunaf falls to Darchok, there will be nothing in this world that will keep us safe. I, and all the drageals, know, because he has never held his tongue on the subject. Darchok feels the only race of intelligent beings that should exist in this world are drageals. And these days, he feels only drageals that agree with him should be allowed to live."

Rusalei, no longer able to maintain her silence, interrupted. "It then seems our only options are to die fighting or cowering in fear? I, for one, believe Zab is correct in wanting to join the drageals and fight."

"Did you come to that decision because you believe it to be the right course of action, or because of the feelings you have for the young man?" Haoule asked.

Rusalei flushed scarlet. It took her a moment before she calmed enough to reply. "Even if I did have feelings for Zab or anyone, I would never allow them to influence my decisions on matters of state. I am appalled you would even make such a statement!" Rusalei's words were clipped, the emotion she was trying to control evident.

"Enough!" Aneesyma snapped. "This is neither the time nor the place for petty squabbles. I do not care what the underlying cause of your opinion is or where it comes from, I only care about your counsel on this matter. If you cannot do so in a civil fashion, I will be forced to dismiss both of you and to make all further decisions myself."

The two ministers bowed their heads, but remained silent.

"That is better." Aneesyma turned to Zabaneja, whose face had also reddened at Haoule's insinuation concerning Rusalei and himself. "Zab, please continue."

"As I was saying, I feel if we do not join forces with Pheunaf, no one will be safe. Of course, this proposal will be of no consequence if Pheunaf declines our assistance. I also think we will not be alone in siding with the Pheunaf."

"Why do you say that?" Aneesyma asked.

"It is not just humans Darchok hates. He wishes to create a world inhabited solely by drageals. I think other races will also be willing to join forces against him. We just need to find a way to do so."

"Other races?" Haoule asked.

Zabaneja nodded. "My sources assure me there has been communication with some of them. Which ones, or their response to the requests, I have not heard."

Haoule shook his head and chuckled. "A very short while ago, I would have thought a conversation discussing other races to be madness, and now I do not blink an eye. How things have changed."

"Zab, you sound as if you think there is a possibility Pheunaf might decline our offer of an alliance," Aneesyma said.

"That is a possibility. Mind you, it would not be because she thinks less of humans. More likely it would be because the combat is in the air and we are not."

"Have you thought about what we should do if that occurs?" Aneesyma asked.

Zabaneja nodded. "If it comes to that, humans and others still need to prepare for the worst."

"Go on."

"If Pheunaf rejects our help, I feel we must go forward and prepare to defend ourselves. To that end, I think we should go ahead with the other facets of our plan. Send Guentza to Siggurna and allow me to contact the others."

Aneesyma nodded and turned to his ministers. "Your opinions, please."

Haoule cleared his throat. "While I still have my reservations about joining a war that, at the moment, does not involve us, I understand the situation a little better. Whether we like it or not, we will be involved in this conflict in some way. So, in the long run, I feel it will be better for us to seek an alliance with Pheunaf and the others than to wait and be at Darchok's mercy."

"I agree," Rusalei said.

"I, too, believe Zab is right in his assessments." Aneesyma turned back to Zabaneja. "When will you approach Pheunaf?"

"With your permission, My Lord, I would like to leave tomorrow at dawn. I think the sooner we get this plan in motion, the better we will all be."

"Of course."

Zabaneja nodded. "Then I will take my leave and prepare to go to the drageal camp."

"Good. I will draft the petition to the King and send Guentza to the capital within the next few days," Aneesyma replied. "So then, that seems to be all we can do at this time. We will reconvene once we have more information as to which direction Zab's plan will take."

All rose, bowed to Aneesyma, and departed.

CHAPTER THIRTY-EIGHT

RUSALEI, RELIEVED HAOULE had gone in the opposite direction, followed Zabaneja into the courtyard.

"If you are following me to say Haoule's comments about your feelings are false," Zabaneja said as he turned to her, his sudden change of direction causing her to almost run into him, "do not worry, I did not believe any of it."

"Of course. I did not think for a moment you had," Rusalei replied. "I actually wanted to talk to you about your mission to the drageal camp."

Zabaneja nodded. "What would you like to know, My Lady?"

"I thought we had agreed you would call me Rusalei when we were alone?" she said.

"I am sorry... Rusalei. It is a difficult habit to break."

"Please try."

"Of course." Zabaneja nodded. "What may I help you with?"

"I, um... well... I was wondering if you might allow me to accompany you."

Zabaneja looked shocked. "No! Absolutely not!"

Rusalei was surprised not only at the speed of Zabaneja's

response, but by his outright refusal. "Why, not?"

"It will be an arduous journey under far from ideal conditions, and I will not have you subjected to such things. You must remember who you are."

"What do you mean, who I am?"

"Rusalei. You know what I mean. Not only are you a minister of Lord Aneesyma's council, you are nobility. This mission is not going to be a mere lark. I will be riding all day and well into the night with very little rest. This is no kind of trip for a lady, especially one of your status." He stopped when he saw the look on her face. A look that conveyed both hurt and anger. "Not to mention, I have no idea what sorts of dangers I might encounter. I cannot, and will not, put you into that kind of peril."

"That is nonsense. I can ride as well as you, perhaps better. As for protecting me, I am almost as skilled with a bow and better with a sword than you."

"That may be. But even with conditions and danger aside, I still have no intention of allowing you to come with me. It would not be proper for a woman, any woman, to travel alone with a man."

"Pfft... What if Lord Aneesyma gives his permission?"

Zabaneja smiled. "If you get his permission, I will be more than happy to allow you to accompany me. But, I must either hear it directly from him, or you must get it in writing. HIS writing!"

"Oh, so you think I would lie to you?"

"I most certainly do! And do not try to tell me you had not thought about it. I know you too well, Lady Rusalei."

Rusalei harrumphed and stomped off.

Damn that woman! Zabaneja thought as he watched her walk away. *What will I do if she somehow convinces Aneesyma to let her come with me? And why am I so against it?*

Zabaneja shook his head to clear his mind, turned and headed toward his quarters. There was much to do before his departure in the morning, and he could not allow anything to interfere with the task ahead.

#

"Damn it," Rusalei grumbled. "How am I going to get Lord Aneesyma to agree to this? I cannot tell him I want to be alone with Zab, away from the trappings of the Keep. That will not do." She shook her head, trying to think of another reason. But what? She had to come up with something quickly, because at daybreak Zabaneja would be off and her chance would be gone.

She found Aneesyma walking toward his rooms.

"My Lord, I am sorry to interrupt you. I have a request."

Aneesyma smiled, certain he knew what she was going to ask, but curious about the pretense she would present. "What might that be, Rusalei?"

"As you know, Zab is leaving in the morning to approach the drageals with his plan."

"I do," Aneesyma said, not surprised he was correct.

"And, as we all know, when things do not go his way, Zab can become, oh, how shall I say it, a bit headstrong. I think it is safe to say we both realize this situation will require a great deal of diplomacy. Especially if the drageals, or any of the others he will be approaching, do not immediately agree with his proposition."

Aneesyma smiled and waited for her to continue.

"With your permission, I would like to accompany him."

"I see. Well, you may not realize this, but drageals do not require the same level of diplomacy humans do. They are far more direct in how they approach things, so Zab is far better suited to deal with them than any of us."

"I was not aware of that."

"If I were to entertain the idea of having someone else accompany Zab, why do you think you would be the most qualified?"

"Well, I am one of your ministers..."

"True, but you are also the youngest and most inexperienced."

"I do not think either of those things should have any bearing on my request."

Aneesyma smiled. "No, I am sure you do not. But, you see, I do. Both of those things have a great deal to do with the situation at hand. Not to mention we are talking about Zab dealing with drageals, with those who raised him, his family. I am sure he will need no further assistance."

"But what of the other races?"

"And you have a history dealing with them?"

Rusalei blushed and Aneesyma could see she was trying to formulate another argument.

He held his hand up. "Regardless of what you say, you do not have my permission to accompany him."

"But, why?" she sputtered.

Aneesyma looked at her, his face no longer showing the joviality it previously had. "Young lady, I am under no obligation to give you reasons for my decision. There will be no further discussion on this topic."

She nodded, remaining silent.

"Good, I am glad I have made myself clear."

"Yes, My Lord, you have."

"Then we are done here."

She nodded. As she watched Aneesyma walk away, she clenched her fists in anger. She did not care if she did not have permission. She would find a way to follow Zabaneja.

CHAPTER THIRTY-NINE

ZABANEJA RETURNED to his room, packed the things he would need and went to draw a hot bath. No matter how many times the others tried to explain how they were able to deliver hot water on demand to anywhere in the castle and the barracks, he still did not understand. But it was one of the few things humans had created that he admired and would miss when he returned home and had to once again bathe in frigid lakes and rivers.

He stripped out of his clothes and climbed into the deep tub, allowing his body to slowly sink into the steaming hot water. He let out a sigh, closed his eyes and rested his head on the back of the metal enclosure.

He did not intend to fall into such a deep state of relaxation, a state just this side of sleep, nor did he know how long he had been soaking in the soothing hot water, when he suddenly felt a splash on his face. He opened his eyes and saw Rusalei.

He bolted upright. "What in the world are you doing here?"

"I came to tell you I spoke to Aneesyma."

"What did he say?"

Rusalei did not answer. Instead, she unbuttoned her tunic.

"What are you doing? Stop that!" Zabaneja commanded.

Rusalei smiled, undid the last button and dropped the shirt to the floor.

"You must stop this," Zabaneja insisted.

"If you want me to stop, you will have to make me." She smiled defiantly at him as she untied the laces that held her trousers. She let her pants drop and pool around her ankles, then stepped out of them.

"Rusalei, put your clothes back on!"

She looked at him and ran her hand over her breast, making her nipple harden. "Do you not like what you see? You tell me to stop," she continued, now caressing her other breast, "yet, I see you cannot take your eyes off me."

She was right, he could not avert his glance from her bare skin, which made his desire escalate.

In the next moment, before he even saw her move, she was in the tub on top of him. Zabaneja was stunned. He could not move. Could not speak. Could not think.

"I know you want me, Zab," she said. "What are you waiting for? What more do I have to do to give myself to you?"

Zabaneja lay immersed in the now lukewarm water, Rusalei leaning against his thighs with his ever hardening erection just in front of her. Still, he could do nothing. Rusalei took his hand and kissed his palm, then ever so gently ran her tongue in ever-widening circles into it. Then she placed it on her breast.

"Rusalei... stop this..." Zabaneja croaked, finally able to muster a few words. "It is not right... a woman of your status..."

She ignored his protests and leaned forward until her lips touched his. "But I want you," she whispered and then pressed her lips hard against his, pushing her tongue deep into his mouth.

Zabaneja tried to resist, but she was relentless. With each breath, she whispered, "I want you."

She reached for his manhood and stroked it. Zabaneja moaned and surrendered. He squeezed her nipple between his fingers until she arched her back, pushing herself deeper into his hand. She let out a small cry. He moved his hands to her hips and raised her up and gently pushed her to one side of the tub as he slid to the other.

"What are you doing?" she cried.

"This is not the place for this. When we make love, it must be in a place of comfort."

He managed to get himself out of the tub and then helped her do the same. He reached for a towel, but Rusalei knelt down and began licking the water from his body. Before she got very far, he realized if he did not stop her, neither would get what they wanted. He lifted her into his arms and carried her to his bed.

He laid her on the sheets, sure she had never had such common material touch her delicate skin. Then he straddled her and began kissing her, first her forehead, then the tip of her nose and then her lips. Her tongue tried to enter his mouth, but he pulled back and kissed her chin. He ever so lightly ran his tongue down the side of her neck, making her moan and squirm.

She tried to reach for him, but he gently pushed her hand away. "Not yet."

When he felt he had fully explored her neck, he moved his hands and mouth to her breasts, alternating between gentle and rough pinches and nibbles, all of which made Rusalei writhe with pleasure. As he continued to suckle her nipples, alternating from one breast to the other, Zabaneja's fingers gently skimmed over her belly until they came to the tuft of curly hair. He played with it for several seconds, knowing full well what it was doing to her.

"Damn you, Zab," Rusalei breathlessly cried, her voice husky. "You are driving me mad."

He released her nipple from his teeth, looked up at her and

grinned. "I know. And I am not done yet." Zabaneja slid down her body, running his tongue along her belly. "This is what happens when you present yourself to me as you did."

He slid further down until he was between her outstretched legs. He lightly ran his fingertips over her inner thighs. She pushed her body toward him, trying to make him touch her more forcefully. He touched the outer lips of her sex and felt the hot, slick wetness as he rubbed his finger roughly over her nub. At the same time, he felt his own sexual arousal getting ever so near its climax. But he needed to keep himself in check until he took her to the point where she felt if he did not enter her, she would explode.

He moved himself back up her body again, kissing or licking her as he moved. He saw she had the coarse sheets clenched tightly in her fists, her breathing heavy as she looked at him.

"Please..." she gasped. "If you want me to beg, I will."

He kissed her lips. "As you wish, My Lady."

He thrust his sex deep inside of her. She cried out with a sound that was a cross between satisfaction and excitement. And the two of them began a perfect sexual dance, each knowing exactly what to do to please the other.

Zabaneja held out as long as he could, wanting to relish each strong, deep thrust into her, but too soon he knew he could delay his need no longer. With one final thrust, he too exploded into his own orgasmic ecstasy.

He slumped down on top of her, and she slowly, gently stroked his back.

"You realize, this should never have happened. You should never have come here. I should never have allowed myself to succumb to my desire for you."

"This is what I wanted. What we both wanted. What we both need — each other, now and forever."

"Yes, each other, now and forever," he whispered and closed his eyes, still clinging to Rusalei's naked body.

#

Zabaneja opened his eyes, still smiling and murmuring 'each other, now and forever' only to find himself in a tub of very cold water. He was alone. There was no Rusalei. It had all been his desire, his imagination, a dream. He now had no choice but to admit the fact he had not been consciously aware of—he desired Rusalei more than anything in his life.

He was relieved when he realized the mission to the drageals would take him away from this place, and her, for a while. Hopefully, during that time he would be able to come to grips with this situation. Right now, he needed to sleep. He got out of the tub, dried off and retired.

CHAPTER FORTY

RUSALEI STOLE DOWN to the kitchen, thankful she was known for always appearing at odd hours to get food. Today, she would visit several of them to avoid arousing suspicion when she took more than she could conceivably eat.

She returned to her room and added the food stash to her already packed bag. She attached her sword to her waist and put the bow and arrow quiver over her shoulder. It was still several hours until the sun would rise, so she should have no problem slipping out and getting a head start on Zabaneja.

As expected, the courtyard and stable were empty. She swiftly saddled her mare and led her silently through the unguarded side gate.

She planned to ride on ahead for several miles and wait for Zabaneja, knowing if he discovered her too close to the Keep, he would send her back. As she approached the first fork in the road, she realized it offered him several options, so her original plan would not work. She decided her best course of action was to hide there and wait. Once he committed to a path, she would let him get ahead of her then follow, staying hidden. Hopefully, by the time he discovered her, which would eventually happen, they would be too far from home for him to send her back alone. She intended to rely upon his sense of duty, which would not allow him to delay his mission by escorting her back.

#

Zabaneja rose before his page came to wake him. By the time the young boy entered, Zabaneja was already dressed. He dismissed the boy's apologies and requested his meal.

Within a few moments, the boy returned with the tray, set it down and left. Zabaneja quickly finished the food, gathered his gear and departed.

He reached the gate, relieved to see no sign of Rusalei. After that dream, he needed to be alone for a bit. He exited the Keep, but as he passed the first fork in the road, he had the strange sense he was being watched. He stopped and looked around, but saw no one.

After a moment or so, he proceeded. As the day wore on, he continued to sense someone or something following him. By mid-afternoon, he decided to test his theory. Without warning, Zabaneja took off at speed and hid far enough ahead so anyone following him would not see him leave the road.

He waited until a horse galloped toward his position. He remained hidden and allowed the hooded rider to pass before he gave chase. He reached his pursuer and before the stranger could react, Zabaneja reached out and knocked him to the ground. He then circled back, jumped from his horse, and put his sword to the rider's back.

"Why are you following me?" Zabaneja demanded.

The fallen rider rolled over, Zabaneja's sword still pointed at him.

"Rusalei? What are you doing here?" Zabaneja demanded as he withdrew his weapon.

Rusalei stood and brushed the road dust from herself and smirked.

"You still have not answered my question."

"I am accompanying you to the drageal camp."

"I told you the only way you could come with me was if Aneesyma gave you written permission," Zabaneja snapped. "Did you get it?"

Rusalei snickered. "If I had, would I be following you this way?"

"Well, My Lady, you are going to turn yourself around right this minute and return to the Keep."

"No, I am not. I am going with you."

"Rusalei, you cannot come with me. You know that. If it was a good idea, on any level, Aneesyma would have given his permission."

"The only way I will go back to the Keep is if you drag me there."

Zabaneja shook his head. "You are acting like a spoiled child, not a council minister. Are you saying you would jeopardize my mission for your own desire to see drageals? Is that more important than what is best for our people?"

"I do not care what you say. I will not go back. I am going to the drageal camp. If I cannot ride alongside you, then I will follow behind you. Either way, I am going!"

Zabaneja threw his hands up in the air, turned and walked a few feet away from her. "Even if this journey did not involve danger, surely you know the two of us traveling alone is not proper by any stretch of the imagination."

Rusalei laughed. "Are you worried about your reputation, sir?"

"That is not funny, Rusalei! You know exactly what I am worried about!"

"If I am not concerned about what others think, you should not be either." She put her hand on his shoulder. "Zab, give up. You will not win this argument. Whether you like it or not, I am going with you. So, we can stand here and argue until it is too dark to continue, or we can be on our way. I will leave that decision up to you."

"So, there is nothing I can say to change your mind?"

She smiled. "Not a thing."

He shook his head slowly and accepted his defeat.

She smiled again.

"Come then, let us be on our way." He turned and walked toward his horse. "Remember, this is not going to be an easy journey and there will be no pampering."

"I am well aware of that," she said.

"You will have to deal with Aneesyma when we return."

Rusalei nodded. She hoped her rash behavior would be worth it.

CHAPTER FORTY-ONE

"HAVE YOU DECIDED how you are going to present your plan to Pheunaf?" Rusalei asked when they stopped for the night.

"Yes, if I get to speak to her directly."

"Because you are not of a high enough social status?" Rusalei asked with more than a hint of sarcasm that made Zabaneja bristle. "She is your mother, surely she will see you."

"Yes, but she is also in charge of this war. She may be too busy or elsewhere to see me."

She squeezed his hand. At her touch, Zabaneja's desires from the previous night resurfaced. He wanted to pull away, but knew that would require an explanation. One he could not give her. When she released his hand, he tried to quell his growing passion. Hopefully, she had not noticed his dilemma. He reminded himself to be more careful and keep his distance from her.

"How long until we reach their camp?" Rusalei tried to sound calm even though at the feel of his touch, her heart pounded so hard she felt sure it would leap from her chest. She hoped the innocuous question would hide her emotions.

He walked a few steps away. "If my calculations are correct, we will get there in three day's time, probably late afternoon or early evening. However, if we are not at the base of the hills at least a few hours before sunset, we will have to wait until the following morning to approach."

She looked at him, not understanding. "Why?"

"The hills are treacherous to maneuver in daylight. In darkness, they are near impossible."

"Oh, of course," she said. "How stupid of me not to have realized that."

#

The following morning, they woke to gray skies. The rain began shortly after they started out. The winds, coupled with a torrential downpour, forced them to seek shelter. They found a cave, just large enough for them to be comfortable without being too close.

"Hopefully, we will be off again in a few hours," Zabaneja said as he tried to get comfortable as far from Rusalei as possible.

"That is good to hear."

By early afternoon, the storm strengthened, proving Zabaneja's forecast wrong and forcing them further back into the small cleft until they were uncomfortably close together. They were quiet, both afraid if they spoke, the dilemma each felt would be revealed.

After a few hours, Zabaneja scooted forward and looked at the sky. He slid back inside and shook his head. "From the looks of it, I fear this is not going to stop for some time. I think we may be spending the night here."

Rusalei was not sure, but she thought she sensed a heavy strain in his voice that seemed more than the frustration at not being able to move on.

"So it does."

\#

"We cannot make a fire in this space nor out in the rain," Rusalei said, "so it is a good thing I brought food that does not need to be cooked." She bent over her saddlebag and began digging in it. "Where is it?" she mumbled to herself.

Suddenly her foot slipped, and she went tumbling backwards, landing on Zabaneja's lap. She sat up and saw his face turning red. At first, she thought not to comment, but then found herself rubbing on his trouser front. Her mind whirled. She wanted to strip off her clothes and make love to him.

"Rusalei…" Zabaneja croaked.

She smiled at him and then purred. "Oh my, what have I found here?" she asked and ran her fingers along his crotch.

"Stop it," he said, his voice still not normal.

She was not sure how she did it, but in the next moment she found herself straddling him. She knew from the look in his eyes he was fighting an internal battle between his desires and what he thought proper. *I knew it,* she thought. *You want me as much as I want you.*

He reached to move her, but she grabbed his hands and forced them to her breasts. As he touched her, she wanted to cry out with pleasure. *If he can make me feel this way by just touching me, what will he do to me when he actually takes me?* The thought excited her.

He struggled to pull away, but with the close quarters and the way she was positioned atop him, he could not move. She took his one hand and pushed it under her tunic. She moaned with pleasure as he touched her bare skin. She arched her back, pushing her breast harder into his hand. Again he tried to pull away.

"You know I want you and I can see you feel the same, why not surrender to our desires?"

She leaned forward to kiss him, but suddenly found herself on the ground as Zabaneja jumped up and stormed out of the cave into the rain.

She snapped her head around to glare at him. "What are you doing?"

"No. The real question is, what are YOU doing?" he asked and went toward the horses.

Wait. Had she misjudged his feelings for her? No, that could not be. She knew she was right. She saw it in his eyes, both his lust and the struggle to deny it. Had her rash actions pushed him too far and too fast?

"Oh, do come in out of the rain," she said after a few minutes. "You will catch your death out there."

"Only if you promise to stop this... this... this, whatever it is you are up to," he replied without turning to look at her.

"If you insist, but... "

He turned and glared. "There is no but. You either stop acting the way you just did, or I will ride on without you right now and damn the rain."

"Fine, I will stay as far away from you as possible. Now, please come back." She smiled, hoping to soften the anger she had invoked, and watched as he slowly returned.

He sat at the very end of the shelter, as far from her as he could. She shook her head and tossed him a meat pie.

"Thank you," he said as he began to eat.

For the rest of the afternoon and into the evening, Rusalei snuck sideways glances at him. He still looked flustered, though no longer angry, and she was certain her intuition about him was correct. He had feelings for her, and tonight she would make him prove it to both of them.

#

Zabaneja had all he could do to control himself. *What was she up to? Or is this another dream, and I will wake to find her acting normally!* But this time he knew it was not a dream, and that made it even worse. What was he going to do? He could no longer deny he wanted her. Wanted to explore every inch of her, to become one with her. As those thoughts ran through his mind, his body reacted to them. *Stop! Stop even thinking such things,* he shouted at himself.

CHAPTER FORTY-TWO

RUSALEI HAD NOT INTENDED to fall asleep, but was glad she woke before dawn. She listened and to her delight, Zabaneja was still asleep. Now, she needed to decide whether to let the events of yesterday end where they had or push the situation further. It did not take long to make up her mind. Even if she could only have him during this trip, or even only this night, she wanted him. She had always wanted him, probably from the first day she had seen him. But now, it was more than want, now she needed him.

She turned and in the dim moonlight saw he was sleeping on his back. She smiled. *How convenient.*

She crawled out from beneath her blanket and stripped off her clothes, shivering slightly as the cool night air licked at her bare skin. Silently she crept across the cave until she was by Zabaneja's side. She was glad to see he had removed his heavy outer garments and was in only his shirt and trousers under the blanket. Rusalei sat for a moment watching him sleep, took a deep breath and put her plan into play.

She slowly pulled his blanket away, moved her hand to the front of his pants and gingerly began to undo the buttons. He did not move as the first button was released. As she reached for the second, he stirred. She stopped and held her breath, but he did not wake. Once sure he was still asleep, she continued. She realized opening his pants was the easy part, getting him aroused without waking him until she wanted him so, would take some luck.

To her surprise and delight, when she opened his pants, she found he was already hard. At the sight, Rusalei's insides tightened. She quietly stood up and straddled him and slowly lowered herself until she was sitting on his thighs.

As her buttocks touched his legs, Zabaneja awoke. His eyes flew open, and he tried to bolt upright. This time, Rusalei was ready. She threw her arms around his neck, held fast, and pressed her lips against his. Zabaneja tried to push her away, but Rusalei did not let go.

"Just this once, surrender," she whispered.

He looked into her eyes, sighed, grabbed the back of her head and pulled it towards his own. She heard him say 'vixen' before he pressed his lips to hers in a bruising kiss, followed by his tongue stabbing its way into her mouth. Rusalei met his actions with her own.

Before she realized what was happening, she was on her back with Zabaneja on top of her. She could tell by the strain on his face that he had lost the battle to refrain from seeking satisfaction. She bit her lip to keep from crying out with passion as the full length and width of him entered her and they began moving in the same sexual dance. He pleasured her in ways she did not think possible until finally, they both reached the pinnacle of ecstasy together. He stroked her face and gently kissed her lips. She closed her eyes, hoping for more, but realized he had gotten up. She looked at him as he readjusted his clothes and walked to where the horses were tethered.

"Where are you going?" she asked, her voice cracking.

"You need to dress. It is almost daylight, and we must be on our way," he replied without turning to look at her.

She was taken aback by the deliberate manner in which he spoke, as if he were delivering his report to the council. She stood up without covering herself, walked to him and wrapped her arms around his waist.

He pulled away. "What occurred tonight can never happen again."

She was stunned. After the way he had so fully given himself to her and she to him, the things he had done to evoke pleasures she had never known before, she assumed she had broken through his barriers.

"What do you mean? Why not?"

"What happened was a mistake," he said. "We both know that to be true."

The pained look on her face tore at his heart. But in the next moment, her stubborn pride took over. "That is not how you acted," she snapped. "I do not remember hearing you protest as you spewed your seed in me. Nor when you fondled my breasts." She grabbed his hand and tried to pull them toward her nakedness, but he pulled away and pushed past her.

"I will not deny what we shared was extraordinary, probably the best lovemaking I have ever experienced. But even with that being said, it was still a mistake." He saw the rage in her eyes. "Rusalei, you know we cannot be anything more than colleagues, perhaps friends."

"Rubbish!"

"It is not. Even if we put aside the class differences, it has never been my intention, nor desire, to remain with the humans. As soon as the time my mother and Aneesyma agreed upon comes to an end I will return to the drageals."

"Then I will go with you. I, too, will live amongst them."

Zabaneja shook his head. "You cannot."

"Why not? You did."

"Because of who you are; how you were raised. It may sound like a good idea, an adventure, at the moment. But there will come a time when the reality of such a life, one without even the smallest of luxuries you are accustomed to, will become clear to you and then your love will turn to hate. Hate towards not only me but yourself. For that reason, there is no way for us to repeat what happened here unless we only want each other as plaything or conquest..."

Her anger exploded, and she flew at him, slapping him squarely across the face.

"Is that what you think of me? Of what happened? Of humans?" Her words were choppy as she tried to control both her anger and, more importantly, her emotions. She would not let him see her cry, no matter how much his words hurt.

He rubbed his face to lessen the sting of her slap. A slap he knew was more than deserved. One that came as a result of him finally telling her, and himself, the truth.

"Of course, not. But that is the only explanation your father and Aneesyma will accept. If you were thinking rationally, had thought this through..."

"So, now I am not only your latest conquest, I am also irrational." This time her voice cracked, and she felt her eyes welling with tears.

She quickly turned from him and went to the pile of clothes she had discarded the night before. She retrieved them, dressed, then picked up her saddle.

"I will get that for you, Rusalei," Zabaneja said and started towards her.

She turned on her heel to face him. "You will address me as Lady Rusalei. And yes, it is YOUR place to pick up my things and wait upon me. Now do so."

He was not shocked by the venom in her voice or her words. He had brought this upon himself—both her anger and his life sentence of loneliness. But he had no choice.

"Yes, Lady Rusalei," he replied and bowed at the waist. "As you wish."

He helped her into the saddle, though on any other day she would have scoffed at even the slightest offer of aid, then proceeded to mount his own steed.

"My Lady, I believe we are within two days' ride of the drageal encampment."

She did not reply. Instead, she pulled sharply on the reins, turning her mare in the direction of home. Had the ground been open field, she would have taken off at a gallop, but it was not, so she was forced to move more slowly.

"I am not going to the drageal camp," she called without looking over her shoulder. "I have no desire to share any more time on the road with the likes of you. Please be sure not to allow your distaste for humans to cloud the purpose of your mission."

Zabaneja stood dumbstruck as Rusalei disappeared from sight. When he finally regained his senses, he found himself wondering what to do next—to go on to the drageal camp or to follow her and see her to safety.

There was no question, he had a responsibility. One far more important than his personal feelings. He took a last glance at the path Rusalei was on, made a wish to the heavens for her safety, and took off to complete the mission he had been tasked with.

#

As soon as was safe, Rusalei pushed her mare to a full gallop. Once sure she was out of Zabaneja's view, she stopped and allowed the tears she had been holding back by sheer will and stubbornness to flow. She sat, sobbing uncontrollably until she had no more tears to cry for him or, more importantly, for herself. She wiped the dampness from her cheeks and repositioned herself and her weapons, then departed for home.

On the journey back, she rebuked herself for her stupidity. How many times had Zabaneja said, or hinted at, those things? Things that, until this morning, she had not realized were his truth and reality. Why had she not listened? She shook her head. *NO!* she shouted into her own mind. *It is not true! He cares for me as much as I care for him. I could not have been just been fooling myself.*

She took a deep breath and continued home.

CHAPTER FORTY-THREE

ZABANEJA REACHED the base of the mountain in the late afternoon on the following day. He knew his arrival was not a surprise. He had felt a drageal presence, a talent he had even as an infant, from just after Rusalei had joined him.

He rode halfway up the mountain, stopping a good distance from the camp. He loosely tied his horse's reins to a tree, knowing it would not take kindly to the presence of drageals. Then continued the rest of the way on foot. At the summit, he was greeted by Phrynia, the young drageal he had met at the Keep.

"Nanetscka ordered me to bring you to her upon your arrival."

"Thank you, Phrynia. I appreciate the escort. How goes it here?"

The young drageal was somewhat surprised this human remembered her name, but then again, he did speak dragealian.

"As well as can be expected, I guess. You will need to ask Nanetscka and the others for details. I have been relegated to menial camp duties and am told nothing. What a bore!"

"Do not be so quick to wish yourself into battle, young one. The reality of it is far more gruesome than anyone ever expects."

The young drageal stopped and moved until her massive snout was almost touching Zabaneja's tiny, by comparison, face. She snorted, her hot breath blowing back his hair. To her surprise, Zabaneja did not flinch.

"So, you do not fear us, eh," she said as she turned from him.

"Do I need to?"

"Why would he fear us?" Nanetscka asked from a few paces behind the young drageal.

If drageals reddened with embarrassment, Zabaneja was sure Phyrnia would be doing so. But he was not here to embarrass her, so he said nothing.

"Ah, Nanetscka. It is good to see you again."

The two old friends nodded. Nanetscka directed Zabaneja to go on ahead and, though he could not be sure, he felt the heat of an aunt's look and words upon an errant child before she joined him.

"That one is a such a handful."

"I am sure you can deal with her. After all, were we any different at that age?"

Nanetscka snickered. "Where is the female you had with you?"

"Um, well..." Zabaneja sputtered. While he had expected them to know of his coming, he had hoped they had not seen Rusalei. "She had to return to the Keep for some reason or another."

"I see."

Zabaneja hoped his flustered response to Nanetscka's questions would escape the drageal, but knew better. Before they had a chance to discuss it further, they arrived at their destination. As they approached Pheunaf, Nanetscka whispered, "We will talk more about her later."

#

He approached Pheunaf, who was deep in conversation with several others, and stood silently to the side. Those gathered either knew him or knew of him, so their conversation continued freely.

As the others prepared to leave, Pheunaf turned to him.

"Pheunaf," he said, addressing her formally while the others were still within earshot, "or is it General now? It is good to see you again, albeit not under the circumstances I would have preferred."

"Alas, circumstances have seemingly thrust such a title upon my shoulders. But from you, dear boy, I expect to be called Mother."

Zabaneja smiled.

"So, you are here on the business of Aneesyma and your people..."

"Drageals are my people," he blurted out in a sharper tone than intended.

Pheunaf nodded. "Of course. As I was saying, before we get to the business you are here for, let us take some time to catch up and reminisce. It has been a little while since last we met."

"I am sorry, I would like to see you more, but..."

"That was not the bargain we struck, child."

He nodded.

The pair sat and talked for quite some time. As much as Pheunaf's tales of how he was found naked and abandoned on the mountainside embarrassed him, he could never deny her the pleasure she received from recounting them. So, he gave her a few minutes respite from the horrors of the current situation and let her indulge in her memories.

When she finished reminiscing, Zabaneja reached into his pocket and withdrew the purple gem she had given him at his departure.

"Here, Mother, I am returning this to you as you had planned." He held it out to her.

She looked first at the stone and then at him and smiled. "Not yet, son. Keep it a bit longer."

He nodded, surprised by the relief he felt at her refusal.

Before he could ask her why, a young drageal had brought a tray filled with hunks of raw meat and a pitcher of dark orange liquid.

Zabaneja looked at the pitcher, then at his mother. "Is that what I think it is?"

Pheunaf nodded.

"Do you know how long it has been since I had aykopyra? Not to mention meat as it should be eaten."

"I can fathom a guess, son. I did not think you could obtain this in any human taverns or inns, can you?"

He shook his head as he lifted the large, by human standards, pitcher with both his hands and carefully poured the dark orange liquid into what he knew was the smallest goblet the drageals had. He lifted the goblet, again with both hands, to his mouth and took a small sip.

"Oh my, this is even better than I recall. Thank you so much for remembering, Mother."

"As if I could or would ever forget your fondness for it. Even as a babe…" she said and smiled.

He did not understand her reference and she did not elaborate, so he took another sip and savored every drop that trickled down his throat.

"Now, son, tell me more of what is going on with your life? Am I to assume you have yet to find a mate?"

He shook his head.

"What of the one who was traveling with you?"

Zabaneja coughed nervously. He tried to calm his thoughts before he spoke of Rusalei. He wanted to tell his mother only that she had wanted to meet the drageals, but then changed her mind, which was, to a degree, the truth.

That was his plan. But he had almost forgotten that when one looked into the eyes of a drageal who wished the full truth, intentions, no matter how good, got lost and one could only speak the truth in its entirety. And so it was with this conversation. His wish to leave much unsaid was lost and instead, he spoke of everything that was in his heart, things that up until this moment, he had not been aware of.

The angst and pain in his voice broke her heart, but Pheunaf said nothing. She listened to him reveal his true emotions, because she knew he would not say such things to anyone else. When the last of his story had been told, Pheunaf silently opened her wings and beckoned him into her embrace. He immediately obeyed and let out a sigh of relief as the black and gold feathers engulfed him in a cloak of security and love.

Neither Zabaneja nor Pheunaf allowed his self-pity to linger. In only a moment or so, Zabaneja had collected himself and Pheunaf opened her wings.

"I am sorry, Mother," he said, shaking his head. "I am acting like a mewling babe over something I have no way to change."

"We all have our hearts broken at one time or another and if we do not allow the emotion out, it will fester until it eats away at our very core, making us vile and wicked. And, as for your lady, I think you do not give her enough credit for being her own woman intent upon forging her own path. After all, no son of mine would ever fall in love with a sniveling child. But I am sure things will work out as they are meant to."

He did not reply.

"Now, let us get down to the reason for your coming here this day."

Zabaneja nodded and proceeded to tell her his plan to get the other human provinces, as well as some of the other races, involved in the war against Darchok.

He looked into her eyes and shook his head. "I am not sure what land dwellers can do against those of the sky, but we cannot, must not, sit idly by. If Darchok wins this war, no one will be safe from his wrath."

Pheunaf nodded. "I agree. Have you approached any of the other factions?"

"Not yet. I did not want to do so until I was sure you would welcome our meager assistance."

"Of course, I do."

"Good. May I ask that one of the drageals take a message to Guentza, the captain of Aneesyma's guard, the one who also assisted with your fallen comrade? He is waiting in a secluded place for word before he continues to the capital city to approach their King on this matter."

"Naturally, tell us where he is. And the other groups?"

"Kalini has been meeting with the chetoga and has set up a meeting for us with another race called the emuranda. She feels their herd queen, Jucara, may be willing to join our cause."

"I have heard the emuranda are a noble race," Pheunaf said. "When will you leave?"

"As soon as possible, I am afraid."

"Of course, but you must at least stay the night. You have many friends here who have missed the pleasure of your company."

"And I, theirs."

#

The rest of the night was spent reminiscing and discussing the best ways for the land dwellers to be of assistance to the drageals.

"What if none of the humans or the others agree to your plan?

What will you do then?"

Zabaneja recognized Phrynia's voice.

"I can guarantee the help of Aneesyma, the ruler of the land where I currently reside, whether or not anyone else joins."

"And what good would one small group of humans be in our fight?"

"Phrynia, hold your tongue," Nanetscka snapped at her niece.

"That is a valid question. We had the same discussion before I was dispatched here. And truth be told, we do not know. Perhaps, we will be no help at all."

Phrynia stared at him, surprised by his response.

Nanetscka nodded. "Do go on."

"Even if we are of little or no help to you, we cannot stand by and do nothing. As you know, the Keep has already been affected by the war. When your comrade died in our courtyard, some of our people were lost and many others injured. And, less importantly, the damage done to structures and livelihoods. So, you see Phrynia, while we may not be able to mount a great assault, we still feel we must help. For everyone's sake."

Phrynia's embarrassment did not allow her to respond at first, but when she looked at Zabaneja, the kindness in his eyes and the nod he gave her made her feel better.

"I am sorry. I was rude and out of line."

Nanetscka looked at her niece with amazement. Only later that night, as everyone was departing, did she tell Zabaneja this was the first time Phrynia had ever apologized to anyone.

Just after the sunrise, Zabaneja bade his mother and the others farewell. He walked down the mountainside and found his horse still contentedly tethered to the tree. Zabaneja patted the horse on the rump and left for his meeting with Kalini.

CHAPTER FORTY-FOUR

ZABANEJA ARRIVED and found Kalini with two others. Emuranda, he assumed. They looked nothing like anything he had ever seen nor imagined; as if someone had sewn bits of several animals together—a horse's head, moose's antlers, and hair that hung like thick ropes to the ground.

Kalini motioned him to join them. As he approached, he felt an odd sensation within his mind and remembered emuranda did not speak out loud but rather directly into your mind. If you did not know how to speak back to them, they would merely read your thoughts, all your thoughts.

:Jucara will meet with you. Follow us.: Zabaneja heard in his mind a few moments later.

Zabaneja and Kalini did as instructed, with no further communication from their escorts. About an hour later, they entered a clearing. He looked around, but saw no one. They continued to follow the two emuranda until told to stop and wait. The two guides walked away but said no more.

"I see all went well with Pheunaf," Kalini said, breaking the silence.

Zabaneja nodded. "And what of the chetoga? Are they in agreement?"

"Most are. There are still some holdouts. They feel we are too small for something so large as a drageal to even take notice."

"They do not know Darchok."

"No, they do not and I hope they will never will," Kalini added.

Zabaneja twitched a little, as if trying to shake something off of him.

Kalini smiled. "Do not fear. The sensation is merely the emuranda looking into your mind."

He looked at her, somewhat surprised. "I thought you said they would not do that."

"I did. And, those we will be dealing with in the negotiations will not. But, like in the drageal camp or in the Keep, the herd contains more than diplomats, and as I told you, emuranda have no concept of privacy nor so-called politeness."

Zabaneja nodded.

:It has been quite some time since you crossed into our land, Kalini. Why have you come now? And with a human,: they heard as a large emuranda approached.

Kalini chuckled. "Jucara, do not try to use subterfuge on me, you are not skilled at such ploys, and are fully aware of the reason for our coming. Zabaneja and I are here to discuss the war raging between the drageal factions and how it will affect us all. And, more importantly, what we can do to help end it."

Jucara nodded and laughed into their minds. *:Very true, Kalini. So this is Zabaneja. We have heard of you, human. You are unique, to say the least. I would have never thought a human could be raised from birth by drageals, but then again, Pheunaf is quite extraordinary herself.:*

"That she is." Zabaneja said.

Jucara smiled. *:I find it interesting that even with your ties to the drageals, you do not blindly support them. You have your doubts about not only if the humans can get involved, but if they even should.:*

"War is never something to be entered into without extensive scrutiny, even if its reason is just," he replied, not reacting to the fact she was in his mind.

She nodded. *:I, too, have been contemplating many of the same things and have come up against the same dilemmas. I feel all sentient races of this world must take action. For if Darchok's forces defeat Pheunaf, none of us will be safe. But how can we assist in a war that takes place in the air, where we hold no dominion?:*

"I have no answer. Only that I know we must find a way," Zabaneja said.

:I see in your mind, perhaps in places you have yet to explore, the seed of a plan.:

He was surprised she saw something he was not aware of.

:Between us, I believe we can devise a strategy that will benefit all. The first thing is to gather allies. I am aware you have requested support from the humans. That is good. I will approach those races you and Kalini have no dealings with.:

"Thank you, Jucara," Kalini said. "Time is of the essence in getting this alliance together. We need representatives from any group who agrees to join us to meet and form an actual plan." She looked at the others and saw agreement. "I suggest we meet three weeks from today. There is an area about a half day's travel east of here that can easily accommodate all of us."

"Three weeks..." Zabaneja said. "That long."

:I do not think we can feasibly get the others together any sooner.:

He reluctantly agreed.

:I look forward to our next meeting, young Zabaneja. And, yes, I do believe there is a way for you to learn how to talk with us and thereby only share the thoughts you wish rather than all of your mind.: She smiled as she watched him digest her words. Zabaneja did not bother to question her comment, he knew if she was going to give him any more explanation, she would have already done so.

#

Two days later, after briefing Pheunaf on his meeting with Kalini and Jucara, Zabaneja was on his way back to the Keep. He wondered if Guentza was having as much success at court as he had with the drageals and the others.

Zabaneja tried to keep his mind on the plans to ally with the others, but his mother's words about Rusalei kept creeping into his thoughts. As wise as Pheunaf was, she knew little of human emotions. He barely understood them himself. She could not understand how his words and actions had affected Rusalei; how they forced her from love to hate. And, the fact he had done such a thing to her, hurt him more than anything he had ever known.

During the day, he was able, with some success, to put such thoughts out of his mind. Nighttime was a different matter. Whenever he closed his eyes to sleep, all he could see, all he could think of, was Rusalei. And when he did finally fall asleep, his dreams were filled with her—her sight, her scent, her feel. In his dreams, he relived their night together. Upon waking, his breathing was heavy, his body sweating and every fiber of his being ached with desire for her.

The last day of his journey he woke to the realization that once back at the Keep, he would be forced to face her. He wondered how they would handle it. Ha! She would not be the one struggling with the situation. She was a noble and, as always, would handle herself with decorum. If anyone was to make a fool of themselves, it would be him. He took a deep breath and prepared for the day's ride.

CHAPTER FORTY-FIVE

RUSALEI KEPT TO HERSELF upon her return, refusing to tell anyone, even Aneesyma, where she had been. She considered resigning from the council and returning to her father's house to avoid Zabaneja, but instantly rebuked herself for such thoughts. She would not sacrifice everything she was, all she had worked so hard to attain, for a man who clearly did not want her. On more than one occasion, she wondered if his plan all along was to toy with her, tease her by denying he wanted her until she pushed herself upon him? Then, as she pathetically begged, he could take her, enjoy the pleasures of her body and what she could do to his, then toss her aside as a trivial conquest. She shook her head. A short time ago, she would have fought anyone who would have even hinted Zabaneja was that kind of man. Now, she was not so sure.

Still, there was a problem. Once he returned, they would be unable to avoid each other. If she acted rudely or ignored him completely, questions would be asked about her change in attitude. No, she had to treat him the same as she always had and she would make sure he treated her as the noble he insisted she was. If he chose to act differently, then it would be him, not her, who would need to explain. And, should he tell anyone she had seduced him, she would most emphatically deny such an accusation.

#

A week or so after Rusalei's return, word came that Zabaneja had been sighted approaching a nearby village and would arrive at the Keep by midday. With that news, Aneesyma called the council to session. As usual, Haoule arrived first, followed by Tuzzern's replacement, Jakaher. Rusalei arrived a few moments later.

"Have we any word from Guentza in Siggurna?" Aneesyma asked after everyone was seated. The three ministers shook their heads. Aneesyma chuckled. "I am not surprised. I doubt if dealing with the court is as straightforward as dealing with drageals or the others. If we get no word by end of day tomorrow, we will send a messenger bird to the capital."

The ministers agreed.

"What do you think Zab will have to say about his mission?" Haoule asked.

Rusalei involuntarily snickered.

"Have you something to say, Rusalei?" Aneesyma asked.

"I am sorry, My Lord. But is Zab's success not a foregone conclusion?" The ministers and Aneesyma looked at her but did not comment. "Surely he would not be returning if he had not completed his mission to his personal satisfaction."

Aneesyma nodded. "Still, we need to hear the details. And we need to determine the status of our troops."

"I have asked Canackell, the acting captain of the guard in Guentza's absence, to gather the data and bring it to us. She should be here shortly," Haoule replied.

"Good," Aneesyma said.

"May I be allowed to speak, My Lord?" Jakaher asked.

"Of course, in this council you are always free to speak," Aneesyma answered.

Jakaher thrummed his fingers nervously on the table and gathered his thoughts. "While I am not against aligning ourselves with Pheunaf and her forces, I wonder how large of a commitment this is going to be. I mean, how many of our men and women will we be attaching to this effort?"

"That is what we are here to discuss, Jakaher," Zabaneja said, startling the group around the table who had not heard him enter.

Haoule and Jakaher jumped from their seats and went to the young man, patting him on the back and shaking his hand. Rusalei stayed in her seat trying to control her conflicted emotions. The desire to slap his face and call him a string of unladylike names or to jump in his arms, wrap her legs around his waist and thrust her tongue deep into his mouth. Instead, she sat, clenching her fists in her lap.

"So, Jakaher, you are the newest member of the council. As always, His Lordship has made an excellent choice," Zabaneja said and pushed his way past the two ministers.

He saw Rusalei sitting there and his heart soared. He nodded at her and, though she nodded back, the cold look in her eyes made his heart plummet. He bowed to Aneesyma.

"It is good to have you back, Zab," Aneesyma said and patted him on the shoulder. "I hope you bring us good news."

Aneesyma motioned Zabaneja to be seated beside him. He nodded to the servant in the corner. The boy immediately left the room and returned with a tray piled high with meat pies, fruit, and pitchers of cider and ale. He placed the tray on the table in front of Zabaneja and began to serve, but was motioned away by Aneesyma. The young boy bowed and left the room.

Aneesyma looked at Zabaneja. "Do help yourself. I surmise you have not had a decent meal since you left the drageal camp."

Canackell knocked and entered the chamber.

"Perfect timing, Canackell," Aneesyma said. "You can give us your report while Zab catches up on a meal or two."

Canackell nodded and began, stopping to answer questions. Though given only a short time to gather the information, the council was impressed with both the completeness and accuracy of her report.

"Thank you, Canackell," Aneesyma said as the young woman concluded. "Gentlemen. Lady. Are there any other questions on this matter?" He looked around the table and when there were no questions, he nodded to Canackell to be seated and continued. "I must say, we are in a better position number-wise than I would have expected."

All agreed.

"And now for your news, Zab," Aneesyma said.

Zabaneja nodded. "Before I begin, is there any news from Guentza on his progress with the King?"

Aneesyma smiled. "We were discussing that before you arrived. And, as I was saying, I am sure Guentza is having to navigate a lot trickier diplomatic waters than you did."

"Yes, I am sure that is true," Zabaneja said. "As for my mission, I met with Pheunaf, as well as representatives from the chetoga and another race called the emuranda. All think an alliance between our peoples is a good idea. In fact, the emuranda leader is contacting other groups to try to get them to join the effort."

"And have you and the others come up with a way that we will be of use to the drageals?" Rusalei asked.

Though her voice appeared normal, Zabaneja felt a coldness not there when she questioned Canackell.

"Not yet, Lady Rusalei. That is one of the things each group is being tasked with—to come up with possible solutions before we all meet again in about two weeks."

"I see," Rusalei replied.

"And if we still do not have a response from Siggurna by then?" Haoule asked.

"I would hope the wheels of the King's court and council do not turn that slowly," Zabaneja began. "But, if they do, my recommendation is to send our envoy as planned. Unless the decision has been made to only join the alliance if the other provinces do."

Aneesyma shook his head. "No, we have already seen, albeit on a small scale, the devastation the conflict can cause, so we are committed."

Zabaneja breathed a sigh of relief.

"If Siggurna and the other provinces decide to join us, they can do so at a later time," Aneesyma said and saw the others also in agreement.

"Our next step then is to strategize ways we can be of use in this war. I want each of you to meet with whomever you feel can be helpful in this endeavor. Remember to consider all possibilities, regardless of how far-fetched they may at first appear," Zabaneja said.

The others nodded.

"Good, then we will meet again tomorrow afternoon."

All around the table rose, bowed, and headed for the door.

"Zab, please remain," Aneesyma said.

When the others had all left the room, closing the door behind them, Aneesyma motioned Zabaneja to sit. He did so as Aneesyma poured two glasses of ale and handed one to him.

"To a successful mission," Aneesyma said as the two men clinked their glasses. "So, Zab, how is your mother?"

"As well as can be expected. Though I can see the war and its casualties, to drageals and all others, weigh heavily upon her brow."

"If it did not, she would not be the leader she is."

Aneesyma knew from the moment Zabaneja walked in the council chamber there was something troubling him. He assumed it might have to do with his mother. Yet, as their discussion of Pheunaf and the rest of Zabaneja's kin progressed, Aneesyma felt certain that, while the young man was concerned about his mother, there was something else weighing on his mind. Something he did not want to discuss.

CHAPTER FORTY-SIX

ZABANEJA WENT TO CHECK IN with Canackell for an update on what had been going on in his absence. As expected, she was in the barracks. As he entered, she and several others came to welcome him back.

"I did not mean to interrupt you, Canackell," Zabaneja said. "Please continue with what you were doing."

Canackell nodded. "Thank you, sir. We were discussing ways we might be of use against Darchok and his forces."

"And have you come up with anything?"

"Well, we have some ideas, but to be honest," said one of the younger female recruits, "I am not sure any are feasible."

"Yes, unlike you, Zab, none of us had never seen a drageal until the unfortunate incident in the courtyard," one of the other men chimed in. "So, we are really not sure what..."

The man hesitated, and Canackell finished his thought. "What would be appropriate behavior?"

Zabaneja was confused. "What do you mean?"

"Well, would they allow someone to ride on their backs? Or would they consider that, oh I do not know, demeaning or worse."

Zabaneja thought for a moment. "In my clan, when I reached a certain size, we devised a way for me to fly on the backs of my friends."

While it was now common knowledge Zabaneja was raised by drageals, those gathered had never considered he had actually taken to the sky with them. They immediately began bombarding him with questions.

"Hold on, now." Zabaneja chuckled. "You must remember that just because those in my clan had no issue with me flying on their backs, I cannot speak for other clans. I cannot even say with certainty that my clan would allow others to do so."

The enthusiasm for Zabaneja's initial statement instantly ebbed.

"Still," he continued, "we will not know unless we ask. So, I suggest you continue to work on ideas, regardless of how far-fetched or implausible they may initially sound. The very nature of this war will require unique actions never before tried."

Those around the table looked relieved at Zabaneja's words.

"That is a good way to look at it," the older soldier said.

Zabaneja nodded. "Canackell, if I may tear you away for a moment, I would like you to catch me up on the aftermath of the drageal tragedy."

"Of course, sir."

Over the next few moments, Canackell gave her report. Sadly, there had been additional deaths, the final total was fifteen, but most of the other injuries turned out to be minor and were no longer requiring the aid of the healers. As for the tower, that was coming along more slowly. A great deal of the rubble had been removed, but most was so badly damaged it was not reusable. And acquiring new material was proving both costly and time consuming.

"At least it was the tower and not any of the dwellings,"

Zabaneja said. "We can do without a clock in the courtyard, but cannot face the seasons without a place to live. If that is all, I will let you get back to your duties. If you need me, I will be in my quarters."

"Of course, sir," Canackell said. "You deserve a good night's rest. I do not foresee having to disturb you."

#

Zabaneja leisurely strolled to his rooms. There was little to be done at that moment, so he decided a long hot soak would be in order. He climbed the stairs and found a set of clean clothes lying on the bed waiting for him.

He went into the adjoining bathroom and began to draw the hot bath. As the tub filled, he pulled off his boots and then stripped out of his clothes, which were covered in road dirt, and left them on the bedroom floor. He climbed into the tub and sank into it until he was completely immersed in the soothing hot water. He closed his eyes. As he did, he remembered the last bath he had taken and was torn as to whether he wanted a repeat of that night.

For good or not, the dream did not return and as the last bit of warmth left the water, Zabaneja stepped out of the tub. He shook his head like a dog, wrapped himself in a towel and returned to the bedroom to find the bed turned down and the dirty clothes removed. He poured a large glass of spiced mead from the decanter on the nightstand and proceeded, still wrapped in the towel, to climb to the roof.

He stood by the low wall and slowly sipped on the sweet yet spicy liquor. He looked out across the horizon and watched the sun go down. Being this high up always made him homesick for his life among the drageal, soaring high in the air, the wind blowing across his face. Still, he was glad for this place.

He finished his drink and headed downstairs. He poured another drink, dropped the towel on the floor and went to the bookcase on the opposite side of the room to retrieve a book that, though he had read it before, was one of his favorites. He tossed it onto the bed then lit the bedside lamp and doused the others. He crawled into bed and let out a sigh as his body settled into the soft comfort of the luxurious feather bed. He picked up the glass from the table and took a large sip, opened the book and began reading. Long before the lamp extinguished itself, Zabaneja was fast asleep, book on his chest and half full glass of mead on the table.

CHAPTER FORTY-SEVEN

THE NEXT DAY, a messenger bird arrived from the capital. While some of the other lords were initially reticent to join the alliance with the drageals, claiming it was not their fight, the king felt differently. In the long run, he reminded them, the conflict would eventually impact everyone, not only in his kingdom but in all corners of this world. On more than one occasion, he reiterated to everyone that borders were of no consequence to drageals. Finally, after some persuading, he convinced all of his provinces to agree to join the alliance. The message said Guentza and an envoy from the king would depart immediately after the bird was dispatched and should arrive at the Keep within three days.

"That is good to hear," Zabaneja said. "Now they will be able to attend the meeting with the others."

Aneesyma nodded. "Yes, but I sense you still have some concerns."

Zabaneja smiled, he was no longer surprised when Aneesyma seemed to read his thoughts. "I was merely wondering what kind of people the king will be sending."

"Ah, I forgot, you have never met His Majesty. I will tell you, he is one who puts duty above all else, so I am confident whomever he sends will be the most suited for the task at hand."

"So, you are a lot like him then, eh?"

"That is one of the highest compliments anyone could pay me."

#

Zabaneja was summoned to Aneesyma's chambers later that evening. He entered to find Aneesyma and Rusalei sharing a meal. Zabaneja felt his entire body stiffen at the sight of her. He tried to calm himself, hoping his inner turmoil was not evident.

"My Lord. Lady Rusalei." Zabaneja bowed to them. "You needed to speak to me, sir?"

"Yes." Aneesyma pointed to the chair beside Rusalei.

Almost as soon as Zabaneja was seated, a young servant girl appeared and placed a plate of food in front of him. He ate as Aneesyma and Rusalei exchanged some inconsequential conversation. Zabaneja listened, but did not comment.

"Ah, you are done." Aneesyma said as the same servant girl refilled everyone's drinks and took Zabaneja's empty plate away. "I am sure you are both wondering why I called you here."

Zabaneja and Rusalei nodded.

Aneesyma rose and walked across the room. "The obvious reason, of course, is to discuss who will be attending the meeting with the drageals."

"Should that not be discussed in the council?" Zabaneja asked.

"It will be, but I also wanted your personal opinions."

The pair nodded.

"But, before we get to that, I have another, more pressing, subject to discuss. I want to know what is going on between you two." He looked at them and tried to hide a smile as their faces became as red as winter apples.

"I do not know what you mean, My Lord," Zabaneja sputtered.

"Nor do I," Rusalei added.

Aneesyma threw his head back and laughed. "Oh, please. You are not fooling anyone, least of all me."

The pair stared at him, neither daring to look at each other.

"I am sorry, My Lord. I am not sure what gave you the idea there was something other than business between the lady and myself, but you are wrong," Zabaneja said.

Rusalei nodded.

Aneesyma shook his head. "All right, let us say I believe you. What do you think if both of you are part of our envoy to the talks?"

Zabaneja swallowed hard, realizing his deepest fear about this mission was coming to pass. "Lady Rusalei would be an excellent choice. She has a keen sense of diplomacy, as well as a knack for seeing the big picture in all situations. And, though they may not be necessary here, her combat skills are unrivaled."

"No! No, I would most definitely not be a good choice," Rusalei said, her voice cracking.

"Why not?" Aneesyma asked. "Do you disagree with Zab's assessment of your abilities? Or do you have another reason?"

Rusalei, who was now wringing her hands in front of her on the table, sighed. "I am flattered by Zab's confidence in my abilities, but I believe, in this situation, he is mistaken."

"And why is that?" Aneesyma asked, noting neither of them had yet to look at the other.

"Because My Lord..." She hesitated. "I would be too much in awe of the drageals and the others to be able to think clearly."

"Well, Rusalei, I appreciate your candor, though I do not agree with it. With that said, I think we are done here."

Rusalei and Zabaneja nodded and rose from their seats, bowed and proceeded to the door. Zabaneja allowed Rusalei to leave first. Once outside, the couple quickly parted without a word.

#

Two days later, Aneesyma met with the council along with Zabaneja, Guentza, and the members of the king's envoy to announce the Keep's representatives to the upcoming meeting. As expected, Zabaneja and Guentza were named. Then, to everyone's surprise, Aneesyma revealed he and Rusalei would also be attending.

"My Lord," one of the king's men began, "I must express my apprehension regarding your being part of this expedition. I fear it is not wise."

"I expected someone to say that, but I have thoroughly thought this through and my decision stands."

The man nodded but still looked concerned.

"Is there something else troubling you?" When Aneesyma saw the young man's reluctance to respond, he continued, "Oh, do go on, man, you are here as an advisor so do that—advise. Tell me what is troubling you?"

The man coughed nervously, then took a deep breath. "Well, My Lord, to be perfectly honest, I am concerned over your mode of transportation. Do you plan to travel in a carriage with a swarm of servants buzzing around you? If so, and please forgive my frankness..."

Aneesyma smiled. "Continue."

"If that is your intention, I fear you will not only slow us down, but you might also attract unwanted attention from, at the very least, bandits or, at worse, Darchok and his forces."

"What would you have me do, besides stay home?"

"As much as I would like that, I see your mind is made up to the contrary. So, my suggestion is you travel incognito, dressed the same as the rest of us, with no servants."

"That is an interesting suggestion." Aneesyma chuckled. "As you can see, good sir, none of my people voiced the same concern because they already know that is my plan. They are aware I am perfectly capable of tending to my own needs on the road. So, that should not be an issue."

"I apologize, My Lord. I was not aware of that," the man said.

"Nor did I expect you to be. I am glad you brought it up." Aneesyma then turned to Zabaneja. "There seems to be something weighing on your mind, as well."

"I fear we have too large a company to travel as a single group or even by the same route. If someone is indeed watching, which may or may not be the case, the mere size of the group could draw unwanted attention."

"Go on."

"We should divide ourselves into smaller groups, perhaps three at the most, with each group leaving on a different day and traveling via a different route."

Aneesyma smiled at the attention to detail, accompanied by just the right amount of suspicion that made Zabaneja so good at his job.

"I agree wholeheartedly. And since there are nine of us, three groups of three is the perfect breakdown. Zabaneja, Rusalei and I will comprise one group..." Aneesyma had all he could do to contain himself from breaking into uncontrolled laughter at the looks of horror on both Zabaneja's and Rusalei's faces at his statement. "And we can split up the King's men so two of them travel with Guentza and two go with Rikar." Aneesyma turned to the young man, "I understand you are now one of the King's staff, Rikar, but I still count you as one of our own."

Rikar smiled. "Thank you, My Lord."

"So, are there any other comments? Questions? Protestations?" Aneesyma asked.

Zabaneja wanted to argue. To say it would be better if someone from the king's group came with him and Aneesyma, but knew any dissension would be squelched.

"Good. Then it is settled." Aneesyma then turned to Zabaneja. "You and the others can map out the best routes for each group. I will prepare for the trek. Just send word where and when we will meet."

It took only a short time and little discussion to chart the routes for the journey. Since each group was to follow a different path, the first group, Zabaneja's, would arrive in five days and each of the others a day or so after.

CHAPTER FORTY-EIGHT

ZABANEJA, RUSALEI AND ANEESYMA, the first group, departed the Keep just after sunrise. Once on the road, the talk turned to the upcoming meeting. And, for the time being, Rusalei and Zabaneja put aside their complex personal relationship and engaged in lively discussion.

Just before midday, the group stopped to eat and rest. Aneesyma immediately set to tending to the horses. An action that shocked Rusalei.

"Should we not be doing that rather than having His Lordship perform such menial labor?" she whispered.

Zabaneja stifled the laugh forming in his throat. "You can try, but I do believe he is not only capable but willing to pull his fair share." Zabaneja saw Rusalei's disbelief at his words and continued. "And I would wager he rather enjoys getting away from the flurry of attention paid to him every time he even looks as if he wants or needs something."

"Of course," Rusalei said. "His day-to-day life is even worse than mine when I go to my father's house—every time I so much as take a breath someone is flitting around me and trying to do something to help me. I cannot stand it! I guess I never imagined he would feel the same." She looked at Zabaneja's smile, experiencing a pang of desire deep within her and quickly turned away.

Once the horses were tended to, the three sat and ate the meat pies they had packed.

"You seemed to be very concerned about me earlier, Rusalei," Aneesyma said between mouthfuls of pie. "Did you not think I knew how to tend to a horse?"

Rusalei almost choked on her food. As she coughed and tried to explain herself, Aneesyma slapped his knee and laughed.

"So, Zabaneja, do you think Pheunaf herself will attend this meeting?" Aneesyma asked, changing the subject.

Zabaneja nodded. "Unless something has changed since last we met, she will. She was very keen upon being there for both its enormity and precedence. I do not believe there has ever been a uniting of so many groups before, well, at least not in any of the tales I have heard nor the histories I have read."

"Well, if you have not read of it, then it did not exist." Rusalei added and then saw the quizzical looks on her companions' faces. "Well, he has read—no, more like devoured—nearly every history book in existence within the kingdom."

Aneesyma laughed. "Yes, our Zab has become quite the scholar."

"Do you think I will be able to introduce myself to the others in dragealian, Zab?" Rusalei asked without thinking.

"Oh ho," Aneesyma laughed. "And, just when did you learn to speak dragealian, young lady? Was it when the two of you were off alone together?"

Both Rusalei and Zabaneja began to sputter.

"Off together?" Zabaneja asked.

"We were never off together," Rusalei added, then looked to

Zabaneja for confirmation.

"I have no idea what you are speaking of, My Lord."

Aneesyma smiled, certain their reaction had confirmed his previous suspicions.

"As a matter of fact," Zabaneja continued, "I taught Rus... Lady Rusalei a few words in dragealian after Nanetscka and the others had removed the felled drageal from the courtyard."

Zabaneja's stumble over Rusalei's name was not lost on Aneesyma. "Oh, did you now?"

"Yes, My Lord, I heard him speaking with the drageals and asked him if he could teach me a little something."

Aneesyma nodded. "Oh, I see. So, have you learned any?"

"Only a word or two. We were interrupted by his mission to Pheunaf."

"And there were no more dragealian lessons during those, was it two or three, days you were together after you followed him. No wait, actually you left first, waited, and then followed him. If you were not learning dragealian during that time, what on earth were you doing? Especially on that night when the rains were so heavy you had to take shelter from the elements."

Rusalei wanted to confess all—her love for Zabaneja, what happened that night, everything. But Zabaneja's icy stare stopped her.

"I am sorry, My Lord, you are mistaken. I know not where you heard such tales of folly. The Lady Rusalei would never do such a thing as chase after the likes of me, and I would never do anything so inappropriate as to allow her to travel with me without proper escort."

Aneesyma threw back his head in laughter. He walked to where his two companions sat, nervously fidgeting. He placed his hands under their chins and lifted their faces toward him. He stared deeply into their eyes then released their chins and stood silently staring at them for a few moments, reveling in their confusion and guilt. After what seemed an eternity to Zabaneja and Rusalei, Aneesyma finally smiled.

"The both of you are horrific liars, you know. The sexual tension in the air around you is so thick, one could cut it with a knife."

"But... " Zabaneja sputtered.

Aneesyma laughed. "Do not even try to deny you have sated, at least once, your lust for each other. You each bear the mark of the other on the visible parts of your bodies. And, I am sure, that, if stripped naked, well..."

Zabaneja and Rusalei stared at Aneesyma and then looked at each other as if trying to see if there was such a mark. It had been more than a month since their encounter, and any residue from that night had surely been washed away. Yet Aneesyma knew everything. But how?

"I doubt if either of you were aware such a thing existed. Only those, like myself, with a certain gift can see it," Aneesyma lied.

The pair now looked directly at him, afraid to look at each other for fear of what other sign they might convey. The couple, whose faces were now a shade of crimson even the royal dyer could not achieve, bowed their heads in as much embarrassment as shame.

"You love each other," Aneesyma said, all sarcasm or amusement gone from his voice, "so why do you deny it? Especially since I must assume the experience you shared was unbelievably satisfying."

The pair was silent while Aneesyma sat waiting patiently.

Finally, Zabaneja looked up and cleared his throat. "Whether it be by the gift of some special sight or by spy, you apparently know all that went on between us," he began, his voice barely above a whisper and shaky. "But you, of all people, having lived through a similar situation, know I have no right to dare to have feelings for Lady

Rusalei, much less pursue or make love to her. She is nobility and I am not."

"I will not elaborate on my situation, but know it is not the same," Aneesyma said.

Zabaneja shook his head. "I see no difference."

"Even so, I think there is something else going on here. Something other than just class differences."

"And what is that?"

"I am not sure. You have told me many times there are no classes amongst drageals, so your use of that is an excuse. Why then do you mask your true feelings? Is it because you still do not trust us? That you still do not consider yourself to be one of us? That you have no intention of remaining with us, your own kind?"

"You are not my kind!"

Rusalei was shocked not only by the tone of Zabaneja's voice but also by the anger bordering on hatred in it. She had never heard him speak so vehemently to a servant, much less his lordship. Yet, Aneesyma did not seem surprised nor upset. No, it was almost as if he had not even heard him.

"Alright, Zab, I will say no more on the matter." Aneesyma had risen and was now standing beside the young man. He put his arm around Zabaneja's shoulder.

Zabaneja broke from Aneesyma's grasp and bolted. He threw himself up on the back of his unsaddled horse, grabbed onto its mane and took off at a gallop.

#

Aneesyma stood shaking his head. After a moment he turned to the dazed Rusalei.

"So, will you tell me what went on or do you also intend to bolt, leaving me to have to carry two extra saddles?" he asked as he sat beside her.

Rusalei looked into Aneesyma's eyes but remained silent. Then, almost against her will and better judgement, she began. "From the moment he arrived at the Keep, dirty and illiterate, barely able to speak, I was drawn to him. Sometimes I had to actually stop myself from chasing after him. Eventually, I badgered Father into letting me enroll in weaponry classes, just to get to know him. All was going well, or so I thought, but as soon as we completed our training, he changed. He became distant, especially once I was appointed to the council. Every time I approached him, even as a friend, he would push me away saying it was not proper for someone of my class to associate with him, even though he had no problems associating with you and the other nobles."

She looked at Aneesyma to see his reaction and saw him nodding as if he knew exactly what she meant.

"And when did you decide to pursue him more aggressively?"

The young noble woman blushed and looked away. "I thought if we were alone and away from the Keep, we could both admit our feelings."

"And is that what happened?"

"In a way..." She hesitated, and Aneesyma did not press her. He waited patiently for her to gather her thoughts, and her courage.

Once she began, she told him the occurrences of their rainy day and night together and how the passion turned to pain the following morning. She repeated Zabaneja's hurtful words. She spoke of how she wept openly on the road home and how it took more than a few days to come to grips, at least to a degree, with her feelings.

Aneesyma's heart broke for her, but knew this was no time to show her pity. That was not what she needed.

"Why does he still feel he does not belong with us? she asked.

"I do not know," he said. "Only he can tell us for certain."

She nodded but said nothing more.

#

Zabaneja was livid as he rode. When he felt he was far enough away from them, he stopped and took several deep breaths to regain his composure. When calm, he turned the horse around and returned. Regardless of his personal issues, there was a mission to be accomplished that far outweighed the problems of any one individual.

Zabaneja slowly approached. He stopped and slid off his horse's bare back and walked silently toward Aneesyma.

"I apologize for my rude and childish behavior, My Lord." Zabaneja bowed deeply.

"I understand," Aneesyma replied.

"If you and the lady are almost ready, we should be on our way."

Aneesyma nodded and Zabaneja walked to the horses and began re-saddling them. Aneesyma and Rusalei gathered their things and within a few minutes, the trio was on the road again. Unlike the morning's ride, which had been filled with talk about the mission, they rode in silence.

Before sunset, they found a spot to make camp for the night. As in the afternoon, Aneesyma took care of the horses, Rusalei gathered wood for the fire, and Zabaneja retrieved the evening's meal from the pack. After everyone had eaten, Rusalei broke the uncomfortable silence that had permeated both the afternoon's ride and the evening meal, asking if they were still on schedule.

"If we cover the same distance we did today," Zabaneja began, "and, barring any unforeseen problems, we should arrive as planned."

"And the other factions? When do you think they will arrive?"

Rusalei asked.

"The meeting is not scheduled to begin for another seven days, so everyone should be there by then. Though, knowing Pheunaf and the other drageals, they will be monitoring the area for everyone's arrival."

"Will we be the first?" Aneesyma asked.

"Of the humans, yes. I am not sure about any of the others. As for the rest of our people, they should arrive over the next two days after we do." Zabaneja replied.

Aneesyma nodded his approval at the assessment. "Well, we have another long day ahead of us tomorrow, so I suggest we get some rest."

It did not escape Aneesyma nor Rusalei that Zabaneja set up his bed as far to the edge of their camp as he could.

CHAPTER FORTY-NINE

BEFORE SUNSET on the fifth day of their journey, a few hours after they had originally planned to arrive, they reached the meeting place and found they were the first there.

"I thought you said the drageals would be here," Rusalei said as they set up their camp and sat down to their evening meal.

Zabaneja motioned to the sky. "They have been here all along."

"Who do you think will be the next to arrive?" Aneesyma asked.

"I am not sure who is actually coming, so it could be the chetoga, the emuranda or someone else."

"Ah, the emuranda," Aneesyma said. "You say they do not really speak, correct?"

"Not as we think of it."

"Oh, yes, I had almost forgotten about that," Rusalei added nervously. "They talk directly into our minds."

Zabaneja nodded. "In a way, they read our minds to find our replies."

"So, they can basically see anything we are thinking?" Aneesyma asked.

"Yes."

"That seems a bit unethical," Rusalei added.

Zabaneja smiled. "Perhaps, but as I was reminded, emuranda, like most other beings, do not hold themselves to the same so-called morality humans do. You will find they do not understand much of what they find in our minds. So, do not be surprised if one of them asks you to clarify something you would likely never discuss in public."

Rusalei reddened at the thought of some things in her mind the emuranda might see and worse want to talk about.

"But the good thing is, whatever they ask will usually be only to you, so no one else will hear," Zabaneja added.

Aneesyma had all he could do not to laugh at her sigh of relief at Zabaneja's last statement.

A few moments into their meal, Zabaneja stood. "The drageals are landing," he said, and walked toward the open field.

Neither Aneesyma nor Rusalei had felt nor seen anything, but knew better than to question Zabaneja when it came to drageals. Before they could say anything more, three massive drageals landed in a circle around Zabaneja, virtually hiding him from view. Rusalei drew in a breath of awe and found herself staring. She rose, wanting to run over to where they were, but Aneesyma gently grabbed her arm.

"Give him a moment," Aneesyma said.

Rusalei reluctantly sat down.

#

"Mother," Zabaneja said as the drageals landed around him. "I am so happy to see you again."

"And I you, son." Pheunaf looked at the silhouettes of the two people sitting off in the distance. "Is this all of your party?"

"The King sent an envoy, five of his most trusted aides. But I thought a party of that size might draw attention to the eyes of anyone who might be looking."

Pheunaf nodded. "Very smart, my boy."

"Thank you." Zabaneja turned to the others. He nodded to Nanetscka and waited to be introduced to the third drageal.

"Zabaneja, this is my second-in-command, Brendirum."

Zabaneja and the drageal nodded to each other.

Zabaneja stepped out of the circle and motioned to Rusalei and Aneesyma to join him.

Rusalei jumped up and was ready to run to them when Aneesyma again touched her arm.

"Decorum, my dear. Remember who you are and what you represent here. This is not a social visit."

Rusalei took a deep breath and waited. Aneesyma walked slowly to the open field and Rusalei walked silently behind him.

"Is that your young lady, Zabaneja?" Pheunaf asked as she saw the other two approaching.

Zabaneja coughed nervously. "She is a friend."

Pheunaf chuckled.

"Ah, Aneesyma, it is good to see you again," Pheunaf said, reaching a taloned hand toward the man. Zabaneja, as he would for the duration of the meeting, acted as interpreter.

Aneesyma bowed. "I feel the same, Pheunaf."

"I am Rusalei," she said in broken dragealian, bowed, then returned to her native tongue to continue. "I am honored to meet you, Lady Pheunaf."

"Thank her for her words and tell her her dragealian is quite good," Pheunaf lied. As Zabaneja turned to speak, Pheunaf went on, "She is quite pretty, son. You will make beautiful babies." Pheunaf chuckled, knowing Zabaneja would not translate her last words.

Aneesyma saw Zabaneja redden at Pheunaf's words and smiled, imagining what she said.

Zabaneja sputtered a bit. "Mother compliments you on your dragealian. She is also glad to meet you, but you need not address her as lady."

Over the next hour or so, the two factions talked about various things, but avoided any talk of the war. The drageals were interested in the other members of the human group, while Aneesyma and Zabaneja wondered who else would attend. For the most part, Rusalei, still in awe of the drageals, was silent, only speaking when someone spoke directly to her.

After a bit, the two groups separated and retired for the evening.

CHAPTER FIFTY

ZABANEJA ROSE before the sun and joined the drageals while Aneesyma and Rusalei slept.

"Tell me more of this female. Did you tell her what I said last evening?" Pheunaf asked, already knowing the answer.

Zabaneja shook his head. "Mother, Rusalei is a noble. As I said at our last meeting, within the human world, unlike ours, there is distinction based on birth and family. Even if I had feelings for her..."

Pheunaf laughed, "Even 'if'? Zabaneja, you are deeply in love with her and dare I say from what I can see, she feels the same way about you. Can you honestly tell me I am mistaken?"

"You already know how I feel."

"What does Aneesyma say about your relationship? I feel he, too, is aware of it. Does he condemn or condone it?"

"It does not matter what he thinks or what I want or how I feel for her, or she for me. When I come home, she cannot follow. So, there is no future for us—not now, not ever."

Pheunaf did not respond. *We shall see, son. We shall see.*

Before they could continue, Rusalei and Aneesyma joined them.

"Good morning," Pheunaf said. "It looks like we will have a

good day to greet the others."

Aneesyma looked to the clear sky and nodded. "If Zab's calculations are correct, our second group should be arriving later today and the last tomorrow."

"That will be good. I think the others should be here by then as well."

#

The next day everyone—humans, emuranda, chetoga and several others who preferred to stay in the shadows and communicate through the emuranda—had arrived and the meeting began.

As she had done with her previous meetings with Pheunaf, Kalini's magic allowed everyone to hear the others in their own tongue. The humans found both that and the emuranda in their minds odd, but in a very short time all adapted. Almost immediately, the discussion centered around the question of how the landbound could be of assistance to the flighted drageals.

"Before I begin," Aneesyma said, "I want it to be made clear our suggestions are in no way meant to offend the drageals or any other group."

"Go on," Pheunaf said.

"I am aware Zab had a flying seat that allowed him to ride on the back of a drageal. What I am unsure of is if such a thing would be agreeable to other drageals, thus allowing humans to fight with you in the air."

"We, too, thought of the same tactic but were concerned no others would be open to flight as Zabaneja is," Pheunaf chuckled. "He loves to fly as much as any drageal."

A sigh of relief came from the humans as they heard Pheunaf's response.

:The emuranda will remain on the ground,: Jucara said to everyone and smirked. *:Though I will not admit to being afraid.:*

Everyone smiled at the emuranda's remark.

"The chetoga, too, would prefer to remain with our feet firmly planted on solid ground. We will leave flight to those who it comes to naturally or who desire it," the large silver chetoga, sitting with his black-tipped tail wrapped around him, said. "I think the best way we can contribute is by doing what we do best, being invisible."

"Good," Pheunaf said. "We are all in agreement and have already begun to build a good infrastructure for our alliance."

"Before we go any further, I foresee an issue with the human part of the plan," Zabaneja said.

The others looked at him, surprised by his reaction to the suggestion of flight, and he chuckled.

"How will the human riders communicate in flight or even on the ground? It is not as if we can teach the humans dragealian nor the drageals the human tongue in the short time we have available to us. And I doubt if Kalini will be able to maintain her magic across the distances that will need to be covered."

Kalini nodded. "It is true I would be of little help in those situations."

"I had not thought of that," Aneesyma said, shaking his head.

:I believe we can be of assistance in that,: Jucara said. *:We can teach you to mindspeak.:* She saw most did not understand what she meant, and she laughed. *:How I am speaking to you. And you can speak this way to one person or many at once, like you do when you speak aloud.:*

Zabaneja shook his head. "I was not aware that would be possible. That would be the perfect solution."

"Are you saying everyone can learn what you call mindspeech?" Aneesyma asked.

:It is possible some cannot, but I assume those chosen for this task will not have that issue.:

The discussions went on for several more hours with each group making suggestions or asking for clarifications.

"We have made great progress today," Pheunaf said as the sun began to set. "And now it is time to celebrate this momentous occasion."

#

Over the next two days, those present drew up plans to be brought back to their respective leaders and groups.

"I have a question," Rusalei said after being quiet for most of the talks. "What has Darchok been up to lately?"

"What do you mean?" Pheunaf asked.

"Where has he been? Have there been any attacks or battles since the one that brought your fallen drageal into our courtyard?"

"Neither Darchok nor we have been idle," Nanetscka said. "The fighting has moved to the skies above other areas."

Rusalei looked embarrassed. "Oh, I am sorry, I should have realized."

Nanetscka smiled and touched the young woman on the shoulder. "There is no need to apologize, my dear. There was no way for you to know that. Had I been in your position, I would have wondered the same thing."

Rusalei looked grateful.

"If there are no further questions or issues to discuss," Pheunaf said, "I believe this meeting has reached its conclusion. Before everyone leaves, I would like to ask for a contingent from each group to remain for a few days or so to allow them to learn to mindspeak. Then, when all return they can help the others of their kind. I suggest the humans be Zabaneja and Rikar since they have already formed a bond with two of the drageals."

The next morning, everyone but the ones chosen to remain behind, bade farewell and set out on the journey home to prepare for the upcoming war.

#

In less than a week, all tasked with learning mindspeech had done so. To their delight, Zabaneja and Rikar found not only could they speak to their drageal partners but to the chetoga and emuranda and all the others. They continued to practice and test the distance limits.

:It has been a very productive week for all,: Jucara said to the group. *:Now it is time for you to return to your respective homes and groups, knowing we will meet again soon, albeit not under such pleasant circumstances.:*

The chetoga and the drageals were the first to leave.

"Should we not be going?" Rikar asked.

Zabaneja looked disappointed. "Yes, I suppose we should. I was hoping..."

As if on cue, Pheunaf appeared and Zabaneja's mood lightened. "You did not really think I would let you leave without saying farewell, did you?"

Zabaneja smiled. "I thought you might be busy with your other duties."

She shook her head and motioned him to her. The two embraced and then Zabaneja and Rikar departed, leaving Pheunaf alone.

Rikar and Zabaneja rode in silence, though they were in constant conversation.

:Now that we know how to do this,: Rikar said, *:how often do*

you think we will try to speak to others like this forgetting they are unable to do so?:

:Probably all the time.: Zabaneja laughed out loud which, had anyone else been around, would have been an odd counterpoint to the silence. *:And, how often will we become angry at them not answering us?:*

Rikar nodded.

#

At the keep, Zabaneja and Rikar were briefed on the progress of the plans.

"I assume you two can mindspeak with each other," Aneesyma said. They nodded. "Any idea on what distance you can cover?"

Zabaneja chuckled. "Did I not tell you he would ask that?"

Rikar smiled.

"We are not sure and have been wondering the same thing since we left the camp," Zabaneja said.

"Zab will likely be able to do so further than I will," Rikar said.

Aneesyma looked confused.

"I am able to contact Phrynia and she me even from here, but Rikar cannot reach his partner. So, it may be that each mindspeaker's range will be different."

"I see," Aneesyma said. "What did Jucara think? Is the distance limit something inherent or if, with practice, can it be increased?"

"She was not sure. This is the first time they have taught mindspeech to anyone."

"Zab and I already decided once I leave for the capital tomorrow, we shall contact each other every evening to test our limits," Rikar said.

"That is a good plan," Aneesyma said.

CHAPTER FIFTY-ONE

THE FIRST HUMANS to arrive at the training site were from the Keep. As they had done before, their forces were split into smaller groups for travel to avoid unwanted attention. Aneesyma, against everyone's advice, insisted upon being an active part of the war effort and so was appointed the commander of the human forces. Upon arrival, he went to greet Jucara and Pheunaf while the others set up camp.

"It is good to see you both again," Aneesyma said as he surveyed the area.

:To answer the question in your mind, the chetoga and the others will indeed be joining this alliance. They will be arriving over the next few days,: Jucara said. *:Though, do not be surprised if you are unaware of the presence of some of them.:*

Aneesyma smiled. "I had forgotten how open our minds were to you, Jucara. May I ask if you have already devised a plan for the training?"

:Mindspeech training will be the first order of business. It will do no good to teach the humans to fly if they are unable to communicate with their drageals and each other. That will also allow us

to identify any among those chosen from all groups unable to achieve the desired results so they can be replaced if need be.:

"As expected, a very sound plan," Aneesyma said. The three leaders spoke for a bit longer. "Jucara, please tell Pheunaf I will send Zab to her shortly."

:Of course,: the emuranda said as Aneesyma bowed and departed.

A short time later, Zabaneja joined his mother and the other drageals.

"I see you had your riding seat duplicated for the others," Pheunaf said. "I had wondered why you took it with you when you left."

"I knew no one in the clan had the facilities to make as many of them as would be needed. And, the Keep's craftspeople made some refinements to the original design, which will make it more comfortable, for both human and drageal. We have also added a ladder of sorts to allow the rider to mount the drageal regardless of the terrain," Zabaneja said.

"What a good idea."

"I would like you or Nanetscka to try it out with me to see if we have, indeed, made it better and if anything else needs to be done. One of those responsible for crafting the seats came with us, and she will be able to make any additional changes as well as repair the seats as needs arise."

"I wonder if you are not merely angling for a way to fly again before the others?" Pheunaf said with a chuckle.

Zabaneja smiled. "Well, flying for the mere pleasure of it would be an added bonus."

"Yes, it will," Pheunaf said. "Now, let us put aside the talk of war preparations and enjoy a meal and the company of friends this night."

#

Mindspeech training began, and though all had been warned by the ones who had already learned it, the oddness of having voices in their heads was still unsettling. It did not take long for all to became comfortable with it and soon, all were able to speak to each other, individually or in groups.

:This is the quietest gathering I have ever been a party to,: someone said to the group, resulting in an outburst of laughter that shattered the silence to everyone's delight.

After the drageals and humans had mastered mindspeech, it was time to face the next task—flying. As had happened with Rikar and his drageal, natural partnerships between human and drageal formed.

"I understand you might be feeling a bit apprehensive about flying, but believe me, once you feel the wind in your hair, you will love it," Zabaneja told the humans before the first lesson.

"How is this going to work? You are not really planning on just strapping us into that contraption," one of the young men said and pointed to the pile of flying seats, "and have us take off into the sky, are you?"

Zabaneja smiled. "Of course not, even though I will admit that is exactly what Pheunaf and I did to Lord Aneesyma on his first flight."

Gasps of disbelief erupted from the humans.

Aneesyma nodded. "It is true, that is precisely what they did. I obviously survived, and it was one of the most exhilarating events of my life. My flight was short, and I did not have to do anything more than sit and enjoy myself. But now, we will all be meticulously trained so when we encounter the enemy, flying will not be an obstacle to us."

"The drageals and I," Zabaneja said, "have come up with what we think is a good training program to allow both rider and mount to become comfortable with each other, as well as many scenarios to mimic actual combat. And, I cannot stress this enough, if you, any of you, have any suggestions for improvement to any aspect of the training, do not hesitate to bring it to us."

Those from outside of the Keep were quite surprised at Zabaneja's statement, while the Keep's soldiers simply nodded.

"Now let us join the drageals and get started."

The riders climbed into the seats. To everyone's delight, very few adjustments to the original design were needed, so the training began.

"That certainly is a sight to behold," Phrynia said as she watched the training.

"We are having them start with the drageals simply running on the ground to allow both rider and drageal to get used to each other," Zabaneja said. "Once that is achieved, they will fly. Close to the ground, at first but then… "

"Do you think any of them will fly as high as we do?"

Zabaneja shrugged. "Only time will tell." He smiled, knowing her competitive side would not let that happen.

#

With drageal rider, what they dubbed themselves, training complete, the teams were dispatched to the various alliance camps and the next phase of the war began—to go on the offensive against Darchok and his forces.

:I think we will find my brother keeps all of his people together in one place. He does not trust command to anyone but himself,: Pheunaf said to the others.

:So, now it is a matter of finding their location,: Aneesyma said.

:We began the search as soon as the alliance was formed,: Jucara said. *:And, as amazing as it sounds, Darchok not only keeps all his forces together, they do not move their camp as we do.:*

:Are you saying you have found them?: Pheunaf asked. *:Why*

have you kept this information to yourself?:

:We were waiting for you to be ready to plan the attack.:

Pheunaf laughed. *:I should have suspected you knew his where-abouts since you always gave us such good information about his upcoming attacks. Now, the time has come for us to go on the offensive.:*

#

On a near moonless night, the assault on Darchok's camp began. The alliance hoped to kill Darchok, knowing if he was eliminated, the others would scatter.

The skirmish began with a small number of drageal riders silently swooping in and attacking with fire and arrow to try to keep as many of Darchok's drageals on the ground as possible. Simultaneously, swarms of chetoga scurried about, throwing things that burned or exploded into the eyes of the enemy. As Darchok's troops attempted to defend themselves from the tiny creatures, they were next assaulted by humans, shooting arrows and slashing swords, mounted on emuranda, who also attacked with massive antlers and hooves that tore through feather and underlying scale.

Against the alliance's hopes, many of Darchok's forces, including Darchok himself, escaped both the ground and initial air attacks. But as they took to the sky, they were surprised to be met by even more alliance troops attacking with claw, fire, and arrows. As dawn broke, the battle ended with Darchok and his remaining forces retreating into the rising sun.

:This is not the time to chase,: Pheunaf said as her troops began to follow.

Reluctantly, the alliance troops obeyed her orders.

CHAPTER FIFTY-TWO

A WEEK OR SO after the initial raid on Darchok's camp, Zabaneja and Phrynia were returning from a reconnaissance mission. As they approached the alliance camp, they spied a group of beings unlike any they had ever seen, heading toward the camp. They flew high above the group, and were surprised when one of them looked skyward and waved.

:That cannot be!: Phrynia shouted. *:Even a drageal would be hard pressed to see us at this height.:*

:Yet, it clearly knows we are here.:

:What should we do?:

:From the way they carry themselves, they do not appear to be hostiles. Regardless, we need to inform the others of their approach.:

Phrynia nodded as Zabaneja mindspoke to his mother of the strangers' approach. Pheunaf told him to keep the group in sight and to let her know if they changed course. Zabaneja and Phrynia did as instructed. It soon became clear the group was headed for the alliance camp. They relayed the information to Pheunaf. Within a few moments a group of humans and emuranda approached the strangers.

The newcomers were quickly deemed not to be an imminent

threat, and Zabaneja and Phrynia were told to resume their mission. As they flew off, the pair saw the strangers following their escort. The stranger in the lead raised its face to the sky and again waved at them, though it should not have been able to see them. The being's behavior made them even more curious.

#

The strangers and their escort were met with stares from those in the camp. The newcomers bore an ever-so-slight resemblance to humans, yet there was something distinctly different. Most obvious was their height. They were very tall, even the shortest of their group stood at least a head above the tallest human. Also, every part of their body, except for their pink skinned faces, was covered in long, silky white hair. But there was something else, something felt, not seen—an overwhelming serenity that permeated the very essence of everyone the strangers looked upon.

When they reached Pheunaf, the one who had been able to see Zabaneja and Phrynia so high in the air stepped forward and bowed.

"Pheunaf, we have watched you for many years," she said in perfect dragealian. "Allow me to introduce myself, I am Varlama."

"I do not wish to appear rude, Varlama, but may I ask who you are and where you come from?" Pheunaf asked. "I am afraid neither I nor Jucara, whom I have the distinct impression you have already spoken with, are able to recognize your kind from acquaintance, tale or legend."

Varlama threw her head back and laughed. "My apologies, dear ladies. I doubt anyone who now inhabits these lands would know of us. We are the tazzamira, an ancient race said by some to be the first to walk this world long before the birth of any others. And long ago, when the newer races, like yours, came into existence, we moved to the tops of the highest mountains where we have since lived." She watched as the two women tried to digest her words and sensed their doubt, knowing both the emuranda and drageals inhabited the high mountains.

"I assure you both, our mountain homes are located higher than your people have ever ventured."

It did not take Pheunaf longer than the blink of a dragon's eye to regain her composure. "And what brings you down from your mountain now, Varlama?"

"This war."

:If your people have stayed hidden, by choice or chance, from view for so long, why do you now choose to concern yourselves with the affairs of others?: Jucara asked.

"Ah, the bluntness of an emuranda." Varlama smiled. "Do you mind if my companions and I sit? It has been quite a long journey."

Pheunaf nodded and the group of tazzamira, in a single, graceful motion, sat on the ground.

Varlama sighed. "That is better. Now, to answer your questions. While we may not walk among your peoples, we do watch what goes on in your world, our world."

:If you never leave your mountain top, how do you do so?:

Varlama smiled enigmatically. "Suffice to say, we have our ways."

Both women sensed the tazzamira would say no more and chose to drop the matter. At least, for now.

"This war troubles us. When it was merely drageal against drageal, it was of little consequence, like siblings quarreling over one thing or another. And, truth be told, if your two factions wiped each other off the face of this world, it would be of little consequence to the ultimate scheme of things." Pheunaf was about to interrupt, but Varlama continued. "Mind you, I am not saying it would not be a terrible thing to lose the entire race of drageals. You are, after all, magnificent creatures. But many races of magnificent creatures have left this world. And I am sure many will leave in the future. That is how the world works."

:And you call the emuranda blunt?: Jucara interjected.

Varlama smiled. "As I was saying, when the conflict involved only drageals, we felt no need to act. But Darchok's escalating madness threatens us all. He must be stopped."

The two women nodded.

"That is why we formed this alliance..."

Varlama put up her hand and nodded. The look in her eyes showed both sorrow and compassion. "I am aware why your alliance was formed. It had to be done. Darchok desires his group to be the only intelligent beings to inhabit this world. You were right in your actions and that is why we are here. To help in your fight against the evil, the insanity, Darchok has become."

Pheunaf nodded. "Are you aware of his latest plan? To burn every inch of land and kill every living thing in his path."

Varlama's expression darkened. "That was what precipitated our coming to join and help you."

"Then we welcome you and yours to our alliance."

CHAPTER FIFTY-THREE

:WHO DO YOU THINK THEY ARE?: Phrynia asked as she and Zabaneja returned to their duty.

:I have no idea, but whoever they are, Pheunaf seems to trust them. I guess we will have to wait until we return to camp to find out.:

:Drat! By then everyone else will know exactly what is going on. I hate being the last to know things!:

Zabaneja laughed, and the pair continued their mission.

#

By the time Zabaneja and Phrynia returned from their duties, Phrynia's worst fears were realized. The camp was abuzz with talk of the newcomers. Not that anyone really knew anything about them, but they had seen them up close and Phrynia had not.

Zabaneja laughed and reminded her their first order of business was to report to Pheunaf and Jucara. She grumbled under her breath.

"Phrynia, sometimes you are as dense as a summer fog. Think about it. The strangers were brought to see Pheunaf. We have to go see Pheunaf..."

When the young drageal still did not understand, Zabaneja laughed even harder. "Good gracious, girl! If they are still with Pheunaf, we will get to not only see them but more than likely talk to them."

Finally, the young drageal nodded her massive golden feathered head. "Oh, I see what you mean."

"It took you long enough," Zabaneja replied. "It is a good thing you are quicker in air battles than you are on the ground, or else we would both be in trouble."

Seeing the twinkle in his eye, the drageal knew he was teasing.

"Come then, let us get over there before the strangers slip away and your curiosity is never quenched."

The pair hurried off, bantering about who was more interested in the strangers.

#

"I believe your son and his partner are approaching," Varlama said a moment before Zabaneja and Phrynia came into view.

"We beg your pardon, we were not aware you were with the newcomers," Zabaneja lied as he and Phrynia bowed. "Forgive us, we will come back later to make our report."

Without looking, Zabaneja felt Phrynia's glare, but did not respond.

"That will not be necessary," Pheunaf said, fully aware of the disappointment that would ensue if she sent the pair away.

"Yes, please do stay, children," Varlama said, enjoying the ire her words evoked. "I mean no disrespect, but when you are as old as I am, even Pheunaf and Jucara are children to me."

"With your permission, Varlama," Pheunaf said. The tazzamira nodded and Pheunaf turned to Zabaneja and Phrynia. "Please give me your report."

:Mother, who are these beings and why are they here?:

:Do not be rude, boy. If you have a question for our guests, ask them directly. If you show some patience, you will likely find the answers you seek.:

Zabaneja cleared his throat and hoped the embarrassment at his mother's rebuke did not show on his face. "Other than these visitors," he turned to look at the group seated on the ground, "we encountered nothing out of the ordinary. There was no sign of Darchok's scouts."

"If I may," Varlama said, bowing her head slightly to Pheunaf. "They are correct in their assessment. Darchok has moved his forces further east while he regroups for his next attack. Your attack on his previous encampment showed him the error in his ways and he will likely not stay in one place too long again."

Without thinking, both Zabaneja and Phrynia simultaneously blurted out. "And how would you know that?"

"Are you spies sent here to feed us false information so that devil can swoop in from another direction while you have us looking elsewhere?" Phrynia snapped.

"Phrynia!" Pheunaf shouted. "Hold your tongue!"

The young drageal's golden feathers instinctively ruffled, rising in anger, but she said nothing more as she glared at Pheunaf.

The older drageal turned to Varlama, "Please accept my apologies. The spirit, and tongues, of youth are oft times hard to control."

"No offense was taken."

"That still does not answer the question," Zabaneja whispered to Phrynia.

Pheunaf turned and glared at him. "If you two cannot control your tongues, I will send you away."

"Sorry," the pair said in unison.

"Do go on, Varlama. I believe some of our reconnaissance confirms what you have said. Many of our teams stationed elsewhere have reported seeing Darchok's forces avoiding encounters and heading east."

"No one informed us of such a development," Zabaneja blurted out.

"And, when either of you become leader of the alliance, you will be kept apprised of all gathered intelligence," Pheunaf snapped. "You may be our best scouts, but in this war you are two amongst many."

Zabaneja's face reddened. "Yes, ma'am."

"We had, in fact, been thinking of sending our best long range scout team," Pheunaf nodded toward Zabaneja and Phrynia, "out tomorrow to search for the enemy's camp or at least to find out more about their movement."

Zabaneja and Phrynia looked at each other in surprise.

Pheunaf continued. "But, if I am to understand you correctly, Varlama, you already know, or at least have a good idea where Darchok and his troops are."

Varlama nodded but said nothing.

"Still, you offer no explanation as to how you know where they are," Pheunaf said, her voice calm with no hint of sarcasm or anger.

"Not at this moment." Varlama smiled. "And, as Jucara is finding out, it is of no use to probe my or any of my companions' minds, for you will find nothing."

Pheunaf looked toward Jucara, who gave her the slightest nod to confirm the tazzamira's words.

"Do not fear, we do not take affront at your actions. After all, you are emuranda and that is what you do," Varlama said. "I would have been surprised, and concerned, if you had not attempted such a thing."

"Concerned?" Pheunaf asked. "Why concerned?"

"Concerned you took a group of total strangers at only their word without trying to find out everything you could about them. I am sure we can all agree, there is no better way to find the truth of another's intentions than by having an emuranda, especially one as gifted as Jucara, journey through their mind."

Both Pheunaf and Jucara nodded, though Zabaneja and Phrynia still seemed unconvinced.

"For right now," Varlama continued, "I ask you, though the young ones will disagree, to trust me." As she said those words, both Pheunaf's and Jucara's minds were flooded with images of who and what the tazzamira were.

"Very well. My heart tells me you can be trusted," Pheunaf said.

Zabaneja almost burst holding in his protest at his mother's actions, but knew better than to interrupt. Later, after the others had gone, he would ask about her response that he considered both foolish and reckless.

"Thank you. Thank you both," Varlama said, bowing slightly. "Now, with your permission, we would like to get some rest. It has been a long day."

"Of course," Pheunaf replied, then turned to Zabaneja. "Please take our guests to the..."

"That will not be necessary, Pheunaf. We saw a lovely spot to the north of your camp that will be ideal for us. We will take over that area for the duration of our stay, with your permission of course."

"Of course. If that is what will suit you best."

"Good."

"Will you need anything? Supplies? Food?" Pheunaf asked.

"No, thank you. We have all we need. Now, we will take our

leave until the morrow." Varlama bowed her head and then, as if on cue, her entire company rose as one and followed.

#

Zabaneja and Phrynia turned to leave as well.

"Where do you two think you are going?" Pheunaf asked.

The pair stopped.

She nodded to Jucara and the two women stood in silence, though Zabaneja and Phrynia were sure they were deep in conversation.

After a few moments, Jucara departed. Pheunaf turned to Zabaneja and Phrynia, the look on her face displaying deep displeasure at their earlier behavior.

"The two of you do realize you were out of line in your behavior, do you not?"

Both Zabaneja and Phrynia, speaking at the same time, argued that they felt they did nothing wrong. They had only voiced their concerns.

"And you think such actions are advisable in the face of an unknown faction? A faction you are unsure of, both in motivation and allegiance. A leader, or a diplomat, does not reveal all in the face of his potential adversary."

The two young people looked at each other in stunned disbelief.

"We did not think... " Zabaneja began.

Pheunaf cut him off. "Exactly! Neither of you took even a second to think before you rashly spoke!"

She glared as if waiting for them to even attempt to make an excuse for their actions. They did not.

"Had this been a sensitive negotiation, you gave away everything to your opponent. The negotiations would be over and you, and your people, the loser."

Pheunaf drew in a breath as if to try to calm herself while Zabaneja and Phrynia waited in silence. She shook her head.

"If either of you are to become leaders, this is a lesson you must learn, and learn quickly."

Zabaneja and Phrynia looked at each other.

"Leaders?" Zabaneja asked.

'Us?' Phrynia added.

"I am sorry, Mother, but I do not understand. And let me say, I mean no disrespect nor am I trying to be impudent, but if we were so completely out of line, why did you let us go on so? Why did you not stop us sooner?"

"Why did you allow us to stay?" Phrynia added.

Pheunaf smiled. "Good questions, both of you. Since I had already, almost from the first moment I laid eyes upon Varlama, accepted the tazzamira as allies, this was a sort of test for both of you."

"A test?" Zabaneja asked.

"I do not understand." Phrynia said.

"I expect not. You two still tend to act rashly in many situations. An often admirable trait in a warrior, but not so in a leader."

"We are not leaders," Phrynia stated.

"I doubt either of us will ever lead much more than what we already do," Zabaneja said.

"Perhaps." Pheunaf smiled coyly.

"But," Zabaneja said, shaking his head, "I still do not understand how you can so quickly trust these outsiders, these tazzamira. How, just by looking at her, did you feel so strongly she was friend? Are she and her people wielding some magic over you? Over all of us?"

"Magic? What sort of magic do you think she could possess that could sway an entire camp at the same time?"

Zabaneja shook his head. "I do not know. I am not well versed in such things, but it seems there is something odd about these people."

Pheunaf smiled. "Now, you are thinking like a leader. I did, and still do, have some reservations about them. There is much they are not telling us, not revealing about themselves and their ways. Does this mean they are our enemy? My gut tells me not."

"And if your gut turns out to be wrong?"

"Well, then, better to keep them near at hand, where we can observe them. If they prove to be something other than what they say... well, they will be close enough to be dealt with accordingly."

Both Zabaneja and Phrynia nodded, once again stunned by the drageal leader's insight.

CHAPTER FIFTY-FOUR

"HOW DO THEY always seem to know where we are?" Darchok growled at Ysernon as they settled into yet another new camp.

"Perhaps we stayed in the same place too long, thus allowing them to find us," Ysernon replied as he had done each time Darchok posed that question.

Darchok glared at his second-in-command. "That is still not a valid answer, no matter how many times you repeat it."

Though none would dare question his actions, ever since his sister's forces had attacked and killed so many of his followers, Darchok's rage had escalated to the point of mania. Still, he did not believe any of it was his fault and continued to search for other reasons for the debacle. And each time Ysernon even hinted otherwise, Darchok took his anger out on him.

Ysernon did not respond.

"Get the others, we have plans to discuss."

The others gathered in silence.

"I have a question," Darchok began. "Why is it we continue to lose battle after battle?"

"I do not understand," one of the drageals dared to reply.

Darchok turned to face him. "That is apparent. None of you understand, and that is why we continue to fall victim to my sister's forces."

"We are doing the best we can, Darchok," Ysernon said.

"Clearly, that is not good enough," Darchok roared. "So tell me, what are we to do to turn the tide in our favor?"

The others looked at each other in confusion. Darchok had never asked their opinion on tactics, or anything else, for that matter.

"What? No one has a single idea? Am I the only one here capable of doing anything right? The only one who knows how to face the enemy?"

Again no response.

"Of course, not. None of you do, and that is the problem!" Darchok shouted.

"The problem as I see it," Ysernon began much to the surprise of the others, "is that they seem to know our plans even before we do."

The other drageals began to murmur their agreement.

"Are you saying there is a spy among us?" Darchok asked, his nares flaring to the point the others backed away as he lashed out at his childhood friend. He knocked Ysernon down and pinned him to the ground.

"That is not what I mean," Ysernon cried.

"Then how do you think they know what our plans are?"

Ysernon shook his head. "I do not know."

Darchok became unhinged. "Is it you, Ysernon? Are you their spy in our midst? The one who betrayed me?" Darchok roared. "Too often, as of late, you have voiced your disagreement with our goals. Have you defected to the other side?"

The others stood frozen. No one could believe Ysernon, of anyone, would be disloyal to Darchok. But all knew to stand up to

Darchok, especially when he was this angry, would turn his wrath against them as well.

"I would never betray you," Ysernon cried. "You know that. I have always been your most ardent follower."

But the words came too late. Darchok's rage had overtaken his rational mind and, in the next moment, he tore out Ysernon's throat. The others looked on in a state of shock.

"What are we to do?" one of them whispered. "He is clearly out of control."

"I am sure he had grounds, evidence, for the accusation he made against Ysernon. He would not have acted against him without it," a second drageal said.

The others said nothing. Although some had their doubts, none possessed the courage to oppose their leader, especially not at this moment.

After a short while, Darchok regained a bit of his composure. He looked at the others. "Do any of you have anything to say?"

There was no response.

"Good," he said and pushed the body off the edge of the cliff. "Now, tell me, what information do you have about Pheunaf and her forces?"

"Darchok, our last intelligence tells us she is still in the area where we last confronted her," said one.

"Are you sure?" Darchok hissed. "That does not sound like something Pheunaf would do, not a tactic she has followed in the past."

The drageals squirmed where they stood. They looked at each other, trying to decide what to do next.

"That was the last intelligence we received, but I am not sure if it is the most recent. I do not know if Ysernon had additional information he had yet to share with us, planning to present it to you at this meeting," said another drageal, then held his breath in anticipation.

But Darchok did not attack. He merely shook his head. "Then, you will need to find that information." The first drageal nodded and Darchok turned to the others. "As for the rest of you... "

He did not finish his sentence. He did not have to. They knew. They all knew.

#

"What do you mean you cannot find them? They are drageals and a great number of them, they cannot just hide under a bush," Darchok roared.

"We have looked everywhere. We can neither find Pheunaf nor any of her troops," the first drageal said. "It is as if they have disappeared."

"That is impossible," Darchok hissed and looked off into the distance.

The others stood in silence, unsure what Darchok would do next.

"I have it. I know how to bring my sister and her foolish allies out into the open. An action they will be unable to ignore. An attack so massive, they will have no defenses against us. One that will turn the tide in our favor and allow us to be done with the others once and for all."

CHAPTER FIFTY-FIVE

"IT SEEMS HIS MIND has finally unravelled," Nanetscka told Pheunaf. "He is turning on his own. He killed Ysernon after accusing him of being a spy."

Pheunaf shook her head. "He is still so blind."

"And let us hope he remains so to the true spies—the birds and smaller animals that are so natural to have around few even notice their presence. I placed an enchantment upon them, allowing them to understand dragealian and mindspeak it back to us," Kalini said. "That is how we heard of his latest plan, one which is hard to believe even he could devise."

"I always knew he was vicious." Pheunaf said. "But, even after all he has done, it is still hard to believe he could really be planning to raze the entire countryside and kill all living creatures in his path. Still, whether we believe he is capable of it or do not want to believe it will come to pass, we cannot ignore it. We must prepare for both the battle and its aftermath."

Zabaneja looked confused. "What do you mean?"

"If I may be so bold as to speak, Pheunaf?" Aneesyma asked.

Pheunaf nodded.

"This will likely be the final battle. Its outcome will decide the war. And there is little doubt the price will be high on both sides," Aneesyma said.

"Exactly. I fear many, too many, will fall. But not facing him would cost the world more."

:Mother, will this battle truly be that dire?:

:Perhaps worse.:

:Worse? How could it be worse?

:I am not sure. I cannot put it into words. It is just a feeling,: she replied.

Zabaneja felt she knew more than she was saying, and that worried him. But knew it would be a waste of time to pursue it.

"Pheunaf, you have led us well with honesty and honor. And you have never diminished the magnitude of what we faced," Brendirum said. "I, for one, am willing to follow you until the end, whatever that might be."

Everyone gathered immediately voiced their agreement with Brendirum's words.

#

"You look worried, Zab," Aneesyma said as the young man approached.

Zabaneja ignored his words. "You should return to the Keep, Aneesyma. Now. This night."

"Why do you say that?"

"Your people need you. If this battle turns out as Mother thinks it will, you will be in far too much danger. And if things do not go our way, they will need you there to lead them."

"You wish me to run away?" Aneesyma asked.

"That is not what I am saying."

"But if I return to the Keep now, before this battle, would I not seem a coward to my people? Even if my motive was not to run and cower, would it not seem so to the outside world?" Aneesyma asked, and before Zabaneja could reply, he continued. "No, I will not leave. My place is here in the thick of it, defending my people."

"And if we fail? What will your people do without you?" Zabaneja asked.

Aneesyma shook his head. "My dear Zab, if we fail, my being there will not do any more for my people than my being here will."

"Are you sure? I think you underestimate the power of your presence and how it can bolster their morale and calm their fears. And if it is to be the end of us all, would it not be better for you to be there with them?" Zabaneja asked.

"I must get back to the others. We will talk again soon," Aneesyma said, not answering Zabaneja's questions.

#

The next day, as Zabaneja prepared for the upcoming battle, two of the drageal riders approached him. "Good morning."

The two nodded.

"To what do I owe the pleasure of your visit?" Zabaneja asked.

The two young people squirmed a little and looked at each other.

"Well?"

"We are sorry to disturb you, sir," the young woman said. "We are concerned about something we heard from one of the drageals."

"And, what was that?"

"If we were to lose, she would rather die in battle than be taken prisoner and suffer the torturous wrath of Darchok and his forces," she said.

"Surely that is an exaggeration," the male rider added.

Zabaneja shook his head. "You have both been around drageals long enough to know they are not prone to exaggeration. It is not in their nature."

"So, you are saying it is true," the young man said. "If we fail to defeat Darchok and survive, he and his troops will..." he hesitated.

"Darchok is not known for his kindness. So, yes, if we do not defeat him, anyone who was not with him, not one of his followers, will die, eventually, but not before they are made to suffer."

The two riders drew in a collective breath.

"As we feared."

"And?" Zabaneja asked.

The pair looked at each other.

"We will need to make sure he does not win," the young man said emphatically.

"I am sure he will be no kinder to those who did not join in the fight against him, either," the female rider added. "So we, the fighters, must defeat him, not only for ourselves but for the defenseless we have left behind."

Zabaneja nodded. "I am glad you feel that way."

After the two riders departed, Phrynia came up to him.

"You did not tell them all, Zabaneja," she said.

"No, I did not," he replied. "They are young and already troubled by what they know. Telling them any more would do none of us any good."

Phrynia chuckled.

"What? Why are you laughing at me?" Zabaneja asked.

"I am not laughing at you," she replied. "I am amused that my aunt's words are indeed true."

"And, what did she say?"

"That you are very much like your mother."

Zabaneja smiled. "Well, I am not so sure about that, but to be so would indeed be the greatest honor I could achieve."

"Now it is my turn to ask you something, and I need you to promise you will answer truthfully," Phrynia said.

"Well, that sounds ominous," Zabaneja said with a chuckle.

"I am serious," Phrynia said.

Zabaneja was surprised. Even in the short time he had known the young drageal, he had never seen her so somber.

"All right, I will answer as truthfully as I can. I promise," Zabaneja replied.

"Are you afraid?" she asked.

"Of what?"

"Stop. You said you would be truthful."

"I am. What are you asking? Am I afraid of Darchok? Of dying? Or of what will happen to those we love?" Zabaneja asked.

"Yes. All of those."

"In your heart, you already know the answer."

She nodded. "Is there something, some one thing, you are most afraid of?"

Zabaneja thought a moment. "I guess that would be failing to defeat Darchok and leaving the others, especially those ill-equipped to fight him, at his mercy."

Phrynia nodded. *So like your mother,* she thought.

CHAPTER FIFTY-SIX

DARCHOK AND HIS FOLLOWERS took to the sky with the first light of dawn. They approached the first human settlement they planned to decimate that day and saw several of Pheunaf's drageals circling the area. Darchok thought nothing of their presence; this was a tactic his sister frequently used in an attempt to protect those on the ground. It was a ploy that had seen some success in the past against small groups of Darchok's forces. That would not be the case today. Today, Pheunaf's paltry band of sentries would be no match for his entire clan. As expected, at the sight of the number of opponents, the drageals fled. Darchok motioned for several of his drageals to give chase and for the rest to begin the attack.

Before the assault commenced, another group of the alliance drageals appeared. Darchok was surprised when they, still fewer in number than his force, chose to engage rather than flee. But after a brief skirmish, they too fled. Darchok and his drageals shouted derisive taunts as all gave chase.

Some distance away from the initial target, the alliance drageals turned to face their pursuers. Darchok's combatants whooped in frenzied excitement at the thought of killing their enemy. But the alliance drageals neither advanced nor retreated, rather they seemed to be waiting for something.

Then, as the sky around them filled with more alliance forces, Darchok's drageals realized they had been lured into a trap and were now surrounded and outnumbered. Their excitement turned to rage.

"Surrender," one of the alliance drageals shouted. "You cannot win."

Darchok roared with laughter, raised his head and spewed fire into the air above him. The two sides attacked each other and filled the sky with dragon fire so bright, the sun paled against it. But the beauty of the sky was quickly replaced by the reek of burning flesh and feathers and the shrieks of the wounded and dying. As the battle raged, combatants on both sides tried to put some distance between each other in an attempt to gain an advantage.

#

Darchok did not immediately join the battle. No, at that moment his focus was to find his primary opponent—his sister. Where was she? Was she such a coward that she sent others into danger while she remained safe elsewhere? That was not what he had heard before, others had encountered her during previous attacks. So, where was she?

To improve his vantage point, he flew high above the others, hoping to catch sight of her. As he searched the sky, he surveyed the scenario below. He watched with glee as his forces mercilessly attacked the drageals with humans on their backs, slashing the straps that held their seat and attempting to set them ablaze as they fell.

He was surprised how quickly the alliance drageals came to each other's aid. Even if it was a single drageal, if it was in trouble others suddenly appeared. It was as if they were communicating with each other. But that could not be, the noise of the battle made it almost impossible to even hear yourself, never mind someone else.

He continued to watch and was shocked to realize not only were the alliance drageals helping each other, they were also co-ordinating attacks which were successfully defeating his forces. One by one he saw his drageals fall or, worse, retreat. The wrath within him reached new heights, and he swore he would defeat his enemy even if he had to do it alone.

Darchok scanned the sky for a target and saw a lone young drageal. He began his descent toward him and then found an even better target. Him! The bane of his existence—his sister's filthy human on the back of a young golden drageal. He changed his target and silently approached the pair from behind. He knew exactly what he would do. He would swoop in and snap the drageal's wing so she could not escape and then wrench that whelp from her back with such force, the drageal's spine would break and she would helplessly fall to her death. As she did, he would turn his attention to the filthy human. But he would not kill him, not just yet. No, he would squeeze the boy until he was almost crushed. As he begged to be put out of his misery, Darchok would then find Pheunaf and when he did, he would tear the boy apart before her eyes.

As Darchok was almost upon them, the golden drageal made an evasive maneuver and avoided his attack. Darchok's rage intensified as he saw others come to its aid, but they did not matter. None there were a match for him. He spewed fire in their direction. As the others scattered, he again dove at his prey but once more they evaded him. He howled his rage as he saw his intended target and the others flee.

#

: That is darchok,: one of the drageals cried as Phrynia and

Zabaneja avoided his second attack.

:We are no match for him,: Zabaneja shouted. *:We must call for reinforcements.:*

Zabaneja sent a mindcall to others. Almost immediately his mother came into view. She flew at Darchok and as she shouted his name, he turned and saw her.

:She cannot take him on alone,: Zabaneja shouted to Phrynia. *:We must help her.:*

Phrynia did not respond nor did she turn toward Pheunaf's position.

:What are you doing? She needs our help.:

:Our, your, presence will only hinder her in the fight against Darchok. We must leave this battle to her.: Phrynia shook her head and took off to help the others.

Zabaneja screamed at the heavens, but in his heart he knew his friend was right.

CHAPTER FIFTY-SEVEN

DARCHOK'S ANGER turned to elation at the sight of Pheunaf. At last he would have his revenge for all the trouble she had caused him. Surprisingly, she stopped before she reached him.

"Waiting for others to come to your aid, sister? Afraid you are still no match against me?" Darchok taunted.

"Just the opposite, brother. I want to ensure there is no one else nearby to interfere."

Darchok was surprised not only by her words, but the calmness in her voice.

The two siblings dove at each other ferociously, snatching and clawing to get a grasp on the other. As Darchok attacked, almost blindly, Pheunaf realized madness had overtaken his mind and senses, clouding his focus and allowing her to get a firm grip on his shoulder. She dug her talons into his flesh, shocking Darchok with her strength, still, his bravado would not allow him to even consider she could beat him.

"I was benevolent to father and allowed him to die quickly. You shall not be afforded the same courtesy," he hissed, not realizing she was pulling him in closer. "You, dear sister, will suffer a much different fate—physically and emotionally. But I will not kill you outright. No, first I shall incapacitate and paralyze you. Then, as you lie helplessly on the ground, I will go after that thing you made me endure for so long and bring him before you, letting him see you broken and then I will slice him to pieces before your eyes. Oh, how I will enjoy the anguish and pain the two of you will endure. And when you have seen your precious human reduced to nothing more than bloodied strips of flesh, and with his final screams of pain still ringing in your ears, I shall finish you, slowly and painfully savoring every moment of your torment."

"You are wrong. Zabaneja will not be the one to die today, but you will," she whispered in his ear, "and it will be at my hand for I shall avenge not only Father, but all the others you have so callously and viciously murdered."

The ruthlessness of her words and tone permeated him and, for the first time, he knew fear. He tried to escape her grasp only to realize how entwined they were. He flailed to free himself but she would not release her grip.

"Goodbye, brother," she said as she punctured his skin with the tip of her talon and began to drag it across his neck.

As he realized he would not escape, he wrapped his wings tightly around her. "If I am to die, so will you," he said as she slit his throat.

Pheunaf instinctively knew how near to the ground she was and how little time she had to extricate herself. She sliced at his wings and was able to free herself and thrust Darchok's lifeless body from her. She went to ascend and realized her wing was broken in such a way she could neither right herself or slow her descent. She thought to call for help but knew the only ones close by were too small to catch her without putting themselves in danger. She closed her eyes, took a deep breath and waited.

#

The nearby drageals saw Darchok and Pheunaf dive at each other and immediately become what looked like a single mass of red, black and gold feathers. They watched the struggle, barely able to imagine the pain each inflicted upon the other. All held their breaths, helplessly watching the mass of feathers falling to the ground, both too caught up in their battle to be concerned with their positions in the sky. At last they saw Pheunaf free herself, but their joy turned to panic when she failed to ascend and continued to fall out of control. The group raced toward her, aware they might not be able to catch her but knowing they had to try. As they approached, they realized her descent was too rapid. All watched in horror as she crashed to the ground below.

Phrynia landed a short distance from Pheunaf's bloodied body, and Zabaneja ran to his mother's side.

"Mother," he cried as he fell to his knees beside her. He stroked the side of her face and she smiled.

"My beloved boy. My only wish for you now is to be happy," she said in a voice just above a whisper.

"Shh, mother, save your strength. We will get help. I will save you."

Pheunaf coughed. "It is too late for that. The war is over. Darchok is dead. I leave it to you to ensure our people, in their grief or rage, do not descend to the savagery of Darchok and his followers."

She took a final breath and was gone.

#

Zabaneja fell upon her body and wailed. Then, with his mother's words ringing in his ears, he rose, wiped the tears from his face and turned to Phrynia. Neither said anything aloud or within their minds, they did not need to.

They approached those gathered near Darchok's body. Some, human and drageal, were beginning to show their anger toward their fallen enemy, calling for the mutilation of his body.

:Stop! That is not who we are. We are not like him. We will not foul my mother's legacy by turning into the same monsters we fought,: Zabaneja shouted.

:And what would you have us do?: someone cried out from the crowd.

:To stay true to what this alliance is. What my mother was,: Zabaneja said.

:And what of the survivors, do we let them go free?: another in the crowd called.

:Do not be absurd,: Phrynia said. *:That is not what he is saying.:*

:If they are to be executed, then so be it, but we will do so justly and without cruelty. We will not treat our enemies as they would have treated us. We will not stoop to their level. We are beings of honor. That was my mother's final wish to me and, if you choose not to abide by that, if you choose to act like the savages we fought, then I will walk away from all of you in shame.:

A collective murmur went through the crowd, and they dispersed.

#

As news of Darchok's demise spread, many of his clan tried to flee while others surrendered. The fleeing drageals were chased down, captured, and returned.

:What will we do with the enemy survivors?: one of the drageals asked.

:Confine them. We will deal with them after we have tended to our wounded and dead,: Zabaneja told him.

A short time later, one of the drageal riders came running up to Zabaneja.

"What is it?"

"Aneesyma," the rider said, "and his drageal."

"What of them?" Zabaneja asked.

"We cannot find them," the rider said. "They are not answering anyone's call. And they are not among the wounded or the dead."

"That is impossible," Zabaneja said. "They must be somewhere. They could not have just disappeared."

"Shall we go look for them?" Phrynia asked. She could only imagine what was going on in his mind. First, to lose his mother and now not to know the fate of the human he was closest to. He must feel as if his entire world was crumbling around him.

Zabaneja nodded.

They took to the air and flew further than the others had and finally came upon Aneesyma's drageal, but he was no where in sight.

"Where is Aneesyma?" Zabaneja asked as he knelt beside the mortally wounded drageal.

"He fell. We were alone when we were attacked by three of the enemy. They came out of nowhere... " The drageal coughed and continued. "One flew at my face while the second slashed the seat strap, causing Aneesyma to fall from my back. I tried to go after him but the enemy surrounded me. I fought, but... I could not save him... I am sorry..."

"Where? Where did he fall?" Zabaneja asked. It was too late; the drageal was dead.

Zabaneja turned to Phrynia. "What do we do now? Where do we search? I must find him."

"I know. We will find him. I promise." Phrynia said, putting her hand on his shoulder. "And if we alone cannot find him, we will have everyone else join the search."

They took off and scoured the lands, first nearby where the drageal was found and then further out. Though neither would say it, they knew they would not find him alive. At last they spied a crumpled mass. Phrynia flew lower and saw it was Aneesyma.

CHAPTER FIFTY-EIGHT

IN THE AFTERMATH of the battle, the responsibility of ensuring everything that needed to be done—tending to the alliance wounded, taking care of the dead, dealing with the prisoners—fell, almost naturally, to Nanetscka and Zabaneja. While neither had sought out the position, both rose to the task.

"Have you thought what you will do?" Nanetscka asked when the two were alone. "Will you go back with the humans or come home with us?"

Zabaneja shook his head. "With both mother and grandfather gone, I have no family, so, do I really belong with the clan?"

Nanetscka looked hurt.

"I am sorry. I did not mean to imply the rest of the clan does not matter to me. It is just..."

"I did not ask to make you feel uncomfortable."

"I know. And I appreciate your concern and interest." Zabaneja said.

"So, you will return to the humans," Nanetscka said.

"I am not sure," Zabaneja said.

"What do you mean? If you do not come home and you do not

go with them, where will you go? With the emuranda or one of the other groups?"

"I do not know if I belong with anyone."

"You cannot just wander alone. That is no life. You need to be around others. Be they human, drageal or someone else," Nanetscka said.

He did not respond.

She sighed. "Just know, I will support you in whatever decision you make."

"I know, old friend," Zabaneja said. "Right now, I need time alone."

#

"Zab, we need to decide what to do with our dead. Do we try to bring them home or bury them here or something else?" Guentza asked.

"I am not the best one to make that decision," Zabaneja said. "We burn our dead."

"Ah, yes. Well, I have given it some thought and realize there are problems with all options. If we bring them home, we have to deal with rotting bodies on the journey. If we bury them here, that would require able-bodied people, who are few in number, to dig graves. Burning them will be the most efficient thing to do, but may upset some of those back home."

"It is quite the quandary, but I feel you have already made up your mind without any input from me," Zabaneja said.

Guentza chuckled. "You know me well. The most efficient and humane action would be to burn the bodies along with the drageals, if that would be allowed."

"That would not be a problem. They fought and died together

so it would be fitting they be sent to their final end together. And those in their homelands? What if they have issues with that decision?"

"If it comes to that, I will explain."

"And if they are still not satisfied?" Zabaneja said.

Guentza shrugged. "If there is one thing I have learned, Zab...an...e....ja, it is there will always be someone who has an issue with whatever you say or do. You just have to do what you feel is best in the situation. What is best for the majority, not just the few."

"You are wise, Guentza. Wait! You called me by my full name."

Guentza laughed. "I have been practicing. Still not an easy name to pronounce, I hope I did not butcher it."

"It was a noble effort," Zabaneja said. "But perhaps, you should just continue to call me Zab."

Both men laughed.

"I have another question," Guentza continued. "What are your plans once all has been taken care of here?"

"Not you, too? Are you and Nanetscka conspiring against me?"

"I do not know what you mean."

"She asked the same question earlier this morning," Zabaneja said.

"We are concerned. I know, with both Aneesyma and Pheunaf gone, you are no longer obligated to return to the Keep. But we would be honored if you decided to do so."

Zabaneja turned and took a few steps away. "I do not know. I really have no idea what I will do."

"I see," Guentza said and put his hand on the young man's shoulder. "You are a very special person, Zab. Aneesyma knew it, as did Pheunaf. That is why they both tried so hard to give you the best of both worlds."

"I see that now," Zabaneja said. "I only wish I had told them before they were gone."

"Do not fret. They knew. No matter how much you moaned and groaned and fought them, they knew deep in your heart you understood."

"I certainly did not make it easy on them."

"No child ever does," Guentza said with a laugh and a slap on Zabaneja's back.

"What of the Keep?"

"What do you mean?" Guentza asked.

"With Aneesyma gone, who will be the lord?" Zabaneja asked. "Is there a chain of command for the succession since he has no heir?"

Guentza shook his head. "No, the rule of the land does not work like the military. If the lord dies with no heir, it falls to the king to appoint a new lord unless there are unusual circumstances."

Zabaneja looked confused.

"The noble can designate someone, not necessarily a relation, to succeed after his passing." Guentza said.

"Oh, I see," Zabaneja said. "Do you have any idea who might succeed, Aneesyma?"

"That will depend," Guentza said

"On what?"

"If the king accepts Aneesyma's suggestion and, more importantly, if the designee decides to return to the Keep."

"Wait. No," Zabaneja said, realizing what Guentza's words implied. "Surely you cannot mean me."

Guentza smiled and nodded. "Of course, I do. Who else would Aneesyma have wanted to succeed him if not you?"

"I would have thought you would be his successor."

"Me? No, that would never do." Guentza said. "Why would you even think that?

"You know the workings of the Keep and all that encompasses

and you are a native of that land. Surely you would be a far better choice. The people would readily accept you. They know and trust you."

"But I am no politician. No diplomat," Guentza said.

"And you think I, of all people, am?" Zabaneja asked, his mouth open, his face reflecting his shock.

Guentza laughed again. "It does not matter what I think. Anee-syma thought so."

"I cannot believe that." Zabaneja said. "Surely the king will not allow me to take over the Keep, I am not even of your land."

"At one point in time we all came from different lands. You fought well to defend us in this war."

Zabaneja shook his head. "I did not fight to defend you or your lands. I did so for my people. For the drageals."

"Perhaps that was your original intention, but that was not how you finished."

Zabaneja shook his head.

"Of course, all of this is a moot point if you choose not to come back to the Keep."

Zabaneja did not reply.

"I will not attempt to force my will or influence upon you," Guentza said. "You are the only one who can make that decision. And, it must be made out of desire, not obligation or a sense of duty."

Zabaneja nodded.

"Then I will take my leave and allow you to be alone with your thoughts. Please know I am here if you need guidance or someone to speak to in order to aid you in the decision process."

"Thank you. I appreciate your kind offer."

#

With the alliance wounded being tended to, the task of preparing the funeral pyres began. A line of twenty or more shallow ditches were dug then filled with the grass and such that had been cleared from their paths.

The bodies of Pheunaf and Aneesyma were, as would all the others, treated with herbs and scented oils meant to offset, though even they could not fully remove, the odors of the cremation process. They were then placed on the first two pyres. It was decided these pyres would hold only them, while all others would receive bodies of numerous drageals, humans and others though each would be burned individually.

As Pheunaf's body was laid to rest and before the fire was lit, Zabaneja knelt beside her. He removed from his pocket the large purple gem he always carried and placed it under her wing. "You would not take this from me before, Mother, but I will return it to you now so you can have it with you forever." His tears freely flowed as he leaned over and kissed her cheek then rose and returned to his place by the others.

The fires were lit. Pheunaf and Aneesyma's bodies burned. All gathered regaled them with songs and tales celebrating their honor and valor both in battle and in life.

Then, one by one, the other alliance members of all races were laid upon the flames. As a testament to their sacrifice, all who were able remained, stood vigil, wept and sang tributes for each, whether they knew them or not.

As the crematory fires burned, Guentza approached Zabaneja. "What of those to be executed?" Guentza asked. "What will come of them?"

"Do you fear the drageals will be barbaric and kill them in a vile and torturous manner? Do you think that little of us? Or do you have some macabre fascination with execution I was not aware of?"

Zabaneja asked.

"Of course, not. That is not what I mean at all," Guentza said. "One of the things I have learned in my time with the drageals is they are far more civil than many humans I have known. Especially in war, far too many humans seem to revel in taking revenge upon their enemies once they have defeated them. That is most definitely not what I see with drageals. There is little revenge, little malice within them."

"Good," Zabaneja said. "I am glad you see that in us. So, what is your question?"

"How exactly will they be executed and what will be done with their corpses and the bodies of those of Darchok's fallen forces?" Guentza asked.

"Ah, I see. The executions will be swift. They will have their throats ripped out."

Guentza cringed.

Zabaneja shook his head. "Do not fear, it is not as gruesome as it sounds. A drageal's talon can behead most creatures with a single swipe. The prisoners will be dead before their bodies hit the ground. As for disposal," Zabaneja began, "they will be burned just as any other drageal, but theirs will be on a communal fire. They will have no show of honor."

Guentza nodded. "As I said, far more civil than many humans. Far too often I have seen humans leave their enemy's dead to be picked upon by beasts."

Zabaneja nodded. "Drageals are not the monsters of your children's tales, are they?"

Guentza shook his head. "No, far from that."

#

As the ashes of the last of the alliance dead cooled, Darchok's remaining troops were executed. Before each was slain, they were reminded theirs was a much nobler end than they deserved. Their deaths, as Zabaneja had told Guentza, were swift and compassionate.

The enemy's bodies, including Darchok's, were piled onto only a few pyres, isolated from the camp and the others, and were set ablaze together. As they burned, the only sounds were the crackle and hiss of the fires. There were no prayers, no songs, not even a word of farewell. The only ones in attendance were the sentinels there to ensure the fires burned true.

CHAPTER FIFTY-NINE

AFTER THE CREMATORY FIRES were quenched, a cavernous silence befell the camp and lasted until the farewells began a few days later. One by one, the groups departed, leaving behind only the humans from the Keep and drageals. As Guentza prepared to depart, he asked Zabaneja one last time if he was going with them. The young man declined.

"So you are returning to the drageals. I am glad to hear that," Guentza said as he bid farewell to the young man who had been his subordinate.

"No."

"I do not understand."

Zabaneja stood silent. After a few moments, Guentza realized he would get no further explanation.

"Just know you are always welcome at the Keep, even if it is only for a visit," Guentza said and gave the young man a bear hug.

"Thank you," Zabaneja said.

#

After the humans departed, Nanetscka and Zabaneja shared a meal.

"I am glad to see you have not lost your taste for raw meat," Nanetscka said. "I do not understand why the humans burn their food so."

"Nor do I," Zabaneja said and managed a weak smile. "You do not know how much I miss eating meat this way or how hard it was for me to eat it cooked."

Nanetscka laughed.

"So, when are you and the clan leaving?" Zabaneja asked.

"At dawn," she replied. "And you? Since you did not leave with Guentza or any of the others, does that mean you are coming with us or are you to meet them later?"

Zabaneja stood and walked a few paces away from Nanetscka.

"What is it?" Nanetscka asked. "What is bothering you? I understand if you want to go with the humans. You deserve to be with your own kind, especially that young female."

Zabaneja shook his head and turned back to face her. "That is not it. I am not going with the humans."

"Wonderful," she said. "So you are coming home, coming with us."

"No," Zabaneja said. "I am not doing that, either."

"I do not understand. If you are not going with them nor coming with us, what will you do?" she asked.

"I am not sure." He turned away again.

Nanetscka knew he was lying, but she chose not to challenge him. "Well, you are always welcome to return to the clan. All you need to do is call. We will come for you."

Zabaneja turned and walked to her. He threw his arms around her neck. "You have always been and will always be my dearest friend, Nanetscka. I will never forget you."

"Nor I you," she replied.

The pair stayed in the embrace for several moments, neither sure if this would indeed be the last time they would see each other.

"Would you like one last flight tonight?"

"Are you serious? You know you need not ask twice."

"Good, then find your seat and we will be off." Nanetscka said.

Too soon, although they could have been aloft forever and it would still have been too soon, the flight came to an end.

"The other riders do not realize the pure joy of riding without having to worry about tactics and battle. Thank you so much, Nanetscka." Zabaneja then thought, *you were the first I rode with in a saddle and now you will be the last.*

"As always, my dear friend," Nanetscka said. "It has been my pleasure, and I look forward to us riding together again in the future."

#

The following morning, Zabaneja came to bid farewell to Nanetscka and the rest of the clan.

"Where is Phrynia?" he asked.

"She is gone. She wanted to catch the first rays of sunlight, or so she claimed. I think she did not want to say goodbye to you," Nanetscka said.

"Please tell her I missed seeing her again, but I understand. Flying at the break of dawn has always been my favorite time as well."

Nanetscka and Zabaneja embraced again, and she joined the others. He was thankful to be able to hold back his tears until the last of the drageals were well aloft.

He stood, eyes skyward, for several minutes after the last drageal disappeared from sight. He turned and walked to Pheunaf and Aneesyma's final resting place. Even though it was now nothing more than a pile of ashes, Zabaneja sat in silence and wept.

After some time, he heard a noise, a cracking branch, as if someone was trying to creep up on him. He reached for his weapon, but realized it was not at his side. He sat frozen, unsure if he was going to be attacked, and then realized he did not care. He waited but heard nothing more. Perhaps it was his imagination. As he relaxed, he sensed more movement behind him, but at the same time he heard a voice in his head.

He turned and saw Kalini.

"My boy, while I am glad to see you, why you are still here and alone?"

He shrugged. "Why you have returned?"

"Much as you have been doing, I have come to pay my final respects to your mother and Aneesyma, as well as homage to all those we lost."

"Is that the only reason you have come?" Zabaneja asked.

Now it was Kalini's turn to chuckle. "Are you accusing me of ulterior motives, child?"

Zabaneja smirked. "I am not the boy you first met so long ago."

"No, you are not." Kalini said. "I will admit, I am worried about you. Why are you not on your way home by now?"

"Home?" Zabaneja snorted. "Do I actually have such a thing?"

"I do not know what you mean. From what I understand, you have two. Both the drageals and the humans want and love you," Kalini said.

"Yet, I do not feel I belong with either of them."

"What in the world are you saying? You are a rare being, my dear. One that has crossed into multiple worlds," Kalini told him.

"That may be, but I am also the reason this war happened. Had mother not found me, not taken me to the clan, Darchok would not have begun this war. And all these people of all the races would not have had to lose their lives."

Kalini laughed.

"What are you laughing at?" Zabaneja bristled.

"You."

"Me?"

"You are indeed a far cry from the shy, angry, little boy who once hid behind his mother's wing. Now you feel you are so important that your mere existence caused a war." She shook her head and did the closest thing to a tsk a chetoga could. "Do you really think yourself so significant to this world that you, and you alone, were the cause of the war? That if you were not here, the war would not have occurred?"

"No, but maybe my living with the clan, so close to Darchok, ignited a hatred in him that might not have emerged had I not been there."

"Darchok was always a hateful being. Had you not been there it would have been something else, perhaps a scent on the wind would have set him on the same path. This war would still have happened. And, if you were not here, if you did not have the life you did, with a toehold in both the human and drageal worlds, would the alliance that defeated him have even been possible? And if there was no alliance, would there have been a different outcome to the war? Or perhaps it might have lasted longer, been more devastating. Who is to say?"

"It does not matter. I do not plan on living in either of their worlds."

"That pains me to hear you say that. You are not meant to be alone."

Zabaneja did not respond.

"Are you sure you really want to spend your life with no one to talk to, to laugh with, or to do all the other things social creatures such as humans and, for that matter, drageals do? And what about Rusalei? Are you just going to leave her behind without even an explanation?"

"She will get over it. She and I were never meant to be anything more than friends."

Kalini shook her head. "For one so bright, you are blind when it comes to those around you, your friends and, even more so, those who love you."

"Love me... " Zabaneja turned away.

"Do you think they," Kalini said, pointing to the ashes piled in front of them, "would want you to be alone or to be happy?"

He did not respond.

Kalini sighed. "That is all I had to say. And now it is time for me to leave." She walked to Zabaneja. He reached down and hugged her.

"I thank you for coming to pay your respects. They both always considered you a dear friend," Zabaneja said.

"It was not only them I came to see, sweet boy. But you know that." Kalini smiled. "Remember, I will never abandon you even though I fear you are trying to abandon yourself."

Zabaneja forced a smile as he watched her walk away.

#

He slept beside his mother's ashes that night. He woke exhausted, but had made a decision. One he hoped was the correct one.

He bid a final farewell to his mother's ashes and departed for anywhere he could be alone.

CHAPTER SIXTY

SHORTLY AFTER THE NEWS of the victory and the loss of Aneesyma arrived at the Keep, word was received that the surviving troops were returning. Debate arose about what should be done.

"While we continue to mourn those we lost, we must not forget to honor those who survived. And to remember the sacrifices all made to keep us safe," Rusalei said to the crowd gathered by the castle steps.

She was happy to see, even in their grief, so many agreed.

"You have become quite the stateswoman," Haoule, the eldest minister, said. "Aneesyma was wise in choosing you against the guidance of his council.

"Thank you."

#

On the day of the troops scheduled return, Rusalei's excitement nearly overwhelmed her. She had long since forgiven Zabaneja. Now, a part of her wanted to ride out alone, find him and throw herself at him without a care for decorum or protocol. But she did not. More because she knew the embarrassment it would cause him. She hoped with all that had happened, he would no longer hold himself or her to his perceived class distinctions. So, she waited with the other members of the council for the men and women who had fought so hard and so bravely to appear.

When at last they did, with Guentza in the lead, she could barely hold back her excitement. She was surprised not to see Zabaneja beside the captain of the guard. She had expected him to be there. She reminded herself that the first riders would get the biggest cheer and onslaught of well wishes, so he was probably riding nearer to the back, possibly wanting to slip in unnoticed as the last rider. Or maybe he would try to blend in with the others somewhere in the swell of troops. So, she looked into every face, but none was the one she longed to see. When the last rider entered and the Keep gates were closed, she was shocked to realize Zabaneja was not among them.

She was struck with the most primal of fears. Was he dead? Had he fallen in battle and no one had sent word to them, to her? No, that could not be. He could not be dead. She would have known, would have felt a hole in her heart. She tried to reach Rikar or Guentza or any of the others she knew, but she could not get close to them. They were surrounded by well-wishers and dignitaries, and the crowd seemed to be pushing her further away. She frantically began to ask about Zabaneja's whereabouts to anyone who would listen. No one seemed to know.

She did not know what to do when a hand grasped her arm and yanked her aside. She turned, ready to punch her assailant when she saw it was Rikar.

"I have been looking for you, Rusalei," he said. Releasing her arm, he motioned her to follow him. "Why were you not on the balcony with the others?"

"I went looking for Zab," she replied as she followed him. "Where is he? Where are you taking me?"

Her heart soared. He had snuck in and wanted to meet privately. That was where Rikar was taking her—to meet Zabaneja.

Rikar did not answer, he could not. He did not have the words or the heart to tell her the truth. That he would leave to Guentza.

At last they reached their destination. Rikar opened the door and motioned Rusalei to enter. In the next moment, her hopes and excitement were dashed when she saw Guentza not Zabaneja standing there.

"Where is he? Where is Zab?" she cried. "What has happened to him? Why is he not here?"

Her mind ran in a thousand directions, found a million explanations, but none was close to the truth. The truth that would shatter her world.

"Why are you not speaking, Guentza? What are you hiding from me? What are you not telling me?" she cried as she pounded on the man's chest.

Guentza took hold of her wrists. She looked up into his face.

"I will not, cannot believe he is dead. That cannot be," she sobbed as she saw the look in Guentza's eyes.

He shook his head. "No, he is not dead."

"Then where is he? Is he wounded? Is he somewhere else having his wounds tended? Tell me where he is, and I will go to him."

Guentza released her. "No, Lady Rusalei, he is not dead nor he is wounded, at least not in the physical sense. But he is not coming back."

"What do you mean?" she cried. "This is his home."

Guentza shook his head. "I believe that and so do you, but Zab does not. He does not think of the Keep as his home. With both Aneesyma and Pheunaf gone, he is no longer bound to this place."

She sobbed and then smiled. "He went home to his beloved drageals. That is good. He loves the drageals. Now he will be able to soar high in the sky every day."

Guentza's eyes welled, something she had never seen happen in all the years she had known him. "He did not go with the drageals, either."

"What? Then where did he go?"

"I do not know," Guentza replied. "I do not think he knew."

"How could you let this happen?" she shrieked. "Why did you not force him to come back, to come home? Could you not have done that?"

"My dearest lady, I did the best I could to convince him," Guentza said. "But Zab is a grown man, not a child. One does not just throw another over a horse and ride off with him to some place he does not wish to go."

"One does, if the other one is clearly not rational," Rusalei insisted.

"I have something for you," Guentza said ignoring her remark. He reached into his coat pocket. "It is from Zab." He held out an envelope to her.

She stared at it for several moments.

"Take it, My Lady," Guentza said. "Whether you take it or not, he is still not here, so please. It is what he wanted."

She slowly reached for the letter and brought it to her chest.

Guentza bowed. "I will leave now and ensure you are not disturbed."

He turned and headed for the door.

"Guentza," she said.

"Yes, My Lady?" he replied, his voice cracking a little.

"Thank you. Thank you for everything."

"It has always been my pleasure, not just my duty, to serve you,

Lady Rusalei," he replied and left the room.

#

Rusalei stood for several moments staring at the door and clutching the letter to her chest. She was torn. She wanted to read it, to see what he had to say. How he was going to explain why he had not returned to the Keep. To her. Had everything they had shared been a lie? Had she only imagined that he cared for her, wanted her, perhaps even needed her?

She could not stop the flood of questions that filled her mind. She felt like she was drowning in her own thoughts, in her own fears. She knew the only way to find the answers was to open the letter, to read what he had to say. But that meant she would encounter another level of fear.

She held her breath, then slowly and carefully, causing as little damage to the envelope as possible, opened it and removed the meticulously folded paper inside. She again hesitated. She closed her eyes, told herself it would be all right, took a deep breath and unfolded it.

> *My dearest Rusalei,*
> *I am so sorry, but I will not be returning. I cannot. I cannot*
> *explain why. You would not understand because I do not. I*
> *only know it to be what I need to do.*
> *Please forgive me.*
> *Forever your servant, Zabaneja*

She refolded the paper, returned it to the envelope and put it inside her sleeve. She took a deep breath and tried to stop her tears. When they finally did, she wiped the moisture from her cheeks, turned and slowly left the room. She was glad to see Guentza had not posted a guard at the door to ensure she would be alone. For that is what she wanted, to be alone, now and forever more.

#

It took some time, almost a month, for Rusalei to venture from her rooms. It did not matter who attempted to bring her out of her doldrums, they failed to succeed. She did not want to be around anyone. What she wanted, she could not have. She wanted Zabaneja. One minute she was angry at herself for not being what he needed to make him want to come back. Then she was furious at him for not even giving her the opportunity to accompany him wherever he had decided to go. She cursed him for always thinking she was too pampered to be able to stay with him no matter the lifestyle, no matter how rough or soft.

Finally, she accepted the truth. There was nothing she could do. As much as she wanted to run to him, to find him, to tell him he was wrong, to convince him they, both of them, were better together than apart. She knew it was impossible. She did not know where he was, and no one else did either.

At last, she emerged from her self-imposed solitude and went to rejoin the council. If they would still have her.

CHAPTER SIXTY-ONE

"HAOULE AND I have been summoned to Siggurna," Guentza informed the council, "to discuss the succession of rule since Zab, Lord Aneesyma's choice, has not returned."

"Are you sure he will not come back?" Rusalei asked.

Guentza shook his head. "I do not know. But the Keep cannot be left leaderless indefinitely while we wait."

Rusalei reluctantly agreed. "Do you have any idea who the king may appoint? Will it be someone from here or an outsider?"

"I would not even dare to guess."

"When will you leave?" Rusalei asked.

"Tomorrow morning."

"We wish you safe travels and an auspicious outcome."

#

"I do not understand your decision, Majesty," Guentza said. "Why would you choose me to take over the rule of the Keep? I am neither diplomat, nor ruler. I am a soldier."

The king smiled. "Be that as it may, you are not only well

respected by everyone, including my staff who fought alongside you, but you are a leader. And since the one Aneesyma chose as his successor has not returned, nor does it look likely he will…"

"Surely there must be someone else," Guentza interrupted.

"I agree with you, Sire," Haoule said. "Guentza, as much as he may protest, is indeed the best person for the position in the absence of both Lord Aneesyma and Zab."

Guentza continued to voice his disagreement with the king's decision, but he soon realized, short of leaving the Keep, he had no choice but to accept.

"All right," the captain of the guard finally relented, "if this is, indeed, what you think best for the Keep."

The king and Haoule were about to congratulate him when Guentza raised his hand. "I will accept with one condition."

"And what might that be?" the king asked.

"If Zab returns, he will take over the rule of the Keep."

"And do you think that is truly a possibility?" Haoule asked.

"I am not sure. I hope so. He should not be sentenced, even self-imposed, to a life alone."

The king pondered the request, and after a few moments, nodded. "I will agree to that, but I will add my own stipulation. I give you permission to change your mind and remain as the Lord of the Keep even if Zab returns, if you decide to do so."

Guentza nodded.

"Good, then it is settled."

"One more thing," Guentza said, "I do not want any pomp and circumstance, no fuss, over my appointment. Merely a proclamation stating I am the new Lord will be fine."

The king laughed. "Why am I not surprised? Yes, if that is your wish, there will be no formal ceremony."

\#

"So, Lord Guentza," Haoule said and smiled as the former captain of the guard bristled at being addressed so, "what will be your first action as Lord of the Keep?"

"To not be called Lord," Guentza replied.

Haoule laughed.

"Thanks to the way Aneesyma ruled, there is not really anything that needs to be changed from the way it is."

"Does that include the council?" Haoule asked. "Have you given any thought to replacing the current ministers with those of your own choosing?"

"I see no reason to do any such thing. Aneesyma chose you for a reason. As far as I can see, each of you are the best person for the job. Not to mention the differences in opinion you display allow all decisions to be looked at from every view point."

"And the position of captain of the guard? Will that go to Canackell?"

"She is the logical choice since she handled the role so efficiently in my absence."

"One more thing... "

Guentza shook his head. "Is this what my life is going to be from now on? Policy decisions all day long?"

Haoule laughed. "The only difference between this and your previous position is the nature of the questions."

"If you say so."

"Now, you do realize even though you do not want an elaborate ceremony you will need to do something, even if it is just a wave of your hand to the people in the courtyard, for your appointment to be official."

Guentza winced. "If you insist."

CHAPTER SIXTY-TWO

ZABANEJA WANDERED AIMLESSLY, never lingering in any
one place. The passage of time did little to assuage the overwhelming
grief that filled his entire being.

Without realizing it, he found himself at his mother's gravesite.
He sat alone and stared at the now barren ground. Suddenly, he felt
a touch on his shoulder. He turned to see Nanetscka. He wanted to
run, but knew she would not allow such a thing.

"Well now," she said with a chuckle, "you have become quite
the scruffy mongrel since last we met. Not to mention you did not
even sense my presence. How are you surviving if you allow others to
sneak up on you?"

He stared blankly at her.

"Oh, come now, you cannot tell me you do not know who I am.
Or, has all this time in isolation wiped your mind of all you ever
knew?"

"Of course, I know who you are. I was not expecting to see
anyone," he said in a hoarse whisper.

Nanetscka shook her head. There were so many things she wanted to say to him, to chastise him for his current way of life, but this

was neither the time nor the place for that. "You are fortunate I recognized your scent lest I might have mistaken you for a meal."

He did not respond.

Nanetscka shook her head. "You do realize tomorrow is the anniversary. Many others will be coming soon to honor the fallen."

A look of panic came over him and his eyes scanned the area for a way to escape. "I must go," he said, and tried to get past the drageal.

"Why?" she asked as she grasped his arm. "Have you not punished yourself long enough for something that was not of your making?"

Knowing he would not be able to lie to her, he said nothing. After a moment, she released him.

"Very well, if that is how you feel, I will not stop you from running away yet again. But you must realize all who know you feel your self-imposed exile is foolish. Do you really think Aneesyma would want that for you? And more importantly, would this have been her wish?" She nodded to Pheunaf's final resting spot.

He shook his head and ran for the nearby trees.

Nanetscka growled under her breath, "You are being so... so... Oh, I do not know what you are being, but whatever it is, it is not right." She turned back to the gravesite and bowed her head. "Please, Pheunaf, find a way to help him," she prayed in a whisper.

#

As the others arrived, Nanetscka saw Phrynia scanning the horizon. "He has been and gone."

Phrynia was shocked. "What do you mean? You saw him? What did he say? Where did he go?"

"He was here, but said little before he ran off. Sadly, he still cannot forgive himself for all of this."

"I must go. I need to find him. I need to see him for myself. I need to talk to him," Phrynia said and took off into the sky.

"I hope you have better luck than I did."

#

Phrynia flew as low as she dared, trying to catch sight or scent of Zabaneja. After several unsuccessful hours, she abandoned her quest and returned to the others. By now, the gathering had grown in size and included drageals and humans and a few others. As everyone reacquainted themselves, the conversation was both lively with current happenings and sad with memories.

When Guentza and the others from Hammarsh Keep arrived, all craned their necks, hoping to see Zabaneja amongst those gathered.

:This should be a time to joyfully and lovingly honor the memories of those we lost. The time for tears has passed,: Nanetscka said into everyone's minds. *:They would not wish us to dwell upon their demise but rather to celebrate their lives.:*

:Here! Here!: cried most of the crowd as they raised their goblets in a toast.

As the night wore on, everyone began to break off into smaller groups.

:It is good to see you again, Guentza,: Nanetscka said. *:I am glad your ability to communicate this way has not faded.:*

:Sadly, it has. I can no longer use it across any distance.:

She nodded. *:I fear that is what is happening to all of us. And, as for Zabaneja, I doubt he will return while everyone is here,:* she said.

:Return? He was here?:

She nodded. *:But I doubt even you would have recognized him.*

His time alone has not done well by him.:

:What did he say?:

:Not much.:

Guentza chuckled. *:Well, that is true to form for him, I guess. Like a drageal, he is not one to indulge in conversation. But you say he does not look well. Is he ill?:*

:I could not tell. My gut says physically he is fine but his mind and emotions are still... : She paused, unable to continue without breaking down.

Guentza took her hand. *:Say no more, dear lady. I understand. I had just hoped... :*

:As did we all, but perhaps the time will come when he feels able to return to us.:

Guentza nodded.

#

As they watched the others depart, Guentza and Nanetscka lingered, holding out hope Zabaneja would appear.

:I am surprised the chetoga and emuranda did not come,: Guentza said.

:Their beliefs in regard to the dead differ greatly from ours, so I did not expect them,: Nanetscka said.

:Still, I thought Kalini would be here...:

:Yes, that does surprise me. Perhaps she will come after everyone is gone.:

:I would have liked to see her again. And now my dear lady, it is time for me to take my leave as well.: He took one last look around, still hoping to see Zabaneja.

#

It had been three days since everyone had departed. Only then did Zabaneja come out of hiding to pay his respects. He returned to his mother's gravesite and sat in silence.

After a while, he sensed something. He looked skyward and saw the glint of golden feathers glistening in the last rays of the sun's light. He began to run, but the incoming drageal would have none of that. She swooped down and grabbed him.

"Phrynia, put me down," he shouted. "You are hurting me."

:I will let you go if you promise not to run.:

:I promise,: he replied.

They landed and Zabaneja considered running, regardless of what he had said, but knew any escape attempt would be futile.

"Why have you returned?" he asked.

"I could ask you the same question? And, by the way, you look terrible. And your stench! Maybe I should have dropped you in the river."

He did not respond to her chiding. "You have not answered me. Why did you return?"

"I came back because I knew in my heart you would. And, before you panic any further, though why you should is beyond my comprehension, no one else is coming. Now, stop acting so foolishly. Come, sit and visit with me. I swear I will not try to force you to do anything you do not wish to do."

For the first time since he had gone off on his own, Zabaneja welcomed the nearness of another living being.

"Why did you leave that morning without saying goodbye?" he asked, breaking the awkward silence.

"Umm... Well..." she looked away. "I could not bear the thought of you not returning with us. But I never imagined you would go off alone. If I had known that was your plan, I would have gone with you."

Zabaneja smiled. "No, that would not have worked. I needed to be alone and you, well, you are far too gregarious a soul to ever be content with me as your only companion."

"Still, I would have done so if for no other reason than to ensure you bathed and ate. You are half the man I remember and most of what remains is the hairiness on your face and head. When was the last time you ate?"

He broke out into a deep laugh. "Wait! Is this truly you, Phrynia? I mean, you sound more like my mother than my former partner. Since when did you start worrying about how I looked or if I ate?"

She shook her head and smiled. "Since you stopped doing so. I am being serious. Are you really all right?"

He reached for her hand. "I could say yes, but you would not believe me. In all honesty, I do not think I even know what 'all right' is anymore."

She put her other hand over his. "You endured a much greater loss than the rest of us. But that does not mean you cannot go on with a life that is both meaningful and happy. You do not have to continue suffering."

He pulled away. "Do you wish me to forget what happened? Forget her?" he snapped.

"Of course, not. We can never forget, even when we try. Those memories are always with us, but they must be kept as just that, memories, some to be cherished and others to be cried over. But, they cannot be allowed to rule our lives as you are letting them rule yours."

He looked into her face and saw she too was crying. "I am sorry. Sorry for my rudeness. For my accusations. For... for everything."

She took his hand again. "There is no need to apologize to me. I am not the one who needs your forgiveness."

He looked puzzled.

"You need to forgive yourself. To let go of the guilt you bear for things you were blameless in."

"I want to. I really do, but after all this time, I do not think I know how."

"Then, let me help you," she said as she pulled him into her and wrapped her wings around him. She was not surprised when both of them openly sobbed.

#

"Have you given any more thought to what we discussed last night?"

"Yes. I have decided it is time for me to return," Zabaneja said.

Phrynia was shocked. "What changed your mind?"

"I was sitting beside the gravesite, watching the first rays of dawn when I saw something glistening in the sunlight. Something that had not been there before. I went to see what it was and found this." He held out his hand to reveal a large purple gem.

"What is it?"

Zabaneja stroked the stone. "This is the stone my mother gave me when I left for the Keep. It was her most precious possession."

"I do not understand."

"I placed this on her body that day."

Phrynia still looked confused.

"Do you not see? This is a sign from Mother. It is her way of telling me that she does not hold me responsible for not being able to save her."

Phrynia put her hand on his shoulder. "Is that not what we have been telling you all along?"

Zabaneja nodded.

"But I still sense a hesitancy within you."

He walked a few paces from her. "As much as my head tells me I am welcome in both places, there is a part of me that has its doubts. Perhaps it is pride. Maybe I fear looking foolish. Like a child who ran away from home only to return with his tail between his legs to the admonishing glares of friends and family."

"Is that all?" she shouted. "From what Nanetscka says about your youth, that was an everyday occurrence for both of you. Have you fallen so low that if people did think such a thing, which I doubt anyone would, it would break you? That is definitely not the Zabaneja I knew. Not the one I called partner and friend. And if that is who you are now, then perhaps it is better you stay off by yourself so no one can hurt your precious feelings." She stood and walked away from him.

A few moments later, she felt his hand on her arm. "I am sorry. I have been wallowing in self-pity for so long, it just became my normal way of thinking. You are right. I do not need to worry about what others think of my actions. I never did before, so why do so now? And now that I know I have mother's blessing... " He stroked the stone then put it in his pocket.

"So you will return?"

"Yes. I think it is time."

"And where will you go?" she asked, full of hope and trepidation.

"To the humans."

"I see," she said, trying to mask her sadness at his decision.

"As much as I love the drageals and know they are my true kin, I feel it is the humans who need me more. Perhaps, by living with them, I can be of more help... make more of an impact. And then there is Rusalei... if she will even have me after the way I treated her."

"If she is half the person you think her to be, she will understand, though I highly recommend you clean yourself up before you see her. You look more like a wild beast than a human!"

The two friends laughed.

"I wish you were returning to us, but I am glad you will now abandon this life of solitude. You deserve so much better, my friend."

CHAPTER SIXTY-THREE

THE DAY BEFORE Zabaneja was to arrive at the Keep, Rusalei was summoned to the castle and found Rikar waiting for her.

She threw her arms around his neck and hugged him. "Rikar, it is so good to see you. It has been a very long time. Let me take a look at you and see how being the King's Guard…"

"King's Personal Guard, m'lady" Rikar said with playful haughtiness.

"Oh, excuse me, sir," she said with a giggle. "Allow me to see how being a part of the King's Personal Guard is treating you."

He stepped back and came to attention. She walked around him, eyeing him up and down, rubbing her chin and saying 'Hmm' and 'I see'. Finally, she seemed to have finished her inspection and stood in front of him.

"Well, Lady Rusalei? Do I pass your muster?" Rikar asked, trying to keep a straight face.

She, too, tried to maintain a stern facade, also with little success. "Well, Rikar, you seem in fine form. I think your new post suits you very well."

As soon as the words left her lips, the two old friends broke into laughter.

Once the pair were finally able to stop laughing, Rusalei looked at him and said. "So, why was I summoned here? Surely you are far too important these days to take time out for those of us living in the backwaters of the kingdom."

Rikar chuckled. "You seem to forget how backwater my roots truly are, Rusalei."

She smiled.

"There are two reasons I wished to speak to you and both involve Zab," he said.

"Oh yes, I think I heard something about him coming back." She took a step back and turned away from him. "There is nothing I want to hear about him, from you or anyone else."

"I know you are hurt," Rikar said, "but please hear me out."

She turned and tried to walk past him, but he grabbed her by the arm. "Please, Rusalei. If you feel the same when I have spoken my piece, then I will not stop you from leaving."

She wanted to go but could not get her legs to move. Finally, she nodded. "If you must, but, be advised, I doubt anything you say about him will be of interest to me."

Rikar pointed to a chair by the fireplace. "Please, let us sit. I do not often get to relax in such luxury, and with such lovely company."

She smiled again and took a seat, noticing a decanter of wine and two glasses on the table beside the chair. Rikar filled the glasses and offered her one, which she took with a slight nod of her head.

"So, what do you need to tell me about Zab?" she asked after a few moments.

"How much do you know about the war, specifically the final battle?" Rikar asked and put his glass on the table.

"As much as anyone else, I would guess," she replied.

"So Guentza never spoke to you of Zab's involvement that day?

What he did? What he saw?" Rikar asked.

She shook her head. "No, no one, most especially Guentza, has ever spoken to me about the battle. I can only imagine it must have been a horror."

"That is where you are wrong, you cannot. Especially not what Zab went through. I was there, I was a drageal rider in the midst of everything and even I cannot fathom it."

Rusalei looked at him. "What do you mean?"

"Did you hear how Pheunaf died?" he asked.

"In a battle with Darchok," she said.

"It was more than that, much more. Darchok and Pheunaf were embroiled in an aerial battle, as all the battles with the drageals were, but those two were fighting as if they were in hand to hand combat. From a distance the pair looked like a single mass of feathers with no distinction where one drageal began and the other ended."

"Oh my," she said.

"At some point, Pheunaf got the upper hand and was able to slash her brother's throat, killing him, but they were too interlocked in each other's grasp and close to the ground for her to recover, so she and Darchok's now lifeless body crashed to earth."

"I had no idea," Rusalei said, her eyes filling with tears.

"It gets worse," Rikar said.

"Worse?"

He nodded. "Zab was the first to get to Pheunaf. She was still alive, but she died a few moments later with him by her side."

"Oh, no," Rusalei said, tears streaming down her cheeks. "How terrible for him."

"Yes, but that was still not the end of the horrors of that day."

"What else could have happened?" she asked. "Did the battle, the war, not end once Darchok was killed?"

"Yes, for all intents, the war ended, but the fighting took a bit more time to conclude. And, even then, there is so much more to war than just the battle, the fighting."

Again Rusalei looked confused.

"Forgive me if my description becomes somewhat graphic, this is not usually the stuff of parlor talk, but…"

"I understand. Please go on," she said.

"Once the fighting is over, there is still the task of dealing with the dead and wounded. Unless you are a barbarian, you do not just leave them to rot or die."

She nodded. "I guess I never thought about that."

"Most people do not," he said. "As we began to deal with those things, we realized there had been no contact with Aneesyma nor his drageal since early morning. They were nowhere to be found amongst the living or the dead. So Zab and Phrynia took to the sky to find them."

"Oh my."

"I suppose no one has been told how Aneesyma died, have they?"

"No."

"Not even the council?" he asked.

"All we were told was, he died in battle. The look on your face makes me fear there is much more to it."

"From what we could piece together," Rikar began, "enemy drageals attacked and sliced the straps that held Aneesyma's seat. With no allies in the area to catch him, Aneesyma plummeted to the ground from a great height. Zab and Phrynia knew nothing of this when they first set out to find the pair. They first found Aneesyma's drageal, but Aneesyma was not there. Zab and Phrynia again took to the sky to find him. When they did, the sight of his mangled body was far worse than either Zab or Phrynia had expected, even after all the death and destruction they had seen thus far."

"Poor Zab," she said, her tears now openly flowing.

"So, Rusalei," he said, "I do not wish you to judge his decision to stay away too harshly. I was there with him after the funerals, first of Pheunaf and Aneesyma and then the others. He stood vigil through all of them. And, let me tell you, the pyres burned for days. Even when he was urged to go, to rest for a bit, he refused. He felt every alliance warrior deserved his respect."

Rusalei managed a smile. "That sounds like him."

"Yes, very much so. Even in his own personal grief, he still felt he could not shirk his responsibilities to those who looked to him for guidance and leadership, even if they were no longer in this world," Rikar said. "I spoke to him afterwards. After the flames had been quenched. After he finally took a moment to reflect upon his personal loss."

Rikar looked at Rusalei, and it surprised her to see his eyes welling with tears. She took his hand, and he nodded.

"He was a broken man, Rusalei. I had never seen him so, even when he first arrived here and thought his world had been shattered. Never had he been so low."

The pair squeezed each other's hands.

"He felt he no longer had a place where he belonged. That he was not of the world of man nor drageal."

"How could he think that?" Rusalei asked.

"I do not know. As I said, he was broken," Rikar said. "I tried to reason with him, to tell him he did indeed belong in both worlds. But he did not believe me. Even when Guentza told him Aneesyma had chosen him as his successor, his feelings did not change."

Rusalei shook her head and squeezed Rikar's hand again.

"I tried to convince him to come home with me. With Guentza. I begged him to come here, or if not here, with the drageals. I know the drageals, his childhood friend Nanetscka and his partner Phrynia and others, I am sure, also tried to get him to go with them. But his answer was always the same. He would not argue. He would merely look at us with a sadness that broke our hearts and quietly decline. None of us wanted to leave him. But we had no choice. Short of tying him to the back of a horse or drageal."

Rusalei smiled. "That is what Guentza said."

Rikar laughed. "Why does that not surprise me?"

"Are you certain he is coming back now?" Rusalei asked.

"Yes," Rikar said.

"How can you be so sure?" she asked.

"Phrynia had apparently met with him when he made the decision to come back to the Keep, and she contacted Guentza with the news."

"I wonder what made him change his mind?" Rusalei asked, more musing than actually expecting an answer.

"The only one who can tell us that will be him," Rikar said. "And, as we both know, that is highly unlikely."

"True." Rusalei said.

Rikar refilled their glasses. "So that is what I wanted to tell you."

"Thank you," she replied. "I appreciate that you shared this with me."

"And?" Rikar asked, not being able to control his curiosity any longer.

Rusalei smiled and took a sip of her wine. "And what?" she asked coyly.

"Do not toy with me," he said. "I know you still love him, and I know he hurt you by not coming back. But have I been at least able to help you understand why he may have done what he did? Do you forgive him?"

She looked down into her wine glass and then back at her friend. "Yes. I forgive him."

Rikar drew in a sigh of relief. "I am glad to hear that. Not that you should not give him a good tongue lashing for his actions."

She smiled. "Oh, I fully intend to do that."

"Good," Rikar said.

The pair lifted their glasses, clinked them in a toast, and sipped.

"But you said you had two things to tell me regarding Zab. What is the second?"

"Oh that, well, the second thing is really of little matter to you. It never has been."

She looked confused. "What do you mean?"

"Your title."

"Oh, that."

"Yes, that," Rikar said. "One of the things that has always kept Zab from fully allowing himself to love you. That obstacle has now or very soon will be removed."

Rusalei looked confused.

"Silly girl, he is going to be the Lord of the Keep. He, too, will have a title."

"You are right. I never thought of that, it never even crossed my mind." She felt more gleeful than she had in a very long time.

"That is because he was the only one who ever thought about it!"

CHAPTER SIXTY-FOUR

IT TOOK OVER A MONTH of travel for Zabaneja to reach the outer borders of the Keep's lands. On more than one occasion, he almost turned around. But each time those feelings surfaced, he felt as if his mother's hand was on his shoulder, urging him to continue on.

As he crossed the border, he was surprised to be met by a group of riders, members of the guard.

"Zab," one called out. "We have been waiting for you."

"I do not understand," Zabaneja said. "How did you know I was returning?"

The guardsman shrugged. "That is not for me to say. My orders were to escort you to the Keep."

"Very well," Zabaneja said.

As Zabaneja and the others rode, they were greeted by throngs of people who stood along the sides of the road, cheering and calling out their thanks.

"What is all of this?" Zabaneja asked.

"Everyone knows what you did," the guardsman said.

"I do not understand. What did I do?"

"What do you mean, what did you do?" asked one of the men Zabaneja remembered from his time at the Keep. "Have you forgotten that little thing called the war?"

Zabaneja shook his head. "I did no more than everyone else, than any of you who were there."

"Perhaps," a familiar voice said from behind.

Zabaneja stopped his horse and turned around in his saddle to see Rikar.

"Rikar!" Zabaneja cried out as his old friend rode up beside him.

The two reached out and grabbed each other's arm in an embrace.

"What are you doing here?" Zabaneja asked.

"Like the others, I am just following orders which are to make sure you do not change your mind and turn back before you reach the Keep."

The ride to the Keep continued to be slow, courtesy of the people gathered along the roadside and shouting Zab's name.

"I do not understand, how did they know I was returning?" he asked.

Rikar shrugged.

#

They arrived at the castle. Zabaneja, accompanied by Rikar, mounted the steps, and the gathered crowd burst into an ear splitting cheer followed by a thunderous round of applause.

Zabaneja's initial response was to just run inside. But that was not to be the case, not this time. As the two men reached the top step, Rikar stopped, blocking Zabaneja's path.

"What are you doing?" Zabaneja asked. "Let me go inside."

"No, you need to address them."

Rikar took Zabaneja by the shoulders and turned him around to face the gathered throng. As Zabaneja's face came into view, the crowd cheered again. He raised his hand, and the crowd silenced.

"Thank you. Thank you all for your support," Zabaneja said, quickly turned and slipped past Rikar into the castle.

Rikar smiled broadly as he caught up to his old friend.

"That was not a very nice thing to do out there," Zabaneja said.

"Really? I found it quite amusing. Shall we go to the council chamber to meet Guentza?"

#

"Zab, I am not sure you have ever been introduced to His Majesty," Guentza said, gesturing to the man seated beside him.

Zabaneja bowed deeply. He was shocked when the king rose and embraced him. Zabaneja was not sure what to do, so he stood motionless, stiff as a board. This was not a normal reaction from nobility, never mind royalty. Finally, the king released his grip on Zabaneja and took a step back.

"My boy, I wanted to personally let you know how very grateful I and the entire kingdom, the entire world, are to you and your efforts in the recent war."

"Majesty, you are mistaken. I had no more to do with the victory in the war than anyone else did. I was one of many," Zabaneja said.

The king laughed and turned toward Guentza and Rikar. "You were right, gentlemen. You said he would say that."

"It is true, Majesty," Zabaneja said.

"Whatever you say, Zab. Or should I say Lord Zab?" the king said.

"Lord? Was not Guentza made Lord of the Keep?" Zabaneja

asked.

Guentza shook his head. "My acceptance of the position was with the clear understanding that it was only until you came back to assume it permanently. As Aneesyma had planned."

The king nodded. "That is true. He insisted upon that stipulation."

"And now that you have returned," Guentza said, "I can go back to doing what I do best—being a soldier."

"But the real question, my boy, is will you accept the position Aneesyma desired you to have?"

Zabaneja looked off into the distance, then replied. "If that is your wish."

CHAPTER SIXTY-FIVE

"WHERE ARE YOU taking me now?" Zabaneja asked as Rikar dragged him inside the castle.

"You will see soon enough."

"Well, I hope wherever it is, it will be more pleasant than where we were."

"Oh, really. So you are not happy you are now the Lord of the Keep?"

Zabaneja shook his head. "I would not exactly say that, it is just..."

Rikar slapped him on the back. "You cannot be telling me there is still a part of you that feels unworthy."

Zabaneja did not reply.

"Seriously, Zab, after all you have been through, you must know not only are you a capable leader but that you are both a valued and, dare I say, loved member of both the drageal clans and the Keep, no, the entire kingdom."

"I guess I am beginning to see that, but... "

"I know. It is still hard for both of us to realize how far we have come from our less than humble beginnings."

"How could I have forgotten that you, of all people, would understand how I felt," Zabaneja said and then smiled. "But you still have not told me where we are going. This is not the way to the barracks nor the tavern."

"Patience, my friend. We are almost there."

#

"Wait, this is the way to Aneesyma's private chambers," Zabaneja said.

"They are your chambers now, and there has been a slight modification to them since last you were here," Rikar said as they reached the door.

"Everything looks the same as I remember," Zabaneja said, his voice cracking a little.

"This way."

He followed his friend to the inner chamber and saw a staircase that had not been there before. "What is that? Where does it lead?"

"See for yourself."

Zabaneja climbed the staircase to a door at the top.

"Well, do not just stand there. Open it," Rikar said.

He opened the door and stepped out onto a roof garden he knew was not there previously. Zabaneja turned to Rikar.

"Guentza had it built for when you returned. He wanted you to have a place where you could be close to your beloved sky."

"But how did he know I would come back? I was not even sure of that."

Rikar shook his head. "Perhaps it was just something he hoped for."

Zabaneja walked around and was surprised as he turned a corner to see Rusalei standing there. "Lady Rusalei," he sputtered and looked back at Rikar.

Rikar chuckled. "That is the other part of the surprise."

Both Zabaneja and Rusalei glared at him.

"You could have told me," Zabaneja said.

"And where would the fun be in that?"

"Why does that not surprise me?" Zabaneja asked no one in particular.

"Just like old times, eh? The three of us together," Rusalei said.

"Yes, but back then you were the only one with a title," Rikar said. "Zab and I were just riffraff. And now I am the only remaining riffraff of the group."

The three friends laughed.

"The King's Personal Guard riffraff, I believe," Rusalei reminded him.

"Yes, that is so. Speaking of that, I must be going to attend to those duties," Rikar said as he left.

Zabaneja walked to the edge of the rooftop and looked out at the distance in silence.

"There was quite some time after you did not return when I truly despised you," Rusalei said after a few moments.

He turned but did not approach her. "And now?"

She shook her head. "The fact I am standing here should answer that question. But, it is not how I feel that matters. It never was. You know that. It was always you who placed barriers between us." She paused. "But you have yet to tell me why you did not return."

He walked to the other side of the rooftop.

"Your silence tells me I have been mistaken about your feelings for me. I apologize, My Lord. I will not bother you again."

She bowed and walked to the door and put her hand on the knob. She turned to look at Zabaneja, to see if he had any reaction to her words, but his back was still to her. She opened the door and left.

#

"What the hell happened?" Rikar asked as he returned to the roof. "What did you do to make her leave in tears?"

Zabaneja turned toward him. "She asked a question I had no answer for."

Rikar shook his head. "You may be the Lord of the Keep, but you are still a damn fool! You love her. She loves you. And now you have the silly title you always worried so much about. What could she possibly have asked you that you would let her walk away?"

"She wanted to know why I did not come back."

"Really? That is it?"

Zabaneja shook his head. "I had no answer for her."

"Why did you not just tell her that? She would have understood."

"I do not understand myself. How could she?"

"You need to go after her. Tell her what you just told me. Give her the chance to make up her mind whether she believes you or not. She will understand, I know she will."

There was no response from Zabaneja.

"Do I have to tie you up and drag you to her?" Rikar asked. "Because, Lord of the Keep or not, if that is what it takes, that is what I will do."

Zabaneja half-smiled. "I believe you would."

#

Rusalei raced past Rikar without a word. She hoped he did not see the tears she could no longer hold back. When she reached her rooms, she slammed the door and stood crying.

"How could I have been so stupid as to think things would be different? Why did I believe him when he said the main impediment to our relationship was my title? I have been such a fool," she said to the empty room.

She stared blankly at the wall until she was roused by a knock on the door. She opened it and saw Zabaneja. She tried to close the door in his face, but he blocked her action.

"Please, Rusalei, hear me out."

"There is nothing you have to say that I want to hear. You made your position perfectly clear earlier."

"No. That is just it, I did not," he said. "Please, let me in. Let me explain. Afterwards, if you feel the same, I will leave and we will never broach the subject again."

She wanted to say no. Wanted to slap his face and tell him to leave forever. But she could not. She opened the door and motioned him in.

"I am truly sorry about the way I have treated you, both today and before."

She listened but did not respond.

"You asked a perfectly logical question earlier," he continued. "One I have asked myself on so many occasions since the war's end."

"And?" she asked, trying to keep her voice from cracking.

"And the reason I could not answer your question is, I have no answer. I truly do not know why I did not return either here or to my clan."

The sadness in both his eyes and voice made her want to run to him, but she resisted the urge.

"What made you come back?" she asked. "Why here and not with the drageals?"

He shook his head and lied. "I have no real answer for that either."

She turned away to hide the tears she knew were coming.

"I understand," he said. "I want you to know I am truly sorry for the pain I caused you." He waited, and when she did not respond, he continued. "I will be going now, but before I do, know the night we spent together was the best night of my life, because I do truly love you."

"I was crushed by your actions, first sending me away and then not coming back. And the few lines you wrote held no comfort."

"Can you ever forgive me?"

She thought for a long moment. "There was a time when the answer to that was no. But Rikar told me of what you experienced and, while I can never fully understand, it did allow me to know what you did—not coming home—was not done out of malice but out of a grief and a melancholy so overwhelming you had no idea how else to deal with it. After hearing that and now seeing you, yes. Yes, I can, because no matter what, I will always love you."

"And I you."

CHAPTER SIXTY-SIX

THREE DAYS AFTER his return, Zabaneja officially became the Lord of the Keep. After the ceremony there was a huge party. Zabaneja wanted to run away; he still hated being the center of attention. But that night there was no escape. It seemed every person in attendance wanted to shake his hand and congratulate him. Finally, he slipped away to a side room, and he fell into a chair and let out a huge sigh of relief and a barrage of profanities.

"Is that any way for the new Lord of the Keep to speak?" Rusalei asked from the shadows on the other side of the room. "You should not be here. You need to be out there, amongst your subjects and well-wishers."

"Ugh, I have had enough handshaking and backslapping to last a lifetime."

"That is not the point. Come, let us return."

#

The following day the king met with Zabaneja, the council and Guentza.

"Is there anything I can do to help you with your transition into your new role and title, Zab?" the king asked.

"There is one thing I would like to request, but only if it is acceptable to the person involved," Zabaneja said.

The king looked puzzled. "And what might that be?"

"If he is willing and, of course, if it is convenient for Your Majesty, I request that Rikar join me as my chief advisor and second in command," Zabaneja said.

Rikar, also in attendance, looked shocked.

"Hmm, an unusual request. Rikar is one of my best men."

Zabaneja nodded. "I understand, Majesty."

"And while it will be a loss to my staff, if he wishes to join you, then he goes with my blessing." The king turned to Rikar, "Well, what is your decision? Do you wish to come back to the Keep and aid your old friend Zab? Or stay in my service?"

"Meaning no disrespect to you or the position and opportunity you gave me, Majesty," Rikar said, "I would be honored to come back and be of any and all assistance to Lord Zab."

The king smiled. "Well, Zab, it seems you have yourself a new chief advisor. And I need to find another personal guard."

#

The king and his entourage left the Keep later that day.

"Will you miss all the pomp and circumstance of the royal court?" Zabaneja asked as he and Rikar sat in the drawing room.

Rikar shook his head. "Not really. It was exciting and very different from what I had ever known or seen, but after a while, well..."

Zabaneja smiled. "I thought you felt that way when we were together during the war. That is why I decided to ask you to join me here."

"About that," Rikar said.

"Are you saying you really do not want the position?"

"No. I do. But what about Guentza? He was always Aneesyma's chief advisor and…"

"I understand your concern, but in all honesty, it was actually Guentza who suggested the change," Zabaneja said. "He said he was ready to retire and let, as he put it, the young ones take over."

Rikar shook his head. "Really?"

"I think the loss of Aneesyma impacted him more than even he realized. They were friends since childhood," Zabaneja said.

Rikar agreed.

"Now, I need your advice as both my chief advisor and my friend," Zabaneja began.

"Yes, you should ask Rusalei to marry you," Rikar blurted out before Zabaneja could even ask the question.

"How did you know that was what I was going to ask?" Zabaneja asked with a chuckle.

"Because at this very moment, she is the most pressing matter on your mind. And before you doubt yourself like you always do, she will say yes."

"Are you sure?"

Rikar shook his head and laughed.

#

Zabaneja surprised himself at how easily he fell into the role of Lord of the Keep. He assumed it was merely because Aneesyma had been such a good leader that all he had to do was carry on with few changes.

On more than one occasion, Rikar reminded him that while that might be true, Zabaneja himself had brought a new perspective to the role. One that took into account the skill and talent of all people, regardless of their station in life.

"Aneesyma never discriminated against anyone," Zabaneja would respond.

"That is true. He did try to include everyone and their opinions, but he was still a noble by birth. Because you were not and for so long felt yourself unworthy of so many things, the people feel you empathize more with them than even he did." Rikar laughed at the wince on Zabaneja's face. "Do not give me that look. We both know it is true."

"Perhaps."

CHAPTER SIXTY-SEVEN

A YEAR OR SO after becoming Lord, Zabaneja was petitioned by a group of former soldiers and their families. They wanted to create a commemoration to the war that had so threatened their very existence. But they were not sure what to do. They did not want a mere plaque on a wall or a statue in the square. No, the very nature of this war warranted something special, though none had any idea what. Everything they thought of was mundane and would not do. Zabaneja took their request to heart and said he would think about it as well.

Several days later, he was drinking wine from a colored goblet and noticed how the light came through the glass. He wondered if it was possible to create a window, a colored glass window with a painting in it. He brought the idea up to Rikar and Rusalei at dinner. To his great delight, they both loved it.

"How large are you thinking of making the window?" Rikar asked.

Zabaneja pointed to the back wall in the great hall. "The size of that wall."

Rikar drew in a breath. "I see being raised by drageals taught you to never think small, eh?"

Zabaneja laughed. "I guess not. Do you think it is possible?"

Rikar shook his head. "I do not know. I have seen such colored windows at the palace in Siggurna, but they were much smaller than what you have in mind.

"But we will never know unless we talk to the Glaziers Guild. If this project is even possible, it will likely require more than one master craftsman," Rusalei said.

The request to the glaziers was met with differing responses. Some thought the vast size of the window would be impossible. Others looked at it as an interesting challenge that would not only test current methods but create new techniques that would only further enhance their skills. Still, even among those willing to take on the challenge, none would guarantee success. And an additional layer of complexity of the project was the design Zabaneja wanted.

"You are all masters, the best this land has to offer. Surely, you will not shy away from such a challenge," Zabaneja said.

The lord's words were enough for the glaziers to begin discussing the task at hand in earnest. Soon enough, their cooperation made them think the project might not only be possible but also successful.

After much discussion, the five master glaziers who would supervise the project brought in teams and began the task by first making smaller models of the design and then a model of the window in plain glass since none had ever seen even a plain glass window of that size anywhere, not even in the capital.

#

As work on the window began, the anniversary of the final battle in what was now known as the Drageal War neared.

"It is time to travel to pay our respects to my mother and all those that fell in the war," Zabaneja said at breakfast.

Rusalei nodded as she stood beside him. "Yes. I have already begun packing for the journey."

He put his hand on her bulging stomach, fully showing the signs of the child within. "Perhaps, you should forego this year." he suggested knowing better than to forbid her.

"I am with child, not an invalid," she said adamantly. "I am far from being one of those women who needs to be pampered every minute of the day, that swoon at the slightest twinge of pain."

"Pain?" Zabaneja asked nervously. "Is that not a sign the birth time is near?"

Rusalei laughed. "You face the fire of an approaching drageal without blinking an eye, yet the idea of the coming of your child frightens you."

"It is not that I am frightened," Zabaneja said. "It is that I am concerned for your health." He gently rubbed her belly and smiled. "Yours and the babe's."

He kissed her on the lips and whispered, "I would be lost if anything ever happened to you, my love. You are my only reason for living."

"I will be fine."

The trio of old friends, along with numerous others who had seen combat, left the next day.

"Will anyone else be there?" Rusalei asked as they traveled.

Zabaneja shook his head. "Phrynia and the other drageals will be, she contacted me the other day. As for the others, I am not sure."

"I am still amazed that you and she are able to communicate over such vast distances," Rusalei said.

#

"You are late," Phrynia said to Zabaneja as the humans from the Keep arrived.

"No, you are early," Zabaneja replied, and the two friends laughed. "You remember Rikar and my mate, Rusalei, do you not?"

The drageal bowed her head. "She is as lovely as ever."

"Yes, she is, and in just a few months, I shall be a father."

"That is wonderful. Ah, Pheunaf would be so happy to hear that."

Zabaneja felt his eyes welling with tears at the mention of his mother. "Yes, she would."

The others stood silently beside Zabaneja. Though they could not understand what the pair were saying, they knew after the two old friends had caught up on what they needed to say, they would be included.

#

"When will the others be arriving?" Zabaneja asked.

"Nanetscka and the drageals will be here tomorrow," the golden drageal said. "I do not expect the emuranda. Will any of the humans come?"

"I have had word some of the drageal riders will. Sadly, day-to-day life and all that entails will probably make it impossible for all to attend."

"And what of Kalini? Have you heard from her?" Phrynia asked.

"No, and that both surprises and worries me," Zabaneja said. "I would think if all was well with her, she would be here or at least have contacted me."

"I am surprised you doubted me," a small voice from behind them said.

Zabaneja ran over to the chetoga, bent down and threw his arms around her. "I am so glad you are here. When I did not hear from you, I feared something out of your control might have happened to prevent you from coming."

"Only my departure from this life would have kept me away," she said with a chuckle. "And I am happy to say that has yet to occur."

Over the next few hours, more of the former allies arrived, and all greeted each other with tears and joy, as well as tales of the good times with those who had fallen and those that remained.

"What did you think of it?" Rusalei asked as they began the journey home.

"I was glad to see so many old friends," Rikar replied.

Zabaneja nodded. "I fear with each passing year there will be fewer and fewer coming to remember."

"Perhaps, but we will always be here," Rikar said.

#

Zabaneja and the others returned to the Keep and went to see the progress on the window.

"What is going on here?" Zabaneja asked as he viewed what had already been completed. "This is not what the window was supposed to look like."

The head glazier looked at the window and then at Zabaneja. "It is as close to the plans Rikar, Guentza and Lady Rusalei gave us as we could make it."

"The emuranda, Jucara, is as I wanted, but the human looks like me, not Aneesyma. And the drageal is Phrynia, not my mother."

Rusalei took his arm. "This is what everyone decided it should be—the three main heroes of the conflict."

Zabaneja shook his head. "This is not right. I am not the one who should be depicted there."

She squeezed his arm again. "Yes, you are. Everyone but you knows it. Just accept the honor your people have bestowed upon you."

#

It took another year for the massive window to be completed. Under it, a brass plaque was placed with an inscription that read, 'This window is dedicated to those of all races who fought in the Drageal War. Let us never forget we must always stand united if this world is to survive.'

Zabaneja invited all survivors of the war and their families to the Keep for the unveiling of the commemorative window. He was elated to find so many of the former friends and allies accepted the invitation but was disappointed, though not surprised, none of the emuranda nor tazzamira would be there.

The humans and smaller races stayed within the Keep, and a camp was set up outside the walls for the drageals. As the festivities began and the groups gathered, there were as many parties at the camp as there were in the Keep.

The unveiling of the window left all in attendance in awe. All commented that it did not matter where you stood in the hall, the eyes of the three beings seemed to follow you. The drageals were able to glimpse its beauty, especially at night when it was lit from within, by flying outside the wall and viewing the drawings and designs Zabaneja brought them.

CHAPTER SIXTY-EIGHT

"I WANT TO HOLD an event," Zabaneja said to the council.

"A celebration of the anniversary of the window's unveiling?" Haoule asked.

"No. An annual banquet to be held here, within the Keep, open to everyone—farmer, peasant, noble or anyone else. A time when everyone can meet and openly discuss their thoughts and opinions without fear of ridicule or retribution. I want it to be as equal as we can make it — no fancy dress or jewelry, no titles, no separation within the hall by rank or class—with everyone eating, drinking and mingling together."

"Do you think that will be accepted by everyone? I mean, it is something quite out of the ordinary," Haoule said.

"Anyone who feels they are above this sort of thing can stay away. But I would hope we have gone beyond that sort of thinking, at least here. You know, you might be surprised at the opinions the other classes possess." Zabaneja said.

"That was not what I meant," Haoule said.

Zabaneja smiled. "I know, but I want to make it clear to everyone what my feelings on the matter are."

"And when do you wish to have this banquet?" Jakaher asked.

"I think early spring, after the last snow but before the first planting, would be a good time. After a long winter of confinement, I think a celebration, a coming together with friends old and new, would be welcomed by all."

Everyone agreed and initial plans were set in motion.

#

Word of the upcoming banquet quickly spread, and the excitement grew. To everyone's delight, there was little opposition to the idea. In fact, people of all classes offered their help, whether in setting things up or bringing food or whatever else might be needed.

"You were correct in your assessment of how your people would respond," Rikar said as he and Zabaneja walked to the council meeting.

"So it seems. I hope the enthusiasm lasts, and all goes well on the night."

"If what I have heard and seen around the Keep is any indication, there is no cause for worry."

#

Midmorning on the day of the banquet, the courtyard outside the castle began to fill with people. Zabaneja and Rusalei watched from one of the upper windows and were happy to see the gathered crowd was made up of all classes. Some timidly stood watching everyone, while others shook hands and patted each other on the back. And still others gave out trinkets, small gifts or food.

"I am surprised so many people are here so early," Rusalei said.

"It seems the idea of a party to break up the normal routine has gotten the people excited."

"I think we should consider sending food and drink to them later in the afternoon."

"That is a good idea, my dear. But I worry the staff will feel overburdened by the additional work," Zabaneja said.

"Hmm, perhaps if you talk to them. You have such a way with everyone."

Zabaneja flushed a bit. "I am not so sure about that, but I will see what I can do."

#

"Ah, My Lord, I was just coming to see you," the head cook said as Zabaneja entered the main kitchen. "My staff tells me the crowds are already gathering, and we were wondering if we needed to find something to tide them over until the feast."

Zabaneja laughed. "It is as if you read my mind, dear lady. But I was concerned for your staff having to do an extra feeding. I mean, it is bad enough all of you have to work during the feast, at least at the beginning."

"Bah," the cook said. "We are happy to do it. Your promise of a party of our own has made everyone feel quite special."

"Still..."

"To be honest, several merchants have actually already set up stands and are donating food and drink, so the burden on our stores and staff will not be significant."

"I was not aware of that."

The cook shook her head. "You still do not realize how much your people love and respect you, My Lord, do you? Though Lord Aneesyma was well-loved, everyone feels as if you are just like them be they noble or peasant."

"Thank you, I do not know what to say."

She laughed. "Accept it. That is all."

#

Just before sunset, the crowd, now much larger than it had been earlier in the day, hushed as servants lit the torches on either side of the castle doors. Within a very few moments the doors opened and Zabaneja and Rusalei, dressed in modest clothing, emerged. The crowd cheered.

"Thank you all for coming," Zabaneja began, and the crowd cheered again. "Rusalei and I bid you welcome to our home."

The couple took a few steps to the side and welcomed every attendee with a handshake. When everyone had entered the castle, Zabaneja and Rusalei made their way to the great hall. As they arrived, the room quieted. Zabaneja nodded to the servants and the torches around the massive stained glass window were lit to the delight of all.

Zabaneja stood in front of the window. "Please, everyone, help yourselves to food and drink. We hope you will make merry with song and dance and have a wonderful time."

CHAPTER SIXTY-NINE

ZABANEJA TURNED at the sound of the door of his rooftop retreat opening.

"I am sorry, my love. I did not mean to disturb you, but I thought after tonight's event you might welcome this."

Rusalei showed him the bottle of orange liquid and the glass she was carrying. He smiled.

"Aykopyra. You know me too well, my dear."

"With this being the tenth banquet, it seemed everyone was in even higher spirits than usual. And, I know how their enthusiasm drains you."

He took the bottle, uncorked it, filled the glass and took a sip. "Ahh, that is just what I needed."

"Does it remind you of home?" She watched for his reaction.

"It reminds me of my youth."

"I think after the visit to the gravesite this year, you should go with Phrynia and the others, spend some time with them. You know they would love to have you to themselves. And, more importantly, you could again take to the sky. I know you miss it so."

He turned from her and looked out across the horizon.

"We can maintain the Keep for a bit while you are away," she added.

"That is not the problem." He turned back to her. "Why are you bringing this up again? I told you before I would not go there."

"But you did not give me a reason. Will you tell me now?"

She looked at him and was surprised to see fear along with the sadness he always showed when they spoke of the drageals.

"No."

"Why not?"

He turned and walked to the other side of the rooftop and looked toward the sky. After a few moments, Rusalei silently departed.

"I am sorry," he said when he returned to their rooms.

"No, I am. I know that is not something you like to discuss and tonight was not the best time to bring it up."

"That is not it. You do not understand..." He shook his head. "I cannot give you an answer because, just like so many other times in my life, I do not really know why I can or cannot, do or do not act."

She wanted to rush to his side and embrace him. To tell him it was all right, that she was sorry she had even brought the matter up. But something in his eyes told her that was not what he needed or wanted at the moment. So, she waited for him to come to terms with what he would or would not be able to tell her.

"But I also know you still miss being in the sky, do you not?" she asked breaking the silence.

"Yes. But, that is no longer my lot in life. No, those are not the right words. You know I love you and the children more than I ever thought possible..."

"But?"

"There is no but. This is my life. What it was meant to be. What

I chose it to be. I would not change it for anything." He pulled her close. "You are my everything. But I am afraid," he whispered.

"I do not understand."

"Nor do I. At least, not fully. I only know I am afraid that if I went to the drageals, I would not have the strength to leave them. That I would never come back. That I would abandon you and the children and everything I have here." He looked at her and tried unsuccessfully to force a smile. "It does not make sense, I know, but..."

"Is that why you never fly with them when we meet?"

He nodded.

"Then, I will not bring up the subject again. I am sorry. I did not mean to trouble you so."

He smiled and took her in his arms. "You never trouble me, my love. It is always I who does so to you."

#

"It is hard to believe it has been over twenty years since we held the first banquet," Rusalei said as she and Zabaneja prepared to retire.

Zabaneja shook his head and sighed. "So it has."

"What is it, my love? You seem troubled, not yourself," she said and touched the side of his face. "Did you not enjoy the festivities?"

"They were fine."

"But something is troubling you."

Zabaneja smiled. "I never could hide anything from you, could I? Yes, there is something I want to discuss and I am not sure how you will receive what I have to say."

"Is there something wrong? You are not ill, are you?"

"No, nothing like that. It is just I have been thinking about stepping down and handing the rule of the Keep over to Torquhil."

She was taken aback, not just by his words but by the lack of emotion in them. "Well, I must say, I was not expecting to hear that."

He looked at her and saw that, while her voice was calm, her eyes showed a level of distress he had not meant to cause her.

"I suppose not," he said and walked to her side. "I am tiring of all of this, and I have been thinking, now might be the perfect time for us to abandon our roles here and run away together, just the two of us. Perhaps, to the drageals."

She was surprised at his suggestion. "Ah, that does sound lovely. Imagine being so close to the sky and not having to think about everyone else for a change."

"Yes, that would be nice. Now, come to bed, my love," he said and beckoned her to join him between the sheets.

#

Rusalei lie there listening to his soft breathing and pondering his words. Whenever she had brought up the subject of his returning to the drageals for a visit in the past, his response had always been to dismiss it. He had given most of his life to the humans, when, she knew, in reality he wanted to be with the drageals. She smiled. Maybe at last he was ready to do something for himself.

She recalled how often, after seeing the drageals at the gravesite visits, a melancholy overcame him. Not in a way that anyone but she would notice. Those were the times she felt guilty for being the reason he chose the life he did. Not that he ever blamed her, or anyone else. She remembered asking him once why he just accepted so many things and smiled at the memory of his answer. 'It is the drageal way.'

But now, finally, he had decided it was time to go back to the drageals—to go home. And, why not? All was in order at the Keep.

Since his return, he had ensured that not only was the Keep and all its people safe, but during his time as Lord, they had prospered to a level that would have made Aneesyma proud.

And, Torquhil was indeed more than capable of taking over rule. Zabaneja made sure of that. As soon as the boy showed an interest in the workings of the Keep, Zabaneja started teaching him and now... now it was time. But the fact that Zabaneja wanted to take her with him, home to the drageals, made her heart soar.

Yes, first thing in the morning she would tell him that she agreed and they should leave as soon as possible.

#

"Wake up, my love," Rusalei said as she walked to Zabaneja's side of the room, the one closest to the windows. "It is not like you to still be sleeping so long after the sun has risen."

She pulled open the drapes allowing the full light of day to enter the room and, as she turned back to the bed, she realized he had still not woken. In fact, he had not moved since she kissed him the night before. She gasped, ran to the bedside and shook him, but it was no use. She could not rouse him. And she knew he would never wake again.

She climbed back into the bed and sat beside him, leaned over and kissed his now cold lips and cradled his head in her lap. "I wish we could have run off together and that you could have once again soared above the clouds, my love. It would have been so wonderful," she said and wept.

She was not sure how long she sat there and did not care because a part of her did not want to ever release him.

Too soon, there was a tap on the door and one of the servants entered with the breakfast tray. When she saw his lordship still in bed and the tears on her mistress' face, she dropped the tray and ran to Rusalei's side.

Rusalei looked at the young girl. "I am fine. Go fetch Rikar and bring him here, but do not tell him or anyone else what you have seen."

The girl nodded, wiped the tears from her cheeks and ran out of the room. A few minutes later, Rikar entered. Though he did not know the exact nature why he was summoned, he knew something was wrong. When he saw Zabaneja and Rusalei, he, too, wept. As he went to her side, she continued to sit on the bed, stroking the lifeless face of Zabaneja.

"I do not have words," Rikar said. Rusalei nodded and the two old friends embraced.

CHAPTER SEVENTY

"THE PEOPLE WILL NOT take kindly to not burying father here in Hammarsh," Torquhil, now the Lord of the Keep, said.

Rusalei glared at him. "Do you think for one moment that I or your father would care what they think?" she snapped.

"Zab gave the better part of his life to the humans of this land, but in his heart he was still a drageal, so he must leave this world as a drageal," Rikar said.

"I am not saying I would ever try to go against his wishes, I am only saying there will be dissent from the populace."

"Damn the populace," Rikar growled.

Torquhil smiled. "I agree. I have already begun the preparations for father's last journey. We will leave tomorrow morning and though he would have preferred to slip out quietly, that is one request I cannot fulfill. So, Mother, Uncle Rikar, please realize the streets and roadways will be lined with mourners until we are well past the Keep's walls and possibly beyond."

Both Rikar and Rusalei nodded.

"I would expect nothing less from the people who so loved and admired him," Rikar said. "Now, I will leave you two to your final preparations. Unless," he paused and bowed slightly to Torquhil, "His Lordship requires something else of me."

Torquhil had all he could do to not burst into laughter. "I am not sure I can get used to such reverence from you, Uncle. But, please do what you need to do."

Rikar kissed Rusalei on the forehead, bowed to Torquhil and left.

#

As expected, the people crowded the sides of the roads far beyond the walls of the Keep.

"I hope these crowds thin soon," Rikar said, "or else we will never be able to make any sort of good time on this trip."

"Are you in a rush to get there?" Torquhil asked.

"Well, the longer we are on the road the more his body will decay and that is not something I wish your mother to see," Rikar replied.

"Nor do I," Rusalei said as she rode up beside them. "But since it is just past winter, the cooler weather will work in our favor."

"I apologize, Lady..." Rikar began and then stopped as he saw the glare she gave him. "I apologize, Rusalei, I did not mean to appear crass or unsympathetic."

She laughed. "My dearest Rikar, we have known each other far too long and have gone through far too many things in our lives for us to ever stand on ceremony. And, if it were you or I in that caisson Zab would not have been nearly so polite in his language."

The three of them nodded and smiled.

To their relief, the throngs of mourners had all but disappeared by that evening and they were able to travel at a swifter pace the following day.

#

The night before they were to arrive at their final destination, Torquhil joined his mother and Rikar as they finished their evening meal.

"What is it, son? You look concerned. Is something wrong?"

"No. All is well. It is just that as often as we have come to this place to honor those who were lost and though I knew this is where we would bring Father as his final resting place..." He paused and turned from them.

Rikar rose and put his hand on the young lord's shoulder. "Knowing something will happen and dealing with it when it actually does can sometimes be a devastating experience. In some ways, I think I always thought, always hoped, your father would live forever, or at least as long as a drageal. But sadly, as much as I would have liked it to be so, he was indeed a human and as such has left us much sooner than anyone wanted."

Torquhil nodded and patted his uncle's hand, and the two men returned to Rusalei's side.

"Do you think anyone else will be there?" Torquhil asked.

Rikar shook his head. "I do not know. We have no way of communicating with the others anymore. Most of us who could mindspeak during the war found the ability waning with both time and distance. I think your father was the last to be able to still call to the drageals."

"Do you think he did? Would he have told them?" Torquhil asked and then shook his head. "No, that is a stupid thing to say. He did not know he was dying, so why would he call them."

Rikar looked at Rusalei. Later, when Torquhil was gone, he asked why she had not told her son what Zabaneja had said to her. She smiled and reminded him Zabaneja's last words were not meant for her children.

#

The following morning, as they neared the site, Zabaneja's entourage was surprised to be met by a large group of riders consisting of many of the former drageal riders. And, as they looked more closely at the group they realized amongst them was the king.

He rode up until he was beside Rusalei. "My dearest Lady, I hope you do not take our appearance as an affront to your grief. We are only here to pay our deepest respects to your late husband, in whose debt we all are."

"I am honored you and the others have come, Highness," Rusalei said, bowing her head. "I did not expect such a thing. Zab would have been honored."

The king laughed. "Oh, no, he would not. He would have told us all we were making far too big a fuss over him."

Rusalei smiled. "Yes, you are right. Now, please grant us the honor of riding beside us to the site."

"I am sorry, but I must decline," the king said. "This is the place for your family and closest friends. I will follow behind, with the others."

Rusalei nodded. "As you wish, Highness."

#

"You seem disappointed, son," Rusalei said as Zabaneja's body was being placed on the ground where it was to be burned.

"I guess I hoped the others would be here. That they would somehow know," Torquhil said.

"But look at all those who did come."

"I know, but I had hoped for the others as well."

Suddenly there was a rustle in the bushes behind them and the slightest air disturbance overhead. As the humans looked, they saw three groups approaching—chetoga, emuranda and drageal.

Phrynia and Kalini stepped forward and approached Rusalei. The drageal took her hand. "We have come to say farewell to our brother," the drageal said, and as if by magic, at least to Rusalei's mind, the drageal spoke and she understood.

"How did you know?" Rusalei asked.

"I no longer felt his presence," Phrynia said. "And I knew you would bring him here."

# # #

ACKNOWLEDGEMENTS

Thanks to everyone who encouraged me by asking for more and kicking my butt to get on with it when I got lazy.

To my awesome beta readers—Craig Berendt, Zarra Van de Kreeke, Janet O'Neil and Tina Nabor—thanks for all the great feedback and for not letting me cut corners or think I could get away with just hinting at things rather than actually writing them out.

And to my fabulous editors, Pam Sheppard and Laura Taylor, thanks for all the hard work I made you do to get this book to where it is. Maybe someday, I will actually figure out where commas belong – LOL.

About the Author

Born and raised in New York, mostly on Long Island not "The City", Dot Caffrey moved to California after high school and now describes herself as a 'Californian by choice not chance'. She did a three-year stint in the Navy before going to college and getting a Microbiology/Medical Technologist degree.

Her father told her she was a storyteller from the time she began talking (which was at a very young age). But, it wasn't until a few years ago that she decided to take her passion for writing and her love for all things magical or mythical seriously and start writing fantasy novels.

Now retired from her day job, she hopes to fill her time with more writing as well as her hobbies of creating and wearing costumes (cosplay), playing video games (though, she admits she is not very good at it), watching NHL hockey and, of course, hanging out with her friends and many cats.

Follow Dot
https://www.dotcaffrey.com
https://www.facebook.com/DotCaffreyFantasyAuthor

www.ingramcontent.com/pod-product-compliance
Lightning Source LLC
Chambersburg PA
CBHW031928110726
47902CB00001B/91